A Worthy Pursuit

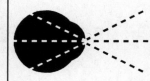

This Large Print Book carries the
Seal of Approval of N.A.V.H.

A WORTHY PURSUIT

KAREN WITEMEYER

THORNDIKE PRESS
A part of Gale, Cengage Learning

GALE
CENGAGE Learning·

Farmington Hills, Mich • San Francisco • New York • Waterville, Maine
Meriden, Conn • Mason, Ohio • Chicago

GALE
CENGAGE Learning

LIBRARY OF CONGRESS CATALOGING-IN-PUBLICATION DATA

Witemeyer, Karen.
    A worthy pursuit / Karen Witemeyer. — Large print edition.
        pages cm. — (Thorndike Press large print Christian historical fiction)
    ISBN 978-1-4104-8221-1 (hardback) — ISBN 1-4104-8221-9 (hardcover)
    1. Bounty hunters—Fiction. 2. Guardian and ward—Fiction. 3. Large type books. I. Title.
PS3623.I864W67 2015b
813'.6—dc23   2015016021

Published in 2015 by arrangement with Bethany House Publishers, a division of Baker Publishing Group

Printed in Mexico
1 2 3 4 5 6 7 19 18 17 16 15

To Laura Baker,
librarian extraordinaire and
the first person
I ever trusted to read my stories.
It is your encouragement and
knowledgeable feedback
that gave me the fortitude
to pursue my dream.
You taught me to see
the world through lenses
different than my own
and deepened my
understanding of the human condition.
You have left your mark on me,
my friend,
and I thank God for the gift.

Be strong and of a good courage, fear not, nor be afraid of them: for the Lord thy God, he it is that doth go with thee; he will not fail thee, nor forsake thee.

— Deuteronomy 31:6

PROLOGUE

February 1891
Austin, Texas
Sullivan's Academy for Exceptional Youths

"I'm closing the school, Miss Atherton, and that's my final word on the subject." Dr. Keith Sullivan shut the attendance ledger on his desk with an ominous snap and pushed to his feet, forcing Charlotte to stand as well. "I've sent wires to all the students' parents, informing them of the closure and offering to reimburse a percentage of the tuition to compensate them for the inconvenience of ending the school term earlier than expected."

A reimbursement of funds? From the man who'd refused to purchase a single new text in the last five years? It was all Charlotte could do to keep her jaw from coming unhinged. There must be another source of income — one large enough to overshadow the loss of tuition. Dr. Sullivan charged exorbitant fees for his exclusive school. Only the most noteworthy students were accepted into the small academy — unless, of course, a particularly wealthy family sought entry for one of their children. In that case, a well-placed donation seemed to make up for any lack in giftedness. Charlotte could only imagine how large a donation would have to be to convince him to close the school entirely.

Backing out of the way as her employer strode around his desk, Charlotte fiddled with the cameo at her neck then marched after him. "What of Stephen Farley? His parents are in Europe. They couldn't possibly collect him before we close the doors. And John Chang is an orphan here on scholarship. He has no place to go."

She paid the Chinese boy's tuition herself out of her monthly stipend and had for the last three years. She'd fought to get him into the school after one of the women from St. Peter's Foundling Home had brought him to her attention. John had been only four at the time, but when he'd climbed onto the worn bench of the secondhand piano in the orphanage parlor and flawlessly picked out every note of Fanny Crosby's "Safe in the Arms of Jesus," she'd known she had to tutor the boy. God had bestowed a rare gift on the child and placed him in her path for a reason. She couldn't have him torn away from her now.

"Arrangements have been made for them to board at St. Peter's."

Charlotte fought down the protest tearing at her throat. Stephen wouldn't last a day there with his penchant for finding trouble. And John. Dear heaven. The boy had been picked on mercilessly by the other children because of his foreign heritage, even as a toddler. He'd been so traumatized, he hadn't spoken a word for months after coming to the academy. He was still much too withdrawn for Charlotte's liking. No telling how far the boy would retreat into himself if he were forced to return to St. Peter's.

And what of Lily? Ice shards speared Charlotte's heart as a new, more sinister possibility cast its shadow over Dr. Sullivan's bizarre behavior.

"Miss Dorchester will stay with me, of course," Charlotte asserted, any other contingency being untenable.

Dr. Sullivan pivoted to face her. "Don't be ridiculous, Miss Atherton. You are headmistress, not mother, to these children, regardless of that piece of paper Rebekah Dorchester had you sign. Lily will return to her grandfather, where she belongs. He

11

plans to be here in the morning to collect her. You," he said with a suddenly beneficent smile that did nothing to thaw the ice impaling her chest, "will surely find a new position in record time. Here." He pulled a paper from a thin stack of folders in his arms. "I've taken the liberty of putting together a list of potential employers for you. These are some of the finest female academies in the country."

Charlotte took the paper from his hand and willed it not to quiver. "Chicago. Boston. Charleston." Her eyes continued down the list. "All so far away."

Dr. Sullivan beamed at her. "You are a brilliant music instructor, Miss Atherton, and have proven yourself quite capable at administration as well. I've already sent glowing letters of recommendation to each of these institutions. Any of them would be lucky to have you."

But none of them would accept her if she had a child in tow.

Charlotte glanced up from the page to meet her employer's eyes — not a difficult task since the man stood an inch below her in height. Neither was it difficult to read the guilt behind his smile. The list of prestigious schools, letters of recommendation, unnecessary compliments — all appeasements for his conscience. He knew how unlikely the staff were to find replacement positions mid-term, just as he knew how wrong it was to turn his back on the pupils he'd promised to educate. Yet he was closing the school anyway. Closing the school and narrowing her options so that she had no choice but to give Lily Dorchester into her grandfather's keeping if she wished to retain a teaching position.

Well, he might think he'd herded her like a heifer into a chute, but if she'd learned one thing in her twenty-eight years, it was that even when backed into a corner, one always had a choice. *Always.*

After Dr. Sullivan nodded to her in that condescending way of his that made her skin itch — as if she hadn't a brain for herself and would be lost without a man to give her guidance — he swung the office door wide and gestured for her to exit. Biting her tongue, Charlotte passed through the doorway and silently resolved to toss his list of schools into the belly of her stove the moment she returned to her room. Her career could be sacrificed easily enough. Protecting Lily took precedence.

With the dark of night cloaking the halls of the school, Charlotte placed her two carpet bags outside her door and gave a final glance over her room. The rug lay properly aligned with the angle of the floorboards. No stray papers across the desk. No wrinkles in the coverlet atop the bed. All as it should be. She gave a little nod of approval, a nod that would have to serve as good-bye as well, for she would not be returning. She'd taught at the academy for ten years — seven as music instructor, three as headmistress. A tiny part of her ached for the loss of the familiar, the safe. Yet she had no time for sentimental attachment. She'd made a promise — a promise she intended to keep, no matter the cost.

Straightening her shoulders, Charlotte turned her back and pulled the door closed, clicking the latch silently into place. Then, careful to stay on the balls of her feet so her heels wouldn't click against the wooden floor, she made her way to the staircase that led to the boys' dormitory. She crept up the stairs then down the hall and eased open the door to the sleeping chamber.

"Stephen," she whispered into the darkness, her eyes not yet adjusted to the full-black of the attic room.

"Here, Miss Lottie."

Charlotte sucked in a startled breath. Heavens, the boy was practically on top of her. How could she not see him? She turned her head in the direction of the sound and squinted until she made out two small shadows a few steps from her elbow.

"John's with me."

A telltale rattle had Charlotte gritting her teeth. "Stephen," she scolded in a hushed tone as she ushered the boys into the hall and closed the door, "you were supposed to leave that paraphernalia behind."

"I only brought the essentials, Miss Lottie. I swear. Just like you said." The boy clutched the sack to his chest and glared up at her. One would think he carried gold coins in that bag, not a collection of gears, bolts, and baling wire. "I can't leave them behind. Miss Greenbriar will throw them in the garbage."

Where they undoubtedly belonged. Nevertheless, Charlotte couldn't deny the boy his treasures. With absentee parents who couldn't be bothered to visit or even write, heaven knew the boy had little enough to call his own.

"All right. But keep them quiet. We can't afford to wake any of the staff."

Some of the rigidity left his shoulders, and he nodded. "Yes, ma'am."

Satisfied, she pivoted to face the door to the girls' dormitory on the opposite side, yet her feet refused to cross the hall.

Drat it all. She hated second thoughts. Horrible, impractical things. It wasn't as if she were stealing the children, after all. She was protecting them. So why did she suddenly feel like a villain? Charlotte huffed out an impatient breath. This was what came of sneaking about at night. It made perfectly innocent activities furtive and played havoc with her carefully laid plans.

Unable to break free of her misgivings, she took hold of both boys' arms then hunkered down in front of them. Stephen looked down at her, a frown tugging on the corners of his mouth.

"Whatcha waitin' for, Miss Lottie? We gotta get Lily. Mr. Dobson's waitin' on us."

"I'm not sure that taking the two of you with me is right. Perhaps St. Peter's is the better option. The safer option."

John slipped his hand into hers and squeezed with a desperate strength. "Stay with you."

It tore her heart out to think of leaving him behind, but if Dorchester somehow discovered where she'd taken Lily . . .

Stephen crossed his arms and glared at her. "I'm not stupid, Miss Lottie. I know something's up or you wouldn't be sneaking us out in the middle of the night. But

I'm tellin' you right now, if you take me to that orphanage, I'll run away. I'm nearly twelve, plenty old enough to find work as a stable hand or errand boy for one of the local shops. But I'd rather stay with you and the little ones. Lily and John need a big brother to look out for them."

"But your parents —"

"My folks don't care two figs about me, never have," Stephen scoffed, shrugging as if such an admission were as insignificant a disappointment as not getting a second helping of pudding after supper. "Only reason I'm here is 'cause they love bragging to their friends about their son being at a school for exceptional youths, even if the only thing exceptional about me is my father's bank account. I know I'm not as special as Lily or John or most of the others, but when you gave me that book about Thomas Edison and Samuel Morse, I figured that maybe if I learned enough, I could grow up to do something important like one of those inventors. That's why I need to stay with you, Miss Lottie. You're the only one who believes I'm worth the trouble."

Without a hint of a second thought, Charlotte pulled Stephen into her arms and hugged him tight as she blinked away the

17

moisture gathering in her eyes. "You *are* gifted, Stephen. Don't you ever doubt it. Lily has her books, John has the piano, but you understand mechanical things in a way that boggles my mind." She released him and stood, brushing away the wrinkles from her gored skirt along with the last of her misgivings. "I suppose we'll just have to write your parents to let them know where you are after we get settled. We can't allow your education to lag just because Dr. Sullivan closed his school, now, can we?"

"No, ma'am."

"Good. Watch John for me while I fetch Lily."

After giving John a quick hug against her skirt, Charlotte yanked on the hem of the snug-fitting traveling jacket that fell to her hips and ran a hand over her hair to check for stray strands. Not finding any, she inhaled a deep breath and straightened her shoulders. Once again in command of the situation, she swept across the hall and entered the girls' room.

Unlike the boys, Lily had fallen asleep. Charlotte gently pulled the blanket down and helped Lily sit up. "It's time to go, sweetheart." The child let out a small, disgruntled moan. "Quiet now," Charlotte murmured around the smile tweaking her lips. "We mustn't wake the others."

Lily rubbed her eyes with her fist then dutifully got to her feet. "Are we going to our new home, Miss Lottie?" she asked behind a yawn.

"Yes." Charlotte helped the girl push her arms through her coat sleeves. "Did you pack your things?"

"Mm-hmm. Under the bed."

Charlotte retrieved the satchel that had once been Lily's mother's. The initials *R.D.* had been stamped into the leather strap above the buckle. She couldn't see them in the dark, but her fingers traced over the indention. *I'll take good care of her, Rebekah. I promise.*

"I remembered to get dressed after the others went to sleep, Miss Lottie. Even my shoes."

"Excellent." Charlotte did up the coat buttons then began straightening the child's bed. "You did everything I asked."

"I promised Mama I'd be a good girl for you."

Charlotte stilled, Lily's bed only half made. "And I promised her that I'd take care of you." The itch of emotion gathering at the back of her throat sent Charlotte back into motion. She finished making the bed and even went so far as to tuck the blanket edges under the mattress.

Rebekah had been gone only a week. Charlotte wasn't so selfish as to wish her back, for her friend had suffered mightily in the last months of her illness, but she couldn't help worrying on Lily's behalf. She'd taught children of all ages, but Dr. Sullivan had been right about one thing — she wasn't a mother.

As if Lily could sense her distress, she placed her hand in Charlotte's palm and squeezed. "Mama said you were the finest woman she'd ever known and told me to stay with you no matter what. It'll all work out, Miss Lottie. You'll see. We can miss her together."

Charlotte squeezed Lily's hand in return. "Yes. I suppose we can."

They exited into the hall, collected the boys, then crept down the stairs. Charlotte steered them back toward her room so she could gather her bags, but the luggage was nowhere to be seen.

"I got yer stuff loaded in the wagon already." The gravelly voice seemed to emanate from the very walls. Charlotte jumped then caught her breath when the school's caretaker materialized from within the doorway that led to the administrative office.

"Good heavens, Mr. Dobson. You gave me a fright." Charlotte reached for the cameo at her throat and fiddled with the pin until she was sure her fingers had ceased trembling.

"Sorry, Miss Atherton. Just thought we better hurry this party along."

Dobson was a strange little creature, sporting more gray hair on his chin than his head, and he never seemed to look her straight in the eye. Yet he was diligent in his work and good to the children. Best of all, he asked no questions. Earlier today, she'd offered him a position as overseer of the property where she'd be taking the children since the academy would be closing, and he'd accepted without once inquiring about the salary. Nor had he questioned her desire to depart in the middle of the night. It was as if he understood her urgency. Perhaps he did. It wouldn't surprise her to learn that he knew exactly what had precipitated the school's closing and what threatened Lily.

She offered him a smile. "Lead the way, sir."

The man had laid a straw tick in the wagon bed and piled a mound of quilts along the edge.

Charlotte nodded approvingly. "You've thought of everything, Mr. Dobson."

He failed to look at her as he helped Lily into the back of the wagon. "Didn't want the young'uns to catch a chill. There's still a nip in the air."

Indeed there was. Charlotte shivered within her coat. Despite the springlike temperatures during the day, nighttime felt like winter. "Bundle up tightly, children, and lay close together to keep warm."

After the three were settled, Charlotte allowed Dobson to hand her up onto the bench. A lap robe and hot brick waited for her. She turned to thank him, but he held up a hand and walked away before she could form the words. He circled around behind the wagon then climbed up beside her. He released the brake and set the horses into motion.

Charlotte held her tongue, realizing her thanks would not be welcome. She glanced over her shoulder at the children then turned to face ahead. Toward her future. This ragtag bunch was her family now, and she'd let no man take them from her.

1

April 1891
Madisonville, Texas

"Whoa." Stone Hammond tugged once on the reins, and his black immediately stopped. "I better climb the rest of the way alone, Goliath." He slid from the saddle, pushing the long length of his duster aside as he swung his leg over the horse's rump. "A behemoth like you is likely to block out the sun this time of day if you crest the hill, and after eight weeks of huntin' I ain't about to let you scare off my quarry."

The black turned his head and gave Stone a look that seemed to imply Stone wasn't exactly a dainty specimen himself then turned his attention to sampling the local prairie grass. Stone snorted. Crazy beast. Always so uppity. But he wouldn't trade him for the biggest bounty on the federal marshal's wall. No, the two of them had been through too many adventures to ever call it quits. They'd battled outlaws, renegades — shoot, even a pair of thievin' circus performers who'd turned out to be devilishly good with knives. He and Goliath bore the scars and carried the years of hard living upon their bodies, but their hearts beat as true today as they had when they'd started a decade ago.

They were retrievers. The best in the state. It was the one thing in life he was good at. Never once had he failed to bring in what he was sent after. And with what this job was paying him, he'd finally be able to buy himself that little place he'd had his eye on, the one far enough away from people and their problems that he and Goliath could retire in peace.

A place not too different from the log cabin he'd spied on the other side of this rise.

Pulling a pair of field glasses out of his saddle bag, he patted Goliath's neck then set out for the top of the hill. Knowing his six-foot-three-inch frame would block out the sun just as much as Goliath, Stone hunkered over as he climbed, going down to his belly for the last few yards. Bracing his weight on his elbows, he sighted the house then held the field glasses up to his eyes and focused in on the details that would tell him how best to approach.

His target had proven unusually cagey. And careful. No witnesses. No discernible trail. No demand for ransom. He'd been forced to do his tracking through society drawing rooms and county registries. Not exactly his areas of expertise. Folks tended to either cower or look down their noses at him in those kinds of places. But enduring the disdainful sniffs of a passel of pinkie-pointin', tea-sippin' ladies had eventually paid off, leading him to a bit of old gossip that gave him his first solid lead. And if he was right, he'd have his quarry rustled up before nightfall.

Stone rolled onto his back and pulled out the photograph he'd taken from the school wall. Three women and a man stood behind a group of two dozen kids spit-shined and dressed for the camera. Two black ink circles blazed up at him. One around a young girl sitting in the front row. Another around a tall woman standing ramrod straight on the far right.

Was the girl dead? Sold? The child was a pretty little thing. Blond hair, bright eyes. A gal like that would fetch a hefty price down in Mexico. But her grandfather didn't seem to believe any serious harm had befallen the girl. He'd simply hired Stone to find her and retrieve her. But what did a pampered rich man know about the seedy side of the world?

Stone had seen evil up close, had trailed men who'd slit a fellow's throat without a second thought, who'd rape a woman then trod on her face for the perverse pleasure of having her beneath his boot. But those who hurt children? Those were the worst of the lot. He prayed the old man was right. He'd never laid a hand on a woman, but God help him, if this Charlotte Atherton person had hurt the child or sold her into the hands of one who would, he didn't think he'd be able to stop himself.

Rolling back onto his stomach, he squinted through the field glasses and ordered his heart rate to calm. No use imagining the worst. Everyone he'd interviewed had given Miss Atherton a glowing character reference. Active in her church, charitable even on her small salary, dedicated to her students. Yet why would such a paragon steal a child? There must be something darker lurking beneath the surface. Something cunning and sly and perhaps a bit demented.

A high-pitched scream pierced the quiet afternoon air. A child's cry. Stone tensed. The toes of his boots dug into the earth, ready to spring him forward. He'd not stand by and do nothing while a child —

A tow-headed girl ran out of the cabin. Stone raised off his belly enough to grab the six-shooter from his right holster. The Colt wasn't the best for long-range shooting, but the sound would draw attention away from the girl. He held the field glasses steady, his gaze glued to the girl as he cocked the hammer.

She screamed again then turned to glance over her shoulder. Stone froze. The girl's face was aglow with . . . laughter. She wasn't screaming. She was squealing. A boy, probably a couple years older than the girl, ran into the viewing area, a long-armed contraption of some sort in his hand. A loud *pop* echoed an instant before a rope shot out from the thing. The girl squealed again and dodged to the left. The rope flopped onto the ground. Admirably close to its target, though. If the boy rigged the rope with a barbed end, he'd have himself a harpoon. Rather impressive.

"You missed!" the girl crowed. She said something more, but her return to normal volume kept the words from carrying.

Exhaling a slow breath, Stone holstered his revolver and settled back in to observe. He tossed a quick prayer heavenward, thanking God that Lily Dorchester was alive and unharmed. For the girl *was* Lily. He'd recognized her features when she'd turned. Now she was dancing around the boy, as carefree as a tawny-haired kitten playing with a piece of string — a string the boy was wrapping up and reloading for another round of target practice.

The dancing halted with a skid. Lily ran up to the boy and cupped her hand between her mouth and his ear then pointed back toward the house. Stone scanned the yard in the direction she'd pointed. A statuesque woman with a laundry basket propped against one hip glided toward a line draped with sheets, towels, and a pair of aprons. Her back was to him, so he couldn't make out her features, but she moved with the refined grace of a society lady. No hurry to her step. Back straight as a board. Hair miraculously unaffected by the wind. At least she wore sensible clothes. Not exactly prairie calico, but her blue skirt was free of frills and she'd rolled the sleeves of her white shirtwaist to her elbows. Add a tailored jacket, and she'd look just like the woman in the picture. Charlotte Atherton.

His pulse sped up a notch at the sight of his quarry.

But he wasn't the only hunter about.

Another had her in his sights as well. One with a giggly assistant who couldn't seem to stand still in her excitement. The boy crept closer to his target, took careful aim, and waited. Waited for her to drop the laundry basket and reach for the first sheet. Waited for her to fold. Waited until the precise moment she leaned over to lay the clean linen in the bottom of the basket.

A *pop* sounded, followed by a less-than-dignified screech as the rope's end slapped against Miss Atherton's . . . end. The woman jerked upright, one hand moving to cover the offended area as she spun.

Now the truth would show itself. Stone waited for the explosion.

"Stephen Farley!"

And there it was. Would she fetch a switch? Perhaps a strop? These tight-laced teacher types always had something around for maintaining discipline. Never a drop of humor in them, and blessed little compassion.

The two pranksters darted out of his vision, but Stone didn't move the glasses to follow them. His attention was locked on the face that had just turned his way.

The photograph hadn't done her justice. Stone's breath leaked out of him in a quiet whistle. Hair the color of sunlight shining through honey. Sun-kissed cheeks and snapping blue-green eyes. Why, if she softened that stern expression of hers, she'd be downright pretty.

"That's quite a clever contraption you've put together, Stephen," she called after the fleeing children. "But if you ever administer it in that fashion again, you'll be writing me an essay on the role of gentlemanly behavior in the advancement of civilization." She shouted the last, ensuring the boy heard her dire threat. If one could call that bit of pudding a threat. An essay? Really? That's what she used to keep the children in line?

Taskmasters the world over were hanging their heads in shame. Wouldn't a kidnapper have to enlist bigger guns to keep her charges from escaping? Locked doors, perhaps. Chains. At least a few threats of bodily harm. A coil of unease tightened in his gut. Something about this situation didn't sit right.

Stone pushed up on his elbows and started to drop the field glasses, but Miss Atherton did something at just that moment that arrested him. She smiled. Small and sweet and oh-so-secret as she slowly turned back toward her laundry. A fondness for the troublesome boy had glowed from within its depths. Not the smile of a madwoman or an abductress tasting future payments, but the smile of a mother.

It must have been that smile that kept him from hearing the nearly silent footsteps creeping up behind him. When the muffled sound finally registered in his brain, his attacker was upon him.

Stone rolled to his back, his hands curving around the grips of both pistols. They never cleared leather. For the gray-haired gnome that had materialized out of the hillside slammed a rifle butt against the top of his head, and Stone's world went black.

2

Stone woke to a pounding head and the disorienting sensation that the world was moving around him. He assumed the dizzy feeling was related to the knot on his forehead until he opened his eyes a crack and saw that the world truly was moving. Or rather, *he* was moving through it. Being dragged through it, actually.

He lay on some kind of litter, one made with pine branches and the itchiest wool blanket known to man. Stone tried to scratch a spot on his neck, but both hands came up together. Bound. He pulled against the rope, contorting his fingers and twisting his wrists, careful not to flail about too much. Better his captor not realize he was awake. The gyrations proved pointless, however. The gnome knew how to tie a knot.

Stone did a quick inventory. Hands bound. Ankles bound. Gun belt missing. Hunting knife confiscated. The blade in his boot was probably still there, but he couldn't be sure. He tipped back his head and caught a glimpse of Goliath's hooves. Indignation roared to life in his chest. His captor had hitched the litter up to Goliath as if the noble steed were nothing more than a pack mule! *Conk me on the head all you like, Gnome, but insult my horse, and I'll make you pay.*

Stone started to roll off the litter and make his stand when his ears perked. Children. Laughing. Calling out to someone named Dobson. His captor? Suddenly the insult to Goliath no longer seemed relevant. In fact, at the moment it seemed downright providential. Rather like the Trojan horse hiding soldiers in its hollow belly. Goliath was dragging him straight into the heart of enemy territory. Where better to gain the knowledge he needed to make his retrieval as clean as possible?

Closing his eyes, Stone feigned unconsciousness and waited.

"What'd you bring us, Mr. Dobson?" A high-pitched voice. Probably the girl's. "What is it? What is it?"

The child sounded like she thought he was an oversized turkey trussed up for Sunday supper.

"Stay back, missy," his captor warned.

33

"He's a mean one."

Him? It was all Stone could do not to scoff aloud. He wasn't the one who'd slammed a rifle butt into an unsuspecting man's head.

"Go fetch Miss Lottie." Saddle leather creaked. Dobson must be dismounting.

Something sharp prodded Stone in the ribs at the same time. The boy. Stone was tempted to lunge upright and growl, but scaring the kid witless wouldn't serve his purpose. So he lay like a lump and let the youngster prod at him.

"Is he dead?"

"Nah. I just tapped him on the noggin." Another prod with the stick. Or maybe it was that harpoon contraption. "Better quit pokin' at him. Don't want him to wake up too soon and scare the missus."

"Aw. Nothin' scares Miss Lottie. Well, except those frogs I slipped into the drawer of her dressing table that one time." The boy smothered a laugh. "She came running out o' her room with her hair flying every which way. It's the only time I ever seen her with it down. Didya know it hangs past her waist? I don't know how she manages to pile it all on top o' her head and keep it there."

Why did the boy have to go and draw that picture for him? Here he lay, forced to keep his eyes shut to maintain his ruse, thereby leaving him vulnerable to inappropriate mental images. Where was a good horse to inspect or a barn door to count knotholes in when he needed one? All he had was the back of his eyelids, and they provided scant protection from the vision of a tall woman with honey-colored hair flowing in long waves down the line of her back. Hard to picture Charlotte Atherton as a tight-laced prude if her hair was all soft and free.

"It ain't proper to discuss a woman's hair, boy." Dobson nearly choked on the words. Was he embarrassed? Angry? Infatuated with the picture himself? That last thought nearly had Stone scowling before he remembered to keep his facial muscles relaxed.

"Go rub down my horse then fetch a bucket of water for the stranger's animal. The beast prob'ly worked up a thirst carting this heavy carcass around." A boot nudged against Stone's hip, leaving no question as to the identity of the heavy carcass being discussed. Stone couldn't say he enjoyed being compared to buzzard bait, but at least the man was seeing to Goliath's welfare.

Plodding hoofbeats retreated as the boy led Dobson's horse away. A gnat buzzed around Stone's nose, making the skin around his nostrils itch something fierce. The infernal bug finally flew away, but the itch remained. And intensified with each tickle of breath. Of all the rotten timing.

Stone directed his mind back to the fetching picture of Miss Atherton with her hair down. Anything to distract him from the need to scratch. Unfortunately, thoughts of all that hair only made him think of how a stray strand dragging across his face would itch like the very devil. Doggone it. He wanted to scratch. Just once. Maybe if he turned his head a little and raised his shoulder he could make it look natural. Maybe not unconscious-natural, but the gnome was no doctor. How would he know what an unconscious man might do?

The creak of a door hinge focused Stone's attention in an instant and saved him from his idiotic rationalizing.

"Mr. Dobson? What on earth . . . ?"

Fabric snapped back and forth in a rapid staccato as Miss Atherton hurried to see what her guard dog had drug in.

"He was up on the ridge, miss. Spying on you and the young'uns. With these."

Ah. Well, at least Stone knew where his field glasses had ended up. He supposed he should be grateful they hadn't been left in the dirt. He'd paid over twenty dollars for the high-powered pair and didn't want to think of them being left out in the elements. The evidence they presented was rather damning, though. He could practically feel her gaze wandering over him, assessing the threat.

Then she was touching him. Her cool hand skimmed over his face until her fingertips rested against the pulse point at his neck. His blood surged at the contact.

"He has a vigorous pulse. I suppose we should be thankful for that."

Too vigorous for an unconscious man. She didn't say the words, but Stone heard the suspicion in her tone. The woman was no fool. He willed his breathing to slow, hoping to compensate for his unplanned reaction to her touch.

"I don't see any blood. You didn't shoot him, did you?"

"No, miss. Just knocked him a good one. He'll rouse afore long. What do you want me to do with him?"

An excellent question, Stone thought. Time to see just how far the teacher was willing to go to keep her ill-gotten gains.

"You'll have to help me get him into the house. I can't tend to him properly out here in the yard."

"Get him into the . . ." Dobson sputtered. "Have you lost your mind, woman? You can't take him into your house. That ain't what I was askin'. I was askin' if you wanted me to cart him into Madisonville to the sheriff or take him out back and work out a more permanent solution. Sure as manure stinks, he's Dorchester's man."

"Probably. But we don't know that for certain. Perhaps he's simply a cowhand with a penchant for bird watching."

Bird watching? Stone nearly jumped to his feet to defend his manhood against the foul slur. Only sissified dandies wasted time on —

Her palm pressed against his chest as if signaling him to stay down. Had she read his mind?

"Bird watching?" Dobson's incredulous voice soothed Stone's pride. "What a load of bunkum. Look at him. He ain't no birdwatcher. He's a mercenary."

Retriever, Stone silently corrected. Not mercenary. His brain was for hire, not his gun.

"Even so," the teacher said, "I can't condone violence against him. The Bible instructs us to love both our neighbor and our enemy, so no matter which category this man falls into, it is our place to offer assistance. Now, help me carry him into the house." Her hand finally slid from his chest, but Stone was too stunned to move a muscle.

She planned to take him into her house? Suspecting he was the enemy? He didn't know whether to applaud her faith or berate her stupidity.

"At least let me fetch the sheriff," Dobson begged.

"And what, precisely, do you expect the sheriff to do? This man hasn't committed any crime. In fact, having the sheriff here would put you in danger. You *did* assault the man. He could call you up on charges."

That shut the fellow up. Well, not completely. He muttered under his breath for nearly a full minute as he unstrapped the litter. When the poles finally fell free from Goliath, Stone's head slammed into the ground with a hard thump. He couldn't quite contain his moan. Only then did the muttering stop.

"Sorry about that." The low, feminine tone resonated near his ear at the same time cool fingers cupped the back of his head. "Now might be a good time to revive, at least temporarily," she whispered. "I'm afraid that with as large as you are, if Mr. Dobson and I try to carry you into the house, you're bound to earn several more bruises."

Not an enticing prospect. And since the one he cared most about fooling wasn't fooled at all, there wasn't much point in continuing the charade. Letting another moan slide from between his lips, Stone lifted his head and made as if to sit up.

Pain speared his skull, eliciting a genuine groan. Careful not to jerk his head around too much, he tugged at his bonds, allowing his struggles to increase as if just then becoming aware of his situation.

A rifle barrel dug into his shoulder. "Settle down, stranger."

Stone glared up at Dobson. "If I were you," he bit out in a low, threatening tone, "I'd watch where I was pokin' that thing."

Dobson paled slightly, but to his credit didn't give up an inch of ground. "I'm watchin'," he blustered. "So don't get any ideas." Dobson jabbed the barrel a little farther into the dip beneath Stone's collarbone for good measure.

Stone's glare promised retribution.

"Are you two quite finished?" The impatient, snapping voice drew Stone's attention back to the teacher. "I swear," she muttered as she leaned forward to take hold of Stone's arm. "It's as if boys never grow up. No matter how old they get, they're still determined to prove themselves the tough-est, fastest, smartest, whatever-else-they-can-think-of-to-compete-about-est. It's ridiculous. If they would just cease their posturing for a moment, they might actually manage to accomplish something worthwhile." She tugged on his arm then, making it clear what she wanted from him.

Bossy bit of goods. But what did he expect from a tight-laced schoolmarm? Actually, he'd expected a lot more running and hid-ing. Tears. A screech or two. Seeing as how she suspected him of being Dorchester's man. Not this quiet determination to see his wounds tended.

What was her angle?

Miss Atherton tugged on his arm again, and Stone complied with her not-so-subtle hint. Rolling slightly to the side, he tried to lever himself up — no easy feat with wrists and ankles bound. The teacher released his arm and gripped him about the waist instead. She wedged her shoulder against the side of his chest to help him find his balance as he stood.

Unfortunately, the sudden change in elevation sent his head whirling in a fit of dizziness. He winced and staggered sideways, forgetting the state of his ankles. The bindings tripped him, and he would

41

have fallen if the teacher hadn't tightened her grip and wrenched him back against her.

"For heaven's sake, Dobson. Untie his feet or we're both going to topple into the dirt."

The bearded fellow came around to the front of them and scowled up at Stone as he pulled a long-bladed knife from the sheath at his waist. "I don't trust him."

"I don't either, but that doesn't mean we have the right to treat him like a prisoner." Miss Atherton grunted a bit as she propped up Stone's weight.

He tried to help her, but his legs didn't seem to be working properly, and the ground kept swelling up and down. He gritted his teeth against the nausea building inside. Acting weak to gain information was one thing, but disgracing himself by casting up his accounts in front of a lady was not acceptable.

"You look a little green around the gills there, stranger."

Great. Now the gnome was smiling. As if the urge to retch hadn't been strong enough already.

"Quit taunting the man and cut him free, Dobson. He's too heavy for me."

Whether it was the woman's authoritative tone or the revelation that she was suffering more from the delay than Stone was, Dobson finally gave in and sliced through the ropes at Stone's feet. Stone immediately braced his legs apart and relieved Miss Atherton of the majority of his weight.

Stone held out his hands toward the little man in front of him, but Dobson's face turned granite hard. Looked like he'd be keeping his hemp bracelets for a while yet.

Miss Atherton urged him forward. Together, they limped to the house.

"John," she called. "Open the door, please."

A tiny Chinese boy swung the door wide and held it open by leaning his entire body against it. His slanted eyes rounded as his gaze traveled from Stone's boots up and up and up until he finally reached his face. He didn't say a word, just kept staring until Stone shuffled past him into the house.

The girl was nowhere to be seen. Odd for such a giggly, curious thing. The way she'd run up to see him when Dobson first dragged him onto the property proved she wasn't timid. So where was she?

Well, no matter. He'd find her. Find her and get her home.

"John," Miss Atherton instructed. "Collect the ewer from my room then go find Stephen in the barn. Ask him to help you fetch some cold water from the well. I'll need to make a compress for this gentleman's head."

The boy scurried around their legs without a word and darted into a room two doors down the hall on the left. A heartbeat later, he dashed out again, pitcher in hand. Casting Stone a wary glance, he made for the opposite side of the house. A door slammed a moment later.

"Does the kid ever talk?" Stone couldn't help asking as the teacher shouldered him along.

"John prefers to keep his thoughts to himself most of the time." Miss Atherton answered his question politely enough but did not expound.

The woman was guarded, deliberate, and doing her best to keep the children away from him without making it look like that was her purpose. She was a contradiction. A lady to the tip of her toes — polite, kind, hospitable — yet a kidnapper with some kind of hidden agenda he'd yet to puzzle out.

They hobbled through the bedroom doorway and stopped at the edge of the bed. She gently slipped from his hold as he lowered himself to sit on the mattress. She stepped back then bent and took hold of his left boot. She tugged until the thing finally gave way then repeated the action with the other foot.

Stone sat and watched her, too dumbfounded to move. A woman — no, a *lady* — was removing his boots. Such a thing had never happened to him before. She probably just didn't want him dirtying her bed linens but still, it was a novel experience. She lined up the footwear inseam to inseam like a soldier anticipating inspection then stood his boots near the door with toes flush against the wall. Once satisfied, she returned, stepped around his knees, and rummaged for something in the drawer of the bedside table. She extracted a letter opener and started sawing at the ropes binding his wrists. Not that it did much good. The pathetic excuse for a blade was duller than dirt. Still, he appreciated her efforts.

"I've got a knife in the back of my right boot. It's probably sharper."

Her head came up, and the full force of her blue-green eyes slammed into him. Man, but the woman had stunning eyes. Nothing prim or staid about them. Dark lashes shuttered them away from him as she dipped her chin and turned to glance in the direction of his discarded footwear.

"There's a small slit in the leather near the back," he explained. "I keep a blade tucked in there for emergencies."

She picked up the boot in question, found the knife, then returned to him. In three slices, she had his arms free.

Stone rubbed his wrists to ease the burn from the rope. At his movement, the teacher leapt back and held the knife up in front of her. Well, at least she had the good sense to hang on to the weapon. He could overpower her in about two seconds if he wished, of course, but there were too many questions he needed answered and only one way to accomplish the deed — winning her trust.

"I ain't gonna hurt you, lady. As soon as my head quits swimming, I'll be outta your hair." He expected to see relief at his pronouncement, or at the very least, a lessening of her wariness. What he didn't expect was for those expressive blue-green eyes to harden into glinting steel.

She backed toward the door and closed it. What was she up to?

She set the knife on the dresser top then stepped closer to him again. Not so close that he could grab her, but close enough to keep her voice from carrying out into the hall.

"You could have shot me from up on that ridge if you'd wanted to kill me." She spoke with such matter-of-fact certainty, it unnerved him. "I saw the arsenal Dobson brought back with him. No cowhand travels that heavily armed. You're here for Lily."

3

Charlotte gave the man sitting on her bed her best truth-inducing stare. She'd ferreted out all manner of little-boy secrets in her time, but this man was no boy. If she didn't know better, she'd think one of Lily's dime novel heroes had come to life. Charlotte had always scoffed at such exaggerated character descriptions — men as tall as mountains with eyes as hard as flint and bare hands capable of punching holes in brick walls. Hardly realistic. Or so she had thought before Mr. Dobson dragged this particular specimen home.

The man was enormous, though not a scrap of him was extraneous. She could still feel the solidity of his chest and the weight of his muscular arm from when she'd helped him into the house. The raw strength in him was daunting, yet she sensed an intelligence in him that offered promise. A brainless lackey would snatch Lily without a thought, but this man . . . this man might be made to see reason. The weathered skin, the tiniest hint of gray at his temples, and the scars on his hands all spoke of experience, of a life lived by one's wits, of a man who had learned not only to survive but to thrive in hostile conditions. This was no hothead, but a man who liked to gather facts and weigh his decisions. Yet he was also a man who could overpower her with a flick of his wrist and take Lily away in a heartbeat, even with his injury. She must proceed with caution.

The man made no response to her declaration about Lily. Just stared at her, his face giving away none of his thoughts.

Please give him ears to hear, Lord. An open mind wouldn't be amiss, either.

"I'm sure Dorchester painted me as a villain," she began, raising her chin a notch, "but I have legal guardianship of all three of the children in my care."

Amber eyes peered into hers with an intensity that tempted her to take a step back. She'd learned long ago not to show weakness in front of a man, however, and held her ground. Lily's future depended on how she handled this moment. Fear was a luxury she couldn't indulge.

The man braced his hands on the edge of

the mattress, his tanned fingers dark against the white of the sheets as they dug into the ticking. Then his eyes slid closed and his features hardened in concentration. Heavens, the man was truly hurting.

She took a cautious step closer to him, hating to see anyone in pain. Even an oversized mercenary. "Are you all ri— ?"

His hand shot out and latched onto her wrist like a manacle. She struggled to pull free, but his grip offered no hope of escape. The swine! How like a man — taking advantage of a woman's nurturing nature. She should have known better.

"Can you back up that claim, teacher?" He growled the question through gritted teeth, his skin taking on an ashen hue.

Maybe it wasn't *all* a deception. There was dried blood along his hairline in addition to a good-sized knot.

"Yes, I can back it up," she said, praying he didn't notice the slight waver in her voice. "I have documents — *legal* documents — to prove what I say is true. I'll show them to you after I see to your wounds."

"I'd rather see them now, if it's all the same to you."

"Well, I can't exactly fetch them with you restraining me, now, can I?" She dared him to release her with a pointed glance then gave another tug of her captured arm. After a slight hesitation, he released her.

Charlotte immediately reinstated the distance between them. The stranger listed sideways a bit and raised a hand to the lump on his forehead. He winced and hissed in a sharp breath, but Charlotte hardened her heart against his pain. She wouldn't be lured in again.

Nibbling on her lower lip, she crossed to her bureau. This wasn't going at all as she'd hoped. She was supposed to tend the stranger's injuries and thereby earn his gratitude and respect before revealing her secrets. But the stubborn man wasn't co-operating.

When Lily had told her that Mr. Dobson had brought home an injured man, and *a mean one* at that, she'd suspected at once who he might be. Thankfully, she and Lily had worked out a plan more than a month ago about what they should do if a strange man ever came around their place.

Hence, the girl was safely down in the root cellar at this moment, reading by lantern light with a tin of soda crackers and a jar of water on hand. They kept a pallet of quilts down there along with a chamber pot, so there should be no reason for Lily to come out until Charlotte came for her. Lily had never minded their practice runs. Even the time Charlotte forced her to stay down there, quietly, for two hours. She'd simply gotten absorbed in one of her books and let the hours pass.

But this time would be different. It wasn't practice.

Charlotte had done her best to assure Lily that there was nothing to fret about when she'd opened the trap door in the kitchen and sent her down into the cellar. Lily had nodded and even smiled, her trust complete. But Charlotte knew the worry would eat at her while she was alone down there.

Watch over her, Lord. Don't let her be too afraid. And don't let me fail her.

"You gonna show me them papers or just stand there wool-gatherin'?"

Charlotte jumped slightly but covered her startle by turning to glare at the beast on her bed. "This is a delicate matter, sir, and I won't be rushed. Besides, in your current state it is unlikely that you'll be able to comprehend the full significance of my documents. I think it better that we wait until your faculties fully return."

"My faculties never left, Miss Atherton." He glared at her, all prickly pride. Men were such predictable creatures. So determined to assert their prowess and deny anything that could be considered weakness. Although, with this particular man, she wasn't so sure his boast was an idle one. Even injured, he exuded far more competency than most men of her acquaintance. "In fact," he murmured, a touch of menace weaving through the words, "my *faculties* are tellin' me that there's a good chance there *are* no documents."

"There most certainly are!" she bristled, letting her outrage overshadow her fear. She marched the remaining steps to the bureau, yanked open the top right drawer, shifted the rolls of sensible black stockings aside, and withdrew the leather document case she'd secreted beneath them. Slamming it down on the dresser top, she spun to face him. "The documents are inside this case. But you won't be seeing them until *after* I tend your injury." That was her plan, and by all that was holy, she would see it carried out. No man was going to bully her into showing her cards before she was ready, and that was that. "Now, just sit there and be quiet until I tell you you can speak."

He raised a brow at her, as if he couldn't quite believe what she'd just said.

She immediately turned her back on him.

Heavens. *She* couldn't believe what she'd just said. He was no pupil to be ordered about in such a fashion. Why, he could snap her neck with two fingers if he chose. She had no way to enforce her dictate, and they both knew it. Yet he made no move to leave the bed. Nor did he say another word.

He'd submitted to her authority.

Why?

Her pulse flickered. The why didn't matter. Whatever his purpose, the fact that he didn't try to dominate her with a show of force proved him to be cool-headed even in his impatience. A man of reason. And a man of reason would listen to reason. Wouldn't he?

A knock on the door stopped her from analyzing the flaws of that particular conclusion. Probably a good thing. Right now hope was in such short supply, anything that hinted of it needed to be clasped to her breast with both hands.

"I've got the water, Miss Lottie." The older boy stood in the doorway with a pitcher and a slightly damp shirtfront.

Stone frowned as he tried to recall the kid's name. Stephen. That was it. The littler one who'd been sent to fetch him was nowhere to be seen. Not surprising. Stone didn't exactly ooze warmth and geniality. Most kids gave him a wide berth.

"Thank you, Stephen." Miss Atherton took the pitcher and walked it over to the washstand on the far side of the room.

The boy stepped through the doorway behind her. He didn't follow her, just braced his legs apart and crossed his arms over his chest. The scowl on his face would have been comical if it hadn't been so earnest.

"Want me to stay and keep an eye on him for you, Miss Lottie? Mr. Dobson told me he wasn't to be trusted."

Stone frowned at the kid. He would have told the boy he wouldn't hurt the teacher, but he didn't want to give up his vow of silence just yet. The kid wouldn't know why he kept his mouth shut, but the teacher would.

Miss Atherton came back around to the front side of the bed and peered at him in a measuring sort of way. "His trustworthiness is yet to be determined."

Her response shocked him. The woman was no fool. She knew he was there to retrieve Lily. She'd admitted as much to his face. Yet she didn't paint him the villain.

His gaze met hers and held. After years of bounty hunting, he knew how to read guilt in an outlaw's face, even when the man protested innocence. Charlotte Atherton's eyes held no guilt. Fear, yes. Intelligence, for certain. And more than her fair share of stubborn determination. But not guilt. At least not that he could see. What he did see was her silent plea for him to offer her the same courtesy she'd just offered him — an open mind.

"Are you sure, Miss Lottie?" Stephen took another step into the room. "He looks pretty shady to me."

The teacher moved to the boy's side and draped an arm over his shoulder. "He's done nothing to deserve our censure, Stephen. Until he does, we will treat him as our guest. We will tend his wounds and offer hospitality until he feels fit enough to leave." She steered the clearly unconvinced kid through the doorway and out into the hall. "Now, go find John and keep an eye on him until I'm done here."

"Yes, ma'am." The boy grumbled as he kicked the toe of his shoe against the wall in protest, but he complied. Although he did make a point to shoot a final glare in Stone's direction before he left.

Stone eyed the teacher as she made her way back into the room, closing the door behind her. What made this woman tick? She seemed oddly determined to be hospitable, even going so far as to scold him into silence when he demanded to see her so-called proof of guardianship. She was stalling, of course, but he wouldn't challenge her on it just yet. He'd rather see things play out. Besides, his head pounded like the very devil. He'd never admit it to her, but he might actually need a little time to recover. Between the throbbing in his skull and the dizziness that set the room to spinning whenever he moved too fast, he wasn't exactly at his best. And with his weapons confiscated, he'd need to be at his best to get the girl safely away.

The sound of water splashing into a basin echoed behind him, followed by a gentle swishing and then a dribbling of excess liquid as Miss Atherton prepared her compress. A moment later, she came into view, her strides businesslike, her expression neutral. Still not meeting his gaze, she halted directly in front of him. One hand held a folded handkerchief. The other lifted to touch him beneath his chin, tipping his head back to give her a better view of his injury.

The touch reverberated through him like a battering ram sending shudders through a fortified wall. Her hand was damp and cool from the well water, yet heat, not shivers, coursed through him at the contact. He'd never felt the like. His first instinct was to shove her away from him and gather his bearings, but he forced himself to remain still. No sense in giving her reason to suspect her touch affected him. It didn't, anyhow. It had just surprised him, that's all. She was his target, an abductor of children, a destroyer of families, a villain of the worst order.

A villain with a very gentle touch.

Stone's eyes slid closed as she dabbed the cool cloth against his scalp.

A villain who smelled fresh and clean, and who mothered the children around her with calm authority and kind words.

Her fingers tunneled through the hair at the back of his head, searching for other wounds and sending a wave of unwelcome tingles down his nape. She found the tender spot where his head had slammed into the earth after Dobson unfastened the litter and dropped him. Stone hissed in a breath. She murmured an apology then immediately moved the compress to the offended area and soothed it with a welcome coolness.

"Here, hold this." She removed her left hand from his chin and reached around to hold the compress in place, freeing her right hand to find his and lift it to the injured spot. "I'll fetch a second cloth."

He opened his eyes and watched her disappear around the edge of the bed.

Solicitous. Gentle. Protective. Of the kids as well as of him. He hadn't forgotten the way she'd forbidden the bloodthirsty gnome from *disposing* of their unwanted guest. She wanted something from him, of that he had no doubt, but no matter how hard he tried, he couldn't quite convince himself she was the villain Dorchester had depicted when Stone had accepted the job.

And if she wasn't a villain, where exactly did that leave him?

4

Charlotte fisted her fingers to still their trembling. Touching him had been a mistake. It had turned him from a theoretical threat into a flesh and blood man. A man with impossibly broad shoulders and a stubbled chin that rasped against her fingers in an utterly disturbing fashion.

Get ahold of yourself, Charlotte. You're twenty-eight years old, a dried-up old prune. What do you care about muscles or broad shoulders or an unkempt chin in want of a shave? He was a man, and men couldn't be trusted. Circumstances had pounded that lesson into her head too many times for her to ignore it now. Besides, this one was working for Dorchester. He'd made no effort to deny it. He was the enemy.

An enemy she desperately needed to win over to her side.

She fingered her mother's cameo then grabbed a second handkerchief from the pile she'd set on the washstand earlier and dunked it ruthlessly into the water. The icy temperature cooled her thoughts and restored her equilibrium. She had a job to do, and Lily's future hinged on her success.

Keeping her eyes downcast, Charlotte strolled back to her patient, careful not to look at him until the last possible moment. The man was just too large. And powerful. Looking at him only served to remind her of her own weakness and vulnerability. If he chose to steal Lily from her, she'd be helpless to stop him. One blow from that tree trunk of an arm and she'd be an insensible, crumpled heap.

Wrenching that disturbing image from her mind, she blotted the last of the dried blood from the knotted area at the stranger's hairline and pressed the compress against the bruised and swollen flesh. The only weapons she could wield against him were kindness and truth. And now that his wounds had been tended, she had nothing left in her arsenal but the truth. She prayed it would be sharp enough to penetrate his defenses.

"What's your name?" she asked as she stepped back from him and forced herself to meet his sharp-eyed gaze.

"So I'm permitted to speak again, am I?"

Charlotte's face grew warm, but she offered no apology. She simply nodded and tried not to notice the way his answering half smile softened his amber eyes.

He straightened his posture, wincing only slightly when he removed the compress from the back of his head. "Name's Stone Hammond."

Of course. How could the man be named anything other than Stone? He was solid muscle from head to toe and had a hard resiliency about him that projected competence — a competence that would have been rather nice to have around had the man not been hired by her enemy.

"Welcome to my home, Mr. Hammond." It was ridiculous, really, to act as if he were a simple traveler passing through when Dobson had bashed his skull and dragged him here with hands and feet bound. But the veneer of civility kept her nerves in check. "I'm Charlotte Atherton, but I suppose you already know that, don't you?"

"Yes, ma'am, I do. And since you know why I'm here, I suggest you quit postponing the inevitable and show me those papers of yours. I give you my word that if they're authentic, I'll take them into consideration."

His word? What value was that to her? Men broke their word all the time. Dr. Sullivan at the academy. Alexander with his smooth promises and faithless actions. All the fathers who promised their children they'd attend their end-of-year recitals then failed to appear. *Her* father.

Charlotte severed that line of thought and flung the remains away before they could undermine her purpose. Her back was to the wall here. She had no choice but to show Mr. Hammond the papers and pray for the best.

"Very well." She turned from him and crossed to the bureau, praying with every step that he would be convinced of the truth. It took only a moment to unfasten the buckle on the case's strap and pull out the papers secreted inside. Holding them to her chest, Charlotte turned to face him. "Before I show you these, Mr. Hammond, I'd like you to state your business plainly. Who are you and why are you here?"

Stone frowned. What game was this? She'd already deduced who he was, who he worked for. What did she hope to gain by asking him to confirm it?

"I'm a retriever," he stated. "The best in Texas. Hired by Randolph Dorchester to find and return his lost granddaughter."

"I appreciate your honesty." Something

solidified in her gaze, if he'd just passed some kind of test. "It's more than I expected from a man working for Dorchester." Her unspoken implication hung heavily in the air. He could sense words piling up in her, words disparaging his employer's character. Yet they never came.

Interesting.

Most people were quick to justify their questionable actions by placing the blame on another. Charlotte Atherton was tempted. He could read the conflict in the way her lips parted ever so slightly, as if the words pressing from the inside had breached the first level of defense. Until she swallowed them.

Respect for her swelled in him, along with a host of questions he had no ready answer for. Why had Charlotte Atherton taken Lily and the others? She'd asked for no money. And she didn't seem crazy. The kids were well tended and obviously cared a great deal for her, if Stephen's earlier attempt at protection was any indication. So what had led an otherwise normal, well-bred woman to abduct three children?

She had gumption, too. Facing him directly. Alone. Unarmed. She hadn't even taken his boot knife. It still lay untouched atop the dresser. Shoot, under other circumstances, he'd probably actually like the woman.

But liking his target wouldn't stop him from accomplishing his mission. He'd never failed to retrieve what he'd been sent after. He wasn't about to start now.

Back straight, the woman walked right toward him. "Your honesty and restraint make me believe you might be a man of honor." She spoke haughtily, but her eyes revealed a tiny glimmer of hope — a hope that made him wish he'd never taken this job. Let someone else crush her spirit. He didn't have the stomach for it. But then, his feelings didn't matter. Completing the job did. "If you are," she continued, conveying with a lift of her brow that only a dishonorable man would disagree with whatever rationale she'd concocted to justify her actions, "when you read these documents, I'm sure you will see that this is all just an awkward misunderstanding. Randolph Dorchester is not Lily's legal guardian. I am."

She held the papers out to him. He took them from her hand, keeping his gaze locked on hers. He'd not be manipulated. Not by her. Not by anyone.

Their eyes held for a long minute, hers filled with as much determination as his, before he finally turned his attention to the documents she'd presented.

He scanned the first page. Signatures from a Joseph and Diana Farley glared up at him from the bottom of the page. Apparently they had granted permission to Sullivan's Academy for Exceptional Youths and any representative thereof to act in one Stephen Farley's best interest in their absence. The second page was practically identical. Only it was an agent from St. Peter's Foundling Home who had signed on behalf of John Chang.

As a representative of the academy, Miss Atherton *could* be acting within her rights. Yet with the school having been dissolved, the agreement would likely not stand up in court. On the other hand, the supervisor at St. Peter's had voiced no objection to the teacher taking charge of young John. Even seemed to believe it was better for the boy. He didn't know if the Farleys would feel the same, but they were apparently still in Europe, according to what his inquiries had ferreted out.

As if reading his mind, Miss Atherton stepped closer to the bed. "I have written to Stephen's parents." She was a picture of calm as she presented that defense, though he imagined a twister reeled inside her. The

66

only indication of her unease was the hand she raised to her throat. It didn't tremble or shake, but her fingers stroked the cameo at her neck once, then twice before she caught herself and lowered her hand. "They have been notified of his whereabouts and assured that he will be returned to their care as soon as they are back in the country."

Stone pierced her with a look, thinking to catch her in a lie. "You didn't worry that they would give away your location?"

Her composure slipped just a notch, but not in the way he'd expected. She didn't glance away or bite her lip in nervousness or hem and haw while trying to come up with a plausible story. No, she scowled at him.

"Don't be a ninny. Of course I worried. But what choice did I have? They needed to know where the boy was. I had Stephen address the letter, using his name as the return address to make it less obvious for someone looking for me, and we mailed it from a town in the next county as an extra precaution. I urged Mr. and Mrs. Farley to correspond directly with Stephen since the school had been closed and hoped that would keep them from mentioning the situation to anyone back in Austin. Did they write to Dr. Sullivan? Is that how you found me?"

Stone shook his head. "No."

She made no response beyond a slight relaxing of her shoulders, but he could feel her relief. The scowl departed next, allowing the composed mask to slip back in place.

She was good. And as far as he could tell, she was not lying. Yet.

He set aside the top two sheets. The boys weren't his concern. She could keep them as long as she wanted if no one made an issue of it. Lily was the one he'd been sent to retrieve.

Stone scanned the third page. Stopped. Then dragged his eyes back to the top to read every word. This couldn't be right. The document had to be a fake. The signature forged. But it had been witnessed by a judge.

A sick feeling pooled in Stone's gut. If this paper was authentic, it changed everything.

5

When Stone Hammond read over Rebekah's will a third time, hope surged in Charlotte's chest like a Thoroughbred straining for the finish line. But she reined it in. This was no quick turn around the track. This was a grueling cross-country race, one where dozens of unforeseen obstacles could appear without warning. The outcome was far from decided.

"I gather Mr. Dorchester failed to mention my legal claim to Lily when he hired you." She paced down to the end of the bed and idly brushed wrinkles from the edge of the coverlet.

The man made no response.

Very well, she'd just have to answer his questions without him actually asking them. "Lily's mother, Rebekah, became a dear friend to me after she enrolled Lily in the academy the term before last. She'd been widowed the year before and had taken up residence in her father-in-law's home in Houston. Something happened while she and Lily lived there. I'm not sure what. Rebekah never told me."

Charlotte wished now she'd had the temerity to ask when she'd had the opportunity. She'd guarded her own privacy for so long, she'd been reluctant to pry into anyone else's. The fewer questions she asked, the fewer she'd be expected to answer in return. Protecting her secrets seemed so pointless now. If she could trade those secrets for information that would help her ensure Lily's well-being, she'd do it in a heartbeat.

"I didn't notice any suspicious bruises on the child when I helped her ready for bed the first night she came to us, so I don't think Dorchester beat her, yet Rebekah had seemed desperate to get Lily into Dr. Sullivan's school. Thankfully, Lily had no trouble earning a place in the academy. She's an extremely bright girl. I recommended her admittance immediately, and Dr. Sullivan concurred. Rebekah nearly wept when I relayed the news. Then she immediately arranged for Lily to board with us through the holidays as well as the school terms. That's when I realized we weren't simply providing education, but sanctuary."

Charlotte paused, lifting her hand from the perfectly smooth end of the coverlet, and turned to face the man called Stone. She prayed the name did not describe the condition of his heart.

"Sounds to me like the mother just wanted to get the girl out from underfoot. Probably had pressing social engagements or maybe a man on her hook that didn't care for having her brat around while courting."

"It's that kind of imbecilic male logic that —" Charlotte stopped. No. She wouldn't explain her fears. It would only weaken her argument. Men wanted facts. Anything that smacked of feminine emotion simply gave them an excuse to discount everything. She would not allow Mr. Hammond to bait her.

"What I meant to say," she amended, her tone calm, collected, "is that you could not be more wrong. Rebekah Dorchester was a devoted, doting mother. She wrote Lily every week, long letters full of news and witty anecdotes about the resident tabby at Dorchester Hall. Those stories never failed to bring a smile to Lily's face. Rebekah visited once a month as well. Nothing kept her away — not rain or freezing temperatures, not the broken carriage wheel that left her stranded three miles outside of town, not even the wasting illness that eventually took her life."

Charlotte took a moment to swallow the rapidly growing lump that always plagued her throat when she spoke of Rebekah's last days. Once certain her voice would not betray her, she continued. "She always found a way to be there for Lily. It is through those visits that she and I became so well acquainted."

Stone Hammond frowned, not at her, really, but at the document residing in his hands. "Still seems odd for a woman to grant guardianship of her daughter to an . . . acquaintance when the child's grandfather was wealthy enough to provide for any need she might have."

"Yes, it is, isn't it?" That brought his head up. His eyes met hers, confusion and mounting impatience burgeoning in his amber gaze. "A rather desperate act, wouldn't you say?"

"Or just plain crazy." He pinned her with his glare, but it wasn't as if she'd not heard this argument before.

"That is what Mr. Dorchester alleges. However, the lawyer who drafted the guardianship agreement as well as the judge who signed it both found Rebekah Dorchester to be of sound mind."

Mr. Hammond scratched at a spot along

his jaw. "I suppose copies of this agreement are filed at the county courthouse?"

"Yes. She filed copies both in Austin and in Houston." So much for hoping the man would accept the documents at face value. It would have made things so much easier. But when had anything in her life ever been easy?

"Then it appears you'll be enjoying my company for a spell." He grinned at her, a full, toothsome smile that would have been handsome if it hadn't been so arrogant.

Charlotte did *not* smile back. "And why is that?"

"I'll need to verify the authenticity of these documents before I can decide what to do. I'll write to an associate of mine in Austin. Get him to make a few discreet inquiries."

She stiffened. "Can this man be trusted?" If Dorchester discovered her whereabouts, she had no doubt he would come for Lily himself. She wasn't so naïve as to believe her piece of paper could get Lily back if Dorchester had the child in his possession. Rebekah had told her the man regularly exchanged favors with a handful of prominent judges and politicians in Houston. He wielded power the way a conductor directed an orchestra, ensuring the people around him played the tune of his choosing. If she lost physical possession of Lily, she'd never get it back.

"I wouldn't work with him if he couldn't be trusted." Mr. Hammond's fierce growl of an answer was oddly reassuring. "He's a Texas Ranger. He'll not be bandyin' the information about, nor will he ask too many questions. What he will do is uphold the law. He's quite a stickler about that." Stone's eyes narrowed. "He'll know if the document's a fake or not."

"I'm not worried about what he'll learn about the guardianship agreement." Charlotte leveled her own stare at him. "I'm worried about another person knowing our location. Lily must be kept safe at all cost."

"Why do you think I'm taking the time to verify your documents?" Stone planted the sides of his hands on his thighs and clenched his jaw against the pain that obviously hadn't fully abated yet. Her papers crinkled in his right fist as he moved to stand. "I've never done anything to put a child in harm's way, and I ain't about to start now. I might have been hired by Dorchester, but I won't be led around by the nose. Not by him and not by you."

Here was the warrior — the man who carried seven weapons on his person and rode a horse large enough to carry two normal men. She should be frightened, yet she wasn't. Stone Hammond might be a barbarian, but he'd just vowed to keep Lily out of harm's way. Perhaps a little barbarism was exactly what they needed.

Stone shoved to his feet. His head pounded, but he ignored the pain. All he wanted now were his boots and room to pace. He needed to think. To figure out what in the world he would do if the teacher's guardianship proved genuine. He strode toward his boots, but a slender figure glided past him, placing herself in front of the door. As if she could stop him if he wanted to leave. Then she took hold of his knife, the one she'd left on the bureau after releasing him from his bonds.

"I hope you're not thinking of tryin' something, teacher." He flicked a meaningful glance at the knife. "I'd hate to have to hurt you."

Charlotte Atherton raised her chin, fire sparking in her usually cool gaze. "Don't be ridiculous. I'm going to give it to Mr. Dobson to lock away with your other weapons. They'll be well kept until you are ready to leave us."

So she thought to clip his claws, did she?

Not that he would ever use them against her or the kids. Dobson on the other hand . . . Stone ran a pair of fingers over the lump pushing out of his forehead. Maybe locking his arsenal away wasn't such a bad idea. A pen and paper were the weapons he had use of at the moment anyway.

"Fine," he groused, waving her off with a sweep of his hand. "Keep the hardware. But I'll need my other belongings. And if you could spare a spot in the barn for me to bunk down, it'd be appreciated."

"That can be arranged."

He straightened to his full height, planting his toes six inches in front of the teacher's. He waited for her head to tip back, for her eyes to meet his before he made his first demand. "I want to question the girl."

A layer of color drained from Charlotte Atherton's face, but her voice held steady. "Absolutely not."

The schoolmarm tone grated on his nerves, but he'd expected that response. He crossed his arms and pierced her with a look. "Dorchester has his agenda. You have yours. The only party who can testify impartially as to what Lily wants is Lily. Forbidding me from talking to the girl only makes me wonder what you're trying to hide." He leaned an inch closer. "You're not afraid of what she might reveal to me, are you?"

"Not what Lily might reveal, no." The hard set of Miss Atherton's face softened just a bit, as if he'd chinked her armor. "My concern is what you might reveal to *her*."

Stone's arms unfolded. Not the answer he'd anticipated.

The teacher dropped her gaze and let a small puff of air escape her lips. Stone stepped back, giving her space.

"Lily doesn't know her grandfather is searching for her. All she knows is that her mama gave her into my care and that we moved here to start a new life after the school closed."

"Didn't she wonder why you spirited her away in the middle of the night? For I know you did. A Miss Greenbriar mentioned that you departed before dawn and a Mr. Fellows from two doors down remembered hearing a wagon roll past his house a little after midnight. Seems he thought it strange since the street was usually so quiet. He took a gander out his window and saw a short driver with a woman on the seat beside him. Didn't mention any young'uns, but I figure you had them bedded down in the back."

The teacher shrugged her shoulders, obviously unwilling to confirm or deny his suspicion. Not that he needed her to. He had a clear enough picture of how she'd made her initial escape. It was the destination that had stumped him for so long. No train tickets. No innkeepers who remembered seeing a woman and three children. Stone had thought for sure he'd be able to track them with someone as distinctive as John Chang in the group. Chinamen weren't all that plentiful in Texas outside of the railroad camps. Chinese kids even rarer. But the woman had been too clever to room in a public place. She probably rotated the kids, too, letting different ones nap in the back so no one would see the same combination of travelers as they made their way across Texas.

"I don't want Lily to be afraid," the teacher said at last. "I want her to be happy and carefree without shadows of hurt and uncertainty hanging over her head. That's no way to grow up." Something in her adamant tone prickled Stone's intuition. Is that how Miss Atherton had grown up? With shadows and hurt?

"I'm not sure she really understands the threat her grandfather represents," she continued. "All Lily knows is that her mama

· 78

told her I would take care of her and that she wasn't to return to Dorchester Hall because her grandfather couldn't be trusted. If she learned that same man was coming after her . . . well . . . it would change her. And not for the better."

Stone recalled the laughing girl, squealing and playing with Stephen as the two youngsters ran about the yard. He wasn't so cold-hearted as to wish that carefree spirit away, but at the same time, he wouldn't be doing the girl any favors letting her live in ignorance, either. Dorchester had the kind of wealth that would ensure the girl never lacked for anything tangible. Even Miss Atherton herself admitted that she didn't know why her friend hadn't wanted her daughter in his custody. In Stone's meetings with the man, he'd seemed the same as all other rich men — self-important, arrogant, expecting people to jump to do his bidding — but he smiled a lot, too, and seemed a charming sort. Not the type to hurt a child.

There was no way around it. Whether Miss High-and-Mighty liked it or not, he needed to talk to the girl. Stone set his jaw. Separating a child from family was a serious matter. Even if the teacher's documents proved legitimate, a man had the right to see his grandchild. Lily was the only one who could give any insight into why Dorchester should be kept in the dark. If, in fact, he should.

"I'm going to talk to her." When Miss Atherton inhaled — no doubt working up a full head of steam to blast his hide — Stone held up his hand. "Cool your kettle, teach. I won't mention who I work for or why I'm here. It'll take at least a week to get a response from my man in Austin. So in the meantime, I'll hang around the place, help with the chores, let the kids get comfortable with me. Ask a few questions here and there, but mostly just listen and watch. They'll tell me what I need to know. Probably without even realizing they've done so."

Her mouth snapped closed. Her eyes studied him. Stone held her gaze. He didn't need her trust, but it would make things a whole lot easier.

"All right, Mr. Hammond. I'll consent to your *subtle* questioning of Lily."

Stone nodded, grateful for her co-operation.

"But before you leave this room, I need two things from you."

He should have known there'd be conditions. There always were with women like her — women who used their heads for more than just a place to hang their hair. They always gave as good as they got.

"All right. What do you want?"

He didn't think it possible for her to straighten that poker of a spine any more, but somehow she managed it. "First, I want your solemn oath that you will not try to steal Lily away from me before you hear back from your man in Austin."

Stone nodded. "Done." He held her gaze a long minute. He could feel her doubt, her fear, and tried to combat it with sincerity. "I'll not make a move until I hear back from Austin."

She took his measure, looking him up and down as if evidence of his trustworthiness could be determined as much by his clothing as his face. The gun belts, even with empty holsters, probably didn't help much. Nor did the sheaths for his knives or the well-worn duster that made him resemble a gunslinger. The uniform served a purpose when he was working, intimidating men into speaking the truth and keeping unsavory characters from making ill-conceived attempts to steal from him while on the trail. He really preferred not having to shoot or knife some group of idiots who thought a man alone was an easy target. But none of that did him any good in this female's bedchamber, surrounded by lacy curtains and dresser doilies.

Then her eyes rested on his feet. Stone grimaced as he unconsciously wiggled his toes. A man should be wearing his boots when someone took his measure. Not be standing around in his stocking feet. Especially when one sock had a hole on the outer edge. A woman who took the time to line up his boots in a straight line against the wall would probably condemn him outright for that hole.

Yet it was that hole that took just a touch of the starch out of her bearing. She raised her chin back up to face him, acceptance, if not trust, lining her features.

"Very well, Mr. Hammond. Then I only have one other question for you."

Stone shrugged. "Shoot."

Blue-green eyes zeroed in on him. "Does Dorchester know where I am?"

6

Charlotte's heart beat so rapidly in her chest she had to fight to keep her equilibrium. She widened her stance to secure her footing but kept her attention locked on the man in front of her.

"No," he finally said, and for a moment Charlotte felt so light with relief she thought she'd float to the ceiling. Then he clarified. "But he knows exactly where *I* am."

Her mind froze mid-process, somehow unable to grasp what he was saying. Or perhaps not wanting to. All she could manage was to blink dumbly at him.

"I told him of the lead I was tracking down, a property registered under the name of Charles Atherton outside of Madisonville."

How had he uncovered *that* piece of information? She'd never told anyone at the academy about the small home her parents had left her. Her father spent all his time in

New York. Her mother traveled from opera house to opera house in Europe. No one in Austin knew about the little rustic bungalow they'd purchased for the daughter who'd had no love for the stage.

"I haven't had the chance yet to report my findings to him." The gruff statement almost sounded like reassurance, as if he sensed the dissonant harmony her fear had released and was trying to adjust one of the notes to resolve the chord. Compassion? From *this* man? Charlotte peered at him more closely, but as she did, his eyes shuttered against her. He lifted a hand to his forehead. "Ran into the butt end of a rifle before I could get back to town."

Irony. Sarcasm. That must have been what she'd heard. Not compassion. How foolish to think otherwise.

"Will you be reporting your findings anytime soon?"

If so, she'd have to pack up the children and leave immediately. But where would she go? She'd have to take the boys back to St. Peter's and try to start over with Lily in a new town, maybe even a new state, somewhere nobody knew them. Use assumed names. Alter their appearances. Hide their talents so as not to be memorable. No recitations for Lily. *No music for me.*

No music. The very idea scalded her heart like acid. But she'd do it. For Lily, she'd do it.

A large hand touched her arm, slicing off her spiraling thoughts. "Rein it in, teacher. No need to plot your escape just yet. I can put off my report for a couple days. Maybe longer if I can come up with some kind of excuse to explain my lack of findings or some tidbit to tide Dorchester over until I hear back from Austin."

Time. In this situation there was no greater gift. "Thank you," she said, making no effort to disguise her true level of appreciation.

He dropped his hand from her arm and cleared his throat, his gaze darting away from her face. "Yeah, well, don't go all mushy on me. Dorchester ain't the type to be put off for long, and I ain't the type to play hero just because a pretty lady looks at me with gratitude in her eyes." He stepped around her, and Charlotte made no move to stop him. How could she when her entire body was frozen with shock? This virile mountain of a man thought her pretty? Mercy. Mr. Dobson must have struck him harder than she'd originally suspected.

"I've got a sizable paycheck, not to mention my reputation as a retriever, on the line," Stone Hammond grumbled as he grabbed his boots with one hand and shoved her documents back at her with the other. "You're getting a reprieve, teacher, but I ain't surrendering." One long stride took him to the door. He turned the knob and wrenched the portal open. "Not by a long shot."

The reverberation of wood banging closed punctuated his parting statement, but Charlotte didn't flinch. She smiled.

Mr. Hammond might have a rock-hard exterior, but hard shells were known to harbor soft insides, and he'd just given her a glimpse of his. It was reason enough to hope.

Stone stomped his feet into his boots then strode down the hall toward the kitchen. He might be sprouting a goose egg on his forehead, but he was done letting Miss Atherton play nursemaid. No porcelain basins with purple flowers painted on the side. No frilly bedcovers. No female fussing over him every time he tried to move. Especially a tall one. One who could fit far too well against his side and whose mouth was at just the right height for kissing without giving a man a crick in his neck.

And just *what* was he doing thinking

about kissing? She was his target, for pity's sake. A kidnapper and probably crazy to boot. She simply hid it well under that righteous all-I-want-to-do-is-protect-the-child act of hers.

Stone entered the kitchen, so caught up in his inner rant he almost didn't spot the gnome until it was too late.

"What do ya think you're doing?" The whiskered fella set the strip of wood he'd been whittling on the table and stood, the knife in his hand waving in Stone's direction.

"Stayin'," Stone announced, jaw firm, eyes hard. To make his point, he stripped out of his duster, folded it over, then dropped the heavy coat onto the tabletop. "Miss Atherton invited me to stay for a while, so you might as well get used to seein' me around."

The gnome shot him a glare so hot Stone was surprised his skin didn't start sizzling. Dobson would bear watching. Of course, Stone was pretty sure the man would be watching *him* as well, so it shouldn't prove too difficult to keep tabs on the fellow.

"I need to use the privy," Stone snapped, already plotting ways to escape Miss Atherton's guard dog. "This place got a back door?"

Dobson jabbed a thumb over his shoulder. Stone followed the direction the man indicated then traipsed out the door and onto the porch. After clopping down the stairs, he found the path leading toward a weathered outhouse standing a short distance away, half hidden beneath an overhang of branches from a pair of oak trees.

Once out of the direct sight path of the house, Stone veered sharply to the left and circled back toward the cabin. He needed eyes on the teacher. She'd be going to get the girl. Stashing a child somewhere for an hour or two was one thing; leaving the girl cooped up for a week was quite another. Besides, the teacher had agreed to let him talk to Lily. No reason to hide her any longer. *Every* reason for him to discover the cubby hole where she'd been stashed.

If Ashe couldn't confirm Miss Atherton's claims, Stone would need to grab the girl and get away quickly without alerting the rest of the household. The more he knew about where she might be, the easier it would be to ensure the protection of everyone concerned. He'd get Lily out, one way or another, but avoiding a scenario where Miss Atherton or one of the boys ended up caught in the crossfire was paramount.

So he crouched and ran up to the house, careful to keep his over-large body beneath window height. Instinct told him the teacher wouldn't have led him past the girl's hiding place when she'd helped him into the house earlier, so that left the rear. The same area he'd just left.

Not trusting the boards of the porch to stay silent under his feet, he remained on ground level and flattened his body against the wall. The window closest to him was too far away to see anything beyond the far kitchen wall and the cabinets and shelves located there. However, it was close enough that he could hear the growl of Dobson's voice and the higher, melodic tones of Miss Atherton. He couldn't make out their words, but perhaps he didn't have to, for after a minute the voices ceased and a series of scrapes and dragging noises ensued. Things fell quiet for a moment, then a deep thud from inside reverberated with enough force to vibrate the window glass.

A trap door. Root cellar most likely.

A third voice echoed from within. Small. Quiet. Definitely young. Stone smiled to himself. He'd just discovered Miss Lily Dorchester's hiding place.

Now to get back to the privy before

anyone grew suspicious.

Retracing his circuitous route, Stone hurried back to the trees and the narrow shack waiting there. He grabbed the handle and pulled the door wide, but a rustle in the oak's branches overhead drew his attention.

The older boy, Stephen, was sitting on a limb a few feet above the roof of the outhouse. Stone's gut clenched. Had the kid seen him stalking the house? No. His back was turned. Stone released a breath. Then he caught sight of the harpoon contraption and grinned. The boy looked like a hunter scoping out game. He'd done much the same as a kid, shooting stick arrows at imaginary deer, firing finger guns at stray dogs while pretending they were rabid coyotes. It was what boys did, playing at being men. Thankfully, the kid seemed far too intent on his make-believe prey to have noticed Stone's surveillance. Stephen hunched forward on the branch, his homemade weapon at the ready, the shooting end aimed at something on the ground behind the privy.

Leaving the boy to protect his homestead from whatever lurked in his imagination, Stone stepped into the outhouse, closed the door behind him, and took care of business. He had just hooked his second suspender strap over his shoulder when a whoop echoed above him.

"Got you, you thievin' cat!"

Stone chuckled softly, imagining a barn cat snarled in Stephen's rope. Until a feral screech exploded across his senses. That was no barn cat.

Heart pounding, Stone shoved open the door and scanned the branches above him. If the boy had tangled with a wildcat, no little rope would protect him. He peered at the limb where he'd seen the boy perched, but he wasn't there.

"Stephen!" he called, backing away to get a wider view of the tree. He instinctively reached for his belt, but his knife was gone. All his knives were gone. His guns, too. Stone hardened his jaw. Didn't matter.

He turned toward the house and cupped his hands around his mouth. "Dobson! Get out here!" Praying his voice had carried, he sprinted around the outhouse in the direction the kid had been staring so intently.

A child's scream spurred him on. Twigs snapped overhead. Leaves crackled. A flash of spotted gray fur caught the corner of Stone's vision.

God help us.

Stephen had wrangled a bobcat.

7

With a running leap, Stone braced one foot against the tree's trunk and launched himself toward a low branch. He caught it in both hands and used the momentum to swing his legs around. Gritting against the strain, he tightened his stomach and forced his body to finish the rotation. Once his chest was above the branch, he clambered to his feet and immediately scoured the tree for the bobcat.

Stephen was trying to shove through a tangle of branches above Stone's right shoulder. If the boy could just get back to the privy roof, he'd be able to drop out of the tree and escape. But the bobcat was closing fast. Too fast. The beast leapt from limb to limb with terrifying ease.

"Hey! Over here!" Stone yelled and shook one of the branches beside him, trying to buy the boy time. Unfortunately, the cat paid him no mind, too intent on her prey higher up in the tree.

Stephen whimpered and ducked behind the trunk out of Stone's sight. The cat hissed and sprang after him. Her claws dug into the bark of the near side of the trunk inches away from where he'd last seen the boy. She leaned back on her hind legs, poised for her next leap.

Stone recognized his chance. Grabbing hold of a head-high branch for balance with his left hand, he jumped and made a grab for the bobcat's hind leg with his right. He closed his hand around the thin ankle and yanked with all his might. The cat screamed, her front claws frantically scratching at the bark of the trunk. Her wild movements threw Stone off balance. He had to release her to catch himself. But he'd done his job. The cat's yellow eyes were locked on Stone. Fangs glistened as she growled.

"Run for the house, kid!" Stone yelled. "Go!"

Hearing her prey escaping, the cat jerked her attention back to Stephen.

"Oh, no you don't," Stone said. He released the branch steadying him and jumped a second time, this time with both hands free. He snagged the cat at her hips and pulled her down.

Onto him.

Her back collided with his head and chest as they fell from the tree. He crashed to the ground. Pain shot through his head and left shoulder as his back slammed into the dirt. The impact knocked the wind out of him.

Stone released the writhing bobcat immediately, praying she'd run off. Instead, she flipped onto her feet and pounced onto his chest. The cat swiped at his face. He dodged left. A razor slashed across his shoulder. Another pricked his jaw. And still, he couldn't breathe.

The cat's back claws dug into his chest. Stone arched, desperate to free himself, but the barbs only sank deeper. He punched at the beast with his right arm while shielding his eyes with his left. His fist collided with her side then the bone of her hip. But the counterattack only enraged her. Finally he landed a blow against the side of her head. The shock of it stunned her long enough for him to grasp her around the neck with his hands. With all the strength he could muster, he tore the she-devil away from his body and flung her off.

She hit the ground. The whine she made at the contact echoed in Stone's ears. He rolled over onto his hands and knees, his lungs finally working again. He panted for breath. Then pulled his feet under him. The cat shrieked, raising the hair on the back of his neck. He pivoted to face her. Readied himself for the pounce. She bared her teeth. Hissed. Leaned back on her haunches.

Bang!

A gunshot rent the air. The cat spooked, jumping sideways.

"Go on! Get!" Dobson's voice echoed from somewhere behind Stone a heartbeat before a second shot was fired. The bobcat fled.

Stone hung his head, lungs heaving. *God bless the gnome.*

Charlotte clutched a trembling Stephen against her skirts, his face buried in her shirtwaist, his arms wrapped around her midsection tighter than her corset strings. She should probably say something, offer some kind of verbal comfort, but all she could manage was a slight stroking of his hair. Too consumed was she by the vision of the warrior before her, ready to continue fighting a savage beast with his bare hands in order to save a child he barely knew.

She'd never witnessed such selfless courage.

Slowly the man stood and turned. His gaze found Mr. Dobson. He nodded — a single sharp dip of his chin. Mr. Dobson

95

answered in kind. No words passed between them, but then words didn't seem to be required. Respect thickened the air, along with gratitude, and possibly even a grudging acceptance.

Thank heavens Dobson had thought to grab his rifle when Stephen shouted for help. Mr. Hammond could have been . . . Charlotte sucked in an agonized breath. His wounds! *Lord have mercy.* Deep gashes sliced his chest where the cat had buried her claws. Smaller cuts crisscrossed his shoulders and collarbone. Blood oozed through the tattered white cotton of his shirt. How was the man even standing?

"Looks like she got ya pretty good," Mr. Dobson said with a casual air that fell far short of the horror pulsing through Charlotte. He acted as if the man sported only a few minor abrasions. Outrageous!

Dobson shouldered his rifle and gestured toward the small log building he used as his sleeping quarters. "I got some salve we can slap on those cuts down at the bunkhouse."

"Those gashes need more than a slap of salve," Charlotte snapped, finally finding her voice. "Some of them will probably require stitching." She took a step toward the men, keeping one arm around Stephen. The boy had been through too much for her to just unwrap his arms and leave him behind. "Mr. Dobson, ride into Madison-ville and fetch the doctor. In the meantime, I'll tend to Mr. Hammond's injuries."

"I'll help!"

Charlotte turned to find Lily hanging out of the kitchen doorway. Adoration glowed on her face as she stared at the stranger. Charlotte bit back a sigh. As if the situation weren't already complicated enough. Thankfully, John demonstrated more sense, hiding halfway behind the doorpost.

"You'll look after John." Charlotte gave the girl a stern look.

"Yes, ma'am." Lily's crestfallen expression tore at Charlotte's heart, but she held firm. The last thing she needed was for Lily to make a hero out of the man.

Charlotte twisted back to regard Stone and caught his grimace. He tried to conceal the action by swiveling his head away from her when he noticed her attention, but he'd not been fast enough. As if embarrassed by his weakened condition, he turned away from her and started hobbling after Dobson.

"Stephen?" She gave the boy's shoulders a squeeze then gently pulled out of his hold. "I need you to fetch my medicine box, a basin of clean water, and a clean washrag from the laundry basket. Can you do that for me?"

His posture straightened as he tipped back his head to meet her gaze. "Yes, ma'am." He sniffed once then set his jaw.

"Good." She smiled her approval. "Bring them to Dobson's cabin. That's where Mr. Hammond will be staying for the remainder of his visit."

The boy nodded but didn't move, his attention riveted on the man gingerly making his way to the bunkhouse behind Mr. Dobson. "Mr. Hammond?" The call echoed across the yard.

The man stopped, glanced back. "Yeah?"

"Thanks."

A dip of the chin was all the response the man gave, but Stephen seemed to find it sufficient. He mimicked the action himself then bolted for the house and the tasks awaiting him.

Charlotte longed to follow him, to hide from the man who stirred up a storm of conflicting emotions inside her. How could she feel indebted to a man whose very presence threatened everything she held dear? How could she see strength and courage and nobility in him when he was Dorchester's man?

Well, at this particular moment, his

employer's identity was irrelevant. He'd risked his life to save Stephen. He deserved her gratitude along with whatever solace she could offer. Straightening her spine, she grabbed a handful of skirt and hurried after his retreating form. It didn't take long to close the gap. The poor man was limping on top of everything else he'd endured.

"Did you injure your leg?" she asked as she came alongside him.

He didn't look at her, just kept walking with his focus trained on the ground as if he'd topple if he couldn't see the place where his feet connected with the earth. "Wrenched my hip when I fell out of the tree."

Fell out of the . . . ? Mercy. She hadn't seen that portion of the struggle. It was a wonder the man had survived at all.

"Mr. Dobson?"

The caretaker turned to face her and raised a bushy white eyebrow. "Yeah?"

"Hurry on to get the doctor. He could have broken ribs or other internal damage from the fall. I'll see that Mr. Hammond gets settled."

"Nothin's broken," Hammond ground out through a clenched jaw. "Just banged up. No need to bother the doc."

Of all the stubborn, prideful, stupidly *male*

things to say. Charlotte pierced him with a scathing glower, hoping he'd feel the heat of it even if he refused to look at her. "Well, you're on *my* property, Mr. Hammond, so I get to make the rules. And Rule Number One clearly states that anyone who falls out of a tree while being attacked by a vicious bobcat has to be examined by a doctor. So your swollen pride will just have to take the hit."

That got him to look up. She braced for his anger, but when his eyes met hers they danced with laughter. "That's some Rule Number One. I suppose Number Two addresses the consequences for tanglin' with a bear. No, wait. Coyote?"

"Water moccasin, actually," Charlotte replied, barely managing to keep her lips from twitching into a smile. "We do have a lake nearby."

Stone chuckled. Then winced, a keen reminder of what she was supposed to be about.

Charlotte darted ahead and held the bunkhouse door wide. Stone hobbled inside and limped toward an empty bunk. She frowned as she scanned the room's interior. She'd never really paid much mind to this building, seeing as how it was Dobson's domain. But several details would need to be seen to if Mr. Hammond were to take up residence. Sheets, for one. A blanket or two as well. The mattress on the spare bunk was bare, and the nights still got rather cold. And he'd want his saddle bags and whatever else Dobson had confiscated. The floor could use a good sweeping, and the rafters could use a few less cobwebs, but that would have to wait until —

"I don't like leaving you and the young'uns here alone with him." Mr. Dobson's low-pitched grumble pulled her away from her mental inventory. "Even hurt as he is, he could still cause trouble."

"The man just saved Stephen's life," she whispered back. "He deserves our help."

Dobson didn't look convinced. "He did us a good turn, I'll give you that, but I still don't trust him. I'm pretty sure he's on Dorchester's payroll."

Charlotte was *positive* Stone was on Dorchester's payroll, but now wasn't the time to clarify that point. "I don't trust him, either," she said instead, "but neither do I wish him ill. He needs a doctor, and I aim to see he gets one." A quiet groan behind her drew her gaze to the man in question as he lowered himself onto the small bed in the far corner. "He's in no condition to try anything with Lily. Besides, all of his weapons are safely locked away." Well, most of them anyway. She'd left his boot knife on her bureau when she'd gone to help Lily out of the cellar. "We'll be fine."

The caretaker frowned but made no further objection. "If he gives you any trouble, I keep a hunting knife stashed under my pillow. Don't hesitate to use it."

As if she could stomach adding more cuts to Stone Hammond's already too-plentiful collection. But knowing Dobson was simply concerned for her welfare and that of the children, she nodded her agreement. Only then did the grizzled man march off to the barn to saddle a mount.

Stepping into the bunkhouse, Charlotte's pulse fluttered despite her assurances to Dobson that she'd be fine. Mercy, what was the matter with her? It wasn't as if she hadn't been alone with the man before. In her bedroom, no less. He posed no immediate threat. Besides, she owed him a *little* trust after his heroic efforts on Stephen's behalf.

However, when he arched his back and peeled off what was left of his shirt to examine the damage the cat had wrought, Charlotte's pulse moved from a flutter to a full-out gallop. Her step faltered and her mouth went dry at the impressive display of muscles beneath the wounds.

Oh, dear. Perhaps she was in more danger than she'd originally thought.

8

Stone gritted his teeth against the pain that speared him as he stripped out of his shirt. The stretch of muscles pulled at the injured flesh, causing new blood trails to trickle down his midsection and soak into the waistband of his trousers.

"It's a miracle you're still in one piece. Well . . . relatively one piece." Charlotte Atherton's eyes raked his chest, concern and a touch of squeamishness evident in her gaze. Along with something a tad bit warmer. Appreciation? Dare he think . . . attraction?

Stone straightened, the pain somehow not quite as bad as it had been a moment ago. A beautiful woman's regard had a wonderful dulling effect on a man's pain. The cuts and scrapes still stung like the dickens, but not so bad he couldn't enjoy a little feminine admiration.

Her footsteps clicked quietly against the

wooden floorboards as she crossed to his bunk. For a tall woman, she moved with remarkable lightness and grace. Always so cool and calm, so perfectly tidy. Made a man want to muss her up a bit so she didn't feel so far above him.

Stone gripped the edge of the bunk, commanding his hands to behave themselves. There'd be no mussing today or any other day. He was here for the girl, not the woman. Besides, Charlotte Atherton saw him as the enemy. She wouldn't be lowering her guard, let alone her hair, around him anytime soon. And that was fine with him.

"Thank you for what you did." The woman murmured the words in an offhand manner as she collected a three-legged stool that had been shoved into the corner behind his bunk and carried it to where he sat. She stopped about an arm's length away from him, set the stool down, then pulled a lacy handkerchief from a pocket in her skirt and wiped the dust from the seat. Frowning slightly at the soiled cloth, she arranged it dirty side down on the stool before sitting herself atop it. "Your quick actions no doubt saved Stephen's life." She finally looked him in the face. "I'm only sorry that your bravery caused you so much harm."

"Any other man worth his salt would have done the same." Of course any other man would've had a weapon at his disposal and therefore probably would have avoided becoming a human scratching post, but he had no regrets. He was alive. The kid was alive. Shoot, even the cat was alive. He'd count that a victory.

Miss Atherton glanced toward the open door, a tiny line forming at the edge of her mouth. "Most of the men I've known wouldn't have risked themselves to such an extent."

"Then most of the men you've known haven't been worth their salt."

That tight little line at the corner of her mouth relaxed into a hint of a smile. Better. When she turned back to face him, her eyes danced, and his heart drummed out the cadence of another victory. "You may be right."

Their gazes held, and Stone could swear that something tangible stretched between them. Something he'd never experienced with a woman before. Almost as if he recognized her. Not her physical appearance, but *her.*

He tore his gaze away, the jerk of his head restoring the throb from his earlier injury. His head. Of course. That would explain the odd feeling of recognition. Some kind of side effect from all the battering he'd encountered today. First a rifle butt to the forehead, then a crack on the back of his skull while he was feigning unconsciousness, and now falling out of a tree and wrestling with a bobcat. Any man would be off his feed after that kind of day.

Charlotte Atherton perched on the stool next to him, her back straight, her skirt smooth. Such rigid schoolmarm posture should make him think of lemon-faced disapproval, corner banishment, and rulers rapping knuckles. Heaven knew he'd experienced more than his share of such puritanical disdain. Yet *Miss Lottie,* as the kids called her, looked anything but rigid. Her posture struck him as composed. Serene. Warm.

"Stephen should be here any minute," she said as she reached for the cuff on her left wrist. Her slender fingers pushed the button through its hole then rolled the fabric of the sleeve in methodic turns, each fold precise and uniform until it reached a spot just below her elbow. She repeated the procedure on the right side.

Stone watched, mesmerized, until the shuffle of footsteps passing through the bunkhouse door brought him out of his stupor.

Good gravy. Had his mind completely gone to mush?

"Oh, Stephen. Excellent. Bring those things over here." Miss Prim-and-Proper waved the boy closer and relieved him of the basin he carried, placing it on her lap. A damp circle darkened the blue of the kid's shirt where the rim of the bowl had pressed against his chest, but she praised him for his steady hands anyway and for not spilling much during his trek from the house. She lifted the washrag from where it lay draped over the boy's shoulder then pointed a finger at the floor near her feet. "Set my box down there and slide off the lid, please. I'll need the bandages that are inside."

Stephen pulled the box from under his arm, arranged it as instructed, then stood like a soldier awaiting orders. "What else can I do?"

Stone caught him stealing a glance at the gashes on his chest and hated the guilt that flickered across the kid's face. Stone cleared his throat. "Can you fetch me a few sheets of paper, pen, and ink? I've got a letter that needs to be written." Which was true enough. But his real motive was to get Stephen out of the room when the teacher started cleaning. No need for the kid to see more than necessary.

The boy nodded. "Yes, sir." He turned to leave, but Miss Atherton stopped him. She touched his arm, drawing him close so she could whisper something in his ear. Stephen's eyebrows arched as he listened, but when the teacher finished, he stepped back and said, "All right." Then he dashed out the door.

Charlotte Atherton dipped the cloth into the basin and squeezed out the excess liquid. The trickling water echoed loudly in the quiet room. She lifted the wet cloth to a spot above the largest of the wounds and tightened her fist until a small stream of water dribbled into the hole. He hissed a breath at the cold sting. His abdomen sucked in automatically, but he caught himself and willed his muscles still.

"I told Stephen you wouldn't need those writing supplies for a while." Her eyes made no effort to meet his, whether from shyness or attentiveness to her task he wasn't sure. "He's going to take John to the parlor and let him play on the piano so Lily can start warming up the leftover stew for supper." She rinsed out her cloth and flushed out the second tear in his flesh near the bottom of his ribcage. "That will keep him occupied for a while. John will play the piano for hours if I let him."

Kid seemed kinda young to have that kind of attention span, but some kids liked banging on things and makin' noise. Odd, since the boy himself was so quiet. To each his own, though. If it kept Stephen away from the gory reminder of what had happened, Stone was all for a little piano banging.

"Good idea." He fought a wince as she scrubbed the cloth over the smaller cuts on his shoulder. "This mess is too ugly for the kid to have to look at."

She didn't say anything, yet the way she tilted her head when he finished speaking felt like agreement. She continued working, and he continued watching her.

The woman never seemed to hurry. Her movements just sort of flowed. No rough jostling. No nervous shaking. Just gentle, smooth motions. By the time she'd finished cleaning his wounds, his breathing had slowed, and the muscles in his neck and back had relaxed in response to her calm manner. If his chest hadn't been on fire, he would've curled up on the bunk and taken a nap.

"I'm afraid this next part is going to be rather unpleasant." Her hands released the cloth to slip silently into the basin on her lap. She set the bowl onto the floor then reached for the medicine box. Her graceful fingers closed around the neck of a tall corked bottle. The lovely lethargy he'd been feeling vanished.

Whiskey.

He shifted on the cot, steeling himself for what he knew was to come. She looked at him, an apology in her eyes. He flashed his best cocky grin. "And here I had you pegged as the teetotalin' type." He dipped his head toward the bottle. "I ain't a drinkin' man myself, but if you need a sip for fortification, I won't judge."

"How open-minded of you, sir." Her tone sounded prissy, but her eyes sparkled with humor. His grin spread wider.

She pulled out the cork, the small *pop* echoing between them. Her nose crinkled at the pungent fumes. "As tempted as I am, I'm afraid this particular spirit has been set aside for medicinal purposes."

Stone shrugged. "Suit yourself."

Miss Atherton retrieved the water-soaked rag, squeezed it out, then met his gaze, all humor gone from her eyes. "Are you ready?"

Stone braced his arms on the bunk behind him to make the torn flesh more accessible. Then he tightened his jaw and gave a quick nod.

She held the cloth below the first gash and dribbled the liquid fire from the mouth of the bottle into his wound. Stone's fingers clenched around the edge of the bare mattress. Every muscle in his body pulled taut. But he didn't make a sound. Not even when she repeated the procedure on the second gash. Pride intact, he barely even flinched when she dabbed some of the liquor on his other scrapes. Breathing in through his nose, he forced his body to relax as she finished.

"All done." Something in her voice brought his focus to her face. Tears shimmered in her eyes. "I'm sorry I had to hurt you." And she was. Genuinely.

His gut twisted in response. He hoped to heaven he didn't have to return the favor and hurt her as well. Stone frowned and turned his face away. What did he have to feel guilty about? She was the one who had stolen the kids, not him. If he ended up taking Lily away from her, it would all be above board with the full blessing of the law.

So why was he starting to hope that her claim superseded Dorchester's?

The teacher capped the near-empty whiskey bottle and returned it to the box at her feet. "I don't want to put any of Mr. Dobson's greasy salve on your wounds until the doctor has a chance to examine them. However, it will be at least an hour before my caretaker returns from town, and I don't want any dust or dirt to undo the cleaning we just did. So I thought we'd go ahead and bandage you up. It will help stem the bleeding as well."

Stone eyed the worst of the gashes. Most of the alcohol had already evaporated from his skin, but a new wetness oozed from the openings. It had a pinkish hue as new blood mixed with whatever other fluid was leaking from his body. "Seems like a sound notion."

She shifted on her stool. "If you'll just . . . ah . . . hold these two dressings in place, I'll . . . ah . . . wrap the bandage . . ."

Stone shot a gaze at his nurse. Was the always-serene Miss Atherton actually flustered about something? Her cheeks were definitely turning pink. And her eyes were making a valiant effort to look everywhere except at his chest. Which, of course, meant that was exactly where she wanted to look. Was it the anticipation of touching *him* instead of just his wounds that had her suddenly ill at ease?

He straightened a little, ignoring the painful pull of the skin around his injuries, and reached for the cotton pads she offered. Biting back a grin, Stone glanced down to fit the dressings over the center of each of the large gashes. By the time he raised his head, he had his expression fully stoic and under control. "Ready when you are, teach."

She startled a bit at his voice then rose off her stool to stand over him. "Of course." She pressed the end of the bandage against his side, her fingers cool against his overheated skin. Slowly, she unrolled the cotton strip and passed it over the dressings. The back of her hand brushed against his, the touch sending odd little prickles down into his belly. Then she leaned close in order to reach the bandage behind him. Suddenly he was the one trying to look everywhere but at her. He stared at the ceiling as she continued binding his wounds. His breaths grew shallower with each pass she made. Even when he didn't look at her, he could smell her. Clean. Like fresh-washed linen. Probably because of the laundry she'd been doing earlier in the day. But there was something else there, too. Something sweet he couldn't quite name.

"There. All done." She stepped away, and Stone finally managed a full-sized breath.

He had just mumbled his thanks when Stephen showed up in the bunkhouse doorway.

"I brought the stuff you asked for, Mr.

Hammond. Miss Lottie told me to bring her travel desk. Said it would have everything you needed inside." He held up an oak stationery box that had a series of flowering vines carved into the sides.

Stone waved him in. "Thanks, kid. Set it over here next to me." He cast a sideways glance at the teacher, who was busily packing up her supplies. Should he thank her, too? He opened his mouth to do so, but she gathered up her medicine box, propped the basin on top, and retreated toward the door.

"I'll go check on Lily and the stew. Stephen, keep Mr. Hammond company, would you?"

"Yes, ma'am." The boy set the writing desk on the bunk then plopped himself on the stool she had just vacated.

"But don't talk his ear off if he wants to work on his letter, all right?" A fond smile curved her lips as she instructed the boy. Stephen returned the smile and nodded his promise, eager to please. And why shouldn't he be? If Charlotte Atherton smiled at Stone like that, he'd be hard pressed not to agree to whatever she asked of him, too. Yet when her gaze brushed his as she left, the affection so evident only a moment ago disappeared behind wary concern. She might be tenderhearted and kind, but she still recognized the danger he posed.

Something hard tapped against Stone's knee, bringing his attention back to the boy in front of him. "Here. This is yours."

Stone looked down. Stephen held his boot knife, hilt out, waiting for him to take it. Stone's palm itched to claim his property, but something held him back. It seemed disloyal somehow, a betrayal to the woman who had just tended his wounds.

"Thanks, but I think your teacher intended to lock that one up with the rest of my things. You should probably go give it back to her."

The boy shook his head. "Miss Lottie was the one who told me to fetch it. Said if you'd had it when you went after that cat, you might not have been hurt so bad." He lifted his arm and offered the blade again. "You probably shouldn't let Mr. Dobson know you got it, though. He might not like it."

Stone took the knife from the boy's hand and slipped it into the small sheath-like pocket at the back of his right boot.

She'd given him a weapon. And maybe a touch of trust as well. It was a start.

116

9

Stone found himself trapped in the bunkhouse. The doc had stitched him up yesterday and then warned him not to attempt any strenuous chores for the next several days. Not even saddling his own horse. Which made him insufferably dependent on Dobson. Thankfully, the grizzled fellow hadn't hung around to prod his pride. This morning, he'd dropped off a load of harnesses that needed oiling and left Stone to complete the task on his own. The harness straps filled a few hours, but he'd finished them by noon.

Miss Atherton brought him a heaping plate of skillet-fried potatoes with bacon and sweet onions for lunch. Tasty grub. The woman knew her way around a stove. She also knew how to sidestep a question. When he'd suggested that Lily pay him a visit that afternoon so he could talk to her, Miss Atherton had her excuses ready. The child had lessons to complete. And chores. And Stone needed to rest after his ordeal. All of which was true, but he recognized a dodge when he heard one. The teacher didn't want Lily anywhere near him. So when the girl snuck into the bunkhouse a couple hours later, Stone had to look twice to make sure his head injury wasn't playing tricks on him.

The girl didn't knock, just cracked the door, slipped inside, and closed it behind her. He'd awoken from his doze the moment her tiny feet hit the steps and rolled over to grab the knife from his boot where it sat on the floor. As soon as he recognized her, though, he released his grip on the weapon and moved to sit the rest of the way up. Lily barely spared him a glance. Instead, she pressed her back against the closed door and splayed her arms beside her. Slowly, she turned her face toward him, lifted a hand to her mouth, and set her pointer finger atop her lips.

"Shhh." She glanced both ways, as if searching out threats lurking behind the wool socks Dobson had hung to dry over the rafters or the blanket draped over the side of Stone's cot. "You have to be quiet, Mr. Hammond. I'm playing hide-and-seek with Stephen, and I don't want him to find me."

Stone raised a brow but kept his mouth shut. He wasn't about to risk running the girl off when she'd just given him the perfect opportunity to start his investigation.

She tiptoed with exaggerated precision over to his cot then stopped directly in front of him. She frowned at his chin and then at the bandages visible through the open neck of his shirt.

"Do they hurt?"

"Yep."

"I'm sorry." She tilted her head back to meet his gaze, her own looking far too moist for Stone's peace of mind.

All he needed was for the kid to start bawling. What a picture that would make if the teacher came looking for her and found her in here crying her eyes out.

"You ain't got nothin' to be sorry about, kid," Stone groused. "You weren't the one who scratched me."

She drew back, affronted. "Of course not. I'm a hero. Heroes don't hurt other heroes. They only hurt the bad guys. And then, only when they have to."

So she thought him a hero, did she? That could come in handy.

Stone shifted backward on the cot until his spine rested against the wall. He gave her a dubious look. "I've never seen a hero quite so short."

"Yeah, well . . ." She threw her shoulders back in an effort to look taller. "That's because I'm a hero-in-training."

"In training? Who's training you?"

"Dead-Eye Dan."

Who in the world was Dead-Eye Dan?

"And Angus O'Connell," she continued, gaining momentum. "He was from the first book I read. You'd probably like him. He's a bounty hunter who's trailing a mean bunch of hombres who robbed a bank, only he didn't realize the gang's leader wasn't with them. Duke Mahone never goes on the jobs himself, you see. Doesn't want to risk getting caught. He hides out along the trail instead and picks off any posse that comes after his men with his Henry repeater. That's how he got Angus O'Connell. Shot him in the back and left him for dead. Kinda like how that big cat got you. Ambushed." The girl's eyes glowed as she recounted the bloody story. "Angus didn't die, thank goodness. A lady helped him, just like Miss Lottie helped you. Except with Angus, it was an Indian maiden who nursed him back to health with her herbs."

"You like bounty hunters, do you?"

Lily nodded emphatically then stunned

him by climbing up onto the cot next to him. "Uh-huh. They're my favorite, chasing down the bad guys when no one else will. Sending them to jail. Keeping people safe. That's what I want to do when I grow up. Keep people safe. Just like Miss Lottie."

"Miss Lottie?" This was getting interesting.

"Uh-huh. When my school shut down, Stephen and John didn't have anywhere to go, so Miss Lottie let them come with us."

"What about you?" Stone pressed gently. "Didn't you have a safe home to go to when the school closed?"

"Of course. This one." She looked at him as if she thought him an idiot.

"But what about your family? Why didn't you go stay with them?"

Lily's forehead scrunched. "Miss Lottie is my family. My mama gave me to her when she had to go to heaven."

That last remark brought the misty look back to the girl's eyes, so Stone immediately changed the topic. "Did you know I used to be a bounty hunter?"

"Really?" The girl practically inhaled the word, her eyes growing as round as silver dollars. "Is that how you got the name Stone? All the best bounty hunters have tough-sounding names. Like Dead-Eye Dan

121

and Hammer Rockwell."

Stone worked extra hard not to roll his eyes at the ridiculous monikers. "Nope. My ma gave me the name. Here. I'll show you." He bent forward to retrieve his saddle bag from under the cot, holding in a groan when the movement pulled at his stitches. Once he had the bag, he sat back and caught his breath as he unfastened the buckle. He pulled out his mother's Bible and opened it to the pages at the front, where the birth records were recorded. He pointed to the last name on the list. "See. That's me. Stone Arthur Hammond. If you go up a couple lines you'll see who I was named after. Beatrice Anne Stone. My ma's granny. Everyone called her Bertie."

Lily giggled. "That's a funny name. Granny Bertie."

Stone chuckled along with her. He'd never known the woman himself but liked the idea of having a Granny Bertie. He was about to ask Lily if she had a granny and therefore steer the conversation back toward Dorchester when a knock sounded on his door.

Lily gasped and dove off the bed.

"Mr. Hammond," Stephen called through the door, "is Lily in there with you? I'm startin' to get worried. I can't find her anywhere."

The girl in question crawled on all fours under Stone's bed.

"Come on in," Stone hollered.

"No!" she whispered, but Stone ignored her.

If Stephen didn't find Lily, he'd go after the teacher. And if Miss Atherton found the girl here, she'd likely sic the gnome on him.

Stephen entered, his eyes quickly scanning the room. Stone captured his attention and silently gestured to Lily's hiding place.

The boy's furrowed brow cleared, and a grin stretched his lips. He jumped forward and crouched down to peer under the bed. "Found you, Lily!"

"You cheated!" She crawled out and scowled up at both Stephen and Stone. "You got help."

"Yeah, well, you cheated, too." Stephen crossed his skinny arms over his chest. "You know Miss Lottie told you not to come in here. She's liable to send you to bed with no supper when she finds out."

"You can't tell her!" The scowl immediately transformed into a pair of pleading puppy-dog eyes and a pouty bottom lip. "Please. I promise not to come here again. Please, Stephen."

The boy crumpled under the onslaught.

"All right, but you gotta do the garden weeding for me tomorrow."

"I will," she vowed. Then she turned her pleading gaze on Stone. "You can't tell either, Mr. Hammond. Promise?"

As if he would. He didn't want the teacher to find out, either. "I promise."

"Good." Her shoulders sagged in relief.

"We better go," Stephen said, taking Lily's hand and tugging her toward the door. Once he had her outside, he stuck his head back in. "Oh, and Mr. Hammond?"

"Yeah?"

"Miss Lottie said to remind you that if you're feeling up to it, you can have dinner with us in the kitchen tonight. Around six."

"Thanks. I'll be there."

Ready to continue probing for the truth.

10

Thirty minutes before the time he was expected for dinner, Stone collected the stationery box the teacher had loaned him, as well as his lunch dishes, and made his way to the house. Never hurt to have the element of surprise on one's side. To increase the advantage, he didn't go to the back door but circled around to the front, the door farther from both the kitchen and the bunkhouse. The least likely door for him to use. Then, instead of knocking, he eased the door open and let himself in. All the better to catch them off guard. Get a true picture of what went on in Miss Charlotte Atherton's house.

Only, *he* was the one caught off guard.

First by the music. An intricate melody filled with twists and turns swirled around him and tugged him toward the parlor. More complex than any popular song he'd heard banged out in a dance hall or saloon.

He couldn't even imagine it in a church setting. Too many notes to follow. Not that he would try. This song didn't need a human voice to give it meaning. All one had to do was listen to feel the impact.

"Don't rush, John," a feminine voice called out from deeper in the house, probably the kitchen. "Keep a steady tempo."

John? The little Chinese kid was playing? Impossible.

Yet when Stone rounded the corner on silent feet and peered into the parlor, there sat John Chang, his tiny fingers flying over the keys like a master. His expressionless face seemed at odds with the stunning complexity of the music, as if the notes he produced required no concentration and no personal response.

When Stone had first started investigating Dr. Sullivan's academy, he'd been aware of the "for exceptional youths" part of the title, but he'd just assumed Keith Sullivan had tacked that on to make his school sound more prestigious and thereby attract a more elite clientele. The one time he'd met the esteemed Dr. Sullivan, he'd smelled a bit too much like snake oil for Stone's taste. All the right words up front, but slippery underneath. Big promises, little follow-through. Stone knew the type. Collected

bounties on a couple in his early days —
swindlers so consumed with lining their
pockets that they spared little thought for
the people whose lives they destroyed in the
process. Dr. Sullivan might not deal in
magic elixirs, but he still smacked of
chicanery. Why else would a supposedly
devoted educator shut down his school mid-
term? He must've found a better way to line
his pockets.

Nevertheless, it appeared that the
"exceptional" part of Dr. Sullivan's academy
had not been a ruse. John Chang was the
most exceptional seven-year-old Stone had
ever seen. Did Stephen and Lily have
remarkable talents as well? He studied Stephen, who sat cross-legged on the floor with
what looked to be a gutted mantel clock in
his lap then lifted his gaze to examine Lily.
She looked like any other nine-year-old girl,
curled against the arm of the small sofa,
engrossed in a dime novel. The teacher had
mentioned that Lily was smart, and she
obviously liked to read, but did that make
her exceptional?

Stone peered a little closer, trying to
decipher clues he had little context for
interpreting. Maybe he needed to see her in
her element. After all, he'd thought John
was just a quiet kid who liked to stick close

to the house until he'd seen him at the piano.

"Mr. Hammond!" Lily's squeal of delight soared through the room and brought the music to a jarring halt. John's hands hovered above the keys as Lily threw aside her paperbound book and jumped to her feet.

Stone grinned at the girl and stepped more fully into the room. "You don't need to stop, kid," he said, nodding in the boy's direction. "You play real well. Do you know another song?"

"Play the moon one that Miss Lottie is teaching you," Lily urged. "That one's so pretty." She started humming a three-note pattern and swayed in rhythm before holding out the sides of her dress and executing a fancy turn.

"It's not pretty. It's sad." Stephen frowned at Lily. "Makes me feel lonely."

"Only when Miss Lottie plays it," Lily argued. "Besides, that's part of what makes it so pretty."

Stephen rolled his eyes in Stone's direction as if he hoped for commiseration regarding the illogical nature of females. Stone managed to hold in his chuckle. Barely.

Turning her back on Stephen, Lily poured all her power of persuasion onto John. She leaned against the piano and dug out the puppy eyes. "Please, Johnny. It's my favorite."

The poor kid didn't stand a chance, though he put up a good fight. "I don't know all the right notes yet," he said. "Miss Lottie is making me read the dots on the page for that one."

"That doesn't matter," the girl insisted. "You've heard Miss Lottie play it, and we all know you can play any piece you want once you've heard it. You don't need the sheet music."

Stone looked from Lily to John to Stephen, but none of them seemed to think her statement the least bit outlandish. They acted as if such talent were normal.

John heaved a sigh and adjusted his position on the bench.

Lily clapped and beamed a smile so wide it filled the room. "Oh, thank you, Johnny!" Then she dashed behind the bench, wrapped her arms around him, and squeezed for all she was worth.

John pulled a face and groaned, but he made no attempt to push her away. Stephen rolled his eyes again. Lily just laughed and danced across the rug. The three acted more like siblings than classmates. Of course, that's how they'd been living for the last couple months.

The music started up again, a slow song with deep tones and a beat that seemed to keep the piece moving forward. It was a much simpler tune, yet the boy played it hesitantly, his gaze scouring the empty space in front of him as if for directions.

Then all at once, Miss Atherton appeared in the doorway, drying her hands on her apron. She raised a brow at seeing Stone there but didn't comment on his presence. Instead, she crossed the room to stand behind John, placed her hands gently on the boy's shoulders, and exhaled a long, steady breath.

"Feel the music, John." She spoke so quietly, Stone almost missed it. "Remember? Let it move from your ears . . . through your mind . . . down into your heart . . . and *then* out your fingers."

The boy visibly relaxed. The notes became less stilted.

"Better," she praised. For a moment, her fingers mimicked John's, playing out the notes upon his small shoulders. Then they slid off and disappeared into the folds of her apron. Leaving her pupil to carry on without her, she stepped away from the piano.

Stone met her halfway across the rug. "I

thought I'd return your writing desk. Oh, and the plate from lunch." He held out the stationery box to her, keeping the dish in place on top of it with his thumbs. "I appreciate the use of both."

Miss Atherton accepted the items then immediately handed the stationery box to Lily. "Take this to my room, please." The girl gave a little huff but then grabbed the box and scampered off. The teacher turned back to Stone. "I understand that Dr. Ramsey volunteered to post your letter for you."

"That's right. He took it with him last night. Seemed like a trustworthy fellow. Should I be concerned?"

Her eyes widened slightly. "Oh no. The doctor is a fine man. Extremely responsible. I've no doubt your letter has already been delivered to the post office. I just . . . I wondered how you planned to occupy your time while you wait for a reply."

Stone stepped closer to her, catching a glimpse of Lily running back into the room out of the corner of his eye. "You know exactly what I plan to do, Charlotte." He spoke in a low murmur. Her mouth gaped just a touch at his use of her Christian name, but he was tired of the forced formality between them. It was time for her to ac-

cept that the barriers needed to come down.
No more holding him at arm's length and
keeping Lily away from him. "I plan to
convalesce and enjoy your hospitality.
Maybe help out with some chores around
the place." He gave her a pointed look.
"Spend time with the kids." The tiny lines
between her brows warned that a frown was
coming, so he quickly steered the discussion to less threatening ground. "I never
imagined I'd be treated to such an impressive concert. John has a rare talent."

"Yes. He does." The frown lines didn't
completely disperse, but pride sparked in
her eyes, thawing the frost that had started
to collect around their edges. "They all do.
In their own way." She nodded toward Stephen, who had managed to completely gut
the clock during their short conversation.
"He's taken that clock apart and put it successfully back together three times now.
Faster each time. And each time he finishes,
the clock ticks down perfect time. It didn't
run at all when we first arrived here."

"And Lily?" Stone asked.

Charlotte glanced down to a spot near his
right elbow and smiled. "Let her read a
story with you, and you'll see."

A small hand wormed its way into his
oversized paw and gave his arm a tug.

"Come on, Mr. Hammond. Come read a story with me. It'll be fun."

His fingers closed reflexively over Lily's hand as he allowed her to lead him to the sofa. It felt strange, foreign, to have something so tiny and delicate curled in his fist. His hands were made to wrap around a revolver or rifle, the hilt of a knife, or the horn of a saddle. They were made for subduing lawbreakers, not reading stories with little girls. However, something shifted in his heart the moment she placed her hand so trustingly in his. Something soft yet fiercely protective.

He had the power to change this child's life. For better or for worse. What if he made the wrong choice? The thought sent a shudder through him. The girl was obviously happy here with her teacher and friends, but would that happiness last? Hiding, living on the run, took its toll on a body. How many times had he cashed in on a bounty because a man got sloppy after turning to drink to deal with the stress of always looking over his shoulder? Charlotte might have created a warm little nest for her chicks here, but that nest could become a prison over time. Lily deserved better than that. But was a rich grandfather necessarily better? Would he love her, care for her? Or would she simply be another pawn for him to control, a bauble to display until she grew old enough to be bartered in marriage to the highest bidder?

God, I can't decide this on my own. Show me the right path to take, and give me the courage to take it.

"Mr. Hammond? You all right?" Lily's bright blue eyes peeked up at him from where she sat on the sofa, her forehead crinkled in concern.

Stone shook off the heaviness of his thoughts and grinned. "Sorry, squirt." He plopped down beside her, noting that the illustrious Miss Atherton had retreated back into the kitchen while he'd been woolgathering. "My mind got away from me for a minute there. Now, what's so special about the way you read?"

Her mouth quirked. "Nothing. I read just like anybody else." She handed him the dime novel she'd been engrossed in earlier then turned her back and rested her spine against his arm. She pulled up her knees and leaned the side of her head against the sofa's back cushions. "It's what comes *after* the reading that makes me special, according to Miss Lottie." She shrugged. "It doesn't seem that special to me, but it *is* lots of fun. Especially with bounty hunter stories." She twisted her head around and grinned at him, her enthusiasm contagious. "You start, then I'll show you."

11

Unsure what he was supposed to do, Stone thumbed back the book cover that featured a man who reminded him a bit of Daniel Barrett, his old partner from the early days. The flaming red hair was brighter than the dark rusty color of his friend's hair, but the title of the novel, *Dead-Eye Dan and the Dastardly Duel,* aroused his curiosity — and his suspicion.

Stone turned to the first chapter and started reading. " 'Dead-Eye Dan hunkered behind a boulder at the top of Widow's Canyon, his rifle at the ready. He'd been trailing the Gatling Gang for five days with nothing but a pouch of jerky, hardtack, and his faithful horse, Ranger, to keep him going.' "

Ranger? Dead-Eye Dan *was* Daniel Barrett! Stone barely contained a snort. Did Barrett know he'd been immortalized in print? He couldn't wait to rib his old friend.

He'd have to find himself a copy of this book so he could wave it under Dan's nose.

Lily must have taken his pause as permission to take over, for she started reading, picking up where he'd left off. " 'The posse out of Rockdale had given up their pursuit two days ago, leaving Dan to track the gang on his own. But he didn't mind. Dead-Eye Dan worked better alone, sniffing out trails like a bloodhound, and getting ahead of his quarry. That was how he came to be on the ridge overlooking Widow's Canyon.' " Lily pitched her voice low, as if not wanting to give away the intrepid Dan's hiding place.

Stone turned to smile at her . . . and froze. Lily wasn't reading. She wasn't looking at the book at all. She still had her back pressed against his arm, her head facing the piano.

" 'Hoofbeats echoed from the west. He'd been right! Billy Cavanaugh and his gang of outlaws had circled back.' "

She read . . . no, *quoted* the book word-for-word. Not a single mistake. How many times must she have read this story to be able to repeat it so flawlessly?

" 'He'd found the small box canyon yesterday while scouting,' " she continued, " 'and Dan's gut had convinced him it would be the perfect place for a hideout.

Sheltered. Hidden. A small creek at the back to provide water for horses and men alike. So he'd taken a chance and positioned himself on high ground and waited for the gang's return. His gut had been right. But then, Dead-Eye Dan's gut was always right.' " Lily tipped her head back until her eyes met his. She grinned. "Your turn, Mr. Hammond."

"How many times have you read this story, squirt?" Stone kept his tone nonchalant, careful to mask his astonishment.

Lily shrugged. "Just once. But that's all I ever read anything. Well, except the Bible. Miss Lottie says the Bible is different because God helps you see new things in it each time you read it. Not quite sure what she means by that. I can see the Bible pages in my mind just like I can see the pages of my dime novels and read them there, but she still likes me to read from the actual book sometimes."

Stone said nothing, just tried to absorb what the girl had said with such casualness. She'd only read the book once? And she could quote it verbatim? He couldn't fathom such a thing. "You see the pages in your mind?" he asked.

"Yep. It's kind of like a photograph, I

guess. I see it once, then I can look at it later, whenever I want, inside my mind. It's not that different from what John can do with the piano." Lily turned around in her seat, obviously tired of craning her neck to look at him. "Miss Lottie says we're not to brag about the tricks we can do, though. Especially if we start attending the school in Madisonville next term. She says it's not kind to make other people feel bad if they take longer to learn something. It doesn't make them dumb, it just means they have to work harder."

Stone schooled his features into a serious mask. Nice to know he wasn't *dumb,* just a *hard worker.*

"Once" — Lily leaned in close as if imparting a secret — "Miss Lottie told me about a boy at the academy who could do really hard arithmetic problems in his head without writing anything down. He got so used to it coming easy that when his teacher tried to show him how to do problems that were even more difficult, he didn't understand them right away and got fed up and quit. Left the academy. Miss Lottie says that if God gives us a gift, we have to culti . . . cultivate it." Lily grinned over the accomplishment of recalling the correct word then gave him a look that had Charlotte Atherton written all over it. "That means work hard at helping it grow."

Stone nodded. "It sounds like Miss Lottie is a good teacher." A woman who seemed to believe that teaching character was as important as teaching reading, writing, and arithmetic. A point in her favor.

"She's the best!" Lily bounced on the sofa cushion. "She gives us our lessons every morning after chores. Well, except for yesterday. But that's because you showed up. You threw off her schedule. Miss Lottie's real fond of schedules. I'm surprised she let you stay." Lily tilted her head and considered him, as if finally questioning what he was doing here.

Time for a diversion.

Taking *Dead-Eye Dan* in hand, Stone fanned the pages to a random spot in the middle. " 'Dan dove behind a fallen tree as a hailstorm of bullets rained down around him. The Gatling Gang had come by their moniker honestly, laying down rapid fire that mimicked the output of the famed war gun. Unruffled by the deadly flurry, however, Dan flipped onto his back behind the log and reloaded his Henry repeater with methodical precision. The six-gun at his hip sported full chambers. The knife on his belt was razorsharp and ready for action.' " Stone's voice trailed off, cueing Lily.

She grinned, taking up the challenge like a seasoned gamester. In less than a pair of heartbeats, she located the page in that mental catalog of hers and picked up right where he had left off.

" 'Bullets blasted shards of bark all around Dan, but he just brushed the pieces off his chest with a flick of his wrist. Billy's gang couldn't aim worth a hill of beans. That's why they always sprayed so much lead. It was the only way they ever hit anything. Too often, innocent civilians. Dan scowled, his jaw tightening as he rolled onto his side to steal a peek over the top of the log. One against seven was lousy odds, but Billy Cavanaugh and his crew were vermin that needed e-rad-i-cation.' " She stumbled slightly over the large word, but it didn't stop her. She passed right over it and forged ahead. " 'He'd just wait for them to reload then take them out one by one.' "

Stone closed the book and set it in his lap to signal Lily that she need not continue her recitation. He had no doubt she could quote the entire book to him if he asked it of her. The girl's memory was remarkable. But her teacher had taken pains to keep the girl grounded, and he'd not undo that by gushing over her amazing talent. Besides, there was no telling how many chances Charlotte would willingly give him to speak with Lily unchaperoned.

"You do know this story is hugely exaggerated, right?" He tossed the dime novel to Lily. "There were only five men in the Gatling Gang, not seven. And Daniel Barrett didn't bring them all in on his own. He had help."

Lily's blue eyes glimmered as she rose up on her knees, bringing her face level with his. "Are you telling me you *know* Dead-Eye Dan?"

Stone blew out a self-deprecating breath from the side of his mouth. "Know him? Shoot. He and I were partners back in the day. 'Course no one actually calls him Dead-Eye Dan. He's a foreman at a ranch called Hawk's Haven up north a piece. Gave up chasin' criminals in order to chase cows. He *is* a crack shot, though. Saved my sorry hide more than once." He nudged Lily with his shoulder, nearly toppling her back onto the cushions. " 'Course I saved his hide a time or two myself."

She grabbed his arm to catch her balance but didn't let go once she was steady. No, she held on to his sleeve as if he weren't a stranger dragged in by her teacher's

142

watchdog. She held on to him as if he were part of the family — or the ragtag bunch that passed as family here in Charlotte Atherton's house.

Stone pressed the heel of his hand against the ache that sprang up in his chest. Stupid claw wounds.

"Wait a minute." Lily drew in a breath so large, he expected her head to start swelling. "You're . . . you're . . . Hammer Rockwell. The man who shows up in the nick of time and takes the Gatling Gang by surprise by climbing down the box canyon wall with his knife clenched between his teeth!"

Hammer Rockwell? Knife in his teeth? "Of all the ridiculous, made-up nonsense," Stone sputtered. "I'll have you know, all my knives were safely stowed in their sheaths when I made that climb. And who came up with that outrageous name? Hammer Rockwell. I never heard anything so absurd."

"Don't you see?" Lily giggled, the joyful sound unruffling a few of his feathers. "They just switched your name around. Stone Hammond. Hammer Rockwell. Don't worry — even though you were only in the story for a few pages, you lived up to your name. You were known as Hammer because your big fists were like steel. You smashed the bad guys with your bare hands, knocking them flat." She demonstrated with a pair of enthusiastic jabs, one of which connected lightly with his shoulder. "You only used your knife when one of the gang members tried to shoot Dan in the back. That sorry outlaw became buzzard bait."

Stone raised a brow at her obvious satisfaction in the fellow's demise. "He actually got dragged in with the others after we patched up his shoulder."

Lily frowned. "I like my version better."

Stone snorted. *Figures.*

Charlotte stood in the hall and bit her lip. She shouldn't be eavesdropping. How many times had she admonished her students against such rude and ill-mannered behavior? And here she was, shamelessly engaging in the very behavior she forbade. Definitely not her finest hour. Yet she couldn't seem to manufacture any remorse, because Stone Hammond had been absolutely right. One could learn a great deal from watching and listening.

The man appeared to be unaccustomed to being around children, yet he interacted with each of them with great patience and kindness, never raising his voice or speaking with condescension. True, he had an agenda, but she'd learned long ago that children could sense when an adult was being less than genuine in their attention and typically responded with coldness or defiance. All three of hers seemed to crave Stone Hammond's attention. Even John had stopped playing and moved to the floor next to Stephen, handing him clock parts while trying not to look too interested in the conversation occurring on the sofa.

How could they not be interested? The man was apparently a living legend, immortalized in literature. Well, if one considered a dime novel literature. *Hammer Rockwell?* Charlotte stifled a giggle. Dreadful name. Yet Stone's reaction to it was what made her smile. He'd sounded so delightfully offended.

She had to give the man credit for coping with Lily's giftedness with aplomb. Outside of a question or two to clarify her abilities, he carried on as if he were simply mildly curious. Had he guessed that probing her about it would make her uncomfortable and therefore less talkative? Charlotte wasn't used to dealing with insightful men — men of restraint. And humility. She tipped her head closer to the doorway connecting the parlor to the hall as she listened to Lily and Stone argue over the merits of buzzard bait. He could have played up the embellished tale and his role in it in order to feed Lily's adoration, but he hadn't. Of course, the truth he'd shared was pretty incredible in and of itself.

"So how come Dead-Eye Dan gave up bounty hunting to be a boring old rancher?" Lily asked.

Stone scoffed, and Charlotte could picture the roll of his eyes. Rather warm, amber eyes, if she remembered correctly.

"Ranchin' ain't boring, squirt. It's a lot of hard work. Just because the cattle don't shoot at you don't mean it's not dangerous. Storms, stampedes, an ornery bull that'd gouge you with his horns as soon as look at you. It ain't for the faint of heart. Besides, there comes a time in a man's life when he wants to settle down and build something a little more permanent. A place of his own to call home."

The genuine longing in his voice caught Charlotte by surprise. He seemed so rugged, so self-sufficient that she found it difficult to picture him in a domestic setting. Home and hearth. Wife and family. Although he hadn't really mentioned family, had he? Only a home. Would he be content without someone to share his life?

Charlotte's back stiffened. Exactly what business was that of hers? She frowned at her meandering thoughts and reached behind her to re-tie the bow in her apron strings. Her elbow bumped the wall lightly as she made sure the bow loops were equal lengths. *Really,* she silently fumed, *the future life of Stone Hammond is none of my concern. The man can hide away in a mountain cave for the rest of his days as long as I get to keep Lily.*

"You don't have a home?" Lily's question floated into the hall, distracting Charlotte from her apron strings. She stilled, hating herself for caring about the answer.

"Nope. Not a real one, anyway. Just a few hotels that keep a room ready for me whenever I happen to make it to town. Ain't had a real home since my ma died back in '68. My pa died in the war five years before that, and with times being so hard and me being so young, there was no way for me to hold on to the house. The bank took it, and I struck out on my own."

And he'd survived. More than survived, Charlotte acknowledged. He'd succeeded. Admirably.

"The only thing I took with me from my mama's house, besides my pa's huntin' rifle and a sack of food," Stone continued, "was my ma's Bible. Never go anywhere without it. Reminds me of her, of what home

147

means."

"I have a locket," Lily said quietly. "I wear it every day under my dress. Wanna see?"

Charlotte pictured Lily tugging on the thin gold chain until the oval locket pulled free of her collar. She would open it and show him Rebekah's portrait.

"Your ma was real pretty." Stone's gruff voice held compassion. "Do you ever miss the home you shared with her?"

Charlotte stiffened again. He hadn't mentioned Dorchester Hall, but she recognized the direction his question was leading. Maybe she'd only imagined his compassion. Maybe he'd made up his entire sad childhood tale just to soften up Lily, to manipulate her into sharing details of her own story.

"I miss the tabby cat that liked to curl up by the stove in the big kitchen. She used to let me carry her around and would always try to pounce on my shadow when we went outside to play. But mostly, I just miss my mama. She never really liked Grandfather's big house. She wanted a cozy little place for the two of us, but Grandfather insisted we live with him."

Lily's voice tapered off, and Charlotte held her breath, not sure what the child would say next. If she told Stone she missed

Dorchester Hall, would that be reason enough for him to take her back?

"I think Mama was right, though," Lily said at last. "Miss Lottie's house is little and cozy, and I like it. It feels like home."

"I'm sure Miss Lottie would be very happy to hear you say that."

Did his voice sound closer than it had a moment ago?

"Wouldn't you, Charlotte?" Suddenly, Stone stepped into the hall and eyed her like a seasoned hunter who'd just flushed a dove from the bush.

12

Charlotte lifted her chin, refusing to let Stone Hammond get the better of her. "Why, yes, Stone." She threw his Christian name back at him, a little alarmed at how easily it rolled off her tongue. "Hearing that Lily feels at home here makes me *very* happy." She skirted around him and held her hand out to the little girl who watched the two adults with a puzzled expression.

Lily hopped off the sofa and obediently took Charlotte's hand, but before she could ask her teacher if she'd been listening to their conversation, Charlotte steered her toward the kitchen.

"Come help me mash the potatoes, Lily. The roast is out of the oven." Eager to focus her attention on anything other than the tall man watching her from the doorway, she glanced to the boys on the rug. "Stephen, when you finish with that clock, please find Mr. Dobson and let him know dinner is nearly ready. After that, fetch the apple cider from the springhouse." Both boys' eyes lit up. "Having a guest for dinner is a special enough occasion, don't you think?"

"Yes, ma'am!" Stephen nodded vigorously, and John joined in with a more sedate version of the movement.

"Thank you, boys." Schooling her features, she turned to face Stone. Chin up. Back straight. Smile in place. "Dinner will be ready in about ten minutes, Mr. Hammond. Please make yourself comfortable in the meantime." She tilted her head toward the book still clasped in his large hands. "Perhaps you'd enjoy reading some more of Dead-Eye Dan's exploits. Lily assures me they are quite engrossing."

"They aren't gross, Miss Lottie," Lily corrected with a huff. "They're exciting."

Stone laughed at that — a rich, deep sound that reached inside Charlotte and warmed cold places that had been long neglected. But like frostbitten fingers placed too quickly near the fire, the warmth hurt. So she drew away from the flame, and with Lily trailing behind her, scurried off to the kitchen.

Men were not to be trusted. Especially not charming men. And while no one would mistake Stone Hammond for a suave

151

courtier, the man had a rugged charm that wormed its way under a woman's skin before she could adequately guard against it. Well, he wasn't going to charm her. Not with his bravery. Not with that wide, muscled chest. Not even with his kindness toward her children or his open-mindedness toward her claim to Lily. Just because the sound of his laugh threatened to melt her insides like whipped cream on hot apple pie did not mean she'd forgotten the lessons her father had taught her.

"Didn't you want *me* to do that, Miss Lottie?" Lily's question pulled Charlotte out of her mental tirade.

She glanced down. Her white-knuckled fingers were fisted around the handle of the masher, where eviscerated potato flesh clung to the steel grooves. Good heavens! She didn't even remember pouring off the boiling water or picking up the masher.

"Yes, sweetheart. I'm sorry." Charlotte scooted aside and made room for Lily to set her wooden stepstool next to the counter. "I got caught up in my thoughts and wasn't paying attention to what I was doing." Once the girl was in position, Charlotte handed over the masher. "Here you go. Smash away."

Lily threw herself into the task, pausing

now and then when Charlotte added butter and milk to the mixture. She chattered about Dead-Eye Dan and how Stone knew him and how they used to work together. She wondered aloud over whether or not Stone had ever met an Indian or been shot while trying to bring in a bounty or fallen in love with a female outlaw who had a price on her head. Charlotte made a few noncommittal *hmm*s at appropriate places in order to hold up her end of the conversation, all while wishing desperately for a change in topic. The last thing she needed to imagine was Stone Hammond in love with some beautiful young desperado. Especially when the thought set off a twinge in her stomach that felt remarkably akin to jealousy.

Charlotte dosed the potatoes with salt and pepper then took over the mashing duty and gave the mixture a final beating until it was creamy and smooth. She covered the pot to keep the contents warm then opened the roaster and moved the meat to a cutting board.

She had just started slicing when Lily spoke again.

"Why is he here, Miss Lottie?"

Charlotte's eyes slid closed, the question stabbing into her as pointedly as the prong of the meat fork had just stabbed the roast.

Oh, Lord, how am I supposed to answer? She'd vowed never to lie to the children. Growing up, she'd suffered through enough lies to recognize that the truth, no matter how painful, was always better in the long run. But she'd also vowed to protect her charges. How could she do both?

Setting down the carving knife, Charlotte turned to face the girl she loved like a daughter. "Why don't we sit for a minute?" she suggested as she wiped her hands on her apron. Charlotte nodded toward the chairs encircling the kitchen table, and without a care, Lily hopped off her stool and skipped over to them.

Charlotte followed more slowly. Lily expected Miss Lottie to have all the answers. But she didn't. She didn't know anything. Not about raising a daughter, not about how to handle Stone Hammond, and certainly not how to explain his presence in a way that wouldn't inspire anxiety.

Forcing her legs to continue at their usual sedate pace toward the table instead of whirling around and fleeing out the back door as she wanted to, Charlotte fingered her mother's cameo and silently asked God to give her the right words.

Lily gazed up at her, her eyes full of innocent questions. Yet her mouth turned down a bit at the corners, proof that she'd sensed Charlotte's unease.

"Well now," Charlotte said as she pulled out a second chair and slid onto the seat. She smiled at the girl beside her and reached over to pat her hand where it lay atop the table, hoping at least one of the two actions would serve as reassurance. Heaven knew she wished someone would pat *her* hand and tell her everything would be all right. But that was a child's wish, and she'd ceased being a child long ago. "Let's see if I can explain."

Lily scooted to the edge of her chair, her upturned face glowing with trust.

Charlotte swallowed, brushed the wrinkles out of her apron, then folded her hands in her lap and began. "Do you remember the night we left the academy? How it was still dark outside when Mr. Dobson drove us away?"

"Yes." Lily's eyebrows scrunched together. "What does that have to do with Mr. Hammond?"

"I'm getting to that." Charlotte gave her one of the you-need-to-be-patient looks that Lily collected as frequently as Stephen did his springs and bolts. "The reason we left while it was still dark was because I wanted to keep our leaving a secret. I knew your

155

grandfather expected you to go home with him."

Lily sat straighter and nibbled a bit on the side of her thumb. "But Mama said I was supposed to live with you. She didn't want me to live with Grandfather."

"That's right." Charlotte recognized the lost little girl she once had been when news she hadn't wanted to hear bombarded her despite her wishes. She pushed her chair farther away from the table and opened her arms. "Come here, sweetheart."

The instant the invitation was offered, Lily bounded from her seat and into Charlotte's lap. Charlotte wrapped her arms around the girl and held her tight, leaning her cheek against the top of Lily's head.

"I promised your mother I would take you home to live with me and love you as if you were my own little girl. And I do. Love you. So much." The catch in her voice surprised her.

She was supposed to be in charge — of the children, of her home, of her emotions. Order out of chaos. It was how she survived. Control meant safety, protection. Yet, with Stone's arrival, control had begun slipping from her grasp, leaving her — and those in her care — vulnerable.

Be strong and of a good courage . . . The

verse she had memorized long ago, the one that helped her fortify her defenses whenever she felt exposed, ran through her head. She clung to it, to the promise inherent in the words. *Fear not, nor be afraid of them: for the Lord thy God, he it is that doth go with thee; he will not fail thee, nor forsake thee.*

He won't fail me. He won't forsake me. I can be strong. Strong for Lily. Strong for the boys. Inhaling a shaky breath, Charlotte pushed the emotion back down where it belonged. When she spoke, her voice once again resonated with the calm, steady tone she'd worked for years to perfect.

"Your grandfather didn't like the fact that I took you away without telling him where I was going, so he sent Mr. Hammond to find out where you were. Which he did. However, because Mr. Hammond suffered several injuries yesterday, it didn't seem right to just shoo him off without giving him the chance to recuperate. Especially since he very likely saved Stephen's life. So we discussed matters, and I agreed to let him stay with us for a while."

Lily pulled away from Charlotte's arms and tilted her face until she could look her teacher in the eye. "So he's not going to take me away? Back to Dorchester Hall?

Because Mama told me to stay with you."

Not knowing how to answer that question since Stone hadn't yet made that determination, Charlotte decided to do a bit of gentle probing on her own. "Do you *want* to go back to Dorchester Hall?"

The girl shrugged. "Visiting once in a while would be okay. See how my cat is doing. Eat some of Mrs. Johnson's chocolate cake." A grin curved the girl's lips. "It's my favorite."

"Mmm. That *does* sound delicious." Unfortunately, chocolate was a luxury Charlotte could no longer afford. At least not until she secured another teaching position.

She wished she could go to the cupboard right now and bake the most decadent chocolate cake Lily had ever tasted, but other things took precedence. Like ensuring Lily and the others were safe.

"Would you want to see your grand-father?"

Lily dipped her head and shrugged. Charlotte had been around children long enough to recognize the look of someone who wanted to say no but didn't think she should. "He's always so busy," Lily blurted. She slumped a bit, leaning back into Charlotte's hold. "The only time he ever played

158

with me was when his business friends invited us over for dinner."

"He took you with him to dinner parties?" That seemed odd. Usually children were excluded from such adult activities.

Lily's chin brushed across Charlotte's chest as she nodded. "I used to really like those parties. Grandfather would buy me a pretty new dress and tell all his friends about how smart I was and how I would grow up to be just as good at investing as he was. He would hold my hand and take me around the house, introducing me to everyone and showing me all the different rooms filled with interesting things. Especially the libraries and studies because he knew I liked books." Lily grew quiet for a moment, as if she were reliving the occasion. "I felt special," she said at last, her voice soft. "Grandfather didn't forget about me during those dinners. He wasn't too busy. He was proud of me. Wanted me with him."

Charlotte ached at the longing in the little girl's voice. She recognized it far too well. The longing to be loved and appreciated by the people who mattered. How many times had she practiced until her fingers cramped in an effort to please her father? Pandered to his pride with extravagant compliments

159

when he fell into bouts of melancholy? Organized his music folders, arranged his tutoring sessions, even kept his financial records updated, all in an effort to prove herself important to him. Only to discover she wasn't important enough.

Men like her father, like Randolph Dorchester, stole energy from those around them for their own purposes. So what had Dorchester's purpose been in taking Lily to those dinners? Perhaps he thought to impress his associates with his warm, familial nature by parading Lily around and visibly doting on her. Or maybe he thought to impress another way.

"Lily, did your grandfather ask you to show off your talent to his friends?" Heaven knew her own father had loved making her play to an audience when she'd been a child. She'd submitted but hated every moment of it. All the eyes on her. The fear that she'd make a mistake and embarrass him. Then watching him accept all the congratulations and accolades for himself as if she'd been nothing more than a puppet and he the one holding the strings.

But Lily was shaking her head. "No. He told me to keep it a secret. He said it was part of the game, and if I told anyone, I'd lose, and he wouldn't get me new books anymore."

What kind of game would Dorchester play with a child at a dinner party? And why the need for bribery and secrecy? Those two ingredients rarely came together to make anything good.

"What kind of game did you play with your grandfather, Lily?"

The question was the one that had formed on Charlotte's tongue, but the deep male tones definitely did not originate in her throat. She jerked her head around, knowing what she would find even before her eyes confirmed it — Stone Hammond lounging in the doorway.

13

Stone stayed where he was, leaning his shoulder against the wall. He should've kept his mouth shut. But when Charlotte had hesitated over asking the question burning a hole through his brain, he hadn't been able to help himself. Something told him the answer to that question would determine which course he followed.

"D-did my grandfather put a bounty on my head, Mr. Hammond?" The hero worship had disappeared from Lily's gaze. Worry, if not outright fear, shone in her blue eyes now when she looked at him. "Is that why you're here?"

A sledgehammer to the gut would have hurt less.

"Not a chance, squirt." He wanted to go to her, to squat down in front of her and reassure her. But he held his ground, afraid any movement would scare her. "I gave up bounty huntin' years ago, remember?"

"Like Dead-Eye Dan?"

"That's right. Dan took up ranching, and I took up —" He was about to say "retrieving," but that sounded too much like bringing in bounties. So he opted for the language her teacher had used. "Hiring myself out to people who need help findin' things."

"And you found me." She didn't look completely reassured. Smart kid.

He dipped his chin. "That I did. And let me say that you are much prettier than the stud bull Mr. Haymaker paid me to find last year. Whew! That beast was ug-ly. Stinky, too." Stone made a face and fanned his hand under his nose. When Lily giggled, the vise constricting his chest finally eased.

Straightening slowly away from the doorjamb, Stone shoved his hands into his trouser pockets and ducked his head slightly, trying to make himself look as harmless as possible. "Would it be all right if I joined you ladies at the table?"

For the first time since he'd alerted them to his presence, he focused his attention on Charlotte. Her face gave away little, that serene mask of hers firmly in place. But he sensed outrage simmering beneath the surface. Yes, he'd butted in where she didn't want him, but he needed to be a part of this conversation, and she was intelligent enough

163

to recognize that fact and not try to stop him. Even as he watched, she nodded slightly, granting him permission to join them. Yet her blue-green eyes clearly threatened violence upon his person if he did anything to hurt the girl in her lap.

Stone chose an arcing path, careful to give the females plenty of space as he made his way to the table. He grabbed hold of the ladder-back chair Lily had vacated, scooted it a couple feet farther away to give them a buffer, then flipped it around and straddled the seat. Draping one elbow over the top of the chair back, he glanced at Lily. "Tell me about this game you and your granddad used to play."

The girl looked to her teacher before answering. Charlotte nodded her approval.

"He called it a treasure hunt," Lily said. "When everyone was standing around talking before dinner, I was supposed to slip away and search for treasure. Grandfather said he and his friends liked to hide secrets from each other, and whoever uncovered the other's secret first won. If I helped him win the game, he'd order me whichever book I wanted from the Montgomery Ward catalog."

Stone worked to keep his expression bland even as tension crept up his back and into his neck and shoulders. He didn't like the direction this story was heading.

"The hard part was finding the right treasure since I didn't know what it looked like. Grandfather said the best treasure was usually hidden in the study, in desk drawers. The more buried, the better. If I could wiggle a locked drawer open, that would be worth the most points, but I was never to break anything. That was against the rules. So I was always careful. I only ever got one locked drawer open. I found a paper with lots of signatures on it that looked important. It was about a new railroad line going to a place called Seymour. A bunch of people from the town had written a letter about how they were raising money to get the Wichita Valley line to go there. I didn't understand the rest, but there was a map under the letter, too. When I drew it later that night for Grandfather, he was so proud of me, he let me pick two books out of the catalog."

Stone met Charlotte's shocked gaze above Lily's head. Yep, she understood, too. Randolph Dorchester had made his fortune in land speculation. For a man like him, being able to predict where the railroad planned to build would be money in the bank. Stone didn't doubt for a second that if he went to the land office in Seymour, Texas, he'd find records of Dorchester's company purchasing tracts of land all along the proposed rail line that Lily had so innocently drawn for him. Shoot, the man probably even helped the townsfolk raise the money they needed to entice the railroad to build there. All out of the goodness of his heart, of course.

The man had turned his own granddaughter into a criminal, having her steal company secrets. And now he'd hired Stone to get his little spy back.

"When the books came in the mail, Mama asked where I'd gotten them. When I told her about the game, she got really mad. She told me Grandfather was wrong to ask me to play that kind of game and that I wouldn't be allowed to go to any more parties with him." Lily twisted in Charlotte's lap to face her teacher. "I told her I was sorry, that I didn't know it was wrong."

Charlotte stroked Lily's hair. "She knew that, honey. She wasn't mad at you."

"I know. She told me. She even let me keep the books. But she did make me promise never to play that game again." Lily fell silent for a moment, her head down. When she finally looked up, her chin was wobbling. "But I did play it again. Twice."

"Why — ?" Before the teacher could finish her question, tears started rolling down Lily's face.

The child wagged her head back and forth as if trying to deny her own admission. "I didn't want to, Miss Lottie. I swear! I told Grandfather no, that Mama told me I couldn't play anymore, and at first, he agreed. But then something changed. He got a telegram that must have been terrible news 'cause he started yelling and cursing and slamming doors. Me and Mama stayed out of his way all week until he calmed down."

She glanced at Stone, her tear-streaked cheeks raising a violent need inside him to hit someone or something. Preferably Randolph Dorchester's pointy nose.

"He seemed to be doing better," Lily explained, her voice still high-pitched and shaky, though she gulped in a few breaths to try to calm herself, "but then he came to my room one afternoon and told me we were going for a drive. He smiled at me, but there was something wrong with the smile. It didn't seem happy at all. I told him I needed to check with Mama. He said he already had, and that it was all right for me to go."

"Where did he take you, sweetheart?" Miss Atherton's carefully modulated tones revealed no shock or disapproval, only compassion. Lily relaxed back into her teacher's arms.

"To a big house I didn't recognize. Grandfather didn't take me to the front door, though. He took me around the side of the house where a window was open a little bit. He told me the man who lived there was mean, that he'd threatened to ruin Grandfather's business just because a storm sank his boat. It wasn't Grandfather's fault there'd been a storm. I felt bad for Grandfather, so I let him boost me up to the window and went in. I searched for papers, books, maps, anything I thought Grandfather might like. Every time I came back to the window, Grandfather would make me recite what I'd found. It was never good enough. So he made me stay inside and look longer. I got so scared. What if the mean man found me?"

Stone's teeth ground together at the back of his mouth. How could a man do that to his own grandchild? Force her to steal for him, placing her in danger?

And how could Stone have accepted a job from a man like that? Had his instincts failed him, or had he been so eager for the fat payout that he'd ignored the warning signs?

"But you *did* get out," the teacher soothed, rubbing the girl's arm. "You're here now. Safe."

Lily nodded. "I found a stack of bills on the man's desk. I'd not paid any attention to them earlier because they weren't hidden away in a drawer, but when I recited their contents to Grandfather, he got excited when I told him about the one from someplace called The Red Palace. After I recited that one, he finally let me climb back out the window."

Miss Atherton shot Stone a questioning look. She obviously didn't understand the significance of that find, but Stone did. The Red Palace was an exclusive brothel in Houston that catered to wealthy gentlemen. Perfect blackmail material.

"I thought we were going home then," Lily said, "but he took me to a second house."

Another house? Was one not enough? Of all the heartless, greedy . . .

"He wanted me to do the same thing there. Said we still had an hour before the second man would get home. He'd given one of the servants some money earlier in the day to make sure the window was left open, so I had nothing to worry about." Lily shifted and grabbed her teacher around the waist and hugged her tight. "I didn't want to go in. I begged Grandfather not to make me. He got so mad, Miss Lottie." Her voice fell to a whisper. "His face got all red. He grabbed my arms and shook me so hard my head started to hurt. Then he told me that if I didn't obey him, he would take my kitty, tie her up in a sack, and toss her in the river. I c-couldn't let that happen, Miss Lottie. I just couldn't!"

"Of course not, sweetie."

Now the teacher was crying, too.

Stone squirmed in his seat, his hands gripping the ladder-back chair so tightly he was surprised the thing didn't snap in two.

"I crawled through the window and walked toward the desk. It was dark in the room, though, and I knocked into the edge of a little table. Something fell. It woke the dog."

Stone jerked upright in the chair. "There was a dog?" He nearly roared the question. Lily shrank deeper into the teacher's arms. Miss Atherton shot a glare at him. "Sorry, squirt. I didn't mean to holler."

"That's all right," she said in a small voice. "The dog scared me, too."

He imagined so.

Lily gave a little sniff then continued with her tale. "He'd been sleeping under the desk. He growled at me first, then he

170

jumped up and started barking. It scared me so bad, I screamed. I ran for the window. This one wasn't quite so high off the ground, so I didn't wait for Grandfather to help me down, I just jumped. My ankle hurt when I landed, and I worried that Grandfather would be angry, but he seemed scared by the dog, too. He helped me up and hurried me back out to the coach.

"On the way home, he said he was sorry about making me go into the house. He didn't shake me or yell or anything. Just sat there looking worried. He promised to buy me a whole shelf of books, but only if I didn't tell Mama. Said Mama would get mad at me and think I was a bad girl."

Miss Atherton gently pushed Lily away from her, just enough to look directly in her eyes. "Your mama would *never* think you were a bad girl."

Lily nodded. "I know. She'd told me to tell her right away if Grandfather ever tried to make me play his game again, so I did. She let me sleep in her bed with her that night, and we left the next day to visit a friend of hers in Austin. That's when we found your school."

Lily wrapped her arms around Charlotte's neck and pressed their two cheeks together. "I'm so glad that Mama sent me to live with you, Miss Lottie. I'm never gonna leave. Never."

Charlotte closed her eyes and returned the girl's hug, but Stone noticed she made no response to Lily's dramatic declaration. Probably didn't want to make a promise she wasn't sure she could keep. Thanks to him.

Stone unwrapped himself from the chair and stood, wishing with all his being that he'd never taken this job. Miss Atherton rose as well, setting Lily on her feet.

"Would you set the table for me, please, Lily? The boys will be in with the cider soon. Have them fill the glasses. John can do the napkins. I need to have a quick word with Mr. Hammond, then I'll be back to carve the roast."

"Yes, Miss Lottie." Lily nodded and rubbed the remains of her tears from her cheeks with her sleeve. Then she looked at Stone. "Now that you found me, you can tell Grandfather that I'm all right. He doesn't have to worry. Miss Lottie's taking good care of me."

Stone swallowed. "Yes, she is, squirt. I can see that real clear."

She smiled at him then. Heaven help him. He couldn't take her back. Not to a man who would willingly place her in danger to fuel his own greed.

"Mr. Hammond?" The teacher caught his attention and gestured toward the back door.

Stone dipped his head. "After you, ma'am."

Expecting her to turn and confront him the moment he pulled the door shut behind them, he was surprised when she kept walking. Past the outhouse. Past the garden. She didn't stop until she reached the clothesline. She scanned the yard, her head swiveling from side to side before she finally pivoted to face him. "What are you going to do?"

Well, at least the woman didn't beat around the bush.

"I'm going to wait for that letter from Austin, just like we talked about."

Sparks flew from her eyes. "After what that child just told you, you still have to wait for written proof before deciding that you're working for the wrong side?" She trembled from the force of her outrage. "I should have known. You and your kind words, your heroic deeds. You almost had me fooled. But you don't care about Lily. All you care about is the money Dorchester's dangling in front of you." She spun away from him and started marching back toward the house.

Until Stone snatched her arm and turned

her around to face him. "Hold on there, Charlotte. I never said anything about needing that letter to make my decision. I need it to help me determine my next move."

She scowled up at him and yanked her arm free of his hold.

"Look." He blew out a breath. "I'm sickened by what I just heard. There's no way I can continue working for Randolph Dorchester with a clean conscience." He hesitated, not sure if he should share the rest of his thoughts.

Charlotte must have sensed he was holding something back. "But . . . ?"

Stone held her gaze for a long moment. "But others won't be as discerning."

She grabbed his forearm as if someone had just kicked her legs out from under her. "Others?"

He had the strangest urge to pull her against his chest and console her as she had done with Lily. Yet even as the idea sprouted in his brain, she chopped it down by releasing her hold on him and wrapping both arms around her waist as if warding him off.

"Others are coming? I thought you said you were the best in the business." Panic pushed her voice into a higher octave. "Why would he hire others?"

"To hedge his bets." Stone watched her face. Shoot. Her eyes had a wild look about them, and her lips were trembling. She pressed them together, though, mastering her emotions. He couldn't help but be impressed. The woman had a steel core. "I may be the best, but you did a right fine job of hiding. I've been hunting for two months without much to show for it. Dorchester got impatient. He hired a second man."

"Will he find us here?" Her eyes begged him to say no, but he couldn't offer her false hope.

"It's possible. If Dorchester shares my information with him. With no confirmation from me, he might assume my lead didn't pan out. Or he could grow suspicious. Either way, if he doesn't hear something from me soon, he'll send Franklin to investigate."

"Franklin is the other retriever?"

Why did she have to look at him like that? All scared and brave, begging him for reassurance even as her body clearly signaled that he wasn't to touch her.

Stone exhaled and scratched at the stiches on his chest beneath his shirt. "Yes."

"He's good?"

"Yes." Franklin wasn't as adept at puzzling through clues and fitting things together, but once he got the scent, the man was like a bloodhound. And he didn't care about the hows or whys. He just cared about the paycheck at the other end. Not that Stone would admit as much to Charlotte. She had enough on her plate already. "I'm better, though. That's why Dorchester hired me first. I'll not abandon you to him, Charlotte." Stone moved closer, his jaw working back and forth like the arguments in his head. Stuff it. The woman needed comfort. Ever so lightly, he cupped his palm around her shoulder. She flinched but didn't move away.

"We have a few days to strategize while we wait for that letter from Austin." And he *had* to wait for that letter. He believed Lily's story. She had no reason to lie nor the understanding to fully grasp the ramifications of what she'd revealed. Yet the story alone wasn't evidence. Getting confirmation of Charlotte's legal guardianship would give them the freedom they needed to take action. "In the meantime, I'll need to go to town and wire Dorchester. Give him just enough to hold off Franklin without tipping our hand."

"What will you tell him?"

Stone grinned as he squeezed her shoulder, trying to infuse her with a

176

confidence he didn't feel. "I'll think of something."

14

What would she do if he didn't return? Charlotte let the curtain drop back into place in her front bedroom window after checking the drive for the hundredth time, looking for any sign of Stone Hammond and his monster horse. After their discussion the day before yesterday, she'd known he needed to travel to Madisonville to send that telegram, but he'd been gone four hours. He could have walked there and back in two.

She'd wanted to go with him, to see the message he sent with her own eyes, to make sure he didn't betray them, but he'd insisted on going alone. Said it was better if no one in town saw them together. He even planned to stop by Dr. Ramsey's office to suggest the man *forget* where they'd met. It was the best way to protect Lily if Franklin came looking later on. There'd be no evidence that Stone was helping them.

If he actually *was* helping them. Charlotte's assurance on that point dissipated a little more with every fruitless glance out the window.

He'd left his cache of weapons locked away in her barn as collateral. Surely he wouldn't abandon such valuable items. Didn't men like him feel an attachment to their weapons? She'd seen how well kept they were. Clean. Oiled. The handles worn in places as if they'd been shaped to their owner's hand over time. The leather of his gun belt even bore his initials. He wouldn't just leave all that behind. Would he?

She'd gambled on him. Gambled on the Bible he'd brought in from the bunkhouse that listed his name in the birth records in his mother's handwriting. Gambled on his outrage over Dorchester's behavior. Gambled on his heroic nature. But what if she'd misread him? Money wielded a powerful influence. It took a strong man to escape its lure. She'd known Stone Hammond only a matter of days. How could she possibly judge the depth of his character with any accuracy?

The arguments tugged back and forth in her brain like a logger's saw, its jagged teeth tearing deeper and deeper into her until she was nearly torn in two. Her legs trembled, threatening to topple her. Her breath rasped. She needed a distraction. Needed . . . *music.*

Charlotte wrenched the bedroom door open and made a beeline for the parlor, for the only thing certain to soothe her chaotic spirit.

The piano beckoned to her like a lost love, promising solace. She slid onto the bench and positioned her hands over the keys. Dobson had taken the children fishing down at the lake. There was no one to hear. No one to see.

As a music instructor, she'd played in front of her students countless times, but always when she was in full control. Never when the storm raged so recklessly inside her that she had to play or be consumed. Not when her soul would be vulnerable, exposed. No, those times required privacy. And God's providence had provided precisely that at the moment she needed it most.

Closing her eyes, she let her fingers hit the keys. Chopin. Her fingers needed to fly, and her mind needed the challenge. The dark tones and unconventional chords of the "Prelude in G Minor" told her story. Trapped. Helpless. Questions that had no answers. But the short piece ended too quickly. Her emotions still churned for release. So she chose another piece, one in F sharp minor. Her agitated spirit accepted the frantic pace, stealing her breath as her fingers sprinted over the keys. But it wasn't enough. Chopin challenged her, pushed her, but his music didn't speak to her soul. Not like Beethoven. "The Tempest" — that's what she needed to play.

Lifting her hands away from the keys, Charlotte straightened her posture and let her gaze rest on an indistinct space on the wall over the sofa until the melody of Beethoven's "Sonata No. 17 in D Minor" sang through her mind.

Wait.

She could hear her father's instructions. *"Don't touch the keys until the music is in you. Until your heart is one with the song."*

Wait.

Her fingers hovered above the piano. She breathed. In. Out. Felt the storm build.

Now.

It began gently. Like she had. Wanting to trust. Wanting to believe that Stone Hammond wouldn't betray them as so many men in her life had done before. But in less than two bars, the doubts rained down. She didn't really know him. Why would he forfeit Dorchester's payment? Why would he care?

Yet he'd taken on a wildcat for Stephen without a thought to his own safety. The music slowed again, like a ray of sun peeking through the clouds just long enough to give hope before the gray storm blotted it from the sky. This time the storm raged longer. Her right hand warred with her left as the lighter tones tried to press their way through the roiling seas of the lower hand like a mermaid calling to a sailor caught in a maelstrom, urging him not to give up, not to be afraid.

Unlike the Chopin preludes, Beethoven's sonata stretched long before her, allowing her to fully immerse herself in the swells and currents of the song. Up and down she went, over and over. To trust or not to trust? If she did and Stone betrayed her, what would she do next? How could she protect Lily?

The music became a prayer, the groans of her spirit that were too complex for words. She poured herself out until exhaustion claimed her, the tempest building to its thunderous conclusion before finally giving way to peace. Her spirit gave up the fight as well, spent from the frenzy of worry. She couldn't control Stone or his motives. She had to give that over into God's keeping.

He could be trusted even if Stone couldn't. The Lord would show her what to do when the time came.

So why did the thought of Stone riding away from her leave her so bereft? Something beyond concern for Lily stirred in her breast. Something she didn't want to acknowledge. Yet something her heart couldn't keep quiet as her fingers moved to the soft, aching melody of another Beethoven sonata: No. 14. "Moonlight."

Stone sat on the front porch steps, afraid to move. Scared that if a stair creaked or a floorboard moaned beneath his weight the music would stop. He had no idea how long he'd been sitting there. Fifteen minutes? Twenty?

When he'd ridden in from town, he'd barely been able to hear the piano, it being closed up in the house. He'd assumed John was playing again. Until he'd unsaddled Goliath and noticed that the wagon was gone and recalled the afternoon fishing trip the kids had been chattering about that morning at breakfast.

It had to be her.

Charlotte.

Lily had mentioned something about her playing being different than John's, but he hadn't grasped her meaning. Not until he'd strutted up to the front door and been walloped by a raging storm. It had stopped him in his tracks. Never had he heard such music.

He'd sunk to the steps and braced his back against the side railing. If he tilted his head back just enough, he could make out her face through the window glass, between the half-drawn curtains. That's when his breath had left him. The serene expression she always wore had fallen away like the mask he'd suspected it to be, leaving her true self exposed. She grimaced as if in physical pain as she bent over the keys, the motions of her body adding emphasis to the turbulent tones. Then, when the music lightened, her face would turn toward the sky as if she was begging the Lord for guidance, searching for the hope she'd somehow misplaced.

She doubts me. Stone closed his eyes and let his head drop back against the railing. He couldn't blame her. He *had* come here intending to rescue Lily. Rescue. Ha! As if the girl needed rescuing from the woman who had sacrificed so much to keep her safe.

Hearing Charlotte's turmoil through the piano cut him to the quick. He wanted to go to her. To reassure her that he'd not betray her. That he'd made his choice, and it didn't include Dorchester. But trust couldn't be demanded; it had to be earned. And he sensed that Charlotte's trust would come at a higher price than most.

She took such pains to lock her inner self away from the world. For protection. Someone had hurt her long before Dorchester. And before that fool, Sullivan, and his closing of her school. A suitor? Her father? Stone hadn't dug very deep into the old scandal surrounding her parents. He'd been focused on uncovering properties Charlotte had ties to, not fifteen-year-old gossip. Yet now he wished he'd taken the time to find out.

The music changed.

Stone opened his eyes. That song. The one John had played for Lily. Yet while the notes sounded familiar, the effect was staggeringly different. Stephen had said the song made him feel lonely when his teacher played it. Stone had to agree. Hearing it reminded him of nights alone on the trail, the wind soughing through the trees, creating its own lonesome lullaby — the kind that made him question the future he'd mapped for himself. Would the cabin and property he'd worked his whole life to claim bring him fulfillment or just isolation?

He shook off the melancholy as he'd trained himself to do, yet the music continued to woo him back. Why? Why did it affect him so strongly?

His gut clenched. It wasn't the music. It was the musician. The song drew him to his loneliest place because that's where *she* was. Alone.

Unable to stop himself, Stone rose to his feet and crept toward the right side of the porch. Then to the parlor window. Her eyes were closed, her lashes dark against her pale cheeks. He peered closer. Something glittered on the skin beneath those lashes. Tears? The back of Stone's throat constricted. *Charlotte.* Always so strong, so controlled for everyone else. They leaned on her, depended on her. *Who do you lean on?*

Not having a clue what to say but determined to let her know she wasn't alone, Stone pulled his hat from his head and strode into the house. He halted in front of the sofa and stood there, praying she could see his intention in his eyes.

She didn't jerk away from the piano as he'd expected. No, her hands simply hovered over the last notes before slowly lifting to brace themselves against the wood casing. Her lashes lifted. She turned to face him, tears flooding her eyes.

"You came back."

15

Charlotte stared at the silent man who had thrust himself into her parlor. Into her life. She should feel relieved that he'd not run back to Dorchester. Or perhaps angry that he'd lingered in town so long and caused her to worry. Maybe even embarrassed that he'd caught her playing, or shamed that he'd seen her weakness. Yet none of those emotions flared in her chest. In truth, she was so wrung out from the music, all she could do was stare silently back at him.

Their eyes held for a long moment, and something in the way he looked at her gradually imbued her with renewed strength, as if she were a wilted garden, scorched by the summer sun, and he a gentle rain. She'd been on her own for so long, no one to depend on except herself and a God who too often felt far removed. Yet Stone was there. His arms strong. His shoulders sturdy. What would it be like to lean on him? For just a little while?

Fanciful nonsense — that's what it was — conjured by a heart too weary to protect itself against old dreams that had never fully died. Still, she couldn't quite shake the thirst. The yearning to be loved by an honorable man, one *worth his salt,* as Stone had called it. She licked her lips, almost expecting to taste the tang, but of course there was nothing there. Just spinster skin and foolishness.

Stone must have recognized her lack as well, for he suddenly cleared his throat and shifted his weight. "Of course I came back," he grumbled. "I told you I would." His gaze flitted from her to the ceiling to his boots to the window before alighting once again on her.

Charlotte did smile then. His fidgeting, the hint of insecurity in a man so thoroughly capable, restored a measure of the control she'd lost in Beethoven's sonatas. She straightened her posture and slowly rose from the piano bench. "In my experience," she said, feeling more like her usual self, "a person saying he will do something is not necessarily a guarantee that it will be done."

All signs of awkwardness vanished from Stone's countenance in a flash. He pinned her with a look that stole the breath from her lungs. "I'll make you a deal, teacher. You start judging me by my own actions instead of those of the sorry yahoos who let you down so many times *in your experience,* and I'll judge you by yours instead of lumping you into the same category as the tight-laced, sour-faced, switch-whacking schoolmarms of *my* past that I always loathed."

The comment brought her up short. "I-I'm sorry. I didn't realize . . ."

Had she been unfair? Life had taught her to be cautious of men, but being cautious didn't give her the right to assume all men were guilty of poor character and then treat them as such. A man, or woman, should be presumed innocent until proven guilty. Hadn't she asked Stone to give her the benefit of the doubt before spiriting Lily away? And he had. He'd listened to her, examined her documents, written letters on her behalf, all in the face of evidence that proclaimed her a kidnapper.

Charlotte lifted her chin and forced herself to hold his gaze. "Forgive me, Stone. I've done you a disservice. I . . ." She swallowed. "I can't promise it will never happen again." Habits formed over half a lifetime rarely disappeared overnight. "However, I can promise that I will make every effort to stop viewing your character through a tainted lens. You're right. You deserve to be judged on your own merits."

The lines of his face softened, and he stepped closer. So close she could touch him if she simply lifted her arm. Naturally, she kept both appendages firmly at her sides.

But he didn't.

Stone reached his hand to her face and stroked a fingertip lightly along her hairline then traced the curve of her ear. Tingles coursed over her scalp, and for a moment she feared her knees would buckle. Never had a simple touch shaken her so completely.

"I'm not perfect, Charlotte." His low voice rumbled over her like river water plunging down a cliff in a spectacular fall. "I'm bound to make mistakes, but I swear to you here and now, that I will do everything in my power to keep you and Lily safe. Do you believe me?"

She wanted to. Oh, how she wanted to. Yet she couldn't quite silence the suspicious voice that clawed through her mind.

He knows you're a lonely spinster. That's why he's touching you, looking at you with such intensity. It's a manipulation to gain your cooperation. It's not real. It can't be trusted.

But what if it wasn't a manipulation?

Charlotte examined his face, the lines of his mouth, the strength of his chin, the sincerity in his eyes. Either Stone Hammond was the finest actor ever to tread the streets of Texas, or he was, in fact, a man of integrity. A man worthy of trust. Could she afford to send such a man away when he'd just declared his intention to keep Lily safe?

His hand dropped to her shoulder then slid gently down her arm, coming to rest a couple inches above her elbow. His grip tightened just a little, enough to remind her that he was waiting for her answer.

"Yes," she blurted. "I believe you." Her belief might be reluctant and cautious, but she'd chosen her path, and she'd not turn back unless he gave her cause.

Stone didn't grin in triumph or sag in relief. No, he held her gaze and stroked his thumb in a comforting swirl atop her sleeve. "Thank you, Charlotte." His hand fell away from her arm, and she immediately mourned the loss of the connection, the warmth of his touch.

He turned to leave. Panic flared in her breast.

"Wait." She grabbed his arm. He glanced back, a brow raised in question. Thankfully, his eyes held no spark of irritation, only curiosity.

Charlotte released him and fought to organize the churning thoughts in her head. She needed to sound intelligent, controlled, when she made her plea. Rambling like an idiot would undermine her position. Yet trust would never bloom between them without honesty, and she couldn't demand a full dose from him without offering a helping of her own.

"I need your help," she finally admitted.

He did smile then. "I know. That's why I'm staying."

She shook her head. "Not with Lily. Well, yes, I do need help with Lily's situation, but that's not what I was referring to." So much for not rambling like an idiot. Charlotte sighed, ran a smoothing hand down the front of her skirt, and tried again. "I need help believing. In you."

She winced at the blunt words, but Stone showed no signs of impatience or anger. He simply pivoted to face her more fully then perched on the arm of the sofa, his posture relaxed, open. "What can I do?"

Charlotte fingered the cameo at her neck, caught herself, and balled her hand into a fist. *For Pete's sake. Just spit it out.*

"I'm not very good at blind faith. I need

to know what you are thinking, planning." She stepped toward him, the words coming easier now that she'd started. "I want to be a part of any decisions being made that affect Lily or the boys. Being kept in the dark tends to rouse my suspicions. If you want me to trust your judgment, you'll need to explain your strategy. And . . ." She caught the words before they flew past her lips, but then something defiant rose within her. Something she'd been pushing down since she was a child. A voice that demanded to be heard. "And I expect to be treated as an equal in this partnership. My opinions will be heard and considered based on their worth, not automatically discounted because they originated from a female. I will have your respect."

"Shoot, Charlotte." Stone's eyes smiled even as his face maintained the serious expression he'd adopted when she'd begun her recitation. "You've had my respect since I first took this job, even when I thought you were a half-crazed kidnapper."

Not the most flattering assessment, yet it was honest, and that was exactly what she needed from him.

Stone propped his heel against the sofa leg and leaned back slightly. "Anyone who could disappear with three kids and leave no trace is a force to be reckoned with. I respected your mind from the beginning, but over the last few days, I've come to respect your heart as well."

Charlotte couldn't help it. She smiled. Never before had she stood up for herself with such abandon. It felt good. But what felt even better was hearing his response. He hadn't scoffed or condescended. He hadn't bullied. No. He'd commended her intellect and offered the respect she craved without a moment's hesitation.

"You uprooted your entire life for the sake of these kids and risked the wrath of a powerful man in the process." Stone pushed up from the sofa, his gaze never leaving her face. "It's as plain as day that you love them, and there's nothing I respect more than a mother's love." He rubbed a hand across the back of his neck, his attention slipping down to the floor for a moment before finding her face once again. "It's been a long time since I worked with a partner, and I might not always remember to consult with you, but you can ask me as many questions as you want to help jog my memory."

It took her a moment to find her voice. "Sounds reasonable," she finally managed.

"There might come a time when I have to make a decision on the spot, though," he said, his tone hardening. "If you or the kids are in danger, I expect you to obey my instructions instantly, without question or argument. In a crisis, there's only room for one leader."

Charlotte didn't hesitate. "Of course. Your knowledge and experience in such situations far exceeds my own. I'd be a fool not to listen to you."

He gave a sharp nod. "Good. Then I believe we have a deal, teacher." He thrust his hand toward her, and Charlotte slipped her palm next to his.

His strong grip closed around her fingers, and for the first time since Mr. Dobson had dragged Stone Hammond to her doorstep, she actually believed everything might end up all right.

Her hand felt good in his. So good that Stone had a hard time letting go. He fought against the insane urge to tug her close and hold her against his chest. 'Course if he did, he'd probably scare her half to death and kill the fledging trust she'd just offered him. So he dropped her hand, cleared his throat, and folded his arms across his chest to keep temptation at bay.

"Well," he said, needing to engage his mind elsewhere, "do you have any questions you want answered now?" He'd promised to let her ask anything, and since he had nothing to hide, opening himself to her queries seemed a harmless enough pastime.

As long as she didn't ask him how often he'd thought about kissing her in the last fifteen minutes.

"Actually, I do," she said. "Do you mind if we sit?" She gestured to the sofa.

Stone nodded.

She perched lightly on the edge of the cushion, her spine as straight as a broom handle. Stone wedged himself into the opposite corner, placing his back against the arm in order to face her. He propped his right ankle on his left knee, positioning his bent leg across the seat between them.

"I want to know what happened in town today," she said. "Why you were gone for so long. You did more than send a telegram."

"Yes." He drew out the word, unsure why she was upset.

Then he recalled what she'd said when he'd first walked into the parlor. *You came back.* She'd thought he'd left. For good. But he hadn't even considered such a thing. So he gave a detailed account of his whereabouts while in town, hoping it would reassure her.

"I dropped by the post office to introduce

myself to the fella running the place, told him I was expecting a letter in the next few days and asked him to hold it for me. Said I'd try to get back to town in a couple days to check on it. I didn't want him to see a stranger's name and start asking around all willy-nilly. Best to leave the smallest footprint possible in case Franklin shows up and tries to track us."

"You seem pretty certain that he'll come." There she went fussing with her skirts again. He was coming to recognize the action as her fretting tic. That and the way she touched the brooch at her collarbone.

"I ain't certain about anything," he amended. "But I've found it wise to plan for the worst so it doesn't catch me off guard."

She dipped her chin in acknowledgment yet made no further comment. Taking that as his cue to continue outlining his visit to town, he moved on.

"I strolled through the general store, taking stock of the supplies they had. Never know what you might need in a hurry. Then I headed for the telegraph office."

Charlotte's gaze zeroed in on him like a sharpshooter taking aim at a target. "What did your message say?"

"I notified Dorchester that I'd located

Charles Atherton's house."

A tiny sound echoed from inside her throat, a sound hinting at a whimper. Stone hurried to tell her the rest.

"I also mentioned that some crazy old man came after me with a rifle when I tried to investigate. I offered to hang around a little while and dig a little deeper but told him I didn't expect the lead to pan out."

She expelled a long, slow breath. "No mention of Lily? Of me?"

Stone shook his head. "None. Didn't figure he needed to know that part."

Charlotte touched his knee, her eyes going soft. "Thank you."

Shoot. Now he was back to thinking about kissing her. *Come on, Hammond. Stay on track.*

"I stopped by Doc Ramsey's office, too. Had him check my progress. He said the wounds were healing well. The stitches should be ready to be removed in about five days, around the same time the letter from Austin should arrive. Which works out well. I'd like to have the stitches out before we leave."

"Leave?" She snatched her hand back from his knee so fast he had to glance down to make sure his trousers hadn't caught fire. "When did you decide we'd be leaving?"

He winced at her strident tone. He supposed this was one of those decisions she expected to be part of. 'Course in all fairness, he'd made the plan before they'd had their conversation, so she really had no business being mad.

"I wired my friend Daniel Barrett while I was at the telegraph office," he said without a touch of apology. "Mentioned that I might be paying him a visit with a few extra packages in tow."

Her brows arched with incredulity. "You plan to deliver my children into the lair of Dead-Eye Dan?"

16

"Is there another place you'd prefer?"

He sounded so calm. Infuriating man. As if picking up and leaving everything familiar was a simple matter of packing bags. Well, it wasn't. Charlotte jumped up from the settee and paced back and forth along the length of the floor rug. How was she to protect Lily if she didn't know where they were going or the people they'd be forced to rely upon? She'd barely begun trusting Stone, and now he expected her to trust some dime novel character? He was asking too much.

"Or maybe you think it would be better to stay here?" The man just sat on the sofa, leg still bent across the cushion as if they were discussing nothing more important than whether they should have white or brown gravy on the mashed potatoes at dinner. Didn't he care that Lily's life hung in the balance? "There's a chance Dorchester won't send Franklin to check things out," he said. "About fifty-fifty either way, I'd say. Now, me? I don't particularly care for those odds, but if things check out the way I expect, and you *are* Lily's guardian, the choice will be yours. We could make a stand here and try to stop Franklin before he reports your whereabouts to Dorchester, or we can leave and let him find an empty house with only the inhospitable Dobson in residence to match the report I wired today."

Charlotte stopped pacing, her back to the annoyingly rational man on the sofa. He was right, of course. She couldn't wager Lily's future on the off chance this Franklin person wouldn't follow up on Stone's lead. But could she wager her best friend's child on the reliability of people she'd never met?

An odd warmth climbed up Charlotte's spine and tickled the hairs on the nape of her neck. Her eyes slid closed. He was there. She knew it as surely as she knew the feel of her mother's cameo at her throat. Stone Hammond stood behind her. Close enough for his breath to ruffle her hair. Yet he didn't touch her.

The lack of touch demonstrated his respect for her, his trustworthiness. He wasn't out to seduce. He only meant to demonstrate his intention to stand by her with a physical display of a figurative ideal. So why did she suddenly wish that he would wrap his arms around her waist and tug her back against his chest?

"Trusting me means you also trust my judgment, Charlotte." His low voice rumbled in her ear. "You can ask questions and use your own eyes to watch for any danger I might miss. But understand that I will never expose Lily or the boys to a situation unless I am completely sure of their safety."

"You trust this Daniel Barrett person that much?"

"I trust him with my life."

Slowly, Charlotte turned to face him. "Do you trust him with *Lily's* life?"

He held her gaze and nodded. "I do. Dan and I have saved each other's hides too many times not to be loyal to the bone. After years of trackin' outlaws together, there's a bond between us that's even stronger than blood."

"Good. I've seen blood bonds broken. I'd rather place my trust in something stronger."

Stone caught the bitterness in her reply as she ducked her head. *Oh, no you don't. No more hiding from me.* He cupped her chin and eased her face back up. "What blood bonds are we talkin' about?"

Her eyes widened, and he swore he could feel her pulse jump beneath his fingers. "L-Lily and her grandfather, of course."

Stone shook his head. "Nope. I don't think that's the one. Dorchester's despicable behavior might rile you, but it hasn't wounded you. There's something deeper and more personal eating a hole through your gut." He murmured to her in soft tones, stroking his hands down her arms to unball the fists that had formed at her sides. "Who hurt you?"

Her fingers clamped around his, nearly painful in the force of their grip. He was pushing her too hard. He could read the panic in her face, feel the tension in her muscles.

"You don't have to tell me," he whispered. "I have no right to your secrets; those are yours alone. But if you want help shouldering the load for a little while, I'm ready and willing." He hesitated, waiting for an indication that she might confide in him, that she might let him inside just a little. But she said nothing.

He shouldn't be disappointed. Her trust of him was too new. Yet after listening to her pour her heart into her piano music, he couldn't stop himself from wanting a piece of that for himself. More, though, he wanted to rub salve into her wounds and aid her healing as she'd done for him after the cat attack. Her injuries lingered deep beneath the surface, however, and he suspected she'd lived with them so long, they'd become part of her. Exposing them would hurt. A lot. And hurting her was the last thing he wanted to do. On the other hand, letting a wound fester and grow infected simply to avoid the temporary pain of lancing was no kindness, either.

What do I do, Lord? How do I help her?

No answer shot from the heavens, yet a growing unease about pressing her for details swelled in his chest. They were *her* secrets. She should be the one to decide if and when to share them. It was his job to listen, not to pry them out of her. Trust had to work both ways.

"When you're ready, Charlotte." He slid his hands from her grasp and turned to go. He'd nearly made it to the hall when her voice stopped him.

"My father had an affair."

Stone's jaw clenched at the blurted words. He could hear tears wavering close to the surface, could feel the agony of her admission, and he hated that she'd endured such hurt.

Give me the right words to help, Lord. Or glue my tongue down to keep it from flappin' if that's best. Just don't let me mess this up. Swallowing his nerves, he turned to face her.

Her head hung low, as if the shame of her father's sin had attached itself to her. She clenched her hands together in front of her so fiercely, he worried for her circulation. Stone closed the distance between them with long strides and immediately wrapped his arm around her shoulders.

"Let's sit back down." He steered her toward the sofa, but instead of letting her perch stiffly on the edge of the seat, he kept his arm around her and urged her to lean against him.

She resisted at first then gave way all at once, tucking her head against his chest. Whether she sought comfort from him or simply tried to hide her face, he didn't know. Shoot, he didn't really even care. She felt so good nuzzled against him, he'd hold her there all afternoon if it made her feel better. Heaven knew it made *him* feel better.

He held her for what felt like several minutes, stroking her arm, resting his jaw against the soft pillow of her hair, waiting for her to continue. When no words came, he gave her a gentle nudge. "How old were you?" His fingers never paused in their stroking, conveying a subtle acceptance he hoped she'd recognize instinctually.

"Ten," she finally said, her voice small. She fiddled with the fabric of her skirt, plucking at it, twisting it, then smoothing it again. "He tried to blame his infidelity on my mother, blaming her for leaving him behind in the wake of her success. But even as young as I was, I knew it was a lie. Papa lived for the limelight, and when Mama's career exploded, he was banished to the shadows. At first, he basked in her glory, taking credit for her magnificence as her teacher and manager. Mama played along, humbly proclaiming that she would have been nothing without his tutelage. She loved him, you see, and knew his foibles. She didn't care about the fame. She cared about the music, about bringing it to life and sharing it with others."

Stone tried to recall what little his investigation had turned up regarding Jeanette Atherton. "She's an opera singer?"

Charlotte glanced up, pride flashing in her eyes. "One of the most sought after mezzo-sopranos in Europe."

He smiled at her, and for a moment she smiled back. Then she seemed to remember the tale she was in the middle of telling. Her smile faltered, and she turned her face back into his chest.

"She's played in London, Paris, even Vienna. I believe she's somewhere in Italy at present. But I haven't had a letter in several months, so I can't be sure."

He heard the loneliness in the statement, but oddly enough, he detected no self-pity. She seemed to bear her mother no ill will, though Stone couldn't say he felt the same. He knew Charlotte had been a student at Dr. Sullivan's academy for five years before spending two at the Sam Houston Normal School in Huntsville and earning her teaching certificate. She'd returned to Dr. Sullivan's academy after that and took up the role of music teacher at the age of eighteen.

"My parents had been happy together . . . before. *We'd* been happy." Charlotte shifted slightly and started picking at her skirt again. "Our house was always filled with music. Papa on the piano, Mama singing, me bouncing between the two. We lived in New York most of the year, but Mama insisted on having a place away from the big city to retreat, a home where we could just be a family and not worry about auditions or performances or what the latest critic spewed in the papers. Papa could only bear to be away for about two months out of the year, but he declared himself too in love with Mama to deny her anything, so he had this house built in the middle of nowhere, and we spent every Christmas here that I can remember. This little house became my favorite place in all the world."

Stone could picture it. The three Athertons gathered around the piano singing Christmas carols, laughing, playing. A little girl's dream.

"That's why his betrayal cut so deep." She pulled away from him slightly and met his gaze. "He said he loved us, Stone. He said we were his pride and joy, his life. We adored him. But our adoration wasn't enough. He craved the adoration of the world. And when the world started praising Mama instead, his love died. He found a new protégé to tutor, determined to prove that Mama's success was *his* creation, not simply a product of her own talent and hard work. His next student was a female pianist — young, beautiful, and so terribly grateful to have the undivided attention of such an acclaimed artist as Charles Atherton. How could he resist such admiration?"

"By remembering his vows before God,

that's how," Stone growled. Weak, sniveling little man. A man worth his salt would delight in his wife's achievements, not sit and cry about his own being overlooked.

An odd look stole over Charlotte's face. She tilted her head a bit and regarded him as if he'd just sprouted a third ear from his chin.

"What?" He scrubbed at his chin with the back of his hand just to make sure whiskers were the only appendages growing there.

"Nothing, it's just . . ." She squared her shoulders. "No, it's not nothing. It is a very significant *something.* Thank you, Stone."

He hadn't a clue what she was thanking him for, but he wasn't about to argue with the woman.

"When the scandal first broke," she said, "I tried to defend my mother against the unfair speculation that arose, but I soon learned it was pointless. People believed what they wanted to believe. She was an *opera singer.* Everyone knew that women of the stage lacked morality. Charles Atherton was simply too much of a gentleman to mention whatever infidelities his wife had committed to drive him into the arms of another woman. As if any excuse justified turning one's back on vows made before God. You're the first person I've heard offer reproach on that front."

"The way I figure it," Stone said with a shrug, her gratitude making him itch a bit under his collar, "when God said no man should put a marriage asunder, that included the fella and gal who said the vows in the first place. I'm not sayin' it's easy. There's too much strife and temptation in this world to ride through at a constant lope. Sometimes the bronc you're on will buck and hop 'til your rear's so bruised you think you'll never recover."

Her cheeks colored at his reference, making that itch spread up the back of Stone's neck. He reached behind him and rubbed his palm across his nape. "What I'm trying to say is that if you hang on with all you got during those rough patches, the ride will eventually smooth out, and when it does, you'll be left with a bond that will only make you stronger."

Listen to him, spouting off like he knew anything about marriage. What did he know? He'd never been a part of one. Only example he'd had was his own folks, and they'd died so young he hadn't had time to watch them weather many storms. Stone blew out a breath. "Works with horses, anyway."

She smiled at him and actually stopped

pickin' at her dress long enough to touch his knee. "I imagine it works with more than horses." Her eyes sparkled in that moment, as if a cloud had shifted just enough to let a ray of sunlight pass through. His gut tightened, and suddenly he wanted to be the man who banished all her clouds. Too soon, though, she shuttered her eyes with lowered lashes and pulled her hand away from his knee to rest it once more in her lap.

"I think what hurt the most was that he never said good-bye. I just came home from school one day to find him gone." She lifted her chin but didn't look at him. Her gaze drifted out into the open space of the room. "From the time I was two and he'd recognized I had an ear for the piano, he'd spent hours with me every week, grooming me into a pianist worthy of playing the finest concert halls of the world. I lived for one of his smiles, for a word of praise. I practiced constantly, believing that we shared a special bond as pianists, one even Mama couldn't share with him. Everything I did was to make him proud. Then he left me. No explanation. No apology. He hasn't written me a single letter in all the years since. It's as if I ceased to exist. Ceased to matter."

In that moment, Stone thanked God that Charlotte wasn't looking at him, for he knew he couldn't hide the rage surging through him. How could a man do that to his own flesh and blood? Leave without a word? Let her think she didn't matter? The man needed some sense and common decency knocked into him, and Stone was more than up for the job. His fists were primed and ready.

"Mama told me that he was just too ashamed to face me, and that I shouldn't believe all men were as faithless as he. I tried to follow her advice, even went so far as to let a young man court me when I was at teaching college."

A lump settled in Stone's gut. It felt a bit like a prickly pear. With spines poking out every which way. "You . . . ah . . . had a suitor?"

She nodded. "He was a year ahead of me in school. Quiet. Intelligent. Not one to be at the center of attention. My father's opposite in almost every way. I thought he'd be safe. He invited me to study with him in the library. I agreed. Before I knew it, we were going to the café for dinner on Saturday evenings and taking long walks around the school grounds. We'd been seeing each other for about three months when his sister came to visit. She brought a friend with her, a friend who just happened to be Alexander's betrothed. The shock on his face when they found us would have been comical had he not made it so clear that he was ashamed to be found with me. He tossed out some excuse about me turning my ankle to explain why my arm was threaded through his and begged me with a look to play along." Charlotte's lips tightened into a thin line as color flooded her cheeks. "I limped a few steps to the nearest bench then waved them all away, giving assurances that I would be fine. When they left for home a few days later, Alexander came to me with some pitiful tale about how, since meeting me, he no longer wanted to marry Georgiana. That he much preferred a woman who matched him in intelligence and ambition. I told him I had too much intelligence to allow the attentions of a man who belonged to another. After that, I focused on my education and never stepped out with another man."

Good grief. No wonder the woman had trouble trusting people.

She let out a sigh and moved away from him to perch back on the edge of the seat cushion. "The only man in my life who has proved dependable is Mr. Dobson, and I'm pretty sure the only reason he stays is because he has nowhere else to go."

"Don't sell the fellow short," Stone said, not quite believing he was actually singing the gnome's praises. "He was ready to do me in to keep you and the kids safe. I'd say more than a roof is keeping him here."

Charlotte looked at him then, a small smile budding as she glanced over her shoulder. "Or maybe he just enjoys whacking tall men on the head and dragging them around."

Stone grinned as he rubbed the bruise on his forehead. "It's a possibility."

Charlotte turned away again and stood. Her hands immediately started smoothing her skirt.

Stone rose to his feet and bent down to capture one of her hands. "Dobson's not the only man you can depend on, Charlotte."

She looked at him a long moment before tugging her hand free. "We'll see."

17

Nearly a week later, Charlotte stood at her bedroom window, once again watching Stone canter off toward town on that oversized beast of his. She caressed the cameo at her neck as he disappeared from view, not out of nervousness this time, but with intent. The feminine profile carved into the shell brooch stirred memories. Her mother had given her the pin the day she'd dropped Charlotte off at the Sullivan Academy.

The two of them had tried to make things work after her father left, staying together for over a year. Her mother had employed nannies and private tutors as they bounced from opera house to opera house, but the strain proved too much. All Charlotte wanted was for her mother to take her home to their Texas cottage, to settle down into a routine, to have a *normal* life. Yet she never spoke of such dreams. How could she when it would mean her mother would have to sacrifice the career she had trained for years to achieve?

If only her father hadn't ruined everything. Yet even as Charlotte cast blame, deep down she missed him. Missed his music, too. Every time she'd tried to play, her mother would flee the room, the memories of all they had lost too much for her to bear. After a while, Charlotte stopped playing altogether. That was when her mother decided to send her to Sullivan's academy.

"You have a gift, Lottie," her mother had fiercely declared as she held her child's hands in one final embrace before leaving. "A gift bestowed by God, and I am stealing it from you, just as surely as your father tried to steal mine from me. No one has the right to take another's gift. Not out of greed, or jealousy, or even self-pity. That's why you must stay here, why you must develop your talent and use it as God leads."

"But, Mama, I love *you* more than I love music. Please don't make me stay here. I want to be with you."

Tears had streamed down her mother's face, but she hadn't relented. Like Lily's mother, Jeanette Atherton had been determined to do what she believed was in her daughter's best interest.

"Do you remember the story of Hannah from your Bible school lessons?"

Charlotte nodded, not sure what a Bible story had to do with her mother leaving her behind. "She prayed so hard for a baby that the priest thought she was drunk."

Mama had chuckled at that. "That's right. And in her prayer, she vowed that if God would give her a son, she would dedicate him to the Lord's service. And she did. She took her son, Samuel, to the priest to be raised by him, taught by him. I'm doing the same for you, Lottie. Traveling from city to city is no life for a young girl, and stifling the music in your soul is a sin I couldn't bear to have on my conscience. This is what's best, darling. For both of us."

And that's when Charlotte had stopped arguing. *For both of us.* Charlotte was holding her mother back, impeding her career. Her love for her daughter tugged her in one direction while her love of the stage tugged her the opposite way. She couldn't have both, not with any measure of success. And Charlotte wanted her mother to be successful. She deserved it. Jeanette Atherton's arias could make the hardhearted weep. A talent like that shouldn't be held back simply because her daughter was too afraid to be on her own.

"All right, Mama. I'll stay."

"That's my good girl." She hugged Charlotte to her breast. "I'm going to miss you so much!" Charlotte never wanted the embrace to end, but it did. All too soon. Her mother straightened, fumbling with the clasp on the brooch that perched high among her bodice ruffles. "Take this, sweetheart. I know you've always liked it. Think of me when you wear it and remember how much I love you." She pressed the cameo into Charlotte's palm, caught a sob behind her lacy handkerchief, then dashed for her carriage.

Charlotte had worn the brooch every day since.

At first, like Hannah, Charlotte's mother had visited every year, usually at Christmas. They would escape to their cottage in Madisonville, chatter long into the night about operas and schoolgirl squabbles, and find each other again. But when Charlotte started her studies at Sam Houston Normal School, the visits stopped. Her mother's career had taken off in Europe, making travel more difficult. And Charlotte had grown into an adult who shouldn't need her mother. Yet she did.

Perhaps it was that loss of connection that made her blind to Alexander's true motives and left her susceptible to his charms. She'd wanted to belong to someone, hungered for a relationship that went deeper than the friendly smile of acquaintances passing in the halls. But that longing only brought pain and humiliation, so she boxed it up and shoved it into the darkest recesses of her heart to gather dust. And there it had stayed all these years, safely out of reach.

Charlotte had her students, of course, and her fellow teachers. Yet even with them she'd felt compelled to hold a piece of herself back. For protection against the time when they would leave.

All that changed the day Stone found her at the piano. He'd cracked open her chest with his gentle questions, and all her secrets had tumbled out in a bloody gush. She still couldn't believe she had told him about her father and Alexander. She'd never told anyone about them. Not the teachers she'd worked with at the academy. Not even Rebekah Dorchester. If he hadn't caught her at such a vulnerable moment, she probably wouldn't have told him, either. Yet she couldn't dredge up true regret over it. The memory of his arm around her shoulders was too precious. The feel of his fingers stroking her arm. He'd listened to the whole ugly tale and never once stopped touching her. Accepting her. Soothing her. His comfort had been addictive. Dangerous. It tempted her to clear away the cobwebs from a certain box that was better left unopened.

"Whatcha doing, Miss Lottie?" Lily's question rang out behind her, startling Charlotte from her reverie.

Dropping her hand from her cameo, Charlotte reclaimed the dust cloth she'd abandoned on the window ledge earlier. "Dusting. Do you need help with your grammar lesson?"

Lily skipped into the room. "Nope. I finished it."

Charlotte nodded her approval. "Good. Then you may read for a while, if you'd like."

"But all my Dead-Eye Dan books are already packed, and I'm not in the mood for anything else." She flopped onto the edge of the bed, her body stretched out on her belly, her feet waving in the air. A long-suffering sigh echoed as she propped her chin on her hand. "Do you think that letter will come today? Mr. Hammond promised we could leave as soon as it got here."

Charlotte forfeited the dusting pretense and sat next to Lily on the bed. She ran her fingers through the girl's wavy blond hair, working a tangle or two free as she went.

Ever since Stone had told the children about the trip he'd planned to visit the ranch where Daniel Barrett worked, Lily had been brimming with excitement. Unfortunately, with every day they had no letter from Austin, the child had grown more and more out of sorts. Today marked Stone's third trip to town. For Lily's sake, Charlotte prayed he would come back with a letter.

"Why don't we go check on the boys, see how they're coming on their grammar lesson? Then it will be time to move on to arithmetic."

"Ugh!" Lily rolled onto her back, her head drooping off the edge of the bed like a piece of raw crust dangling over the rim of a pie tin. "I hate arithmetic."

Charlotte bit back a smile at the dramatics. "Come on. It's not so bad. You memorized the multiplication tables in one day. Division is just working backward on the same table."

"But not all the answers are on the table. And those stupid remainders . . . Ugh!"

Charlotte stood and waited for Lily to drag herself off the bed. "You can't always rely on your memory to get you the answers, Lily. You have to learn the mathematic procedures so you can figure out a solution when that internal catalog of yours hits a blank page."

"I know, I know. That still doesn't mean I gotta like it."

After the children finished their arithmetic lesson, Charlotte gave them each a treat from the cookie jar then shooed them outside to play. Her mind lingered miles away from teaching. Six miles, to be precise. In Madisonville. With Stone.

She snatched the loaves of bread that had been cooling on the kitchen counter and began sawing them into slices. Halfway through the second loaf, Mr. Dobson burst through the back door.

"Rider comin' from the east. Ridin' hard."

Madisonville lay to the south, not the east.

Heart thundering, Charlotte dropped the bread knife and sprinted past Dobson, out the door he'd just thrown wide.

"Stephen!" Charlotte ran as fast as she could around the back of the house, praying the kids were playing in the barn as usual and not roaming farther afield. "Stephen!"

She spotted the boy on the top rung of the corral fence. His head whipped around. In an instant, he leapt from his perch and raced toward her. "What is it, Miss Lottie?"

"Rider coming," she managed between heaving breaths. "Help get the others . . . to the cellar."

Stephen took off for the barn without a single question. By the time Charlotte made it to the opening, he had both John and Lily by the hand.

"Hurry, children." She could hear the quiet thuds of distant hoofbeats drawing closer. They didn't have much time. The trees surrounding the house offered some measure of cover, but once the rider turned down the lane that led to the house, he'd have an unobstructed view. They had to be in the house before he reached the lane.

John's shorter legs struggled to keep up with the older kids. Stephen dragged him along, but the younger boy lost his balance and fell.

Panic lent Charlotte speed. "I've got him," she called, waving at Stephen to keep going. Barely breaking stride, Charlotte scooped John up and held him to her chest. His legs locked around her waist and his arms found her neck. Thankful for his secure grip, she dashed up the back steps and through the kitchen door. Dobson threw it closed behind her.

The cellar door had been built into the kitchen floor, and her caretaker already had it propped open, waiting for them. Stephen and Lily scurried down the ladder. Charlotte handed John down to them then gathered her skirts to make the descent herself.

Halfway down, she paused and glanced up at Dobson. "Be careful."

The old caretaker rolled his eyes at her. "Quit your worryin', woman. I'll be fine. I got my rifle and my wits. You just tend to them young'uns."

Charlotte nodded and turned her attention back to fitting her toes to each rung so she didn't tumble. As soon as her head cleared the floorboards, the door above her slammed into place. Darkness stole her breath.

"Miss Lottie?" Lily's tearful voice led Charlotte to where the children huddled against the far wall.

"Shh. It's all right, sweetheart." Feeling her way in the dark, Charlotte found Lily's hand and clasped it tight. "I'm here. Everything's going to be fine. Let's just close our eyes and pretend we're all snuggled up together on the sofa." Charlotte maneuvered herself into the middle of the group, sat on the floor, then gathered John in her lap. Wrapping one arm around Lily and taking Stephen's hand with the other, she hummed a lullaby until she felt the children start to calm.

Keep the children safe, Lord. Whatever happens, keep them safe.

Charlotte couldn't tell if the children's eyes were indeed closed, but hers were wide open and staring straight at the tiny outline of light that ran around the perimeter of the cellar door. Her ears strained to hear any hint of what might be going on above. No shouting. No gunshots. Yet.

Thank heavens Stone had put this plan together. It had been his idea to hide her and the children in the cellar if any strangers came calling. That way Dorchester's man would find only Dobson in residence, should he arrive to investigate. Most of the toys and clothing had already been packed for their journey, so there wasn't much evidence of a woman or children in the house, but a keen eye might still find enough to cause suspicion.

Footsteps stamped against the floorboards above. Charlotte's pulse stuttered. A shadow flickered across the lines of light surrounding the door. She yanked Stephen and Lily across her middle and folded her body over them as best she could.

The door creaked open above her. A shaft of light pierced the darkness. Charlotte bit back a cry.

"Charlotte? It's me. Stone."

Her head shot up. There he was, kneeling at the opening, his beautiful face peering down at them. "Stone. Thank God. I thought for sure Franklin had found us." She unfolded herself and released her grip on the children.

"I took a roundabout route so no one watching from town would guess my destination."

Lily dashed toward the ladder. "Mr. Hammond, you're here! Did the letter come?"

Charlotte grinned as she clambered to her feet and brushed the dirt from the back of her skirt. That girl and her letter. Well, at least Lily was too distracted to be afraid anymore.

"I'm here, squirt," Stone answered. "And yes, the letter came, though I haven't had a chance to read it yet. Come on out of there now."

Lily bounded up the ladder and into Stone's arms. He patted her back as if not quite sure how to return the hug then set her aside as John and Stephen scrambled out. He reached a hand down to help Charlotte next, and she took it gratefully. Once fully emerged, she tried to pull her hand

free of his, not because she wanted to —
the feel of his strong, capable hand surrounding hers soothed her nerves far better
than any tonic ever could — but because
propriety demanded it. However, he did not
release her. In fact, he tugged her closer and
whispered roughly in her ear.

"We have to leave, Charlotte. Now.
Franklin's in town."

18

Stone felt a shiver run through the woman in his arms, but when she stepped away from him, no hint of distress showed on her face.

"All right, children." At her voice, the chatter that had been building around them ceased. "Mr. Hammond's letter has arrived, so you know what that means."

"We get to meet Dead-Eye Dan!"

Stone bit back a chuckle. Daniel was going to have his hands full with this one. Stone couldn't wait to see how his former partner reacted. Uncomfortable around females on a good day, Daniel Barrett would be way out of his depth with Lily.

"That's right," Charlotte continued, "and if you finish packing up the last of your belongings in the next few minutes and help Mr. Dobson load the wagon, we might even be able to leave early. How would you like that?"

Lily squealed. "Hurry, Stephen, John. We gotta go!" Lily sprinted toward her room, the boys on her heels.

Just like that, Charlotte turned the suddenness of their departure from a cause for alarm into a reward.

"You're amazing," he murmured, his gaze finding hers. "I probably would've mucked up that whole exchange and had a bunch of scared rabbits on my hands, but you made them *excited* about leaving. How do you do it?"

She shrugged. "After teaching for a decade, I suppose I've developed a few instincts. In truth, though, I simply don't want them to be afraid. They are aware of the possible danger and know to be cautious of strangers. That's enough for now."

"It's enough for you, too, Charlotte." Stone stepped closer, compelled to do what he could to ease *her* fears. "Franklin didn't see me in town. I made certain of it. And I laid a false trail then doubled back to ensure no one followed me. Doc's the only one who knows where I'm staying, and he won't talk." He laid a hand on her arm, his thumb stroking back and forth along her sleeve in an effort to provide comfort. "Franklin will talk up folks in town tonight, see what he can learn, then head out here to investigate tomorrow at the earliest. We have the jump on him. He won't find us."

At least Stone prayed he wouldn't. A fella could never be one hundred percent sure about anything. But that was his problem to worry about. Not Charlotte's.

Dobson circled around into Stone's line of sight, obliterating the illusion of privacy. "I suppose you'll be wantin' your guns back."

Stone released Charlotte's arm and turned to face the ornery caretaker who was now his ally. "They might prove useful."

"I'll fetch the trunk." Dobson groaned just loud enough to ensure the sound would be heard and appreciated then lumbered toward the door.

"Thank you, Dobson," Charlotte said. "If you'll bring it to the kitchen, I can fill it with foodstuffs after Mr. Hammond empties it."

The wizened little man nodded then glanced back to catch Stone's eye. "Don't prove me a fool for trustin' you, Hammond." He glared the challenge, but Stone heard the real message. *Take care of my family. They're all I've got.*

Shoot. The gnome was starting to grow on him.

"I won't," Stone vowed.

Dobson held his gaze for a long moment then gave a brisk nod and left through the back door.

Charlotte stared after him. "It feels disloyal to leave him behind."

Stone found her hand and gave it a squeeze. "We need him here playing the role of the cantankerous caretaker if Franklin comes by. You know that."

She sighed but didn't let go of his hand. "I know. I just worry about him." She pivoted to face Stone then, her blue-green eyes locking with his. "What if Franklin doesn't believe the charade? What if he resorts to brutality to try to get answers? I couldn't bear it if Dobson were harmed because of me."

Her grip on Stone's hand tightened, and moisture glistened in her eyes. With a tug of his arm, Stone pulled her against his chest and held her there. "Don't worry, darlin'. Dobson's a tough old buzzard. Smart. Sneaky, too. He got the jump on me, remember? He'll manage just fine."

"I pray you're right." She released his hand and stepped away from his embrace. He had to fight the urge to draw her back in. Keeping her eyes averted from his, she moved toward the counter and started gathering up the slices of bread laying across its surface and wrapping them in a towel. "How long will it take to reach your friend's ranch? I need to know how much food to pack."

Stone forced his feet to remain where they were, giving her the space she seemed to want. "It's not too far by road, but we'll need to skirt around the towns as much as possible. We can't afford to be seen together. In fact, I think I'll leave the wagon to you if you feel comfortable driving, and take Goliath cross-country. I'll keep watch on you from a distance, of course, and be close enough to lend aid should the need arise, but if I can take cover among the trees most of the way, that would prevent any passersby from putting us together should they be questioned. I can also scout ahead for campsites and have things set up when you and the kids arrive."

"So two nights? Three?" Charlotte knotted the bread towel and looked up, her brows arched in question.

Scenarios and alternatives ran through his head now that he'd started the ball rolling. As he discarded some and reworked others, it took him a minute to realize he'd never answered her question.

"Two," he pronounced. "If we split up, we can take a more direct route. But getting such a late start today will set us back some. On second thought, better plan for three nights, just to be safe. Never know when a horse will throw a shoe or an axle will break. You are comfortable driving the wagon on your own, right?"

She smirked at him, the rare show of playfulness drawing his mind away from his plans to ponder something much more pleasant. "I think I can manage. An unmarried woman doesn't get to my advanced age without learning a thing or two about self-reliance. If I had to wait on a man to transport me every time I wanted to go to town, I'd fritter half my life away."

"Your age doesn't seem all that advanced to me." Stone rounded the counter and closed the distance between them, unable to leave her self-deprecating statement unchallenged. He ran his gaze slowly over her figure. "Nope. All I see is a woman in her prime." He stepped closer and lassoed her waist with his arm. "Strong." He slowly inched his palm from her waist to the small of her back. "Independent." He climbed higher, to the dip between her shoulder blades. "Loyal and brave." He pressed her closer, until softness brushed his chest and her head was forced back to maintain his gaze. "And so dad-gum beautiful it puts thoughts in a man's head."

He lowered his face toward hers, intent on showing her just where some of those thoughts lay, but a loud scraping from outside stopped him.

"Hammond! Give me a hand with this trunk, would ya?"

Stone swallowed a groan and stepped away from Charlotte, trying to ignore how pretty she looked with that fiery blush lighting up her cheeks. Knowing he'd put it there.

The noise outside escalated to loud banging. Was the man dragging a railcar up the steps?

"You comin', Hammond?"

With a growl, Stone stomped across the kitchen. He'd give Dobson a hand, all right. With all the knuckles included.

The first two legs of the journey passed without incident. Unless one counted skirmishes over who got to sleep next to Miss Lottie in the wagon at night, or Stephen threatening to stuff his dirty sock in Lily's mouth if she didn't quit jabbering about Dead-Eye Dan. More than once, Charlotte had found herself envying Stone his solitary ride away from the wagon, though the dark circles shadowing his eyes this morning proved his exhaustion.

The man had barely slept during the past two nights, standing guard over her and the children the way he did. She'd felt so safe, knowing he was watching out for them, yet she wished for his sake that it hadn't been necessary. Fatigue could slow a man's reflexes, impair his judgment. He'd need to be at his best if Franklin caught up to them. For the children's protection, of course.

Charlotte bit the inside of her lip. That was a lie. Stone was more than a shield or a line of defense. He was a man whose well-being mattered to her, for reasons she dared not examine too closely.

He'd left the wagon before full light, as was his custom, secreting himself and Goliath in the surrounding countryside, deep enough that not even Charlotte could spot them. And she knew where to look. Which she did, far too often.

She couldn't seem to keep her attention fixed on her driving. It constantly wandered back to Stone. And what had transpired, or nearly transpired, in the kitchen the day they'd left. He'd wanted to kiss her. And she'd been about to let him. No. She'd been about to be a fully engaged participant. And oh, how she hated that Dobson had interfered. That too-innocent quirk of his lips as he'd strolled into the kitchen holding one end of the trunk while Stone carried the other with a single hand, showing how superfluous a second man was for the task — yes, Dobson had known exactly what he'd been interrupting. The little meddler.

Charlotte slumped a bit on the wagon bench as she readjusted her hold on the reins. She couldn't be angry with Dobson. He was only being protective. He couldn't know how much she'd longed to press her lips to Stone's. What if that had been her only chance to learn what a true kiss felt like?

She sighed as she adjusted the reins in her fingers to navigate a sharp turn in the road. Stone had kept his distance since then, never even touching her that she could recall. And she was sure she would recall. No, the man had been like another person these last couple days. Like a soldier on duty. Handing out orders and instructions, checking perimeters, inventorying weapons. He barely even took time to eat. And he never smiled.

She missed his smile.

Well, she might as well get used to missing him. Growing attached would be foolish. Stone would have no reason to linger after things with Lily were resolved. And if they *weren't* resolved? Even then, she couldn't expect him to stay with them indefinitely. At some point he'd return to his retrieving, and she'd be left alone to keep Lily out of Dorchester's grasp.

Keep me strong, Lord. Charlotte stiffened her posture and snapped the reins lightly over the backs of the team as the road straightened out once again. *Thank you for sending Stone to help us out of the trouble of the moment, but don't let me depend on him to the point that I'm no longer able to guard Lily myself when he leaves.*

For he would leave. Everyone did. Her father. Her mother. Students graduated. Fellow teachers accepted new positions. Self-serving administrators closed schools. Stephen's parents would collect him when they returned from their travels abroad. And who knew what would happen with John. Charlotte doubted any court would allow a single woman to officially adopt a child, and though she'd hoped that the overcrowding at St. Peter's would cause the agent to conveniently forget about her undefined custody arrangement, she couldn't count on that. If Charlotte made no effort to contact them with John's whereabouts by the end of the natural school term, they could bring up true charges of kidnapping

— charges she couldn't deny.

Even Lily would leave her someday. Hopefully not by Dorchester's hand, but still, the day would come. The daughter of her heart would fall in love with some cowboy hero like Dead-Eye Dan, marry, and start a life of her own.

Stop feeling sorry for yourself, Charlotte. So what if everyone left? She'd been on her own most of her life. She was resilient. Strong. She'd survive.

"Miss Lottie . . . I gotta use the necessary."

Charlotte twisted on the seat to find Lily gripping the edge of the wagon bed, legs crossed, lips in a firm line. She nearly laughed. Here she'd had Lily married off in her mind when the child was barely more than a babe herself.

That's what I get for borrowing trouble.

Stephen leaned across John to frown at Lily. "You were supposed to go before we left camp."

"I didn't have to go then," she countered, scowling back at him. "Now I do."

"All right, children. No need to argue." Charlotte drew the right rein taut and steered the wagon to the edge of the road before bringing the horses to a halt and setting the brake. "Stephen, climb up here and mind the team while I take Lily."

Using the wheel spokes like ladder rungs, Charlotte climbed down from her perch and lifted Lily over the side of the wagon.

"Sorry, Miss Lottie. But I couldn't hold it no more."

"I know, sweetheart." Charlotte took her hand and led her toward a stand of post oaks that would serve as a privacy screen. "But next time, when I ask you to take care of business, I expect you to obey instead of justifying why the instruction doesn't apply to you."

Lily hung her head. "Yes, ma'am."

"Good." Charlotte squeezed her hand to let her know she wasn't angry then released her grip. "Hurry along, now. We have a lot of miles to cover without much daylight left."

Lily dashed around the trees, consumed by an urgency that had little to do with the sun's position in the sky.

Charlotte fought a grin as she turned her back. Out of habit, she scanned the road for any sign of traffic — ahead and then behind. Her ears caught a low rumble. She frowned. Hoofbeats. A lot of them. Coming from around the bend she'd just passed.

"Lily, we've got to go. Now!" Charlotte barged into the trees, her heart beating painfully against her ribs.

Lily squealed, still hunkered over, her drawers around her ankles. Charlotte took her by the arm and stood her up. "I'm sorry, sweetheart, but there's no time." She grabbed the cotton fabric and wrenched it up to her waist.

"Miss Lottie!" the girl protested, not quite grasping the situation beyond the fact that her teacher had just infringed on her privacy.

"Riders are coming." Charlotte grabbed Lily's wrist and started dragging her out of the trees. "The boys are alone."

Finally, the girl seemed to comprehend. Her feet picked up speed, and soon the two of them were running through the brush.

The horses were faster.

Charlotte called out a warning to Stephen, but before the boy could reach under the bench for the shotgun they carried, a group of five men on horseback swarmed the wagon.

"What do we got here?" the lead man drawled as he pulled his mount to a stop at the front of the wagon. He signaled to his companions, and in seconds, the entire wagon was surrounded, with Charlotte and Lily cut off from the boys.

They were ragged-looking men.

241

Unshaven. Unkempt. Disreputable. Charlotte pushed Lily behind her back and forced her chin up.

"You look to be in need of assistance, ma'am. I guess it's a good thing we happened along." The leader's gaze raked her from head to toe, his eyes cold, hard, and full of lascivious intent.

"Thank you, sir," Charlotte stated in her best schoolmarm tone, the one that usually erased a man's interest faster than a cloth erased chalk. "But we do not require assistance. We were just about to resume our journey. Please feel free to continue on."

Instead of dulling the man's interest, her authoritative tone appeared to ignite something in the man, something that had him peering at her face as if he were trying to memorize her features.

Charlotte cast a quick glance at Stephen, thankful to see he'd left the shotgun in its hiding place. It would serve no purpose against so many, beyond putting the boy in greater danger.

"Wouldn't be gentlemanly of us to let a woman travel unescorted," one of the men closer to her said. "A female as handsome as you deserves *special* treatment." He reached out a hand to stroke her cheek.

Charlotte jerked away from the touch,

feeling violated. And more frightened than she'd ever been before. Lord have mercy. If these lechers got their hands on Lily . . .

The men laughed at her show of spirit — dark, ugly sounds that made her flesh crawl. All except the leader. He frowned.

"You're a teacher, ain't ya?" he asked, nudging his mount closer to where she stood.

She didn't answer. Just glared at him defiantly. She'd not cower.

All at once a grin broke out across his face, his tobacco-stained teeth doing nothing to aid his appearance.

"I've got it!" He slapped his knee, causing his horse to sidestep at the sudden movement. "You're that teacher the feller from Houston was lookin' for." He glanced back at the wagon and eyed the boys. "Yep. Three kids, just like he said. Well, boy howdy. Men, we just found ourselves a fugitive with a big, fat bounty on her head!"

Charlotte didn't take time to think. She launched herself at the man closest to her, pulling him out of his saddle even as she screamed for Lily to run. "Run for Stone!"

She threw her body atop the villain and rained blows upon his head, her only thought to create enough of a distraction to give Lily a head start. Stone would be on his way. He always watched over them.

Unless he'd been scouting ahead. *Dear God, please don't let him be scouting.* The men had come at them from behind. Stone wouldn't have seen them coming.

Even as the thought ran through her head, an iron arm wrapped about her middle and yanked her off. The leader had dismounted and now held her firm against his front. She kicked and flailed until she heard a revolver being cocked.

"Quit your fightin', teacher, or Winston'll put a bullet in the boy's head."

She glanced up. One of the riders on the far side of the wagon had his pistol aimed straight at Stephen's temple. She stilled instantly.

"Everett?" The leader nodded to the second man on the near side of the wagon, the one still sitting on his horse. "Go after the girl."

The man kicked his mount and headed off in pursuit.

"No!" Charlotte tried to run after them, but the man holding her lifted her feet off the ground with a shift of his stance, his arm cutting off her cry as it squeezed her middle.

"Don't worry, darlin'," he drawled in that sickeningly sweet tone of his. "You'll be reunited real soon."

Tears blurring her vision, Charlotte watched helplessly as Everett closed in on her daughter.

19

A monster horse crashed through the trees a few yards in front of Lily. The dark figure on the animal's back let out a war cry that nearly set the earth to rumbling. Then a gun exploded. Everett jerked backward. Tumbled from his horse. Lily screamed. Halted. Covered her ears with her hands and bent over into a ball.

Until the newcomer shouted her name and ordered her into the woods.

Charlotte gasped. Then blinked. Hammer Rockwell, just as the dime novels had described him. Brown duster whipping back and forth in the wind, hat pulled low, gun in one hand as he steered his mount in front of Lily, guarding her retreat. Merciless, dangerous, and the most beautiful thing she'd ever seen.

Stone.

The leader's grip around her middle loosened at the distraction, and Charlotte wrenched free. She shoved past her captor and lunged for the wagon, only to have the man grab her from behind.

"Not so fast, missy." He swung her around in front of him like a shield then started backing toward his horse. "I'm takin' you with me."

The other three men opened fire on Stone.

"Stephen!" Charlotte gestured with her head toward the wagon bed. "Take John into the back and lie down." She didn't look away from them until they'd successfully scrambled into the back and taken cover, Stephen sheltering John with his arm as they huddled behind the wooden siding.

The firing continued. Her team grew restless. *Please don't let them bolt,* Charlotte prayed. *Not with the boys inside.* Though it would take them away from the gunplay. These men obviously didn't care about innocents in the crossfire.

Stone did.

The truth slammed into Charlotte with stunning force. He hadn't fired a single shot since the one that felled Everett. He was protecting the children. Protecting her. But that protection left him vulnerable. It emboldened the enemy. Yet he continued to ride toward them. Low in the saddle. As if he were invincible.

She had to do something to help him. But what? She was a hostage, a shield. Yet only her midsection was compromised. Her hands were free. She needed a weapon, something to . . .

Charlotte reached to her throat and tore the cameo brooch from her collar. With a flick of her thumb, she had the clasp open. She palmed the face and brought the silver pin down with all her strength into her captor's thigh.

He cried out and dropped her while yelling a vile curse. She paid him no heed. Instead, she leapt for the wagon, threw herself over the side and into the bed, and immediately jabbed her pin into the nearest enemy horse's flank. The horse screamed and reared up, knocking into the horse beside it.

If she couldn't stop the bullets, at least she could skew their aim.

She sidestepped the boys, intent on reaching the third horse positioned behind the wagon, but the chaos she'd created spooked her own team. The frightened animals jerked in their traces and sent Charlotte sprawling. She dropped her cameo as she threw out her hands to break her fall. The brooch skittered into the corner, near the tailgate. She clambered after it, only to catch sight of a man's boot descending toward her head out of the corner of her eye. She jerked back and twisted away, but the boot still landed a glancing blow at her temple. Down she went, dazed. She blinked and tried to shake off her stupor. A glimpse of her captor straddling the side of the wagon, boot raised for another kick, jarred her back into action. Charlotte curled her arms around her head and ducked.

A quiet whistle sounded above her as something whizzed over her head. An instant later, her tormentor let out a second howl of pain and fell backward, a knife lodged in his shoulder. A roar echoed behind Charlotte at nearly the same moment. She barely had time to turn her head and lurch sideways as Stone leapt from Goliath's back, arms outstretched.

He tackled the two men closest to him. His momentum launched all three of them into the wagon bed. Guns flew out of hands. Horses spooked and ran. Bodies slammed into wood.

It proved too much for the team. They lunged forward until the brake gave way then galloped down the road without a driver at the helm.

Charlotte braced herself against the tailgate as the force of the sudden motion threw her backward. Clinging to the side of the speeding wagon, she gestured wildly to the boys. Stone's momentum had carried the men to the far side of the wagon bed, but they were already stirring. Soon fists would be pounding, legs would be kicking, knives might even be brandished. She had to get the boys out of the way.

Stephen nodded to her, grabbed John's arm, and half crawled, half rolled to her as the fight began in earnest. Taking advantage of his position on top, Stone grabbed the collar of the man beneath him and slammed his head into the wagon floor. Twice. The second man lunged at him from the side, wrapping his arm around Stone's neck as if to choke him. Stone answered with a ferocious backward jab of his elbow into the man's stomach.

"Look!" Stephen pointed behind them as he reached Charlotte's side. "They're leaving!"

Charlotte glanced away from the fight to check on the other men. Sure enough, the one who'd not been injured — Winston, the leader had called him — was fleeing around the bend. The leader, a hand to his chest where the knife had been, sat astride his horse, heading in an altogether different direction. Toward the trees where Lily had run.

"Stone!" Charlotte whipped her head back around. "He's going after Lily!"

Stone heard Charlotte's shout, jammed his knee into the belly of the man beneath him, then twisted far enough to slip his arm through the second man's legs. With a groan, he lifted the man off his feet and tossed him over the side. The pinned man took advantage of his inattention to retrieve a knife. Stone spotted the blade and immediately grabbed the man's wrist.

He didn't have time for this.

Stone curled his tongue and let out a shrill whistle to bring Goliath to him then pounded the man's arm into the wagon until he finally lost his grip on the knife. Once that was done, he smashed his fist against the man's temple with enough force to leave him unconscious then rolled him over the side.

"Hurry, Stone!" Charlotte cried. "He's almost to the trees."

Stone pushed to his feet, widening his stance to keep his balance in the speeding wagon. He gripped the driver's bench as he made his way to the place where Goliath galloped alongside. Stone grasped the edge of the wagon then propped his left boot atop it. His gaze skimmed over Charlotte and the boys, clinging to the tailgate.

How could he just leave them? They could hit a rut and be thrown. The team could veer off the road into a ravine and turn the wagon over. He hesitated.

"Go, Stone." Charlotte nodded at him. "Lily needs you more than we do. I can stop the wagon."

She could fall to her death, too.

"Go!" she demanded.

He did. Stone pushed off the edge of the wagon with his left leg and landed astride Goliath. Pain shot up his right thigh from where one of the bullets had taken a hunk out of his flesh, but he ignored it. With a prayer in his heart for those he was leaving behind, he grabbed Goliath's reins and steered him toward the man disappearing into the trees.

Winded as the beast was after charging the villains and keeping pace with a runaway wagon, Goliath responded to Stone's urging with a champion's heart. His long legs ate up the ground at a pace that matched the thundering of Stone's pulse.

Would Lily know to hide? What if she heard the villain's horse's approach and thought it was Stone coming to retrieve her?

252

She'd run right into the scoundrel's hands.

Stone clenched his jaw and leaned farther over Goliath's neck. Not on his watch. No one was gonna harm a hair on that girl's head.

The terrain shifted from flat prairie to scattered woods as Stone urged Goliath up the slope. Forced to slow in order to navigate the trees and uneven ground, Stone tuned his ears to his surroundings. With all the cover afforded by the trees, he'd be more likely to hear another rider's position than spot the man himself. Of course, his own position could be forfeited just as easily.

He slowed Goliath to a walk. A rustling sounded to the east. Stone peered between the oak trunks. There. A dark brown hat. Moving north. Not high enough off the ground for the man to still be on his horse. Stone slipped his revolver from his holster then dismounted quietly from Goliath's back. Minding his steps, he crept closer, his attention focused on the man ahead and to the right. One of his arms hung uselessly at his side, but the other clutched a pistol — a pistol aimed at a scraggly bush that couldn't quite conceal the pink calico dress quivering behind it.

"Come on out, girl," the man ordered in a

gruff voice. "I ain't gonna hurt ya. I'm gonna help you get home." He took two steps closer to the bush. "There's a feller lookin' for you. Works for your grandpa. I'm just gonna take you to him." Another step. "No reason to be scared."

Stone slid his second revolver from its holster and lifted both guns into position. "On the contrary," he threatened, "there's every reason to be scared."

The man spun toward Stone and fired. At the same instant, Stone dropped, rolled to his back, and fired twice. The first shot relieved the man of his hat. The second, his gun.

Stone cocked his weapons as he rolled into a crouch, his feet once again under him. "I'd prefer not to kill you in front of the girl, but if you reach for that knife at your back, I'll empty the next two chambers into your chest."

The man stilled then slowly brought his good arm out from behind him and raised it in the air.

"Lily," Stone called, "come stand behind me."

He didn't have to ask twice. She dashed out from behind the bush and ran to him. Giving the other man a wide berth, she ducked behind Stone and immediately wrapped her arms around his waist and leaned her face against his lower back.

Stone's muscles leapt at the contact, ready to defend, to protect her at all costs. He narrowed his eyes at the man. "Get on your horse, collect your comrade, and go."

"But Everett's dead. You killed him."

"Nope," Stone contradicted. "But he will be if you don't get him to a doctor." He'd seen the man up on all fours when he'd ridden Goliath past him moments before. He'd been in sorry shape for sure, but not dead. "Fairfield's just a few miles back. You can make it."

The man hesitated, but then apparently decided whatever reward Franklin had promised wasn't worth his life. He edged away from Stone.

"Go!" Stone shouted.

The man ran, leaving his pistol in the dirt.

Stone didn't have the luxury of waiting to ensure the fool followed his instructions. Now that Lily was safe, all he could think about was Charlotte and the boys.

After holstering his guns, he peeled one of Lily's hands from around his waist, clasped it in his own, and started jogging toward Goliath. Once there, he lifted Lily up in front of the saddle horn then mounted behind her. He settled her across his lap so his back would be her shield, then took up Goliath's reins.

"Where's Miss Lottie?" Lily's voice quivered as she asked the question.

Stone wrapped an arm about the girl, hating the broken, bloody images that came too readily to mind, visions of the wreckage he might encounter. He steeled himself against the possibilities and focused instead on the lines of determination that had been etched into Charlotte's lovely face when she'd ordered him to retrieve Lily. Charlotte Atherton was not a woman who failed easily.

"She's with the wagon," Stone ground out, praying the equipage in question, along with its passengers, was still intact. Then he nudged Goliath into a canter and set out to find the truth.

20

How on earth was she supposed to stop this wagon on her own? Clasping the wagon side with both hands, Charlotte gained her feet only to feel a tug on her skirt. John looked up at her from his place in the corner, trust in his eyes and something closed in his upraised fist. She held out her hand, and he placed her mother's cameo in her palm. An inanimate object shouldn't have the power to instill such hope, yet it did. She closed her fingers around it and nodded her thanks to John. Then, before her doubts could re-assert themselves, she stuffed the brooch into her skirt pocket and made her way toward the front of the wagon.

Help me, Lord. Please help me. She repeated the prayer over and over in her mind with each shaky step she took, her body hunched as she gripped the side of the wagon for balance, her hair whipping around her head and slapping against her cheeks, her eyes stinging and tearing from the wind.

She reached the back of the driver's bench and stopped. She had to climb over. No easy task in a long, gored skirt.

"Want me to do it, Miss Lottie?" Stephen touched her arm, startling her. She'd had no idea he'd followed her. "I'm good with climbing stuff."

"Absolutely not!" Dear Lord. If he fell, she'd never forgive herself. "Stay back here and tend to John."

Trusting him to obey her, she turned back to the bench. Using the small trunk of books and clothes that Lily had packed and Stone had tied down at the beginning of their trip as a step, Charlotte hiked her skirt past her calves and swung her right leg over the bench. She held onto the seatback with both hands, rested her stomach across it, and dragged her other leg over. Blowing out a heavy breath, she eased from her knees to a normal seated position and latched onto the bench arm.

The reins had fallen from the brake bar, of course. They dangled above the wagon shaft between her two panicked grays.

"Whoa, now!" Charlotte called to the horses as she gingerly scooted to the middle of the bench. Not that her command did any good. The animals were too crazed to listen. But she repeated it anyway. "Whoa."

The horses thundered on. As did her pulse. She was going to have to retrieve the reins.

Charlotte glanced up. No traffic, thank heaven. The road looked relatively flat. But a curve loomed ahead. A rather sharp curve. More of a corner, really. One they'd never make in one piece if the horses didn't slow.

Twisting on the bench, she hooked her fingers over the back of the seat then leaned forward and stretched toward the reins. Not even close.

If Stone were here, he'd probably leap over the footboard, land on the shaft, grab the reins with one hand, and slow the team with a single tug on the lines. But Stone wasn't here. And if she tried to leap over the footboard onto the shaft, she'd probably slip off the narrow pole and fall prey to sharp hooves and unforgiving wheels. Her heeled boots and long skirts just weren't made for such acrobatics. So what could she do instead?

Whatever she did, she had to do it soon. That curve was only a few hundred yards away.

Not knowing what else to try, Charlotte did the only thing she could think of to

259

close the distance between her and the reins. She slid off the seat onto the floor of the driver's box, raised up on her knees, and leaned over the footboard. She reached for the lines. Stretched her fingers. Still . . . too . . . far. Inches separated her from her goal.

She sagged over the rumbling, rib-bruising board, tears of frustration burning her eyes. "You can do this, Charlotte," she whispered to herself. "You have to."

Throwing caution aside, Charlotte crammed her feet beneath the bench and pushed them against the back of the box to propel her farther over the footboard. She *would* reach those lines. The wooden edge of the footrest scraped down her ribcage to her belly. She reached again. The tip of her longest finger brushed one of the lines. So close!

Too close to give up.

She pushed off with her feet again until her shoes no longer connected with the box. The backs of her heels pressed into the underside of the seat as the footboard slid beneath her belly to catch in the bend of her hips. She reached. Stretched. And caught the two lines on the right.

She reached for the left lines that dragged a little lower. Just . . . a . . . bit . . . closer.

One of the front wheels hit a hole. The wagon bounced. Hard. Charlotte's shoes slid out from beneath the seat. She fell forward. Screamed.

Her hands connected with the shaft of the wagon tongue. She caught herself. And the reins. She'd trapped them beneath her left palm.

"Miss Lottie!"

She heard Stephen's cry but could do nothing about it. She could barely breathe, bent double as she was, gripping the footboard as hard as she could between her thighs and belly to keep herself from falling farther.

She had the reins, but how on earth would she ever right herself enough to get up? That corner had to be nearly upon them.

Please, Lord. Just spare the boys. Save them from —

Her prayer was interrupted by a small body wrapping itself around her left leg like an anchor and a pair of hands grabbing at the back of her blouse from the right, pulling her up.

Charlotte thanked God for brave, disobedient boys as they hauled her over the footboard and back into the driver's box.

The instant she had her feet under her again, she drew back on the reins with all her might. "Whoa!" She stood in the box, leaning backward to add the pull of her weight to the endeavor.

The horses ran on.

Stephen grabbed the reins in front of her hands on the right side, and John imitated on the left. All three of them pulled. All three yelled, "Whoa!"

Little by little, the horses slowed.

"Whoa!" they all yelled again as they reached the corner, their pace still far too swift.

The horses slowed a scant bit more, but the wagon swayed recklessly, swinging in a wide arc around the bend. The back wheels slipped off the side of the road into the grass, but the wagon remained upright.

They made it around the curve in one piece, and a few dozen yards later, the team finally halted.

The boys cheered. Charlotte flopped onto the seat, numb.

Then all of a sudden panic seized her chest and all she could think about was getting off the demon vehicle that had nearly killed them.

She set the brake, tied off the reins, and immediately ushered the boys down to the ground.

"Let's wait for Stone and Lily in that

lovely grass," she said, pointing to a thick patch of green prairie grass just a few steps away from the road. "I think I'm going to need a few minutes to recover."

Drained of all energy, Charlotte lay down flat upon the grass, one boy cuddled into each side. She closed her eyes as the sun warmed her wind-frozen face and thanked God for His timely rescue.

Stone slowed Goliath to a trot when they reached the curve in the road, dreading what he might find around the bend. Every pain in his body intensified. His knuckles, his thigh, his knees from where he'd fallen into the wagon, his throat from the choke-hold, his jaw and side from the hits he'd taken, the spot on his shoulder where a second bullet had grazed him. Everything throbbed, but none of his physical aches compared to the stabbing in his chest as he steered Goliath around the corner.

"Look, Mr. Hammond! The wagon!" Lily bounced in his lap as she pointed. "But where's Miss Lottie? I don't see her."

He didn't either. Not at first. He told himself not to panic. The wagon stood undamaged, the team calm. But what if they'd slowed on their own? What if Charlotte and the boys had been thrown some time before? He'd scanned the sides of the road with care, but what if he'd missed them? What if . . .

He drew Goliath near the wagon. And spotted the flash of Charlotte's blue skirt obscured by the tall grass.

"Charlotte!" Hesitating only long enough to set Lily on the ground, Stone sprang from Goliath's back and sprinted around the wagon. He slid to his knees in the grass beside her, his gut in knots, his eyes scouring her for injuries. But before his gaze could reach higher than her knees, she sat up.

"Stone," she said, her voice slightly groggy, as if she'd been asleep. Then she blinked and sat up straighter. "Is Lily . . . ?"

She couldn't even get the words out before the kid threw herself into her teacher's arms, nearly knocking Charlotte back to the ground.

"Oh, thank God."

Stone silently echoed the sentiment as the two females embraced. Thank God, indeed.

Stephen and John jumped up and grabbed at his arms, the story of their adventure bubbling out of Stephen so fast, Stone could barely keep up. John nodded vigorously throughout, as if eager to share in the telling.

After several minutes, the kids finally turned their attention to one another, Stephen and Lily trying to out-horrify each other with their tales. Stone offered a hand to Charlotte and helped her to her feet. She immediately started fussing with her appearance, brushing grass from her skirt, picking at the torn collar of her shirtwaist, patting down her hopelessly windblown hair.

He captured her fidgeting hand with his and tugged it down. "Leave it."

Her eyes met his, surprise fluttering her lashes.

"I like you a little mussed." He grinned. "Makes me feel less like a dirt clod in comparison."

She blushed then. Just a little, but it was enough to warm his blood.

Charlotte dropped her gaze to her feet. "You're the most heroic man I've ever met, Stone Hammond." Slowly she lifted her face. "I owe you everything."

"Nah." Now he was the one shuffling and fidgeting. "You don't owe me anything." He rubbed the back of his neck. "You did all the hard work." Stone reached out, took her hand in his, and squeezed. "You did good today, Charlotte. Real good."

She smiled at him, her expression softening to a degree he hadn't seen since he'd caught her at the piano. It was as if she'd pulled back the curtain she usually left drawn and allowed him to peek inside to glimpse her vulnerability, her gratitude, and a longing so sad and stark it kicked him in the chest with the strength of a mule. Then she lowered her lashes, and the curtain fell back into place. A heartbeat later, she was gone, seeing to the children.

Stone couldn't move. Could barely breathe. Talk about putting ideas in a man's head. Women never looked at him like that. He was too rough, too coarse, too much of a loner. Ever since his mother died, he'd learned not to expect much softness from life. His ambition had provided income, and his skills had kept him alive. He had a handful of friends he trusted like brothers. It had always been enough to keep him content in the past. But now? He wanted more. He wanted softness. Closeness. Music.

He wanted *her*.

One mountain at a time, Hammond.

First he had to get his charges to Dan's place. The five yahoos he'd just sent off with their tails tucked between their legs were sure to flap their gums about his escort, so there was no point in separating himself from Charlotte again. Not that his nerves could handle such a thing anyhow. His hands were still shakin' from finding her and the boys laid out in the grass as if they were dead.

He'd be driving the team the rest of the way to Hawk's Haven. Give Goliath a rest, and maybe even find a creek to wash up in. Charlotte wasn't the type to arrive somewhere disheveled, and he could probably stand to rinse the dirt out of his scrapes.

"Stone Hammond!"

Charlotte's outraged voice had him spinning around to face her even as his hand reached for his gun.

"What?" He scanned the area for a threat. None presented itself. He looked back at her.

"You're bleeding!" she accused. She marched up to him and started categorizing his paltry wounds. Out loud.

"Quit your fussin', woman. Nothing's serious. It'll keep until we find a stream to wash up in."

"We have a canteen." Then she started throwing out orders. "Stephen, lower the tailgate so Mr. Hammond can sit down. John, fetch the water. Lily, unpack one of my petticoats. I'll need to tear it into strips."

"Bossy female," Stone grumbled as she

forced him to take a seat. He glared at her. She glared right back. Man, but he liked that about her, the way she stood up to him. And if he was honest with himself, he rather liked the fussing, too.

One mountain at a time, Hammond. One mountain at a time.

21

The arched entrance to Hawk's Haven loomed over Charlotte's head later that afternoon. The children exclaimed over the hawk outline burned into the wooden sign, but Charlotte gained no comfort from the symbol. As if she needed another predator stalking her and her charges. Dorchester and Franklin were quite enough, thank you. Not to mention the unknown others Franklin was apparently offering reward money to. How many men like those they'd just encountered waited to pounce? A shiver coursed through her, and she leaned a little closer to Stone as he turned the team down the drive toward their final destination.

A cry from a real hawk echoed in the air. Charlotte's gaze snapped to the sky, but she saw nothing. It was just a bird, she told herself, yet gooseflesh rose on her skin anyway. She rubbed it away with a brutal hand over her sleeve. She didn't have time for such foolishness.

Stone turned to look at her, concern lining his brow. "You all right?"

She forced a smile. "Fine. Still a little skittish, I guess."

"Understandable." He gave her one of his lopsided grins, the kind that made her stomach turn flips. "But we're safe now that we're on Hawkins's land."

Charlotte nodded. She knew that. She just wasn't sure how long that safety would last. Stone had assured her that Jonah Hawkins was a good man. Daniel Barrett had vouched for him, and apparently Stone's friend didn't hand out praise lightly. Yet that was no guarantee he'd welcome them onto his property. Daniel Barrett might owe Stone his allegiance, but Jonah Hawkins could turn them away in a heartbeat, especially if he suspected trouble followed them.

"Ooooh, Miss Lottie, I can see the house," Lily squealed. She stood in the wagon bed behind Charlotte's right shoulder, her hands gripping the driver's seat for balance. The more excited she grew, the more she bounced, and the more she bounced, the more the wooden seatback thumped against Charlotte's spine. But Charlotte didn't have the heart to reprimand her. After the harrowing adventure they'd survived, the girl deserved to bounce and squeal as much as she wanted.

"He's coming, Miss Lottie! I see him." The rattling on the back of Charlotte's seat intensified.

"Where? I don't see anything," Stephen grumbled.

"There!" Lily jabbed her arm straight forward, nearly scraping the side of Charlotte's chin. "A horse. Heading this way."

"That could be anyone." Stephen's voice sounded beleaguered, but Charlotte caught him leaning over the side to look.

"It's not just anyone," Lily insisted. "It's Dead-Eye Dan! I know it is."

Stone chuckled softly. "That's him."

Charlotte cast a quick, reproving glance at Lily. "Remember what we talked about last night. You are to address him as Mr. Barrett. We don't want to offend or embarrass our host."

"Yes, ma'am."

Charlotte turned forward on the seat and started smoothing wrinkles from her skirt. She lifted a hand to check her hair but stopped when Stone scowled at her.

"You look fine," he groused.

And didn't that boost a lady's confidence? Dark frowns always enriched a compliment.

What had gotten under his skin in such a short time? He'd been smiling at her not two minutes ago. Why did he care if she wanted to tidy her appearance? It only made sense to look her best when meeting the man who had the power to either offer them shelter or send them packing. First impressions were important. Unless . . . No. Surely not. She darted a sideways glance at the man beside her. Surely he didn't think she was trying to . . . *attract* Mr. Barrett? The idea was laughable. Why, she hadn't tried to attract a man's attention in nearly a decade. And why would he care if she did?

Her pulse fluttered as the obvious answer tantalized her. She glanced at Stone again. He was smiling now and raising a hand in greeting. Foolish spinster. Of course the man wasn't jealous. He was probably just annoyed by her wiggling. Ordering herself *not* to feel disappointed by that conclusion, Charlotte pasted a polite smile on her face and turned her attention to the man approaching.

The dark red of his beard caught the sunlight as he squinted at her with icy blue eyes, taking her measure, no doubt. Charlotte stiffened her spine and raised her chin as Stone reined in the horses.

"Dan, you old rascal. Good to see you."

Let him look all he wanted. She'd not apologize to him or anyone else for what she'd done to protect Lily. And who was he to judge, anyway? He looked more like an outlaw than a ranch hand, armed nearly as extensively as Stone, minus the ammunition belt and the gun strapped to his back. He did carry a second rifle, though, one long gun slung on each side of his saddle. Only a man accustomed to trouble packed that kind of arsenal.

Or one *expecting* trouble.

Charlotte swallowed. He had every right to scrutinize her. In fact, she should probably be thankful that Stone had a friend with such obvious . . . *talents* . . . they could turn to for assistance. Combing down her hackles, she exhaled and forced her hands to unclench in her lap.

"Charlotte." Stone's voice drew her attention back to him. His eyes held hers, connecting, encouraging. "May I present Daniel Barrett? Dan, this is Charlotte Atherton."

Mr. Barrett touched the brim of his hat and dipped his chin a fraction. "Ma'am."

So stoic. So hard. Did he resent her being there?

"Mr. Barrett." She bent her head to him. "I hope we are not inconveniencing you with our arrival."

"No, ma'am."

She waited for more, but the man didn't seem inclined to offer reassurances.

"I'm Lily." The words burst from the girl as if the dam holding them back had suddenly given way. "And I've read all your books. Do you think I could get your autograph later?"

The man's gaze shifted to Charlotte's left, and his veneer cracked. His mouth twitched and his eyes widened with . . . apprehension? Surely not. What could this hardened warrior possibly fear from a tiny child? Yet his horse shook its head and sidestepped as if sensing his rider's anxiety.

"Easy, Ranger."

"*That's* Ranger?" Lily's excitement grew palpable. "The same Ranger that beat the door down with his hooves to save you from burning to death after Billy Cavanaugh locked you in that barn and set it afire? Wow! Can I pet him?" She scooted past John and Stephen in order to get closer to the edge of the wagon bed and reached out a hand toward the dancing horse. "Maybe you could give me a ride later. Mr. Hammond let me ride Goliath with him once. I know how to sit real still and not kick my legs . . ."

Daniel Barrett wheeled his horse around

and aimed him back toward the ranch. "I'm . . . ah . . . going to make sure everything's ready back at the cabin, Stone. See you there." He nudged Ranger to a trot then a canter and disappeared from sight.

"Way to go, Lily. You scared him off," Stephen huffed.

"Did not!" Lily planted her hands on her hips. "Dead-Eye Dan's not scared of anything. He was just in a hurry. Wasn't he, Mr. Hammond?"

Stone peered over his shoulder. His laughing gaze landed on Charlotte for a brief moment before continuing on to Lily, but in that moment, the humor glowing in his amber eyes lifted her spirits as nothing else could.

"That's right, squirt. I imagine he's gonna let you, Miss Lottie, and the boys stay in his cabin while he and I bunk with the hands. He probably rushed off to pack a bag of clothes and stuff to take to the bunkhouse so he won't disturb you later."

Stephen crowded in next to Lily. "I want to sleep in the bunkhouse. I'm no baby that needs to stay with the women and children."

"You'll be staying with me, Stephen Farley," Charlotte answered before Stone could be tempted to give the boy his way. "I'm the one responsible for you while your parents are away, and I'll not have a bunch of foul-mouthed cowhands corrupting your morals while we're here."

"But Miss Lottie . . ."

"Don't argue with your teacher, boy." Stone's deep voice cut off Stephen's protest. "You'll have plenty of time to hang out with the cowpokes during daylight hours. Nights will be better spent in Dan's cabin, where it's quiet. Believe me. I'd trade places with you if I could. Now settle back down." He flicked the reins over the team and set the wagon back into motion. "Dan's cabin is the first outbuilding on the right. See if you can spot it."

The children started shouting and pointing and bouncing, the commotion deafening. But when Stone turned to her and winked, an altogether different commotion stirred inside her. Heavens, she needed to get control of herself. She bit her lip to keep from smiling at him and concentrated on the image of a calm lake swallowing the pebbles that rippled her surface until serenity once again prevailed.

She might trust him to see to Lily's safety, but allowing herself to develop feelings for the man would be disastrous. At least now that she'd recognized her susceptibility, she could be on her guard.

■ ■ ■ ■

When Charlotte turned away from him and added several layers of starch to her spine, Stone's smile relaxed into a more thoughtful posture. Had his wink offended her? Seemed like a little thing to get her dander up about. No, there was something else bothering her. Something deeper. Not that he had a clue as to what it was. Shoot. He could fit what he knew about women in a bullet casing and still have room for the gunpowder. Better spend his energy focusing on what he did understand — protecting his charges. As soon as he got everyone settled, he'd bring Dan up to speed on the situation with Franklin and Dorchester. His friend needed to know the threat housing them could pose.

When they reached the cabin, Stone maneuvered the wagon around the corner so the back would be closer to the door, then he set the brake. He hopped down and turned to offer Charlotte assistance only to find her climbing down on the far side. The woman definitely had a bee in her bonnet about something.

Shrugging off her rejection, he strode to the back of the wagon, untied Goliath, then led his horse to the hitching post next to Ranger while the kids started scooting the bags and trunks toward the tailgate. He'd just made the porch when voices from inside shot through the open door to halt him in his tracks.

"I told you to get out of my cabin, woman. It ain't proper for you to be here."

"What *ain't* proper is for you to inform me we're having guests a scant twenty minutes before they arrive and then refuse to let me house them in an appropriate manner. Women and children, Daniel? They should be in the house with me, not out here in a bachelor's cabin."

"They're staying here, and that's final, Etta. You don't know Stone the way I do. This isn't a pleasure visit. He brought them here because trouble's on their trail. With your father away on business, it falls to me to make sure you're safe. The more distance there is between you and them, the better I like it."

"Oh, for heaven's sake! You'd think I was a porcelain doll, the way you treat me. When will you realize that I can do more than sit on a shelf and look pretty?"

Light footsteps clicked against the floorboards in a rapid staccato an instant before a tiny woman appeared in the doorway, tossing fuming daggers over her shoulder in what Stone could only conclude was Dan's direction. Stone bit back a grin. Seemed he wasn't the only ex-bounty hunter with woman problems.

"Oh!" The comely female startled when she finally noticed him on the porch. Her anger disappeared in a blink as an inviting smile softened her features. "You must be Mr. Hammond. Welcome to Hawk's Haven."

Stone dragged his hat off his head and dipped his chin. "Thank you, ma'am."

"I'm Marietta Hawkins. I'm sorry my father is not here to greet you as well, but be assured that you and your party are welcome to stay as long as you —"

A blond-headed whirlwind blew past and latched herself onto Miss Hawkins's hand. "Is this really Dead-Eye Dan's house? I can't wait to see inside."

An audible groan came from somewhere inside the cabin, and Stone's eyes met his hostess's, both of them alight with laughter.

Miss Hawkins hunkered down in front of Lily and whispered conspiratorially to the girl. "It is! But you'll have to wait for him to leave before you can explore. He likes to pretend he's simply Daniel Barrett, ranch foreman and expert mule trainer, that

Dead-Eye Dan doesn't really exist. So we humor him. But you want to know a secret?"

Lily's eyes grew round, and she nodded slowly.

"I've seen Dead-Eye Dan in action. One winter, I was thrown from my horse during a snowstorm and had to make my way back to the ranch on foot. A pack of wolves caught my scent and started stalking me. They had me surrounded, and I was sure I was going to be torn limb from limb. But just as the lead dog pounced, a shot rang out and he fell to the ground, dead. Six more rifle shots cut through the air, so fast I could barely count them. But with each shot, another wolf fell until none were left. Dead-Eye Dan saved my life that day. And you know how I thank him for his courageous deed?"

"How?" Lily exhaled the word on a sigh of wonder.

"I never talk about Dead-Eye Dan where he can hear me." She tossed a quick glance over her shoulder to make sure the man in question was still out of earshot. "And I keep my entire collection of Dead-Eye Dan novels boxed up under my bed and only read them at night so he'll never see them. Do you think you can do the same?"

Lily nodded. "Yes, ma'am."

"Very good." Miss Hawkins pushed back up to her feet but kept her voice low. "Maybe I can show you my book collection later."

Skirts brushed against Stone's pant legs, and a shiver of awareness passed over him. *Charlotte.* He turned, intending to place a hand at the small of her back and bring her into the circle to introduce her, but she sidestepped his touch, neatly arranging Stephen and John into the resulting gap.

"I believe you've just made a friend for life," she said to their hostess, her serenity mask firmly in place. "I'm Charlotte Atherton. And this little imp is Lily. The boys are Stephen and John." She gave them a remember-your-manners look and waited for each of them to bob their heads in greeting before turning her attention back to the woman before her. "I apologize for the way we're foisting ourselves upon you, Miss Hawkins, but I thank you dearly for your hospitality."

"Think nothing of it. You are welcome to stay as long as you'd like. And please, call me Marietta."

The sincerity in Marietta Hawkins's smile must have reassured Charlotte, for a touch of true warmth broke through her carefully constructed composure — warmth she directed at a stranger, not at him, but still, the evidence that she hadn't *fully* retreated behind her walls helped loosen the knot in Stone's gut.

Miss Hawkins drew Charlotte into the cabin and shooed him and Dan out, relegating them to the masculine tasks of carting luggage and tending horses. Reluctant to leave, Stone lingered with Goliath out front, checking saddle bags that were already fully secure long after Dan drove the wagon and team to the barn. Why had Charlotte avoided his touch? Stone peered at the drawn curtain in the window, wishing he could see her, talk to her. Was she afraid Miss Hawkins would draw an unsavory conclusion from the innocent gesture, or had she meant the message for him — *Keep your distance?*

Stone worked his jaw back and forth. *Put your barriers up if you want to, Lottie. I'll still find a way to win you over.* Tightening the strap on his saddle bag a final time, Stone untied his horse and led Goliath to the barn, making a point not to look over his shoulder as he went.

22

Stone tossed his saddle bags onto the empty bunk next to the one Dan had claimed and pulled his arms out of his duster. Man, he was tired. He couldn't wait to rid himself of some of the excess weight he'd worn while traveling out in the open. The Colt Special strapped to his back could come off, along with the ammunition belt draped across his chest. He unfastened the inverted holster hanging between his shoulder blades then lifted it and the ammunition belt over his head. It was all he could do not to sigh as the weight fell away, but he'd not have Dan thinking he'd gone soft over the last few years.

"So what kind o' trouble we facin'?" Dan stretched out on his bunk, his arms bent behind his head, his booted feet propped on the end of the too-short bedstead.

Stone shook his head as he bit back a smile. Dan might dip his hat over his face like he wanted a nap, but Stone knew better than to think the man relaxed. Daniel Barrett could still shoot a hole through the button on a desperado's coat from his current position. Which was exactly why Stone had brought Charlotte and the kids here.

"Nothin' Dead-Eye Dan can't handle."

Fast as lightning, Dan rolled to his side and slammed a fist into Stone's shoulder, right where that bullet had creased him. Pain ratcheted down Stone's arm at the same time laughter bubbled up his throat and escaped in a quiet chuckle.

"Don't you start in on that nonsense! I can't retaliate when the womenfolk call me that, but I sure as shootin' can wipe the floor with your sorry hide if *you* do, *Hammer.*"

"So you *have* read them. I'd wondered." Stone kicked his friend's boots off the ledge where he'd just replanted them on the bedstead, taking the glare Dan shot him in stride.

"Had to see for myself what kind of balderdash that city slicker was writing about me," Dan grumbled as he planted his feet on the floor and hung his elbows on his knees. "Seems some of the lawmen we used to work for have loose tongues."

"Or empty pockets," Stone guessed.

Dan shrugged. "Bunch of hog slop, if you ask me."

Stone lowered himself to his cot and pushed his hat brim back. "I know. Lily read me part of one. *The Dastardly Duel,* I think."

"Dastardly title," Dan grunted under his breath.

"Maybe, but that little girl thinks you hung the moon and the stars, and I won't have you ridin' roughshod all over her feelings just because the stories make you grumpy."

"This the same gal who wanted to *pet* my horse?" He scowled. "Ranger ain't a puppy, Stone. He's a warhorse."

"I know. I feel the same about Goliath, but the kids have good heads on their shoulders. They're not gonna braid yellow ribbons through the animals' manes or anything." He shrugged then slapped his palms on his thighs. "Maybe you can let her brush Ranger down one evening or something. That'd probably satisfy her. You can even supervise. Make sure no currycomb hearts end up on his flanks."

A pillow hit Stone square in the face, knocking his hat off his head. He returned the projectile with equal fervor, grinning when Dan's Stetson hit the bunk as well.

"So . . . you ever goin' to get around to

tellin' me why you're here? Not that I ain't glad to see ya, of course." Teasing affection warmed Dan's eyes — affection and something deeper. Loyalty.

"I've had a bit of a hitch with one of my retrievals," Stone admitted. "Seems the grieving gentleman who hired me to find his missing granddaughter is actually a scoundrel who wishes to profit from the girl's unusual talents. And the kidnapper, as it happens, stole the child in order to protect her."

"I take it this is the doe-eyed kid who wanted a ride on my horse?"

Stone nodded. "Lily Dorchester. Miss Atherton was her teacher and a friend of her mother. She's also Lily's legal guardian." Dan's head came up, his eyes narrowed in question. "Ashe verified the claim," Stone assured him. "His letter came before we set out. Dorchester has no legal right to the girl unless he can bribe a judge to overturn the guardianship. Which, from what I've learned about his penchant for garnering secrets that can be used to his advantage, is not outside the realm of possibility. If he doesn't already have a judge or two in his pocket, a little well-placed blackmail could probably sway one to see things Dorchester's way should he manage to gain possession of the girl."

Dan sat up straighter, collected his hat from behind him, and started reshaping the crease. "It's not like you to work for men of that ilk."

Stone's jaw clenched. "I know. It galls me to think I fell for his ruse." Stone shoved to his feet and paced to the window and stared out, seeing nothing. "I should have examined his story more closely, dug a little deeper into the details. But truth be told, the moment Dorchester told me his grand-daughter had been kidnapped, I knew I had to take the job. I can't stand to think of any kid suffering or being under the thumb of some slave driver. No kid deserves that."

A strong hand clasped him between shoulder and neck. No words were needed. Dan understood. They'd both survived life on the street. It made them tough. Hard. And neither of them wished those experiences on anyone.

"I guess it's a good thing you did take the job," Dan said, releasing Stone and coming to stand beside him at the window. "Another retriever might not have questioned Dorchester's story. He would've just snatched the girl and collected the reward."

Stone turned slowly and met his friend's eye. "There *is* another retriever. That's why

287

we're here. I've led Dorchester on, hoping he'd assume I was still searching for Lily, but the man has no patience. He sent Walt Franklin to follow up on my leads. I spotted him in Madisonville the day we left. And he's apparently offering payment to anyone who can help him locate the girl. Ran into a group of mercenaries on the way here."

Dan raised a brow. "How many?"

Stone grinned. "Five."

"Hardly fair odds. Six would have made it more interesting."

Stone shrugged. "Five was interesting enough. They had the kids at their backs so I couldn't use my gun. Evened things up a bit."

Dan looked him over, his gaze hitching a time or two over the evidence of his scuffle. "You don't look the worse for wear."

"Nah. The teacher had the worst of it. Had to stop a runaway team while I was off retrieving the girl."

Dan let out a low whistle. "Wouldn't think a prissy schoolmarm like her would have the gumption."

"Charlotte Atherton's got more grit than most." Pride laced his voice. Enough that Dan looked at him sideways before turning the topic back to the matter at hand.

"Franklin's not one to give up on a job."

Dan leaned an arm against the window frame. "He ain't too clever, but once he catches the scent he's like a bulldog with a bone. He won't let it go."

"I know." Stone rubbed a hand over the three days' worth of stubble lining his jaw. That knowledge was what'd kept him awake the last two nights — imagining the rough way Franklin would handle the sweet little girl who loved her dime novel adventures. Living one out wouldn't be as glamorous. Franklin would probably tie her up to keep her from bolting and gag her to keep her quiet. He'd tether her to a tree at night like an animal so he could sleep without worrying about her escaping. Franklin wouldn't care about the rope burns on her wrists or the way a handkerchief stuffed in her mouth could choke her. All he'd care about was getting her back to Dorchester with the greatest possible speed and least possible bother.

But that wasn't all that worried him. Stone glanced back out the window in time to see Charlotte and Miss Hawkins walk past, Miss Hawkins pointing out buildings with an outstretched arm, no doubt giving Charlotte the lay of the land.

What would Franklin do to Charlotte if she tried to stop him from taking Lily? For she would. She'd fight tooth and nail to keep that little gal safe. Would he use his fists on her? His gun?

"They're safe here, Stone," Dan said, as if reading his mind. 'Course he probably had. That's what had made them successful partners. They could read each other's thoughts without saying a word. It's how he knew Dan had feelings for the little brunette marching around the yard with Charlotte in tow. And how he knew his friend would never act on those feelings. Not when the woman in question was the boss's daughter. 'Course Dan had probably already ascertained Stone's own weakness where Charlotte was concerned. He wouldn't say anything, though. Neither of them would. Admitting weakness was not something men like them did. Friends simply accepted, adjusted, and watched each other's backs.

"We can't stay here forever," Stone finally acknowledged. "I have to find a way to convince Dorchester to call off the hunt. Uncover some kind of leverage to force his hand."

"Hard to do that while you're out here dodging Franklin."

"I thought I'd write Ashe again. Ask him to do some digging into Dorchester's business practices. Lily described some unsettling . . . games . . . he tricked her into playing, games that involved her spying on his business associates and gathering information that I'm sure Dorchester planned to use against them later."

Dan raised a brow. "How much spying could a gal that small accomplish?"

"You'd be surprised." Stone quirked a grin, recalling his own shock when Lily had revealed her gift. "That girl's got a mind like one of them camera boxes. She looks at a page once and can recite it all back to you word-for-word. No mistakes."

Dan's other brow lifted.

"How do you think I came to learn about *Dead-Eye Dan and the Dastardly Duel*?" Stone bumped Dan's shoulder with his own. "She recited entire sections of it to me without ever glancing at the pages. It's like she can see them in her mind and no longer needs the source."

"A skill a blackmailer would find handy." Dan peered out the window to where Lily danced around Charlotte's skirts. John came up as well, reached for his teacher's hand, and clung to her as if frightened by all the newness around him. "No one would suspect a child."

"Exactly."

Stephen ran past the window, calling out

some kind of challenge to Lily that must have been impossible to resist, for she shot off after him. Charlotte turned away from Miss Hawkins in order to keep her gaze on the children. Always so vigilant. So protective. He wished she didn't have to be. Wished she could relax and enjoy life instead of constantly waiting for it to blow up in her face.

"I better get out there before them wild Indians scare the stock," Dan grumbled good-naturedly. "I guess if Ranger can keep his cool in a gunfight, he can probably hold his own with a couple pint-sized hooligans rubbin' him down." Dan plopped his hat on his head and sauntered toward the bunkhouse door. He reached for the knob then glanced back at Stone. "Get some rest, partner. You look awful. I'll keep an eye on things."

Stone wanted to argue, wanted to insist that he, and he alone, be the one to take care of Charlotte and Lily. But Dan was right. He needed sleep. And no one was better qualified to watch over his girls than Daniel Barrett.

"Thanks." Stone reached for his left boot and yanked it off.

"Write Ashe after dinner," Dan said in a gruff voice as he opened the door. "I'll send a man to town to post the letter in the morning."

Stone fell asleep with a half-composed letter in his mind and a prayer on his heart.

After dinner that evening, Charlotte took a seat in one of the rockers sitting on the wraparound porch that covered three sides of the big house. She closed her eyes, letting the cool evening breeze wash over her. The tension she'd been carrying in her muscles over the last three days slowly drained out of her fingertips and toes. They were safe. At least for now.

Dozens of men roamed the area, seeing to their duties. Men who wouldn't take kindly to interlopers. Men who answered to Daniel Barrett. He and Stone were with them now. Organizing a patrol and assigning shifts for guard duty during the night.

The boys played in the yard. Marietta Hawkins had found a set of tin soldiers that used to belong to her brother and had brought them down for Stephen and John to play with before disappearing with Lily into her bedchamber, where the treasure chest of dime novels awaited their inspection. Charlotte smiled to herself, imagining Lily's excitement as she pored over the books, searching for some new tale she'd not yet memorized.

The rocker on her right creaked, startling Charlotte's eyes open.

"Nice evening, isn't it?"

Stone. Her heart, injudicious thing that it was, leapt at his voice.

She held back the smile that begged for release and settled for a polite nod as he leaned back in the rocker and set it in motion with a push of his foot. "Yes, it is." She'd meant to make some further comment on the weather, but her mind blanked when her gaze met his. There was something in his eyes — tenderness, perhaps? — that arrested her thoughts. Uncomfortable with the strength of the sensations his attention aroused within her, she dropped her gaze only to have it fall upon a folded sheet of paper clutched in his hand.

"I'm writing another letter to my contact in Austin." Stone's fingers crinkled the paper. "I'd like your permission to ask him to dig into Dorchester's business dealings. Discreetly, of course. Maybe take a little trip over to Houston and check in with a few of Dorchester's associates. With what Lily has told us, I'm thinking he might be involved in blackmail or some other unscrupulous activity. If we can find evidence of dirty dealings, it could give us the upper hand in convincing him to let Lily go."

Dorchester. That's why Stone had sought her out. Not because he'd wanted to spend time in her company, but because he'd wanted to discuss his plans with her. It was what she'd asked of him, after all. She should be grateful for his consideration. So why did she suddenly want to weep?

She gripped the arms of her chair to keep from reaching for the cameo at her throat and drew in a slow, even breath. "I don't suppose it would do any harm as long as Dorchester doesn't suspect he is being investigated. But it could take months to uncover evidence of that nature. We can't stay here that long."

"Don't worry about tomorrow, Charlotte." Stone's hand — large, strong, and incredibly warm — closed over hers on the rocker's arm. "It has enough trouble of its own. We'll focus on what can be done today. Then, when tomorrow gets here, we'll deal with what it has to offer."

Abruptly, he pulled his hand away and stood. She wanted to grab him back, beg him to stay with her just a little longer. But, of course, she didn't. She simply sat in her chair, stared at the ground, and waited for the retreating footsteps that would signal his departure.

The sound never came. Instead, a pair of boots stepped into her line of vision, and an outstretched hand waved beneath her nose.

"Walk with me?"

She tilted her chin up and met his eyes with her own. Before her brain could stop them, her fingers slipped into his palm. In the next moment, he had helped her to her feet and was leading her away from the house.

23

Stone didn't release her hand when she gained her feet, and Charlotte's pulse rate increased from a fluttery *allegretto* to a breath-stealing *presto*. She mentally cautioned herself, arguing that he simply wanted to discuss more plans with her and happened to be in the mood for a stroll, but her body didn't seem to concur. Instead, her heart pounded in her chest as his fingers twined with hers. Her lungs tightened when he glanced sideways at her. And when he smiled? Well, her knees nearly buckled right there in the middle of the yard.

"Careful." He tucked her into his side and held her there for a moment, allowing her to regain her balance and her dignity. Unfortunately, the increased proximity only played further havoc with her senses as the masculine scent of him filled her nostrils and the feel of his corded muscles had her mouth going dry.

Embarrassed at her reaction, Charlotte stiffened and pulled away from his hold. Stone allowed her to regain some distance between them but refused to relinquish her hand. Even after she'd tugged to free it. Twice.

Fine. He could hang on to the silly thing if he liked it all that much, the big bully. She smoothed her other hand over her shirtwaist then froze. Did he really like it all that much? Holding her hand? The thought shot a blast of warmth through her limbs. A warmth that made her languid and docile. Far too easily led. She recognized this truth with a start as her feet fell into step beside him without her having instructed them to do so. She should demand he release her and continue their little jaunt walking solely under her own power. Yet doing so might make her appear a shrew. Or worse, a coward.

So she kept her hand in his and tried desperately not to enjoy the feel of his calloused palm against hers.

Stone steered her along the length of the corral then around the barn until they were out of view of the yard.

"I really shouldn't leave the children," she protested, glancing back the way they had come even as her curiosity urged her forward.

"They'll be fine." Stone continued moving, moderating his stride to fit hers but not slowing down. "Lily's inside with Miss Hawkins and Dan's around in case the boys get into any scrapes. You've been guarding them nonstop for the last three days. You deserve a chance to breathe for a few minutes."

As if she could breathe with him looking at her like that, all soft and concerned and . . . well, never mind how he was looking at her. She quickly repositioned her attention to the ground in front of her.

"I won't keep you long. I promise," he cajoled.

Was that sudden ache in her chest disappointment? Of course not. Hers was a practical nature. And returning to the yard in a timely matter was eminently practical. So why did she suddenly want to shuck that characteristic like a pair of too-tight shoes in order to run barefoot through a grassy meadow?

They walked down a narrow horse trail that flanked a barbed-wire fence, neither of them speaking. The quiet gradually soothed her, calmed her pulse, and actually became rather . . . comfortable. Charlotte stole a glimpse at Stone only to find his attention focused on their surroundings. She followed the direction of his gaze. A grassy field dotted with cattle stretched before them, clear to the horizon. And above the horizon? A tiny gasp of pleasure escaped Charlotte's lips. While she'd been staring at the ground, God had been painting one of the most glorious sunsets she'd ever seen.

Scarlet clouds slashed across a fading sky. Deep oranges and pale pinks blended into the background, throwing the tops of the trees into black silhouette.

"Stunning," she breathed. Her feet stopped of their own accord, halting the man beside her as well.

Stone released her hand, and for a heartbeat, she thought he meant to view the spectacular sight alone. Yet even as the first hint of regret registered, he banished it by wrapping his arm around her waist and settling her close to his side.

"Other places might have taller mountains or bigger lakes or fancier flowers," he said, his hushed voice reverent, "but none of them can best a Texas sunset."

Not sure what to do about his holding her so close, Charlotte held inordinately still. He said nothing more. Just inhaled. Exhaled. And stared at the sky.

The sight really was too beautiful to spoil

with doubts and questions for which she had no answers. Why did she have to possess all the answers, anyway? Was she really so much of a coward that she'd wall herself off from a man just because he made her heart flutter? No harm would come from enjoying a moment in his company. Fire wouldn't fall from heaven if she relaxed her guard.

Besides, holding herself so rigid was keeping her from truly enjoying the masterpiece God had wrought upon the sky.

Charlotte bit the inside of her cheek and, feeling as if she were leaping off a cliff, softened her posture. She leaned her hip slightly against his. Then her spine curved one vertebra at a time, until she matched the shape of his side.

A movement along her waist arrested her. His fingers. Stretching. Adjusting their hold. Charlotte held her breath. His arm bowed more deeply around her, fitting her snugly against him. His eyes remained on the sunset, though. His lips fixed in an almost-smile.

Releasing her breath, she slowly . . . ever so slowly . . . allowed her head to fall against his shoulder.

Stone closed his throat against the shout of

victory that surged up from his lungs the moment Charlotte's head finally nestled against his shoulder. The woman was as skittish as an unbroke mare, but never had he received a sweeter reward for his patience.

He hadn't been this close to her since the afternoon he'd found her at the piano, her walls already torn down from hours of worry and despair. Today her barriers had been firmly in place. But he'd coaxed them down one brick at a time. Success like that gave a man reason to hope.

Then the sun slipped below the horizon. Stone gritted his teeth, wishing it back. Wishing for any excuse to prolong the moment. He promised himself that when she pulled away, he'd let her go. Give her the freedom to choose when the embrace would end.

She didn't move.

Stone bent his head until the side of his jaw rested gently against her hair. The soft tresses caught in the scruff of his whiskers as he caressed her with his cheek. He inhaled, drawing in the faint scent of lilies trapped within the strands. He shut his eyes, the lingering colors of the sunset no longer holding any attraction for him. Only Charlotte. The feel of her. The smell of her. The sound of her breathing. He wanted to savor it all.

After several minutes, Charlotte sighed, and Stone felt her sag slightly. He opened his eyes. All traces of pink and orange had faded from the sky, leaving only the hazy gray of dusk. He should probably release her. Escort her back. But he didn't. He wanted her to himself just a little longer. So he held his tongue and held his woman. Her breathing matched the rhythm of his as crickets serenaded. It was the single most contented moment of his life.

Until a childish squeal from the other side of the barn brought reality crashing back down upon them.

Charlotte lifted her head from his shoulder and turned in the direction of the noise. "That sounded like Lily. She must be finished looking at Marietta's novels. I really should see about getting the children settled at the cottage."

Excuses poured out of her as she straightened away from him, the few flyaway strands of hair still tangled in his beard the only part of her that seemed willing to maintain contact. He could almost see her reconstructing her barriers as she dropped her attention to the ground in front of her, pretending as if nothing of consequence had

303

just occurred between them. Well, she could build her walls if she liked. He'd just build a door.

"Look at me, Charlotte." His gruff murmur vibrated barely above a whisper. She stilled, her gaze remaining locked on the ground. "Look at me," he said again.

Her face inched upward but stalled before her eyes met his. He placed a curled finger beneath her chin and helped her ascend the rest of the way. Her lashes dipped, cheating him from the sight of her beautiful eyes. So he waited, holding her chin in place until the curtain finally lifted. A smile tugged at his mouth at her shy regard. It made her look younger, fresher, untouched by the world's disappointments. The way she should look all the time.

"When I took the job with Dorchester," Stone said, his eyes delving into hers, "I decided it would be my last retrieval. At thirty-five, it's past time for me to quit living in the saddle and start putting down some roots. But tonight I've changed my mind. I'm gonna complete one more job before I retire."

Charlotte's lashes fell over her eyes again. "Because you won't be able to collect your fee from this one." She sounded so certain of her presumption, so wretchedly understanding about it all.

Stone's smile widened. "Not because of the money." He paused, waited for her lashes to flutter out of the way.

"To reestablish your reputation?" she guessed. "Failing to retrieve Lily for Mr. Dorchester will leave your perfect record tarnished."

Stone shook his head. "I don't need a reputation for what I got in mind. But I *do* plan not to let anything get in the way of my completing this final job."

Her brows furrowed. "You sound as if you already have it lined up. Did Mr. Barrett inform you of someone in the area in need of your skills?"

"Nope. I'll be working solely for myself this time around."

"Yourself? I don't understand. What do you plan to retrieve?"

Stone bent his head close, his heated gaze delving into hers. "You."

Charlotte peered at him, searching. Her own eyes glowed with confusion and a touch of fear, but there was a longing beneath it all that shot straight to Stone's heart and injected a healthy dose of hope.

He opened his mouth to say something — what, he wasn't sure. But before he could utter a word, Charlotte spun away from

305

him, grabbed up her skirts, and fled.

Stone watched her go. Smiled as she halted at the edge of the barn to smooth her clothing and hair. Her shoulders lifted as she inhaled a deep breath, no doubt fighting to reclaim the control his bold proclamation had shattered.

She didn't glance back at him, but he could feel the pull that stretched between them. She wanted to. For now, that was enough.

"Beware, Charlotte Atherton," Stone murmured as she disappeared around the corner of the barn. "I'm coming for you." A smile of anticipation stretched across his face. "And I always retrieve what I set out after."

24

Each of the last two mornings when the sun rose, Charlotte had awoken and begun counting the hours until it would set again. For that's when Stone would court her. She had no other words to describe his actions despite her valiant efforts to explain it away as something else. Kindness? No, it was more than that. Flirtation? Not when he'd declared his intention to *retrieve* her.

Tonight, she sat on the edge of her bed and picked up her brush from the small bedside table, one of the few pieces of furniture in the bedroom of Daniel Barrett's cabin. She tilted her head and brushed the tangles from her hair as she recalled Stone's words to her on their first stroll. A secret smile curved her lips, escaping the confines of her control now that the children were abed for the night on their cots in the main room, and she was alone with her thoughts.

Retrieve her. She should be offended by

the notion. It sounded like something a Labrador would do to a dead bird. Hardly a romantic image. Yet when Stone had said it, his eyes had lit with purpose, and a shiver had danced through her midsection, stirring all manner of dreams she'd thought securely packed away.

Relentless. That's how Lily's novels described him. Would Stone pursue her with the same tenacity he exhibited when hunting down a villain? There'd be no reward spurring him on. Nothing beyond the atrophied affections of a washed-up spinster. She wasn't even sure she knew how to love a man. She'd spent so many years training herself not to, that opening herself to such a possibility made her heart ache like an out-of-use muscle suddenly called upon to heft a great weight.

The brush stilled in her hand. *What would you have me do, Lord? I'm afraid of being hurt again, but I can't let fear rule my life forever. If only I could know for sure that Stone won't ever leave me.*

Charlotte sighed wistfully. A guarantee would make everything so much easier. She'd promise herself to Stone this very minute if she had proof he'd never betray her. But life offered no guarantees — she knew that better than anyone.

Trust in the Lord with all thine heart; and lean not unto thine own understanding. In all thy ways acknowledge him, and he shall direct thy paths.

The familiar proverb rose in her mind to convict her. She'd leaned on her own understanding for all of her adult life. It was how she maintained order, control. How she avoided pain. But what if her own understanding was flawed this time? What if God was trying to direct her paths and her fear of future hurt was impeding his plan? Or what if it wasn't God directing her but her own foolish longings? How was she to know the difference?

Charlotte sighed in frustration and set the brush back on the small table. Gathering the length of her hair, she pulled it forward over her right shoulder and started braiding it.

Once her braid was secured with a scrap of ribbon, Charlotte stood and slipped her arms into her dressing gown. She'd check on the children one last time before going to sleep. The path involving Stone might be unclear, but she had a firm grasp on her purpose regarding Lily and the boys.

Padding on bare feet, she opened the bedroom door and peered into the darkened room. The bedroom lamp allowed enough light to see, but not enough to disturb the young sleepers. Stephen and John shared a pallet in the corner, John in a cocoon of blankets, his small body completely still and contained while Stephen's legs and arms were flung every which way, with only a corner of the blanket clinging to his middle. Charlotte smiled at the odd pair, each so dear in his own way. She glided over to them, bent, and straightened the twisted blanket until it once again covered Stephen adequately. Then she placed a gentle kiss on each forehead before straightening and crossing to the small settee where Lily bedded down.

Her face looked so peaceful in sleep, so untroubled.

"Help me keep her safe, Lord," Charlotte whispered before touching her lips to Lily's brow.

A quiet knock sounded on the front door. Frowning, Charlotte turned. Who would be at her door this time of night? The rapping sounded again. Louder this time.

Stephen moaned and flopped over on his side. The action spurred Charlotte forward. The children needed their rest. Besides, good news never came calling at night. Only bad. The children had had enough upheaval already without adding more worries to their load. Stone had promised to notify her at once if anyone spotted Franklin around the ranch. Perhaps that time had finally arrived.

Her abdomen twisted, but she lifted her chin and hurried to the door. "Trust in the Lord," Charlotte murmured under her breath, the reminder helping her reestablish her composure. He *could* be trusted. He'd sent Stone to protect them, after all.

Only it wasn't Stone outside her door. When she pulled back the swath of burlap Daniel Barrett used for a curtain, she found two cowhands standing on the cabin's porch, their faces too shadowed for her to make out. The one doing the knocking must have caught the curtain's movement, for he stepped over to the window and politely yanked his hat from his head.

"You mind openin' the door, ma'am?" His muffled voice distorted as it passed through the window glass.

Charlotte shook her head. She wasn't about to open the door without them stating their business. Their being here at all was highly improper. She did recognize the one at the window, though, so a few of the knots in her stomach relaxed.

He was one of the young stable boys who tended the horses and kept the barn clean.

311

Jimmy, she thought. He couldn't be more than sixteen or seventeen, judging by the smoothness of his cheeks, but he was as tall as any of the other hands around the ranch. Charlotte had come across him in the stables a time or two over the past few days.

"I'm sorry to disturb you at such an hour, ma'am, but you're needed up at the big house." He crouched down in order to position his face closer to the window so she could hear him better. "Miz Hawkins sent for ya. She took sick all sudden like . . . with an . . . ah, womanly ailment. She's in terrible pain, ma'am, but too embarrassed to let any of us menfolk help her. My brother will watch over the kids while I escort you to the house."

Charlotte nibbled her lip in indecision. She longed to assist Marietta in her time of need, but she didn't feel comfortable leaving the children in a stranger's care. Especially since the second man made no move to step closer to the window.

Dropping the burlap curtain, Charlotte stepped to the door and lifted the heavy bar that blocked the men's entrance. Holding her wrapper closed around her throat, she opened the door just enough to peek her head out.

"I'd be happy to assist Miss Hawkins,"

she said in a low voice, "but I'd prefer it if Mr. Hammond watched the children in my absence. They are more comfortable with him, you see." She turned an apologetic smile to the man in the shadows.

The instant her head turned, the shadowy man charged. He thrust his arm through the slim opening and slammed his palm into her shoulder. Charlotte gasped and staggered back, almost tumbling onto her rump. The man shoved his way into the cabin, throwing the door wide. Only then did she see his face.

One of the attackers from the road.

"Lily!" Charlotte spun and ran for the settee, but the man grabbed her from behind and covered her mouth with his hot, meaty hand.

Charlotte screamed against his palm and kicked out with her legs, twisting and writhing in terror. He didn't even grunt as her bare feet batted him.

Stephen was the first to wake. He bounded to his feet, narrowed his eyes, and let out a war cry. "Let go of Miss Lottie!" Lowering his head like a bull, he charged Charlotte's captor. Jimmy rammed into him first, shouldering him with enough force to send the boy sprawling onto the floor. He crumpled into a heap, moaned, and raised a hand to his head.

Lily screamed Stephen's name, her legs tangling in her covers in her haste to get to him. "You big bully!" she yelled, her eyes spitting fire as she scrambled over to Stephen. "When Stone finds out about this, he's gonna whup you good."

Jimmy darted a glance from the girl to his brother and back again. His chest heaved as if he were suddenly having difficulty catching his breath. The threat wasn't an idle one, and he knew it. "Are you sure about this, Winston? They aren't acting like they've been kidnapped."

"Do what I tell ya, boy. You owe me." Winston's foul breath turned Charlotte's stomach. "Franklin can sort out the details. All I care about is the fifty dollars he promised anyone who could find the girl. If we *bring* the girl to him, he'll up the price. Thar may be a hun'red in it for us. You wanna keep shoveling manure all your life, or you want a real man's pay?"

Awakened by the commotion, John whimpered and clutched the blanket to his chin like a shield. He sat up and scooted his back as far into the corner as he could, drawing his knees up in front of him.

"Grab the girl." Charlotte's captor twisted so he could scowl at Lily. "We're rescuin'

314

you, runt. You'll thank us when you're back with your family."

"Miss Lottie *is* my family," Lily wailed. "My mama gave me to her."

Charlotte nodded her head vigorously against the cowboy's hold, but his grip only tightened, his hand pressing so hard against Charlotte's mouth, her teeth began to ache.

"Jimmy," Winston ground out between clenched teeth, "get to it."

The younger brother approached Lily like one would a cornered animal. Hunched over, arms outstretched to catch her if she tried to bolt. Lily shook her head. "No! I'm not going with you. I'm staying with Miss Lottie and Stone."

"I'm not gonna hurt ya," Jimmy cajoled.

Stephen pushed to his feet and placed himself between the girl and the much larger man. "Leave us alone."

"Can't do that, kid," Winston growled next to Charlotte's ear.

"Sorry," Jimmy murmured as he grabbed Stephen by the neck. He flung him over the arm of the settee as if he wanted to give the boy a soft landing on the cushions. Then he wasted no time lunging for Lily. She screamed, but he was ready. He stuffed a wadded bandana in her mouth and scooped her up, keeping her arms pinned to her chest. She kicked her legs, ramming her heels into his hip, but the lanky young man seemed impervious to the attack.

Seeing Lily in the man's arms snapped something inside Charlotte. She went wild, launching herself upward with her legs as she slammed her head back. Her skull crashed into the forehead of her captor with a satisfying crack.

"Ow!" Winston called her a foul name then threw her against the wall. The force of the collision stole her breath for precious seconds. Just as she found her wind and opened her mouth to scream, Winston thrust an acrid cloth into her mouth. It tasted of sweat and dirt, but Charlotte pushed at it with her tongue anyway. She had to get it out. Had to scream for help.

But it was no use. The man was too strong. In a matter of minutes, he stripped the belt from her wrapper and used it to tie her hands behind her back. He leaned close to secure the gag to her mouth with a handkerchief he'd pulled from his pocket. Stephen, bless him, rushed past, making a beeline for the door.

Yes! Run, Stephen. Get help. Get Stone.

Charlotte thrashed harder, twisting her head from side to side, hoping to distract her captor. Stephen made it to the door, lifted the bar, and had just started to pull it inward when a booted foot kicked it closed.

Jimmy.

Charlotte nearly wept, but smothered the inclination. She'd not give these men that victory over her. Besides, a stuffy nose would make breathing rather difficult with a gag stuffed in her mouth. She'd be strong for the children. Not that emotional strength did her much good when her hands were bound, and now her ankles as well. Winston's boney knees pinned her feet to the floor as he fastened a leather strap below her calves.

The minute he finished with her, he grabbed Stephen and gave him the same treatment — bound his hands and feet and gagged him. Stephen glared daggers at the man — daggers the man ignored. At least Stephen was too angry to be afraid. Poor John must be falling apart. Charlotte glanced over to the corner where the boy had been sitting.

He was gone.

25

Charlotte jerked her attention back to the men stomping about the main room. They didn't seem to notice anything amiss. Never had she been more thankful for John's quiet nature. If ever there was a time for the little boy to slip past someone's notice, it was now. But where had he gone? The cabin only had one door, and he'd not exited there. She would have seen him.

A window? Mr. Barrett had a small one in his bedroom, but the latch stuck something awful. She'd barely been able to pry the thing open herself when she and Marietta had aired out the room that first morning. She couldn't imagine John's tiny fingers managing the task.

Well, wherever the boy was, he was out of sight and out of mind as far as the two villains were concerned, and that was victory enough for now.

"We'll wrap her up in this." Winston flung

the charcoal-gray blanket from Stephen's pallet into the air with a snap. It fluttered gently to the floor. "Lay her down, and hold her arms and legs steady." He was ready with another handkerchief to secure Lily's gag the instant Jimmy relaxed his hold on her to lay her down.

Lily's eyes met Charlotte's. Swollen. Red-rimmed. Glistening with terror. Pleading with her teacher to *do* something.

Charlotte longed for the strength of Samson, to snap her bonds and crack the imbecilic skulls of the cowboys holding her precious Lily down. But she had no such strength. She was helpless.

Or was she?

Charlotte calmed her desperate flailing and straightened her spine against the frame of the settee until she sat with all the elegance of a queen upon a throne. She had no physical strength to offer Lily, but she could fortify the child's spirit. Give her reason to hope. Grant her assurance that no matter what these men intended, they wouldn't win in the end. God would watch over her. And Stone would come for her.

Lily's chin lifted just a hair. Her sniffling ceased. Her legs and arms stilled. Then her head dipped ever so slightly, and Charlotte knew she'd taken the message to heart.

Rescue would come.

"Wrap the blanket 'round the girl good and tight, Jimmy, but leave that top part open to flap over her face when we get to the patrol. The dark color will make her invisible this time of night, but I'll have to sit in the wagon bed with her to make sure she don't wiggle enough to draw notice while you get us past the guard."

The foul man had the audacity to grin as his brother cocooned Lily like an unwilling caterpillar. "Yes, sirree." He rubbed his hands together. "My luck's finally turnin' around. First, I'm the only one of Gordon's gang to get away from that Hammond fellow without a scratch, then when I meet up with my kid brother for a drink at the Coyote, he tells me about Hammond, a teacher, and a group of kids hidden away on the Double H. The very same combination we met on the road. Too good to be coincidence." The wolfish gleam in his eye raised Charlotte's hackles. "Some might say I was *destined* to collect that reward. Hard to argue with that, ain't it, teacher?"

Only because she had a gag stuffed in her mouth. She glared at him since she had no other recourse.

He laughed.

"Let's get outta here before someone

catches us, Win. If I ain't long gone by the time Barrett figures out who took the girl, I ain't gonna live long enough to enjoy that reward. Neither of us will." Jimmy tossed the blanketed bundle over his shoulder like a sack of flour. Lily hung lax. No more fighting. No more weeping. Just a single haughty glare she raised up long enough to drill into Winston as he moved past her to unbar the door. A glare that promised retribution.

The man's step stuttered. He looked away, cursed, then wrenched the door open. "C'mon. That Houston fella should be waitin' on us by now. I wired him about the delivery. If we hurry, we can be out of the county before daybreak."

Jimmy grunted and followed. Charlotte strained against her bonds, desperate to help her daughter, but helpless to do so. Before she could even pull up to her knees, the door slammed shut.

They're getting away!

Charlotte twisted to her side and scooted her rump across the floor until she could reach the arm of the settee with her mouth. She scraped her face against the upholstered edge. Again. The handkerchief refused to budge. Again and again. She had to get the thing off. Had to alert Stone. Finding a rough spot where an upholstery tack jutted out from the fabric, she intensified her efforts, trying to hook it like a fish. She had just found a promising grip when a sharp thump echoed against the cabin wall.

Her gaze flashed over to Stephen. He'd managed to wiggle his way to his feet but stilled at the unexpected sound. A second thump rattled the window behind her. What little light had been filtering in from outside suddenly vanished.

The storm shutters. The men were covering the windows. Locking her and the boys inside. Even as the thought registered, the rapping of a hammer carried through the air. First at the shutters. Then the door. They'd sealed every possible exit.

Charlotte and the boys were trapped. Trapped inside until someone discovered them in the morning. By then it would be too late. Lily would be in Franklin's hands.

Unless John had somehow found a way to escape. He was a tiny scrap of a boy. Even if he couldn't get the window open, perhaps he'd gotten out some other way. A loose floorboard opening into a crawl space beneath the cabin? The hole for the stovepipe in the ceiling? He wasn't exactly the adventurous type, but if he were frightened enough . . .

"Are the bad men gone, Miss Lottie?"

John. His small frame stood silhouetted against the light of the bedroom lamp. Charlotte swallowed her disappointment as the boy crept into the main room, trailing his blanket behind him. He was safe. Unharmed. Reason enough to be grateful.

"Mm-hmm." Charlotte circled her head to direct John closer. Seeing her state, he dropped his blanket and ran to her. He cupped her cheeks in his hands for a moment, turning her face from side to side, then hooked his fingers around the handkerchief and tugged it down onto her neck. She nodded encouragement to him and thrust her chin out so he would remove the gag. As soon as the foul thing was out, she told John to help Stephen then aimed her face toward the newly covered window and screamed as loud as she could.

"Stone!"

Stephen and John soon joined the chorus. "Help us!"

They screamed until they were hoarse, but no one came. The cabin was too far removed. The walls too thick. The boarded-up windows too solid. As foreman, Daniel Barrett lived apart from the other men, his cabin situated in a lovely spot on the front side of the corral. She'd thought it pretty, located near the paddock, away from the smells of the barn and the noise of the bunkhouse. Now it was an isolated prison, keeping her from going after her daughter.

"It's no use," she finally rasped, urging the boys to cease their shouts. "They can't hear us." Defeat brought tears to her eyes, but she refused to let them fall. She leaned against the settee and set her shoulders. If Plan A didn't work, she'd simply have to move on to Plan B. And C and D and on down the list until they found a way out of this mess. Lily was counting on her, and she'd not quit. They were all intelligent people. Surely they could think of something.

She turned her back to John then twisted her neck to glance at him over her shoulder. "Come here, sweetheart, and help me with this knot."

John stepped close, but instead of picking at the knot, he buried his face in Charlotte's neck.

"I'm sorry I hid, Miss Lottie. I should have helped you fight the bad men." Wetness leaked onto Charlotte's skin. "I was too scared."

Charlotte crooked her head around him and raised her shoulder, embracing the boy as best she could while still bound. "Shhh, sweetheart. You did exactly the right thing. Why, if you hadn't hidden away, you'd be just as tied up as the rest of us. But since you were so clever, you can be the hero of our story and set Stephen and me free."

John pulled away and blinked up at her, his short, damp lashes clumped together. "Wh-where's Lily?"

"Waiting for us to rescue her, so we must hurry." Not wanting the child to get worked up again, she nodded toward Stephen. "I need you to untie my wrists. If we can figure out a way out of here, we can send Stone after Lily."

With all the possible exits nailed shut, she found it difficult to grasp much optimism. Still, she scanned the room, examining every section of wall for weakness. Too bad the cabin was made of logs. Not exactly something she could chop a hole in with Stephen's pocketknife.

Barrett had taken all his firearms out of the cabin at her insistence. She hadn't wanted the children exposed to the danger of such weapons. Now, as she examined the top of the tall bookshelf across the room, she prayed he'd forgotten one. A gunshot would bring the men running.

She squinted. There *could* be a rifle or shotgun secreted up there. Close to the

325

door, handy for a tall man to reach up and grab as he left. The shadows tantalized her with imagined bounty. She couldn't see far enough into them from her position on the floor to tell if anything real lingered there or not, but somehow she knew the top of the cabinet would prove to be bare. Daniel Barrett didn't strike her as the type of man who'd lose track of his guns.

Please, Lord. We need to get out of here in time to save Lily.

"I think I know a way to get out." Stephen's words rang through the room as if God himself had sent her an answer to her prayer. His gag drooping around his neck, Stephen hopped over to the door, his gaze assessing both edges. "They nailed it shut on the handle side but not on the hinge side. I've got a screwdriver in my bag. If we can pry out the hinge pins, we should be able to push the door open. At least far enough to squeeze through."

Tears moistened Charlotte's eyes. Never would she let this boy think he was anything less than exceptional. At this moment, she truly believed him the single most exceptional youth the Sullivan Academy had ever produced. "It's a brilliant plan, Stephen. Absolutely brilliant." And undoubtedly God-sent.

Stephen turned to face her, his eyes alight with pride and a hope so fierce it brought her own flagging coals flaring back to life.

"This will work," she said, blinking away the dampness from her eyes. She smiled at Stephen then glanced over her shoulder to nod encouragingly at John, who was busy picking at the tie at her wrists. "I'm sure of it."

John offered a timid smile in answer then went back to work.

Charlotte bit her lip. She wasn't truly sure of anything, but for the first time in a long while, she was willing to hope for the best instead of expecting the worst.

Stone stretched out on his bed and propped his hands behind his head. Sounds from the bunkhouse filtered over him. The click of poker chips and the occasional ruffle of cards from the game in the back corner. The snores from the hands who had early-morning patrol duty. Even the scratch of pen on paper from a lovesick young pup trying desperately to write a half-decent line of poetry for the town girl he was courting. Masculine sounds. Comfortable, easy, familiar. So why couldn't he fall asleep?

Because he didn't want to sleep among a bunch of hairy-faced men who smelled like sweat and smoke, who thought nothing of belching and scratching and walking around in their drawers. He wanted a fussy, prim-and-proper woman who smelled of lilies and fit perfectly against his side during a sunset stroll. He wanted children around him — girls who dreamed about riding herd on outlaws, and boys who built crazy contraptions or who rarely made a sound unless they sat at a piano and spit out jaw-dropping masterpieces. That's what he wanted surrounding him at night. A family.

"You ever think about gettin' your own spread, Dan?" Stone asked in a voice that would carry no farther than the bunk beside his. "Settlin' down with a good woman and havin' some kids?"

"Don't know about the woman and kids part, but I do got my eye on a piece of land not far from here. Thought about training mules. Sold a few in the past, and I keep getting requests for more. Hawkins lets me train 'em in my spare time, but I won't really be able to make a go of it unless I strike out on my own."

Stone slanted a glance at his friend. Something about the way he avoided the discussion of a wife added to Stone's earlier suspicion about Marietta Hawkins. "Seems like a sound plan for a man who's never met a horse he couldn't tame," he probed. "You could make a good living that way. Easily provide for a wife —"

"It ain't the providin' that's the issue," Dan growled. "It's —" He never got to finish, for the door to the bunkhouse swung open on its hinges so hard it slammed into the side wall.

"Stone! I need Stone!"

He was on his feet, gun in hand, running toward her before the words even left her mouth. All it had taken was one glance to know something was terribly wrong.

His prim-and-proper teacher had just barged into a bunkhouse full of strange men in nothing more than her nightclothes.

26

"I'm here, Lottie." Stone reached her side in an instant. Knowing Dan would have his back, he holstered his weapons and opened his arms to her, wanting — no, *needing* — to be her anchor. But Charlotte apparently had no desire for comfort, for she grabbed his wrist and started dragging him quite forcibly from the bunkhouse.

"Hurry, Stone! You must go after her. It took longer for Stephen to free the pins than we'd hoped. They have nearly an hour's lead on you."

Had she hit her head? The woman was talking gibberish. Her grip hadn't suffered any ill effects, though. She continued tugging at his arm even though he was already trotting after her like a faithful hound.

"Charlotte. Stop." He planted his feet. "I can't help you unless I know what's wrong."

She tugged again, deaf to his demand. "There's no time. I sent the boys to the stable to wake the hand on duty. He should be saddling Goliath and Ranger even now." When Stone didn't move, she reached back and grabbed hold of him with a second hand, her sleeves sliding up her arms. Angry red marks glared up at him from around her wrists. Binding marks.

Stone snatched her hands from his arm and held up her wrists. Rage — searing hot and seething — roiled in his gut. "Who did this to you?" His jaw clenched so tight he almost couldn't get the words out.

Charlotte wrenched her arms free of his hold. "The men who took Lily!" The name escaped her on a sob, and finally Stone understood.

"Franklin." How had the man gotten onto the ranch?

Charlotte shook her head, her dark blond hair flying about her shoulders as she pinched her lips together and stuffed her emotion back down. "Not Franklin. One of the men who attacked us on the road. And a Double H man."

"Who?" Dan's sharp voice behind Stone pierced the conversation like an arrow through an apple.

Charlotte's gaze snapped over to him. "Jimmy."

Dan's eyes glowed with fury. Someone

was about to lose his job — and his hide. Stone would gladly volunteer to help dole out the punishment.

"They're taking Lily to Franklin right now," Charlotte said. "Stephen and I fought them as best we could, but they were too strong. They must be taking her back to town. Winston said Franklin was expecting them. You have to catch them and bring her back. You *have* to."

Charlotte wrapped her arms around her middle as the night wind buffeted her white cotton sleeping gown. The outer covering fluttered behind her, doing nothing to stave off the chill of the air. She looked so lost, so scared, so heartsick. Yet there was a fierceness about her, too. A fierceness that demanded he retrieve that which she held most precious. A fierceness that fully expected him to succeed.

Stone straightened. He *would* succeed, God help him. He'd not stop until he had Lily safely back in Charlotte's arms.

He lunged forward and captured Charlotte in his embrace. "I'll get her back for you, Lottie. I swear it." He pressed his cheek to hers, rasping his vow in her ear as he crushed her to his chest.

"I know you will." She leaned into him, making no effort to pull away. "I trust you."

Those three words nearly felled him. Yet at the same time, they galvanized him like a lightning bolt sparking a prairie fire. He longed to let the flames rage out of control, but he couldn't risk Lily being burned in the process. So he banked the fires just enough to see clearly through the smoky haze. He needed speed. Action. But his best chance of retrieving Lily unscathed required strategy.

The stable hand emerged from the barn at that moment, leading Goliath and Ranger, both saddled and ready to ride. The horses pawed at the ground and shook their heads as if sensing the tension around them. They knew what was to come. Stone squeezed Charlotte's middle then released her. Jaw set, he strode for his horse.

Dan tossed him his ammunition belt, his custom shoulder holster, and the knives he'd left in the storage chest by his bunk, then he moved to the horses and shoved rifles into the boots of each of their saddles. Another cowboy jogged forward with Stone's duster and hat. In less than a minute, Stone was geared up and atop Goliath. He cast a final glance to Charlotte and found a boy on either side of her, all six eyes imploring him to bring Lily back to them.

"She's expecting you, Mr. Hammond," Stephen called out. "She'll be ready."

Stone gave a sharp nod. He'd not let them down.

"There's a saloon in Steward's Mill," Dan said as he circled Ranger close to Stone. "One of the few places open this time of night. Logical place for a rendezvous."

Stone forced his gaze from Charlotte's to the road before him. "Lead the way." He touched his heels to Goliath's sides and set out at as fast a pace as the moonlit night would allow.

Thirty minutes later, they pulled their mounts to a halt in front of the saloon. "Do you see the wagon?" Stone asked as he swung his leg over Goliath's back and found the ground.

Dan scoured the overcrowded street and alleyway. Seemed the Lonely Coyote wasn't so lonely, even on a Tuesday. Stone looked over the single horses and frowned. The one he most wanted to see wasn't there. Franklin's palomino. Flashy bit of horseflesh — white mane and tail that would fairly glow under the three-quarter moon that lit the night sky. Unless Franklin had opted to disguise his presence by renting a livery nag, they were too late. Lily had already been handed over.

"There." Dan cut into his thoughts and pointed to a weathered farm wagon just peeking out around the corner. "That's Double H stock." Dan dismounted and cut a path through the horses at the hitching post. Stone followed.

When they neared the team, the horse closest to them nickered and lifted his head in greeting, having recognized Dan's scent. Dan cupped a hand over the sorrel's nose and whispered to him. The animal stilled.

Plenty familiar with Dan's effect on four-legged creatures, Stone didn't linger to watch the exchange. He sidled past the horses, scraping his back against the brick of the building until he reached the wagon bed. Planting a booted foot on a wheel spoke, he grabbed the side and hoisted himself up. Nothing. He hadn't really expected to find her there, but the disappointment was sharp nonetheless.

"She's not here," Stone informed Dan in a flat voice.

Which meant she was already with Franklin. *Hang it all!* Stone slammed his palm against the wagon's side. If that hulking brute harmed one hair on Lily's head, he'd — Stone inhaled and forced the rising panic back into subjugation. Franklin wouldn't hurt her. She was worth too much. The bit of logic did little to soothe him, though. Franklin wasn't the problem. Dorchester was. And the longer the lead Franklin stretched out, the slimmer their chance of retrieving Lily before she reached Houston. Once under her grandfather's control, it would take a legal battle to get her back.

Stone hopped down from the wagon and squeezed his way out of the alley, his narrowed gaze zeroed in on Dan's back. He needed to focus on the problem at hand. Gather information. Sniff out the trail. "Let's hope Winston and Jimmy decided to spend some of their ill-gotten gains before headin' out tonight." He clapped Dan on the shoulder. "Should we take a gander inside?"

Dan nodded, a half smile curving his lips. "After you."

Stone pushed through the batwing doors and slid along the front wall, keeping his back pressed against the paneling. He scanned the faces. One after another. At the bar. At the tables. The men wore hats, some pulled low over their faces, making it hard to distinguish their features. But the hat with the leather band in the back corner looked familiar. Stone studied its wearer. It could be one of the men who'd waylaid them on the road, but he couldn't be sure. Not without seeing the man's face.

The man turned over his cards, grinned at his comrades, then started scraping the pot toward his belly with both hands. "I *knew* my luck had turned!" He lifted his face to make his boast, and Stone's gut clenched.

It was him. The one who'd held a gun to Stephen's head. The one who'd terrorized Charlotte.

Stone pushed off the wall and marched straight for the back table. A girl carrying drinks started to approach, took one look at his face, and ran for the bar. When he reached the table, he didn't slow. He scooped up Winston with a hand to his throat, lifted his feet from the ground, then pinned him against the back wall. "Your luck's turnin' again, Winston," Stone ground out. "And this time it might never recover."

The man's eyes flew wide. "Y-you!" he croaked.

"Yep. Me." Stone pulled one of the knives from his belt and gave the fellow a bit of an impromptu shave, taking care to nick his jaw. "And if you want to survive this here introduction, I suggest you tell me where the girl is." He nicked him again. "Fast."

The sounds of scraping chairs and hurried feet echoed behind him as the poker table emptied.

Winston stiffened, his eyes narrowing at something behind Stone. "My winnings," he rasped.

"Are the least of your worries." Stone tightened his grip on the man's throat and successfully regained his attention.

"Found the other one, Stone," Dan called out.

"Since you found what you're lookin' for, Dan," the man behind the bar said, his deep, booming voice carrying through the room nearly as effectively as the sound of his shotgun hitting the counter, "I'd appreciate it if you'd do your *talkin'* outside my establishment."

"Happy to, Buck." Dan started dragging Winston's companion toward the entrance. "Coming, Stone?"

"Yep." Stone jerked Winston away from the wall and released his neck. While the man staggered to regain his balance, Stone grabbed hold of his right arm and twisted it behind his back. Winston groaned but put up no resistance as Stone shoved him forward.

Stone glared at the lanky kid in Dan's grasp as he rounded the corner to join his partner in the alley. He might not be a day over seventeen, but he'd been big enough to manhandle Charlotte and the kids. That meant he was big enough to pay the consequences for his actions.

The kid swallowed hard. "I-I'm sorry, boss. I didn't want to, but Winston said the girl had been kidnapped."

"And instead of coming to me with your concerns, Jimmy, you broke into my cabin, roughed up a woman and three children under my protection, and sold an innocent girl to a man you've never met?" Dan demanded. "I ought to string you up and save the county the expense of a trial."

Jimmy paled. "It was all Winston's doing, I swear," the kid blurted. "He bullied me into it just like he did when we were kids."

"Shut up, runt," Winston growled. Stone twisted the man's arm a little harder. He arched his back and fell to his knees. If the kid felt like talking, Stone wasn't going to let big brother interfere.

Dan gave Jimmy a little shove, throwing him back against the alley wall. "Well, as it turns out, Miss Atherton *is* Lily Dorchester's legal guardian. She has papers to prove it." He jabbed the boy's chest with his finger. "Which means you and Winston here are the ones guilty of kidnapping. I hope the money jingling in your pocket was worth the time you'll be spending in jail."

Dawning horror spread over Jimmy's face. "J-jail?"

"Yep." Dan glanced down at his feet and shrugged. " 'Course, if one of you were to tell us everything you knew about Walt Franklin and his plans for the girl, we might be willing to put in a good word for you with the marshal."

"H-he took her and rode out. I don't know where." Jimmy all but tripped over himself in his eagerness to gain Dan's goodwill.

"That's not good enough." Dan met the boy's eyes, his hard features leaving no room for mercy.

The kid glanced toward the sky, as if searching the expanse for something useful to pass along. Then he snapped his fingers and grinned. "I heard him say something about needing to fetch his things from the Commercial and catching the morning train."

Dan turned to Stone. "The Commercial Hotel. In Corsicana. If he's riding double with the girl, we can make up some ground on him."

"He only left about fifteen or twenty minutes ago," Winston grunted, obviously trying to get in on the deal. "If you leave now, you've got a chance. Better hurry, though. If you wait for the marshal, ya might not catch 'em."

"No need to wait, fellas. I'm here."

Stone glanced over his shoulder and nodded at the lawman striding into the alley. "Toby."

The marshal fingered the brim of his Stetson. "Stone. Dan." His casual glance passed over the other two men. "Buck sent a messenger to fetch me. Said there was some trouble brewin'. Am I gonna find posters for these two back in my office? Been a while since you two brought me a bounty."

"You might find something on this one," Stone said as he hauled Winston to his feet, "but right now I ain't interested in collecting. I got to retrieve the little girl these yahoos kidnapped before she gets on a train in the morning." He shoved Winston at the marshal. Toby caught him with no difficulty. "Lock these two up for kidnapping and assault. We'll stop by on our way back to give a statement."

The lawman nodded even as Winston started sputtering.

"Assault? We didn't hurt no one. Just tied up the teacher and the kids and nailed the doors and shutters closed so they couldn't

341

escape until morning."

Stone's fists itched to pummel the man just for touching Charlotte, to crush him with blow after blow until he lay as helpless and powerless on the dirt street as he'd made Charlotte feel in that cabin. "I'm sure they just sat idly by and let you bind them," he ground out, his sarcasm slicing like the blade he wished he could wield. "No struggle. No fight. No need for you to use force."

His gut churned at the images flooding his brain. Lily crying and terrified. Charlotte brave and desperate, fighting off two men all on her own. Stephen trying to be a man but being too young to defend the women. And John. Poor kid probably wouldn't talk for weeks after the fright he'd had.

Then all at once, Winston's words hit him. He'd nailed the door shut? And the storm shutters? In his hurry to leave, Stone hadn't paid the cabin any heed. It was a miracle Charlotte and the boys had escaped. Charlotte's ramblings about Stephen freeing the pins finally clicked. The boy had taken the door off its hinges. That's how they'd gotten out. Thank God for smart kids.

"I'll hold 'em for ya, Stone." The marshal fastened a pair of handcuffs around Winston's wrists then looked at Jimmy. "Ya gonna come quietly, son, or do I have to chain you, too?"

Jimmy hung his head and moved forward. Dan divested him of his gun belt and the knife at his waist. Stone gave Winston the same treatment. Toby strapped the belts through his own, letting the holsters slap against his left thigh then pulled his own weapon and started marching the brothers off to the jailhouse.

Stone turned and jogged toward the horses. They had serious ground to make up and not much time to accomplish the task.

"Nice doin' business with you again, Dan," the marshal drawled as he crossed in front of the Lonely Coyote.

Stone didn't pay attention to Dan's reply. He mounted Goliath, grabbed Ranger's reins, and aimed the animals up the road.

"C'mon, Dan. We got a train to catch."

Dan mounted in a swift, easy motion, catching the reins Stone tossed his way, and the two rode off, this time heading north to Corsicana.

27

Goliath and Ranger had both been trained for endurance riding, but the nearly thirty-mile trip stretched them to their limits. Stone pressed them hard at first, hopeful they'd overtake Franklin since he was weighted down with Lily. Then he'd spotted the second set of tracks in the soft dirt of a creek bed where they'd watered their horses. Stone had stared at the marks, his entire body aching as if he'd just been felled by a tree. Dan knelt down beside him, took one look at the tracks, and hung his head. He knew what they meant. Franklin had a spare mount. Overtaking him would be impossible.

After that discovery, Stone slowed the pace, no longer racing against Franklin but against the sun. If they could reach Corsicana before the train pulled into the depot, they had a chance. If Franklin managed to get Lily on board . . . well, the additional witnesses would make things a bit tricky. If they missed the train altogether? The thought twisted Stone's gut. Facing Dorchester in a place where he controlled the stage and all the players would be like battling a wildcat without a weapon. Stone had survived it once, but as he recalled, the cat had suffered very few ill effects. Stone had been the one to lose a pound of flesh. Not exactly a scenario he wanted Lily mixed up in.

So when the sunrise bathed the countryside in golden light, Stone cringed. When the first birds began to sing, he nudged Goliath from a walk to a trot. And an hour later, when a distant train whistle pierced the air, he leaned over the horse's neck and begged him to run.

"Follow me." Dan urged a lathered Ranger into the lead. He nodded to a path leading east through the trees.

Stone nodded. Speed was essential, but so was secrecy. If they could avoid the main road into town without losing time, they might be able to get the jump on Franklin. Oaks lined the path, blinding Stone to what lay ahead. Then all at once, they hit open space. Open space that butted up against railroad tracks. Tracks that still rattled from a train that hadn't yet come to a halt at the station.

Thank you, God!

"Come on, Goliath. Almost there," Stone urged. "I promise to pamper you for a week after this."

The horse, noble beast that he was, stretched his stride just a little wider. Stone murmured praise in his ear and gave him his head. Whatever the animal had to give, Stone would take. For Lily.

The first buildings came into view, and Dan signaled with a wave of his hand for Stone to cross to the east side of the tracks, where stockyards and cotton gins would greet them instead of houses and storefronts. Stone followed without question — until they passed the train station. Where was Dan going? Instinct screamed at Stone to split off down W. 8th toward the depot, but years of proven trust kept him following his partner on the perpendicular trail down S. 9th. They passed a flour mill, a cotton yard, and even a gin before Dan finally turned down E. Collin. There, they crossed the tracks, and Dan directed Ranger south toward one of the many freight platforms along the rail line. A painted sign advertised Frank Root's Livery. At once, Dan's intent became clear. Hide the horses.

Scout the area. Locate Franklin and Lily before giving away their position. Indian-like stealth instead of a cavalry charge. The wiser option.

A man forking hay into a feed rack frowned at them when they brought their mounts to a halt beside the small corral to the right of the main building. He eyed the lather on the horses' chests with stark disapproval. He leaned the pitchfork against the wall and stomped over, no doubt ready to blister their hides for their treatment of their mounts. But when his gaze climbed to Dan's face, the creases of anger on his brow cleared into lines of concern. He broke into a jog.

"What's wrong, Barrett? Never known you to push Ranger like this before."

"A little girl's life never hung in the balance before."

The man slid a leg through the corral's fence slats, bent his body, and emerged on the other side. As soon as Stone and Dan dismounted, he collected their reins and clucked soothingly to the exhausted animals.

"I'll pay double your boarding fee, Frank, if you cool them down for us and see to their care. We pushed them through the night."

"Don't you worry none," he said, already

leading the horses toward the shade of the stable. "I'll reward these two warriors right and proper." He called to a lad already inside and handed the reins over with instructions for the boy to start rubbing them down. Then he pivoted and pierced Dan with a thoughtful stare. "Had another beast come in this morning in similar condition. Wasn't as lathered, but I could tell he'd been ridden hard."

Stone had started scouting the best route to take between buildings to get to the depot unseen when the livery owner's words carried to him. He spun and nearly lunged at the man. "Was it a palomino? Fancy tooling on the saddle?"

"Yep. Along with a dun mare I recognized from Thompson's Livery down in Steward's Mill."

Franklin.

"Did he have a child with him? A girl?"

Frank leaned a shoulder against the livery wall. "Yep. Said it was his daughter. Didn't look much like him, though. Her bein' blond and him bein' dark."

Stone's heart thumped wildly. They'd been here. They were close. "How long ago?"

"First thing this mornin'. Said they was gonna grab a bite at his hotel before catchin'

348

the train. Fellow said he'd send for his horse once he got the girl home."

"How'd she look?" Dan asked.

Stone held his breath, bracing for the answer. *Please let her be all right.*

"Couldn't see much of her. Fellow had her wrapped in a blanket. Carryin' her while she slept. All I could see was her hair." Frank shrugged. "Truth to tell, I was more concerned with the horses than the kid. That palomino was limpin' a bit. Had a rock in his hoof."

Stone shifted his gaze to Dan. "He probably dosed her with laudanum."

Dan nodded. "Good way to keep her from causing a scene when they board. It'll mean she won't be able to run away from him, too. Retrievin' her won't be easy."

Stone clenched his jaw. "Then we'll just have to retrieve *him* instead."

Dan grinned.

"So . . . how do you want this to play out?" Dan asked from his position in the alleyway across from the Commercial Hotel.

Stone scanned the street. Too many people coming and going, what with the hotel across the way and the boarding house on the other side of the alley wall. "Long-lost friend. Anything else would draw too much attention."

Dan nodded then slid his revolver from his holster. Stone opted for a blade.

They'd already scouted the platform and surrounding area. No sign of Franklin. But then, he'd wait until the last minute to board, not wanting anyone to grow too suspicious about him carting around a sleeping child who was well past the age of being carried.

Behind them, a train whistle pierced the morning air with its final call for boarding. A minute later, a handful of businessmen exited the hotel. Then a family with a pair of squabbling kids. Then two ladies with fancy plumes on their hats. Stone scanned each face, tension radiating through him, ready to strike.

Franklin was a hulking brute with long, straggly hair and a penchant for wearing buckskin britches dripping with fringe. The man's costume begged the dime novelists of the world to immortalize him on the page, but as far as Stone knew, no one had. Restored a bit of his faith in the authorial profession.

Another man exited the hotel. Tall. Broad shoulders. Sack suit. Bowler hat. Well-trimmed hair. Stone nearly looked past him until the man tugged a young boy out from behind him. The lad, clothed in worn trousers, baggy shirt, and knit cap, didn't seem to fit with the immaculate man. And he staggered about as if he wasn't sure where the ground was. Stone's nape tingled. Something wasn't right.

Stone took a step out of the alley, needing to get closer, to try to make out the faces.

"What are you doing?" Dan hissed.

"That could be them. The man and the boy. Franklin could have changed their clothes."

Dan edged closer. "Are you sure? If we go now and it's not them, we risk scaring him off."

"And if it *is* them and we don't go, he could get Lily on that train." Pulse roaring in his ears, Stone took another step. If only he could see their faces.

Dan's voice echoed behind him. "Make the call."

Stone hesitated, his gaze combing over the man making his way toward the station with the boy then shifting back to the handful of other people exiting the hotel. No one else matched Franklin's build.

His gut told him to go. His *spirit* told him to go.

"We go."

Decision made, the men wasted no time.

Hiding their drawn weapons in the folds of their coats, they laughed and jostled each other as they made their way toward the depot. Stretching their stride to make up ground, they circled around and came at Franklin from the side. Dan waved at an imaginary comrade to excuse their change of direction while Stone steered them directly toward the boy.

"Walt Franklin?" Stone called out. "Is that you?"

The man's shoulders flinched, but he didn't turn. Stone grinned. He didn't need him to turn. The flinch gave him away.

"It *is* you!" Stone and Dan maneuvered around him, cutting off his path to the station. "I haven't seen you in a coon's age, you old rascal. And look, you're all gussied up. I almost didn't recognize you."

Franklin twisted his face to glare at Stone, finally removing all doubt of his identity. "Get out of my way, Stone," he growled through gritted teeth as he smiled at the few people who had slowed to observe the reunion.

"And the lad," Dan enthused loudly. "You must've grown a foot, boy. I wonder if I can still hoist you on my shoulders like I used to when you were little."

Stone slung his left arm over Franklin's

shoulders, fanning out his coat to disguise the blade that he shoved against his rival's side. He twisted the point just enough to let Franklin feel the threat and release his hold on Lily.

When Franklin's grip loosened, Dan holstered his weapon and with an exaggerated grunt, lifted Lily over his head. Her glazed eyes registered no change as she flopped into her new position like a half-stuffed doll. Dan kept hold of her hands to protect her from falling backward. "Hold on to your uncle Dan now, and I'll give you a ride."

"We don't have time for a ride," Franklin admonished, though Stone's blade kept him from moving to stop them. "Our train is boarding."

"I'll gallop the boy down to the freight platform then meet you back at the main station," Dan said. He took off with a skipping stride toward the freight platform, making appropriate horse noises. Only Stone knew the detour he would take, escaping with Lily back to the livery. Dan would see to her protection.

Stone would see to Franklin.

28

"I don't take kindly to people stealing my bounty." Stone growled through teeth clenched into the shape of a grin for the sake of the other passengers approaching the platform.

"Then maybe you shouldn't have put Dorchester off." Franklin tried to twist away from the point of the knife, but Stone's iron grip on his shoulder held him fast. "The man's not exactly patient, you know. Your little stunt of taking the girl to Barrett's ranch gave me the permission I needed to jump the bounty. If you'd been serious about collectin', you'd have had the girl back in Houston by now."

Stone kept his voice hard as he forced Franklin onto the platform and toward the line of people waiting to board. "There were complications."

Franklin snorted. "Yeah. I heard about your *complications.* Fell for a skirt. Never pegged you for the gullible type, Hammond."

"Tell me something." Stone turned to smile at a passing lady. "Did Dorchester tell you Miss Atherton has legal custody of the kid?"

"Who told you that? The teacher?" He guffawed. "What'd she do? Blink her eyes at you until you believed her lies?"

Stone's fingers bit into the man's shoulders harder than necessary. Hard enough to make the big man bend slightly at the knees to escape the pain. "She had a paper. Signed by a judge. A paper a colleague of mine in Austin verified. Dorchester played us."

"Ease up, man." Franklin winced. Reluctantly, Stone dialed back the pressure. He had a role to play, after all. And it wasn't a chivalrous part.

The family from the hotel with the quarrelsome kids slowed the steady progress of the line as one of the boys threw a tantrum and refused to board. Stone held Franklin back a few paces, not wanting to get too close to anyone. No one besides Franklin needed to hear what he was about to say.

"Why do you think I've wasted all this time wooing a dratted schoolmarm?" Stone turned his head and spat. "I ain't about to be hauled away on kidnapping charges. Even if I snatched the girl and got her to Houston, what's to stop the teacher from pressing charges against me? Or you, for that matter."

Franklin shrugged. "You could kill her."

Stone fought down a gag. Kill Charlotte? He couldn't even pluck a hair from her head without regretting the pain it would cause her. "Better to woo her, gain her trust, and not have to worry about a hangman's noose. You know how fickle women are." He eyed Franklin knowingly. "Give 'em a little affection, make 'em promises, and soon they'll be selling out their own kid for a chance at running away with a handsome devil like myself and the fat reward I'll earn. 'Course, if I happen to take the reward and get the running away done before she catches on, well, that's just a lesson learned, ain't it?"

Franklin shook his head, a chuckle of admiration rumbling from his chest. "You always were a wily one, Hammond."

Stone urged him one step closer to the train. The line was moving again now that the boy's father had wrangled his screaming son and forced him up the steps. One after another, the passengers boarded. Link after link, the chain shortened, until only two people stood between Franklin and the railcar.

"Go to Dorchester," Stone commanded, pressing the knife just a little closer to make sure Franklin understood the importance of compliance. "Tell him I don't appreciate his interference. I'll have the girl to him before the end of the month, and I'll expect full compensation. If he doesn't like the delay, that's his problem. He should've leveled with me from the beginning."

"I ain't your errand boy, Stone."

"No, but you're Dorchester's lap dog. You'll tell him." Stone ushered him a step closer to the train, but a subtle change in the way Franklin moved set Stone's instincts flaring.

In a blink, Franklin reached across his midsection and drew a pistol from a shoulder holster under his coat. Stone did the only thing he could think of — he threw his body hard against Franklin, pinning his still-bent arm to his chest.

"I'm gonna miss you, man," Stone declared, embracing a struggling Franklin to him in a bear hug he hoped looked more like a farewell offering than the stranglehold it was. If Franklin managed to get his finger on the trigger, he could blow a hole through them both. Stone was banking on the man's self-preservation restraining him, but a man eager to make a name for himself was unpredictable at best. Stone needed to claim control. Fast.

Careful to keep his knife arm on the inside of Franklin's coat as he wrapped him up, Stone inched the blade toward the tender flesh of the man's underarm. Just a little higher. There!

He jutted the knife upward in a sharp thrust. Franklin grunted.

"Drop the gun or I push it in to the hilt," Stone growled in his ear. The blade was only about an inch into the fleshy part of his side beneath his armpit. Far enough to draw blood, but not far enough to do any real damage. A full thrust, though, could sever a blood vessel. Franklin stilled, recognizing his peril.

Stone gave him a few rough pats on the back, jiggling the wound painfully against the partially embedded blade, encouraging him to comply. Franklin swore under his breath.

A throat cleared nearby. "Time to board, sir," the porter stated. "We have a schedule to maintain."

"Drop it and get on the train," Stone ground out, "or I'll drop you on the platform with a gusher that will drain you before the doc arrives." He pounded Franklin's back again then raised his voice. "Take care of yourself, Walt." Stone tightened his hug. Franklin groaned.

Finally, something shifted against Stone's belly. Keeping his grip against Franklin's upper body, Stone sucked in his abdomen and pulled his hips back. A hard metallic object slid down his front and thudded onto his boot.

Stone immediately released Franklin, slid his knife free, and gave him a *friendly* shove toward the steps. Franklin stumbled, but righted himself before the porter could offer assistance.

"See you at the end of the month." Without looking down, Stone slid his foot out from under Franklin's pistol then covered it with the sole of his boot. He waved along with the others who'd gathered on the platform, yet he didn't relax his guard until he caught a glimpse through a window of Franklin taking a seat near the front of the railcar, his right hand gripping his left arm and pinching it close to his side. He'd not be making any mad dashes to leap from the train.

Still, Stone pinned his stare on the man, not taking any chances. He didn't look away until the whistle blew and the train chugged past the station. Only when the Houston & Texas Central Railway sported nothing but empty tracks as far as his eye could see did Stone give up his vigil and head back to the livery, one gun heavier than when he'd started out.

Frank Root, the livery owner, met Stone at the stable door. "Barrett took the girl to my place." He pointed deeper into town and gave a handful of directions. "She was still pretty groggy, but she was startin' to come around. Jabbered about Dead-Eye Dan ridin' to her rescue so much it almost put Barrett to the blush."

Stone grinned. Lily was coming back to herself. *Thank you, God!* But the urge to see her for himself throbbed in his chest. He murmured his thanks and set off down the road, stretching his stride to its full length.

"My missus will have the kid back to rights in two shakes," Frank called out after him. "Don't you worry."

Stone lifted a hand to show that he'd heard but didn't break stride. Lily was his responsibility. He was glad for the help, but he intended to see to her care himself from here on out.

When he reached Frank's home, he pushed through a small wooden gate. The creak of the hinges brought a scruffy brown dog out from under the porch like a rock from a slingshot. The mongrel barked and ran circles around Stone's boots, nipping at his ankles. Stone ignored him and marched forward undeterred.

An apron-clad woman materialized at the front door. "Hush, Jasper!" She pointed an imperious finger at the tree shading the porch's corner. "Go sit over there and leave the poor man alone."

Jasper stopped circling and raised his head to look at his mistress. He gave a final defiant bark then sauntered over to the tree as if it were where he'd been intending to go all along.

"Sorry about that," she said, opening the door wide as Stone climbed the steps. "He's extra protective when Frank's away. You Mr. Hammond?"

Stone fingered his hat brim and dipped his chin. "Yes, ma'am. I'm here for Lily."

A smile lit Mrs. Root's face, deepening the lines around her mouth in a way that made it impossible not to curve one's lips in return. "Such a doll, that one. Even with all she's been through, bless her heart. She's inside."

Stone removed his hat and crossed the threshold.

"In the parlor around the corner to the right," his hostess directed, tacitly giving him permission to go on without waiting on her. Permission Stone gladly accepted.

Crossing into the parlor, he was nearly felled by a blond-haired missile striking his knees. Lily threw her arms around his waist and pressed her cheek to his belly.

Stone reflexively reached down and cupped the side of her head with his hand, his thumb running over her soft tresses. She was alive, safe, protected. Suddenly, his throat felt scratchy, and he had to clear it before his voice would work properly. "You seem to be doing better, squirt."

Her sweet face tilted up to look at him. "Miss Lottie said you would come. I knew I just had to be brave and wait. But the yucky medicine that man made me drink kept making me sleepy." She released her hold on his waist and twisted her lips in obvious disgust. "I finally get to have a real adventure, and I don't even remember half of it." She crossed her arms over her chest and stomped her foot. The fierce action threw her off balance. Stone grabbed her shoulder to steady her. Apparently the laudanum's effects hadn't completely abated.

"That man is on a train headed far away

from here, so you don't have to worry about him anymore." Stone patted her awkwardly then stepped back.

"Oh, I'm not worried," Lily assured him. "Mr. Barrett told me you were putting the fear of God into him." She gave a little nod then started reciting Scripture as if she had the book of Proverbs open in front of her. " 'The fear of the Lord is the beginning of wisdom. . . . The fear of the Lord is to hate evil: pride, and arrogancy, and the evil way. . . . By mercy and truth iniquity is purged: and by the fear of the Lord men depart from evil.' " She glanced back up at him. "Now that you've put the fear of God into him, he's sure to be a much nicer man."

Somewhere in the corner, Dan sputtered and coughed. Stone shot a glare in his direction.

"Well, that's not exactly . . ." Was he supposed to tell a nine-year-old child that he'd threatened the man with physical pain and possible death in order to keep him in line? He could just imagine what Charlotte's reaction to that explanation would be. He swallowed. "I did my best to convince him to change his ways, but no one can force someone to fear the Lord. They have to make that decision on their own."

Lily nibbled her lip thoughtfully. "I suppose you're right."

Mrs. Root bustled into the room just then, saving Stone from more truth-skirting. "Look what I found in one of my daughter's old trunks." She held up a blue calico dress with a small lace collar. "It might be a tad longer than you're used to, but I bet it would work." She held out her hand to Lily. "Come on, sweetness. Let's go try it on and get you looking like a girl again."

Lily grinned. "It's so pretty!"

Taking the girl's hand, Mrs. Root led Lily out of the room and down the hall.

Once the sound of a door clicking shut signaled their privacy, Stone strode over to where Dan sprawled in an armchair and flopped into the matching rocker across from him.

"Told Franklin I'd have Lily to Dorchester by the end of the month."

Dan let out a quiet whistle. "Only two weeks away. Doesn't give us much time to gather the evidence we need to pressure the man into calling off the hunt."

Stone tossed his hat onto the settee to his right, leaned back, and grimaced. "I know, but I had to make him think that I still intended to bring her back. Otherwise he'd just send more bounty hunters after us. Now that Franklin knows I have the girl, my options are limited."

"What reason did you give for the delay?" Dan extracted his leg from the arm of the chair where it'd been dangling and planted his foot on the floor to face Stone more squarely.

Stone winced. "Said I needed the time to seduce the teacher into giving me the girl willingly so I could get around her having actual custody of the kid."

"And I thought *I* was bad when it came to women."

"Well, what else would a man like Franklin have believed?"

Dan held up a hand to ward off Stone's defensiveness. "I ain't passin' judgment. It's actually a pretty good ploy. Explains Miss Atherton's presence at the ranch and buys us a little time. But that time will do us no good if we can't get evidence against Dorchester."

The two spent several minutes tossing around ideas, none of which carried much merit. "We need to find a handful of businessmen who'd be willing to testify to Dorchester's unscrupulous business practices. Surely there'd be enough animosity somewhere to flush out the truth." Stone punched his fist against his thigh. There *had* to be a way. *Please, God. Let there be a way.*

Dan huffed out a breath and sagged back into his seat. "But how do we identify who these business partners are?"

"We could use Grandfather's secret ledger."

The childish voice drew Stone's head around. Lily stood in the middle of the parlor rug, her new blue dress swirling around her legs as she twisted from side to side.

"I've never looked inside, but I know where he keeps it. It probably has some names in it."

For the first time since Stone had left Dan's ranch, he found a genuine reason to smile.

29

Charlotte sat at the window of her new upstairs bedchamber, staring down the Hawk's Haven drive until a quiet rap sounded against her open door. Charlotte blinked and slowly turned to find Marietta Hawkins stepping into the room with a tray bearing a bowl of what smelled like beef stew along with a pair of corn muffins.

"You know, the front room downstairs has a lovely view of the road, too. And the time will pass much more quickly with the boys running about, distracting you." Marietta raised her brows in a slightly chiding manner as she set the tray on the desk.

"They're not causing you any trouble, are they?" The broth smelled heavenly, but too much anxiety churned in her stomach to allow an appetite.

"No, no," Marietta assured her. "I think John worries that you've taken ill, though."

Charlotte bit her lip. "I'm sorry. It's

just . . . I *need* to watch for them. I can't explain it. It's as if watching for them, concentrating all my energy on praying them back home, is helping them return safely." Hearing her feelings in words made her shake her head. So foolish. As if her waiting at the window had anything at all to do with Stone's ability to bring Lily home. "I know it's silly —"

"Not at all." Marietta circled the bed and sat on the edge of the mattress near Charlotte's chair. "Women have been praying their men home since Adam and Eve left the garden. And you better believe it makes a difference. I shudder to think about the poor fellows who don't have a mother or sister, wife or sweetheart praying on their behalf. It doesn't matter how strong and capable our men are, they still need the Lord's protection. I might not be able to guard them against an outlaw's bullet or a raging bull's horns, but I can be on my knees, petitioning the One who can." She laid a hand on Charlotte's arm, a touch that communicated understanding while infusing quiet courage.

Charlotte covered Marietta's hand with her own. "Thank you."

She truly didn't know what she would have done the past few days without this kind woman. After the incident at the cabin, Marietta had insisted Charlotte and the children take up residence in the big house, and without Mr. Barrett around to argue, no one gainsaid her. She'd kept Charlotte so busy the first day — in the kitchen, weeding the garden, even performing Beethoven on the out-of-tune piano Mr. Hawkins kept in the front room, all while distracting her with constant, frivolous chatter — that Charlotte hadn't had time to fall apart before Stone's message arrived that evening.

Glancing down at the crumpled paper in her lap, Charlotte slid her hand from Marietta's and smoothed the creases from the small sheet she'd read countless times over the last two days.

Have Lily. Horses need to recover. Be back Saturday.

Such a brief message. So many questions still swirled through her mind. But he'd given her the one piece of information that mattered most. Lily was safe. Stone was safe. The rest could wait.

"Hmm . . . I suppose the view *is* better up here." Marietta stood and moved to the window. For a moment, her features took on a degree of longing that distracted Charlotte from her own thoughts.

Perhaps her new friend's understanding

stemmed from more than just her compassionate nature.

As fast as it had appeared, however, the expression vanished behind Marietta's gracious smile. "Well," she said, turning away from the view, "I promised the boys I would dig out my father's chess set. Better see to it before they accuse me of forgetting." She patted Charlotte's shoulder as she passed but then paused at the door. "Perhaps you'll come down after you've had a bite and play for us again. Mama's piano never sounded so good as when you played it. I know it did *my* heart good to hear the cheerful tunes."

All at once, Charlotte was struck by how selfish she was being. She'd closeted herself away with her own fears, never once considering that others might be just as worried as she. Well, no more. If a little music on an imperfectly tuned piano could bring this dear woman respite, Charlotte would gladly play all afternoon. Prayer was important, but so was trust. Time to leave those who were out of her reach in God's hands and tend to those who were close by. "I'll be down shortly."

Charlotte joined the others downstairs and was immediately swept into the front room

370

and deposited on the piano bench. The boys abandoned their chess game to call out requests, as did Marietta, and soon the house was filled with music. Lively, cheerful tunes to banish the heavy atmosphere hanging over the ranch. Stephen confiscated a pair of spoons from the kitchen and fiddled with them until he found a steady *clickity-clack* rhythm to match her beat. Marietta clapped her hands and tapped her toes while John climbed into Charlotte's lap and started taking over the music without missing a beat.

"Do 'Turkey in the Straw,' Miss Lottie!" Stephen called when the final notes of "The Yellow Rose of Texas" faded.

"All right." Charlotte leaned down and whispered to John, "You take the melody. I'll add some ornamentation."

John grinned. It was their favorite game. He started in on the melody with his right hand, the simple notes clear in the air, his tempo sedate. Then he added the left hand and began to increase the speed. Once Charlotte caught his rhythm, she closed her eyes, listening to the unsung harmonies that danced through her mind. She added a plucky bass line first then stretched around John's back to reach the upper register. Soon there were entire families of turkeys dancing in the straw.

Stephen tossed his spoons aside and jumped to his feet. "Come on, Miss Hawkins. Let's dance."

Marietta chuckled but didn't resist answering his summons. Soon the two were locked at the elbows, swinging about the center of the room. Charlotte laughed along with them, her heart feeling lighter than it had in days. This was what she'd needed — to be surrounded by friends and music and gaiety. Why had she ever thought being alone would be better?

Feeling inspired, Charlotte improvised on her improvisation, adding a military beat in the bass to imitate drums while trilling the upper registers like a pair of flutes. John adjusted the melody to match her new beat and soon Stephen and Marietta kicked up their knees, threw out their elbows, and marched in vigorous circles about the room. After a few minutes of that, Charlotte threw in some syncopation, reminiscent of the Negro spirituals she'd always enjoyed. The dance changed again. Marietta grabbed handfuls of her skirts and swished the fabric in front of her as she bounced lightly on her toes. Stephen kicked front and then back and then repeated it while waving his hands to the sides.

John let go a giggle, a rare sound from the quiet boy. Charlotte kissed his head and sent a prayer of thanks heavenward for the blessing of joy.

The joy of the Lord is your strength. Her mother's favorite verse whisked through her mind. Charlotte had never understood it until now. She'd always thought her mother simply used it as an excuse to sing whenever she felt the urge. When one was already joyful, after all, she didn't really need strength, did she? No, it was when worry and anger and fear consumed a person that she needed God's strength the most.

Only now did Charlotte realize that one could choose joy even in times of despair. God's blessings were so prevalent, a person could always find reason to rejoice. One simply had to trust God enough to leave her problems at His feet and open her eyes to the blessings already provided. Music. Friendship. Laughter. They had been here all the time, but Charlotte had shut them out. Now they flowed through her, strengthening her. Giving her hope, renewed optimism, and a level of contentment she'd never experienced while sitting at the window.

"*I* want to dance!" a newcomer shouted.

Charlotte's head whipped around. "Lily!"

Discordant notes clanged. Yanking her hands from the keys, she wiggled out from beneath John, setting him to the side of her on the bench. Then she shot to her feet and ran across the room. "Oh, Lily!" Charlotte threw herself to her knees on the rug in front of Lily and hugged the girl to her. "You're back. Praise God, you're back!" Tears welled, but she closed her eyes against them and reveled in the feel of her daughter — yes, *her* daughter — pressed against her chest.

"Of course I'm back, Miss Lottie." The fierce way Lily clung to Charlotte belied the outright confidence of her words. "Mr. Hammond always retrieves what he sets out after. Isn't that right, Mr. Barrett?" She looked behind her to the man in question for confirmation.

It took Dan a minute to drag his gaze away from the very lovely Marietta, who was still a tad flushed and out of breath from her dance with Stephen. "Uh . . . yep. That's right." He finally nodded at Lily, which earned him a smile from more than one female in the room. "Stone's got the tenacity of a bloodhound. He never comes home empty-handed."

Stone. Charlotte's gaze locked with his. She stilled at the intensity there. His amber eyes overflowed with promises. To protect. To provide. To overcome. For *her.*

Her breath caught at that last thought. He did what he did because he was honorable and wanted right to prevail. He did it to keep Lily safe. Yet the longer Charlotte held his gaze, the louder the true message sounded in her heart. *For you. He's doing it all for you.*

Charlotte retreated from his gaze and the uncomfortable fluttery sensations it inspired in her belly. Squeezing Lily to her one more time, she took refuge in the familiar affection of children. This she understood. This was safe. And Lily's small body felt so wonderful tucked within her arms after so many days of separation. It was nearly impossible to let the girl go, but she did. For she owed a debt of gratitude to the one who had returned her. A debt she could never repay.

Slowly, Charlotte gained her feet and moved to stand in front of Stone. Chatter rose behind her as Stephen pestered Lily with questions about what had transpired since the night she'd been taken. Marietta quizzed Dan in similar fashion. No one seemed to be paying any attention to Charlotte and Stone.

"Thank you." The words fell softly from

her lips, so inadequate, yet she could find no others. "Thank you for bringing her back to me."

He said nothing. Just nodded. Then he raised his hand and stroked the length of her cheek with the backs of his fingers. Charlotte's eyes fluttered closed. Such tenderness nearly undid her. Nothing else in the room existed in that moment. Just his touch. His nearness. And the desire it stirred in her heart. A desire to belong to this man and no other for all the days of her life.

Her eyes flew open. What was she thinking? Worse, what was she doing? Pulse racing, she stepped back and glanced around, sure she'd find curious or even disapproving eyes on her. But no one was looking at her save John, still standing by the piano.

"Can I play for Lily, Miss Lottie?" he called out to her the moment their gazes met, as if he'd been patiently waiting for her to finish with Stone and look his way. "She wants to dance."

Lily immediately clapped her hands. "Oh yes, Miss Lottie. Please. It looked like so much fun."

And suddenly all eyes *were* on her. Warmth crept up Charlotte's neck and cheeks. "Of course you can play." Anything to get their eyes off of her. "I'll join you in a few minutes."

John scrambled onto the bench again and filled the room with the bouncy melody of "Oh! Susanna." Stephen took up his spoons again while Marietta twirled about the floor with Lily. Even Daniel Barrett slapped his thumb against his leg to the beat as he leaned against the wall.

Charlotte inched toward the piano, finding it surprisingly difficult to leave Stone's side despite her embarrassment at being caught so close to him. She had just begun a strong internal lecture to herself on the importance of proper decorum when Stone placed his hand on her arm and stopped not only her movement but her ability to form a coherent thought.

"Not just yet," he murmured. "I need to talk to you first."

She turned. "About what?"

"Dorchester."

Charlotte's stomach lurched. Was this where he told her he was leaving? He'd taken care of Franklin. Rescued Lily. She had no right to expect more from him. Just because he'd shared a few sunset walks with her didn't give her the right to make demands of him. Heaven knew he'd already done far more for her and the children than anyone else would have in his position.

"All . . . right." She inhaled a fortifying breath. "Shall we step into the hall?"

He nodded and shuffled sideways to let her pass through the doorway ahead of him. His hand found the indention of her back as she did so, and Charlotte had to press her lips together to restrain a sigh of pleasure. Why did his touch always have to melt her insides to syrup? If ever she needed to be strong, it was now. Determined to find her backbone, she pivoted to face him and effectively separated herself from his touch.

"So?" she queried, bracing her heart for the blow to come. "What did you need to tell me?"

"Dorchester's not going to stop coming after Lily, Charlotte. Not unless we make him stop. I've bought us a couple weeks, but I think we should make our move before then. Catch him off guard."

Charlotte blinked. Stone's words were so different from what she'd expected, it took a moment for her mind to sort them out. "What move?"

He smiled at her then, the lopsided grin of one eager to please yet unsure of the outcome. "Dan and I spent the last two days plotting, and I think we've come up with a solid plan, a way to get the upper hand with

Dorchester while ensuring he leaves Lily alone. For good."

"That sounds wonderful!" The fact that he wasn't saying good-bye was wonderful in and of itself, but to think he might have found a way to defeat Dorchester . . . why, it was enough to set Charlotte's heart humming with excitement. "Tell me."

His smile dimmed a bit, his expression growing cautionary. "You're not going to like it."

30

Stone watched Charlotte mentally brace herself. She inhaled, took a small step back with her left foot, then lowered her shoulders as she released her breath. What she didn't do was don that serene mask of hers that she'd always shielded herself with before. This time she looked him straight in the eye. All Charlotte. No wall.

"I'm ready."

Saints above, in that moment, with her turquoise eyes peering up at him with equal parts trust and determination, he couldn't have recounted his plan had Dorchester himself walked through the door and held a gun to his head. Why had he even brought up the issue anyway? They should be in there with the others, singing and dancing and celebrating Lily's return. But, no. In his infinite stupidity, he'd thought it'd be better to get the bad news over with first thing. Give her more time to get used to the idea before they actually had to put it into action.

"Stone?"

"Sorry. I . . . It can wait. I shouldn't have pulled you away." At least not for this. Now a kiss? That would have been a good reason to sequester her in the hallway. Man, he wanted to pull her into his arms like she'd done with Lily a few moments ago. Hold her close. Breathe in her delicate scent. Rub his bristled cheek against her soft hair until the strands tangled in his beard growth as they had during that first sunset stroll.

Charlotte rolled her eyes at him. "For heaven's sake, Stone Hammond. You can't drag a lady away on the pretext of urgent news — urgent, *unpleasan*t news — and then tell her it can wait. I'll be fretting all evening if you don't tell me now."

Yep. He'd bungled it, all right.

Charlotte's toe tapped against the floorboards. "Well? Spit it out."

"I'm going to take Lily back to Dorchester."

All color drained from Charlotte's face. Only then did Stone realize how his words must have sounded. Of all the idiotic ways to spit something out. He reached out, thinking to steady her, but she shook her head at him. Her slender throat worked up

and down as if she were trying to swallow
something distasteful.

"Lottie, I didn't mean that like it —"

She held up her hand to silence him. Then
she straightened her posture, raised her
chin, and met his gaze head-on. He
expected to see accusation. Betrayal. Denial.
But what he saw instead speared his heart
with so much pride, he thought he might
explode from it.

Trust. Her eyes still glowed with trust.

"All right. We take Lily back to
Dorchester. Then what?"

A mass of riotous feelings stampeded
through him like a runaway herd. And like
a steer caught up in the frenzy, he followed
the leader right over the cliff. He grabbed
Charlotte to him and kissed her. Fully. Pas-
sionately. With an ardency that bordered on
wildness.

Stone cupped her face in both his hands,
his thumbs stroking the satiny skin of her
cheeks as his mouth slanted over hers.
Shock vibrated through her, but she didn't
pull away. Instead, she clutched his
shoulders for balance. Taking that as permission, he dragged her against his chest, needing to feel her close, needing to stake his
claim.

She trusted him. This woman, who'd been

382

betrayed by one man after another over the course of her life, *trusted* him. Him — the man sent by her enemy to steal Lily from her.

Stone's arms tightened about her, his palms sliding over her back as he eradicated any distance between them. What little rational thought he retained warned he was moving too fast. He tried to rein himself in, to gentle the kiss, but just as he started to lift his head, Charlotte bounced up on her tiptoes and grabbed at his neck with her hands. As if the threat of losing her connection with him had galvanized her, she broke free of her shock and kissed him back with an innocent fervor that sent blood pounding through his veins far faster than cattle on stampede. Her fingers tangled in the hair at his nape. A tiny mewling sound echoed in her throat. And her lips — her glorious, soft, willing lips — pressed into his until he swore he could taste the same desire in her that raged through him.

The reins were forgotten. Stone reached around her neck to the back of her head, positioning her for his renewed attentions, but the sound of boot heels scuffing along the wooden floor pulled him back.

"I see you're explaining our plan in vivid detail."

Charlotte stiffened at the sound of Dan's voice. Stone immediately tucked her head against his chest to shelter her from their visitor's gaze then shot a glare at his partner, one that promised slow and painful retribution.

"She seems to be taking the news better than we expected."

"Shut up," Stone growled.

Dan laughed. "Oh, don't mind me," he said, holding his hands out in a gesture of surrender that was anything but. "I was just heading to the kitchen to fetch some water for Miss Hawkins. All that dancing has plumb wore her out."

"Get on with it, then."

"I'm goin'."

Yeah. With the speed of a tortoise on a broken leg. Stone narrowed his gaze, zeroing in on the gun belt slung low on Dan's hips and the target it presented in the rear. He calculated all the ways he could land a swift kick in the designated zone, but unfortunately, all methods required releasing Charlotte — something he wasn't yet willing to do. So he bit the inside of his cheek and waited.

"Oh," the limping turtle offered as he finally reached the doorway leading to the kitchen, "I happened to notice that Mr.

Hawkins's study is unoccupied if you wished to continue your *discussion* in there. Might be a good idea to go over the plan someplace where the kids are less likely to see . . . er . . . hear."

The tiny embarrassed groan that leaked out of Charlotte as she turned to hide her face more fully against Stone's chest was the last straw. Stone jabbed his right hand into his coat pocket and pulled out the first object he encountered with sufficient heft. His coin pouch. He hurled it at Dan's grinning face, forcing the man to forgo his snickering long enough to duck. He wasn't fast enough, though. The pouch collided with Dan's hat, sending it flying behind him. Not quite as satisfying as a black eye, but Stone would take it.

"All right, all right." Dan backed away, his eyes still flashing with far too much glee. "I accept your bribe. Mum's the word." He covered his mouth with his hand and backed into the kitchen, finally leaving Stone and Charlotte in peace.

The mood well and truly broken, Stone dropped a quick kiss on the top of Charlotte's head and urged her toward the closed door on her right that led to the study. "Come on, sweetheart. He might be as ornery as a buckin' horse in a cactus saddle, but he's right about one thing. It's better if the others don't overhear."

Lifting her chin, she separated herself from him. Her cheeks blazed like a rosebush in full bloom, but her eyes sparked with determination. "All right, but you'll be staying on your own side of the desk for the duration of this conversation, Mr. Hammond. Understood?"

Stone bit back a grin and nodded. "Yes, ma'am."

As he opened the door and followed her into the study, he couldn't help but notice that the schoolmarm tone he'd always found so off-putting in the past didn't bother him in the least when it came from a mouth still swollen and moist from his kiss.

Charlotte gripped her hands together as she entered the study, trying desperately to still their trembling. What had she been thinking? To allow him to kiss her like that where anyone could walk by and see. Where someone *had* walked by and seen. A new wave of heat flooded her face. Mercy. A teacher could lose her position for such a display.

But then, she wasn't really a teacher anymore, was she? And after worrying about Stone and Lily for three and a half days, seeing them both home — whole and unharmed — she hadn't been able to hold her emotions in check. She'd tried. Heaven knew, she'd tried. She'd not thrown her arms about his neck like she had with Lily, even when her muscles physically ached with the desire to do so. She'd averted her gaze from his face as much as humanly possible and nearly escaped to take refuge at the piano until he'd lured her into the hall.

His touch had shattered her pretense, though, and captured all her attention. Leaving her vulnerable. Exposed. When his mouth met hers, she'd been helpless to resist. All the worry, all the longing she'd stored up since they'd arrived at the ranch, had erupted like a geyser out of a heart long dormant.

She'd thrown herself into his kiss as if it were the key to her survival. That was the true reason Daniel Barrett's interruption embarrassed her so deeply. Not because he'd caught her *allowing* Stone's kiss, but because she'd been such a willing participant. No decorum. No restraint. Just a staggering relief that he was safe, and a love so strong she couldn't contain it.

Love. Charlotte rounded the large mahogany desk and slowly lowered herself into Mr. Hawkins's chair, her right palm pressed firmly against her belly. Keeping her gaze glued to the desk, she fought to shove the word back into the dark prison it had escaped from. This wasn't love. It was just . . . strong friendship? Camaraderie? Her heart was still protected. It had to be.

"You're awfully quiet, Lottie." Stone laid his arm atop the desk, palm up, the invitation obvious. "Don't let Dan's teasing bother you. He doesn't mean anything by it. Just likes giving me a hard time is all."

She stared at his hand. The lines creasing his palm. The relaxed fingers slightly curved. She wanted to place her hand in his — to renew that connection. But she dared not. Not when her self-control was so weak. So she pretended she didn't see it as she lifted her chin and schooled her features into a prim expression. "We're here to discuss your plan, I believe, not Mr. Barrett's antics."

Next, she pretended she didn't see the flicker of disappointment in his eyes as he straightened and withdrew his hand. And after that, she pretended not to feel the stab of loneliness that cut through her when he shuttered his own emotions away. Well, for a few seconds at least. Until the warmth drained from his gaze, and she nearly shivered at the loss.

Thrusting both hands out onto the desk

toward him, she slouched forward. "I'm sorry, Stone. You didn't deserve that." Treating him like a recalcitrant child was unpardonable after all he'd done for her. For Lily. "I just . . ." *Plain speaking, Charlotte. Don't be a coward.* "I'm afraid of what you make me feel."

She dropped her chin. There was no possible way she could look at him after saying *that.* Harsh seconds passed. The only audible sound, the thumping of her own heart. He didn't say anything. Or do anything. Her heart pounded faster, harder. Her throat constricted. She'd done it now. Turned him away. No man liked to talk about feelings. Especially a rugged warrior of a man who probably viewed her company as nothing more than a pleasant way to pass the time.

Even as the thought presented itself, another argued. Hadn't he promised to pursue her when Lily's situation was resolved? A man wouldn't say something like that unless he meant it, would he? Or unless he was a clever rogue who used promises like that to woo women into his arms. No, Stone wouldn't do that. Her heart rebelled at the very idea. Yet hadn't her heart proven untrustworthy in the past?

Moisture gathered in her eyes, but she bit

her lip against the urge to let it roll down her cheeks. How desperate she must seem to him. The lonely spinster craving something so far above her reach. Stone Hammond — handsome, intelligent, valiant as any knight on a steed — he could do much better than her. He was just too kind to say the words. That's why he said nothing.

She needed to leave. Now. Barricade herself in her room. Away from his pity. His apology. Charlotte jerked her arms back toward herself and shoved to her feet, her mind focused solely on escape.

His hands captured hers before she cleared the desk. His strong, wonderful hands. Hands that had rescued Lily from Franklin. Hands that had cupped her cheeks a moment ago as if she were the most precious of treasures. Hands that now held her fast, as if promising never to let go.

"Wait, Charlotte." The raspy whisper didn't sound like the Stone she knew. No confidence. No swagger. He almost sounded as if his throat were as constricted as hers. "Please. I . . ."

She still couldn't bring herself to look at him, but she ceased trying to pull away from his hold.

"My feelings scare me, too."

Charlotte's head whipped around. Her gaze searched his face. The drawn line of his mouth. The tension working in his jaw. His eyes — gracious, his eyes. So intense. So sincere. Yet not without a flicker of unease, making the truth of his admission undeniable.

"I'm thirty-five years old, Charlotte. I'm rough around the edges, not much accomplished with book-learnin', and I've grown so accustomed to the seedy underbelly of life that I'm not sure I would know how to live amongst normal folk. I'm guilty of bloodshed and violence. I'm about as far your opposite as a man can get." He cocked a half grin at her, so self-deprecating it made her chest ache. "You're elegant. Refined. More educated than I could ever hope to be. And the way you play the piano? I doubt even one of God's angels could match it. You're loyal, dedicated, protective of those in your care . . . and honey, you're so dad-gummed beautiful it near suffocates me every time you unleash one of your smiles in my direction."

Charlotte shook her head at him, unable to believe what she was hearing. Stone loosened his grip just enough to caress the backs of her hands with his thumbs.

"I want you in my life, Charlotte Atherton.

391

More than I've ever wanted anything. And it scares the living daylights out of me. Because no matter how hard I fight or how long I wait, I have no guarantee you'll ever trust me with your heart."

The first tear slid past her lashes and down her cheek. Then a second. And a third. He knew. Knew how broken she was. How afraid she was to love a man who might someday betray her. She'd learned to trust him with Lily's safety, but with her heart? The shriveled organ throbbed painfully at the mere suggestion.

"I love you, Lottie, and I want to make you my wife." Stone's low voice rumbled between them. Ardent. Unwavering. Determined. "I'll pursue you," he vowed, "until a parson either joins us in marriage or speaks words over my grave."

It was too much. The riotous joy. The soul-stirring terror. But it was the image of him in the cold ground, lonely and unfulfilled, and the knowledge that she was the one who had put him there that sent her fleeing. A sob in her throat, she tore her hands away from his and ran.

31

Stone caught her before she reached the door. "Don't run from me, Charlotte." His voice was more plea than demand. Perhaps that was why she ceased trying to pull away from him.

He loosened his grasp on her wrist, praying he hadn't just made a mistake. She didn't snatch her arm away, but neither did she look at him. She just stared at the floor as if the answers to all her questions lay embedded in the wood.

He knew he'd frightened her when he'd spoken of his feelings, and perhaps it would have been wiser to let her go, to give her time and privacy to work through her thoughts. But when he'd seen the fear flare in her eyes and realized she was about to bolt, he'd acted on instinct. He couldn't let her go. Not now. Not ever.

Stepping closer, he turned his hold into a caress, stroking the pulse point on her wrist with the pad of his thumb. "We don't have to talk about this now, darlin'." Charlotte had a lot of years of hurt to get past before her heart would be willing to trust a man's love again. So he'd give her time to get used to the idea. And give himself time to prove worthy of that trust. "We have other things to discuss. Like Lily."

That brought her face up. Stone smiled. Nothing like a little prod at the cub to get the mama bear back in a fighting stance.

"Right." She cleared her throat and stood a little straighter. "The plan. You were supposed to explain."

He ignored the touch of accusation in her voice. It *had* been his fault they'd gotten away from the original topic. Stone leaned his shoulder against the wall near the door, his gaze never leaving Charlotte's face. "Lily told us about a secret book her grandfather keeps jammed in a crevice on the underside of his desk drawer. We're pretty sure it's a ledger, hopefully one containing blackmail evidence."

"Hopefully?" Charlotte's eyes narrowed.

Stone didn't flinch. "Just hear me out to the end, all right?" Although the end wasn't any better than the beginning. In fact, the worst part was yet to come.

Charlotte bit her lip, hesitated, then gave

a tiny nod. She was trying so hard, God bless her. He wished he could make it easier, somehow shrink the chasm he was asking her to leap over, but it was what it was. No amount of pretty words would change it.

"Lily said it looked the same as the books Dorchester trained her to find in other men's offices, and those books all contained business records. We have every reason to believe this book will be the same. And the fact that he hides it away increases the likelihood that it contains illicit accounts. Dorchester doesn't know Lily discovered his hiding place, so he has no reason to suspect that we would make a play for it."

"What kind of play are we making?" Charlotte asked. "And when you say *we*, you best be including me because there's no way on God's green earth that you are keeping me out of this. If Lily's going, then I'm going." She tugged her wrist from his gentle hold and crossed her arms over her chest, giving him a glare that no doubt sent lads in short pants scuttling off to schoolroom corners after being caught making mischief.

"I will never take Lily away from you, Charlotte. You have my word." Stone gauged her reaction and inwardly rejoiced when a bit of rigidity seeped from her shoulders.

"Not only are you included in this plan, you play an essential role. I can't carry it off without you."

Her arms didn't uncross, but they loosened. He took that as a good sign.

"Once we get all the details settled, you will travel ahead of us to Houston and position yourself near Dorchester Hall. You'll need some way to disguise yourself, of course, but Dan seemed to think Marietta could assist with that. Anyway, once you are in place, I will arrive with Lily in tow. After my run-in with Franklin, Dorchester will be expecting me. I'll hand her over and demand payment. Then you'll come barging in as if you followed me and make as big of a commotion as you can to keep Dorchester distracted. I'll retrieve the ledger then get you out of the house."

"What about Lily? We can't just leave her there!" Charlotte's arms dropped to her sides. "If Dorchester discovers what we've done, there's no telling how he might take his anger out on her."

Stone pushed away from the wall and placed his hands at her waist, afraid she might try to bolt again. "We'll have to leave her there at least until nightfall. But I'll have my man in Austin watching the house. We can give her a signal to use if she gets into trouble."

Charlotte shook her head in large, fierce wags. "No. It's too dangerous. I won't have her at risk —"

"She already agreed to the plan, Lottie." Stone kept his voice low, steady, hoping to calm her, but she only struggled harder.

"Of course she agreed. She's nine! What does she know of danger? To her it's all a big adventure, like something out of her Dead-Eye Dan novels."

"The child just endured a kidnapping," Stone reminded her. "She's hardly innocent of danger."

"But she's naïve. She simply trusts you to save her again. She doesn't know all the things that could go wrong." Charlotte fisted her hands around the lapels of his coat and shook his entire torso. Or tried. "As impressive as you are, Stone, you can't guarantee that she'll not be hurt. You can't control all the variables. There are too many."

He ran his hands up from her waist to wrap them around her back and slowly pull her to him. She fought against him, but he was stronger. Little by little, he closed the circle of his arms until she stood trapped against his chest.

The fight went out of her then, and she

sagged into him. He tucked her head beneath his chin and stroked the small line of skin along her nape, between her collar and her hair, doing his best to help her relax.

"You're right, Charlotte," he murmured close to her ear. "I can't control all the variables. No human can. All I can do is use the experience and talents God has given me and trust Him with the outcome. There are very few guarantees in this life. The few that do exist come from God. The guarantee that He will love us and be faithful to us. He never promised us a life without hardship. In fact, I seem to recollect several places in Scripture where He promises that we *will* face such things. But even in that, He vows to be by our side through it all, to give us the strength to endure whatever comes."

"I'm scared, Stone." The words were barely audible, muffled as they were by his chest. But he could feel their vibrations against his heart. "I don't want to lose her."

And I don't want to lose you. "We'll both be there, sweetheart. Watching over her. Protecting her. The minute I have the book secured and there's no threat of Dorchester regaining possession, we'll fetch Lily. It should take no more than a matter of hours. Ashe will help us."

She tilted her head back, and he loosened his hold enough to let her meet his gaze. "Ashe?" she asked.

"Robert Ashe, the Texas Ranger I told you about. The one in Austin who verified your guardianship papers. I'll wire him tomorrow after Dan and I take care of a little business with the marshal in Steward's Mill. He'll help us."

"But we'll be stealing Dorchester's property. Surely a lawman would want no part of that."

Stone grinned. "Ashe owes me a favor. He'll cooperate. Shoot, he'll probably try to get me to hand the ledger over to him so he can start building a case against Dorchester."

"That could take months! If it ever even made it to court. Rebekah told me that her father-in-law had several judges and prominent politicians on his payroll. Even if Ashe found someone willing to testify, all Dorchester would have to do is get one of his cronies to throw out the case."

"I suspected as much. Which is why I won't do it. Lily's safety is more important than making Dorchester pay for his shady business dealings." For now. Once Stone convinced Charlotte to marry him, they could officially adopt Lily, thereby permanently removing her from Dorchester's reach. After that, Ashe could pursue Dorchester to his heart's content.

Charlotte's long lashes blinked slowly over her eyes. "You're going to use it as leverage, aren't you?"

She was a smart one, his woman. Stone nodded. "Yep."

Charlotte bit her lower lip. "I don't like it. What if Dorchester calls your bluff?"

Stone raised an eyebrow. "Oh, honey. It won't be a bluff. And I'll make sure Dorchester knows it."

"But what if the book isn't what Lily thinks it is? Or what if he moved it and you aren't able to find it? What if — ?"

"Shhh." Stone placed a finger over her lips. He wasn't going to let her work herself up into a frenzy again. And if it took a heavy dose of reality to do it, that's what he'd give her. "What if we do nothing and Dorchester sends Franklin or another retriever after her again? What if Dorchester puts a bounty on *your* head for kidnapping? He has three different cases he could possibly bring against you. Even if you weren't convicted, the arrest alone could give him the ammunition he needs to seize custody of Lily. The longer we put him off, the more desperate he'll become. And the more desperate he becomes, the dirtier he'll play. The risk is greater if we don't act."

She said nothing. Just buried her head against his chest again and tightened her grip on his coat. At least she still trusted him for comfort. The rest would follow eventually. Stone rested his chin atop her head and held her.

"I love her, too, Charlotte," he said, finally breaking the silence after several minutes. "I haven't known Lily as long as you have, but that little girl already has me wrapped around her finger. I swear I'll do whatever it takes to keep her safe."

Stone rubbed circles across Charlotte's back, seeking solace for himself as well as her. "After I lost my parents, I didn't let myself dream of family." His throat suddenly threatened to close off, but Stone forced the words out. She needed to hear them, and he . . . well, he needed to say them. "I concentrated on physical things that could be purchased or achieved. I dreamed of owning a piece of land with a cabin that no bank could take from me. I dreamed of being a man others respected, a man who would have made my mama proud. Sometimes, in the hardest times, I simply dreamed of a meal large enough to fill my belly."

Charlotte shifted against him. No longer gripping his coat, her hands tunneled inside it to clasp him around the waist, giving comfort instead of taking it.

"I never allowed myself to dream of family because I knew firsthand how much it hurt to lose them."

He heard her indrawn breath, felt the tremor that ran through her. Or maybe the tremor had been his. Thinking about his folks did that to him, made him weak, vulnerable. The lost little boy with no home, no one to depend on besides himself and the God his mama had told him stories about. That God had proven faithful, though. Had seen him grown into a man — one with his conscience intact. Had provided friends, brothers really, like Dan and Ashe. And now, if Stone didn't miss his guess, He'd provided the one thing Stone had never been brave enough to ask for but had always craved.

Stone reached between them and urged Charlotte's face up until her gaze met his. "Over the last couple weeks, I've started dreaming of family, Lottie. Dreaming of a wife, children. Dreaming of a honey-haired teacher with blue-green eyes and a smile that makes my heart buck harder than a fit-throwing mule. Dreaming of a daughter with a love of dime novels and a thirst for adventure that rivals my own. Dreaming of a son whose quiet manner explodes into music whenever he touches a piano. Shoot, I even dream of building a school where a boy with a penchant for tearing things apart can come and study so I don't lose touch with him, because he feels like family, too.

"I dream of you, Charlotte. You *and* the kids. I'll never let Lily go. Not without a fight. Trust me."

32

It took a few days longer to organize his plans than Stone had originally calculated. Ashe had been called away to San Antonio to testify against a cattle rustler his Ranger company had brought down with Stone's help last year, the same rustler who'd nearly cost Ashe his leg.

The bullet he'd taken to the thigh during the shootout had ricocheted off bone and nicked arteries that had bled so fiercely the doc who'd worked on him feared the tissue damage would require amputation. Ashe, stubborn cuss that he was, made Stone swear to shoot the doc if he even reached for his saw. Never one to let a friend down, Stone had made himself a permanent fixture in the doc's surgery and kept one hand on the handle of his revolver during the entire procedure. Ashe pulled through only to fight a second battle with infection.

The doc's daughter, Belinda, had seen

him through that travail and won his heart in the process. She'd been sweet on him for years, but she'd never been able to get him to stay in one place long enough to snag his interest. After a week of nursing him through fever and a month of exercising his leg until he could walk successfully without a cane, if not without a limp, Lindy had earned not only Ashe's gratitude, but his devotion as well. The Ranger with the itchy feet who'd always preferred the saddle to the hearth suddenly found himself requesting administrative duties at the Austin office, not because of his leg, but because he wanted to stay near Lindy. They'd married last December, a mere two months before Stone took the job with Dorchester.

Perhaps viewing their happiness had made it possible for him to imagine his own. With Charlotte.

Stone grinned as he traded in his currycomb for the horse brush, setting one atop the stall's half-wall and collecting the other before continuing with Goliath's grooming. The horse's hide quivered at the stroking, sending a drowsy fly skittering off in search of a more stable resting place.

It was early yet. The sun had been up only for half an hour. The cool of the morning still clung to the air, even in the barn, making it the perfect place to gather his thoughts before things got crazy.

"I'm gonna be gone for a while, boy," he murmured, patting Goliath's neck with his free hand. "Takin' a little trip down to Houston."

Goliath snorted in answer, as if displeased by the prospect of being left behind.

"I know," Stone soothed as he brushed the gelding's side. "I'd rather take you than a train any day, but I've got womenfolk to consider. Not to mention the fact that we're running behind schedule, having to wait on Ashe to get back from San Antonio and all. Dorchester's bound to be pushin' the outer edge of antsy by now."

It'd been over a week since Charlotte had agreed to his plan. Nine days, to be precise. And in all that time she'd never wavered. Not even when she'd learned that Dan's responsibilities on the ranch would keep him from joining them. 'Course, knowing Dan would be around to provide protection for John and Stephen took some of the sting out of the revelation, but it had still been a test of Charlotte's faith to adjust. A test she'd passed admirably. Oh, she'd asked plenty of questions and offered input whether they wanted it or not, but she never fretted openly about what might go wrong nor did she ever let Lily see anything other than confidence on her face when they discussed their scheme.

"I'm right proud of her, boy," Stone said as he stroked the brush over the horse's back.

He'd asked for her trust, and she'd given it to him. And not just for Lily's protection, either. No. She'd started opening her heart to him as well. Taking sunset strolls with him in the evenings. Seeking him out during the day to bring him a glass of water then lingering to make conversation about inconsequential matters. And last night . . . Stone paused in his grooming and smiled. Last night, she'd played "Moonlight," the song that had first fractured the wall between them nearly a month ago. The song that started his dreams of family.

The notes had caressed the air so softly, they'd almost disappeared before his ears could capture them. She hadn't wanted to wake the children. Yet the quiet notes brought their own depth, for he found that if he leaned his head back and closed his eyes, he could feel the music dance over his skin like the lightest brush of a feather. Or a finger. Her finger. Skimming along his arm, his nape, tunneling through his hair until his scalp tingled.

Strange how the song no longer sounded lonely when she played. It had become a love song, one that paired a strong, masculine bass line with a gentle, whispering soprano, weaving them together in a ballad of hope and tenderness and trust.

Placing a hand on Goliath's flank, Stone moved around to the other side and set to work with the brush once again. His thoughts moved from Charlotte back to Lily and the task set before them. A task that weighed heavily on his spirit.

"Don't let me fail her, Lord." Stone stopped brushing and rested both arms on Goliath's back. He rested his forehead against the horse's side and prayed the same prayer he'd been lifting up since the day he'd brought Lily back to the ranch. "I know that 'A man's heart deviseth his way: but the Lord directeth his steps.' I've been meditatin' on that verse all week. We've made the best plans we can, but only you can see where they lead. Help me to trust in *you,* not the plan. Guide our steps. Protect Lily and Charlotte. Bring us all home safely."

"Amen."

Stone opened his eyes and lifted his head. "Charlotte?"

Silhouetted against the morning light

streaming through the barn door, it was hard to make out her features, but then, he didn't need to see her face to know it was her. Her voice carried the same lilt as her music.

"Mr. Barrett has the wagon hitched. I'll be leaving in a few minutes." She took a handful of steps into the barn, the shadows evening out around her, bringing her into focus.

Stone blinked at the severe black gown she wore, so different from the blue skirt and white shirtwaist he was used to seeing her in. The mourning gown had belonged to Marietta Hawkins from when her mother had passed two years ago. It was made of the finest fabric, but the harsh black left Charlotte's skin looking pale and wan. Of course, the prospect of what lay ahead during the next two days could have stolen her color as well.

Running his hand along Goliath's back, Stone exited the stall and met Charlotte halfway. "I didn't realize Dan intended to set out so early this morning." He'd thought he'd have more time with her before she left.

The Houston & Texas Central had a depot in Richland, so they didn't have to travel all the way to Corsicana. Even in a wagon, the trip should only take about four hours with Dan's mules at the helm. He bred the heartiest stock in Texas. There'd be plenty of time to make the early-afternoon train if they left after breakfast as they'd originally planned.

"It was my idea." Charlotte's hand lifted to touch the brooch at her neck. Only it wasn't there. Maybe that's why the black of her dress seemed so overwhelming. He wasn't used to seeing her without her mother's cameo.

They'd agreed it would be better to travel without it. Any men Dorchester might have scouting the train station in Houston would know to look for it.

Charlotte pressed her lips together then fisted her fingers and pulled her hand down to press against her stomach. "One never knows what trouble one may encounter on the road. I wanted to ensure we had plenty of time to catch the train even if we should break a wheel or have an animal go lame along the way."

"I suppose it doesn't hurt to be prepared. Though I had hoped to stroll with you one more time before you left." He gently took hold of the hand fluttering near her waist and lifted it to his lips. He touched his mouth to the soft skin on the back of her hand, his gaze never leaving hers.

Her lashes lowered, and her breath hitched. "I — I wasn't able to sleep much last night, so when the first rooster crowed, I dressed, finished packing, and went in search of Mr. Barrett. It didn't take much effort to convince him to move up our departure."

Stone swallowed a chuckle. Dan's version of arguing with a woman entailed either giving in or getting lost as quickly as possible. Since he wouldn't be able to escape Charlotte today, giving in would've been the speediest resolution.

"Lily and the boys are awake as well. They're waiting by the wagon to see me off." She shifted a few inches away from him and picked at one of the pleats on her skirt. "Marietta is letting Lily borrow her Dead-Eye Dan books for the train ride, so she shouldn't cause you much trouble. I packed a few snacks as well. Boredom tends to make her hungry."

Stone fought not to roll his eyes. They'd been through all of this last night. "It's only a half-day's ride, Lottie. We'll survive."

She met his eyes, and her cheeks flushed a lovely shade of pink. "Of course you will. I just . . ." She shrugged. "I'm not used to letting others take over my responsibilities. I

411

still feel guilty about asking Marietta to watch the boys for me. Stephen can get a little rambunctious at times, and John . . . well, John hasn't been away from me since I took him from St. Peter's to study at Dr. Sullivan's academy. He's so quiet and withdrawn, it's hard for people to know what he's thinking. I —"

"He'll be fine," Stone interrupted, breaking off her rambling with a certainty that brooked no argument. "He's old enough to understand what we're doing and why. And Stephen will be here to interpret anything Marietta doesn't understand. Those two boys are as close as any brothers I've seen. They'll help each other when the waiting grows long."

Stone kept her hand in his and steered her toward the side wall so they'd be safely out of sight of the door. If their time was at an end, he intended to make the most of the few moments he'd been given.

"I know it's hard to leave them, Lottie, but I've been prayin' about it all week, and my gut is still tellin' me this is the right thing to do."

She nodded, her gaze hovering somewhere in the middle of his chest. "I've been praying, too," she replied. "And while I can't claim the same level of confidence, I have found a measure of peace." Slowly, her lashes lifted. Blue-green eyes searched out his. "I trust you to take care of her, Stone. To take care of all of us."

It wasn't the declaration of love he'd been longing to hear, but it was a gift all the same. One that deserved a proper response.

So he bent his head, matched his lips to hers, and poured all the words they didn't have time to say into a kiss guaranteed to linger in both their minds until their paths crossed again.

33

Stone turned his rented horse down the lane that led to Dorchester Hall, Lily in front of him in the saddle.

"I see it!" She bounced in his lap, pointing to the two-story mansion that separated itself from the other homes of the area with a pretentious rolling lawn that spread over the adjoining lots on either side, ensuring that nothing inferior encroached upon its beauty. Not that any other home in the area could possibly compete with its size and ornate architecture.

Dorchester Hall sported Greek Revival columns and double wraparound porches, one on each level. Dark green shutters framed the windows from ceiling to floor in grand style, while the intricately carved oak door left one thinking its purpose was more to keep the undeserving out than to welcome visitors in.

Stone reached across the girl and gently

tugged her arm down. "Easy, squirt. You're not supposed to be all that excited about this reunion."

"Oh. Right." She immediately slumped against him and thrust her bottom lip out in a very believable pout.

"Remember what I said. Let me do the talkin'. All you have to do is act as if you don't like me much. Got it?"

"Got it." Lily gave a sharp nod, her pout never wavering.

"Good girl." Stone scanned the area as the horse made its lazy way down the street. Service wagon outside the house on the left. Grocer's sign on the wagon's side. A vendor making deliveries, then, not a peddler. Good. A door-to-door salesman could complicate matters. Elderly woman on the right pruning rosebushes. Too far away to hear any indoor commotion at the Hall and too frail to remain outdoors for long. Quiet street. Favorable conditions. So far, so good.

Stone made a point not to look at the trees flanking the east side of the house, knowing Ashe would have hidden himself among them that morning before the sun rose. His leg might pain him a bit every now and then, but the man was still as stealthy as an Indian. He'd commandeer the high ground easily enough.

"If your grandfather sends you to your room, unlatch your window first thing."

Lily sighed. "I *know*. We went over that a hundred times last night. I unlatch the window so Mr. Ashe can get to me if something goes wrong. And I'm supposed to signal him if I need help by closing half the curtains."

Stone fought a grin at her beleaguered tone and grunted in response. He had a role to play, too. And with the house drawing nearer, it was high time he got into character.

Thinking of Dorchester's plans to use Lily's remarkable talents for illicit gain was all it took to blacken his mood and harden his mouth into a scowl. By the time he reached the front of Dorchester Hall, he'd worked up a good head of steam. The flash of black he'd caught in his peripheral vision only stirred the pot.

The veiled woman in widow's weeds sitting so stiffly on the bench across the street, a book open in her lap, the wind ruffling the pages, should never have been accused of kidnapping and hunted down like a criminal when she'd been the legal guardian all the while. If Dorchester had hired Franklin first . . . If he had found her . . . It didn't bear contemplating.

With a growl vibrating in his throat, Stone swung down off his horse, one arm still locked around Lily's middle. She squealed, striking out with her legs, but he tucked her under his arm horizontally so her shoes kicked harmlessly behind him. He flicked the reins of his horse through the loop on the wrought-iron hitching post at the edge of the walkway then tramped up the gravel path.

Before he'd even reached the stone steps leading to the entrance, the door opened. A butler in suit and tie looked down his nose at Stone's travel-stained clothes and squirming package.

"Mr. Hammond to see Mr. Dorchester," Stone announced in a thunderous voice as he climbed the steps, ignoring the servant's hauteur. "I'm expected."

He pushed his way past the flummoxed butler and strode into the marble-floored entryway as if he owned the place.

"Dorchester!" Stone hollered even as he quickly refreshed his memory on the layout of the house. Grand staircase to the upper floor. Kitchen behind. Dining room to the left. Sitting room to the front of that. Formal parlor, front right. Study behind. "I've come for my fee!"

"Put me down!" Lily demanded, her voice

high-pitched and furious. "I told you. Mama said I was to live with Miss Lottie, not Grandfather."

Stone squeezed her ribs, a reminder to hold her tongue. He didn't want her drawing undue attention to herself. He needed to be the one drawing the fire. Although he had to admit, her shrieking had done a good job of drawing an audience. The housekeeper had emerged from the kitchen to see what all of the commotion was about, as had an upstairs maid who hung over the balustrade gawking at the goings-on downstairs.

"Dorchester," Stone called through a clenched jaw, "I've got your brat. Come fetch her before I decide to teach her some manners."

"I am *not* a brat!" Lily's fist collided with Stone's thigh. "I'm just not supposed to be here. I'm supposed to be with Miss Lottie."

So much for him doin' the talking.

"Really, Mr. Hammond." The housekeeper ventured into the foyer, her hands wringing but her chin high. "Must you cart the young mistress around like a sack of potatoes? Hand her over to me. I'll see to her."

The woman had more gumption than Stone had expected from one of

418

Dorchester's staff. It spoke well of her. Standing up for the child and all. It was good to know the girl had an ally with backbone in the house. 'Course, whether that backbone would still be standin' straight when facing Dorchester was another matter altogether.

Stone couldn't let the woman take Lily yet, though, not until Dorchester showed. So he shot a harsh scowl at her. "If it's all the same to you, ma'am, I think I'll just hang on to her a little longer." The housekeeper ceased her cautious advance, her eyes widening at his hard tone. "Dorchester owes me a pretty penny for retrieving this package. I ain't lettin' her go for anyone but the man himself."

"Well, you certainly took your own sweet time about it, Hammond."

Dorchester. Finally.

Stone swiveled toward his employer's voice. The man had just opened the study door, his hand still on the latch, his eyes cold and assessing. Stone narrowed his own gaze.

"Maybe if you hadn't lied to me about the circumstances surrounding the package's disappearance," he said, swinging Lily around to stand on her feet, "it wouldn't have taken so long. The

419

schoolmarm was a complication I didn't need." He kept a firm hand on Lily's shoulder, both as a reassurance to her and a show of strength to Dorchester.

The man shrugged as if twisting the truth was of no consequence. "What is one female against a man of your reputation?" Dorchester stepped through the doorway, his shoes sliding gracefully over the marble floor. "Though I'm quite disappointed in your level of efficiency. I expected better from you. Why, as soon as Franklin located the girl, he had her in hand by the next day. It took you weeks."

Dorchester raised a brow in challenge even as a second man stepped out of the study. Franklin.

Stone's scowl deepened. So he had another gun to deal with. And one with a grudge, judging by the dark gaze aimed in his direction.

"You hired me because I'm the best." Stone emphasized the last word as he eased his duster back behind his holster, making sure his draw would be unhindered while giving Franklin a little reminder about who was in charge. "And one of the things that makes me *the best* is the fact that I work within the law. When I retrieve something, you can be sure there'll be no suspicious lawmen showing up at your door askin' embarrassing questions or arresting you on charges that could do serious harm to your reputation. If I hadn't been there to smooth things over with the teacher, you can bet there would have been a company of Texas Rangers breathin' down your neck before Franklin could have even made his delivery. Train might be fast, but last I checked, telegraph is still faster."

Dorchester glared over his shoulder at Franklin before turning back to Stone. "Well, then, I guess it's a good thing I hired the right man for the job, isn't it?"

Stone could feel the heat of Franklin's fury scorching the air between them, but he refused to acknowledge it, keeping his focus on Dorchester.

"And my fee?" Stone demanded.

"We'll discuss that in a moment, after I assure myself that my darling granddaughter is unharmed." Dorchester looked to Lily for the first time, crouching down in front of her and reaching for her hands.

Lily shied away from him, and for a moment Stone worried that she'd turn to him for comfort. Not that his gut wasn't screamin' at him to put himself between her and her scoundrel of a grandfather. He didn't want the foul piece of filth touching her, either, but they both had to ignore their instincts and play the roles they'd been assigned.

"Lily, sweetheart. I've been so worried about you."

So worried that he hadn't even glanced at her once for the past five minutes. Stone's molars ground together at the back of his mouth.

"I'm fine," she choked out. "Can I go back to Miss Lottie now?" The plaintive note in her voice sounded far too genuine for Stone's peace of mind. She spoke to her grandfather, but Stone couldn't shake the feeling that she meant the question for him as well. Brave girl that she was, though, she never broke character.

Dorchester frowned at her question but quickly masked his displeasure with a doting smile, one about as genuine as a string of paste jewels.

"No, dear. You'll be staying with me. With your *family*. Miss Lottie meant well, I'm sure, but your place is here." He made a gesture with his hand, encompassing all the grandeur surrounding them. "You'll have everything a girl could ever want. Books. Dolls. Fancy dresses." He paused then winked at her. "A pony."

"But I don't want a pony. I want Miss

Lottie! Mama said I was supposed to stay with her."

Dorchester made no effort to hide his frown this time. He stood abruptly and grabbed Lily's arm, dragging her away from Stone. "Well, your mother was wrong. You are to stay with me, and that's the end of the matter. I'll hear no argument, young lady. Understand?"

"Y-yes, Grandfather."

It took all the control Stone could muster not to slam his fist into Dorchester's jaw. He maintained his impatient hireling veneer by the thinnest of threads.

Dorchester snapped his fingers and called his housekeeper over. "See to the child, Mrs. Johnson. No doubt she is overtired from her journey. I'm sure she'll be more agreeable after a nap."

"Yes, sir, Mr. Dorchester." The woman hurried forward and wrapped a motherly arm about Lily's shoulders. "Come on, little one. You'll like all the new toys your grandfather bought for you. He's had your room ready and waiting for weeks now, hoping you'd come home."

Lily let herself be drawn away, but not without casting a glance over her shoulder at Stone as she went. He wanted to smile or wink or do *something* to show his support, but with Dorchester looking on, he didn't dare.

Mrs. Johnson rambled on as she led Lily up the stairs. "That tabby you were so fond of is probably sunning himself in your bedroom window right now. It's his favorite room in the house, you know."

Lily turned back to the housekeeper, a tiny smile playing at her lips. She didn't say anything, but her steps lightened a bit as she headed up the staircase.

Forcing his gaze away from Lily, Stone turned back to Dorchester and glared at him as if he were facing the man at ten paces, hand hovering over his pistol, about to draw. Hard. Arrogant. Unmovable.

"Now that the brat's out of the way," he growled, "let's talk about my fee."

34

Charlotte gripped the open book in her lap as if it were her only anchor in a gale-force wind despite the fact that nary a breeze stirred the Houston humidity. Perspiration trickled down her neck as her eyes scanned the upper balcony. She wasn't to move from her bench until Mr. Ashe gave the signal.

Lily and Stone had been inside Dorchester's house for days. All right, it was probably less than fifteen minutes, but still, it was too long. Too long for her to sit on this wretched bench and do nothing.

Charlotte's fingers curled around the edges of the book even harder as she willed herself to remain still. She squinted, trying to get a better view of the tree that was supposed to be harboring their ally. She couldn't see a thing. Infernal veil. It hid her identity well enough, but it impeded her vision to a deplorable degree. How was she supposed to carry out her part of the plan if she couldn't see the signal when it was given?

Robert Ashe was a tall man. Surely she'd be able to make out his form when he emerged from the tree, even with her veil in place. But shouldn't he have made his move by now? Had his leg given out? She'd noticed his limp during their brief meeting last night. What if he wasn't able to get to Lily if she needed him?

Even as the questions swirled in her mind, a dark shape separated itself from the branches of the hickory tree and lithely dropped onto the upstairs balcony.

Charlotte sucked in a breath, waiting for a cry of alarm that would spell disaster for them all. But no servant rushed to throw up a window sash or yell out a warning. Respect for the Ranger blossomed within Charlotte. He hadn't made a sound. Bad leg and all.

Mr. Ashe crept toward the back of the house, checking each window before moving past. Only then did she notice the hitch in his stride. He finally reached the third window and crouched beside it, waiting. A moment later, he stood tall and waved his arm over his head.

The signal! Lily must be safely in her room.

Charlotte leapt to her feet, her heartbeat

taking off at full gallop. She dropped the unread book to the bench and focused her attention on the door across the street. The door that separated her from Lily. From Stone. Her chest heaved as her breathing came in shallow rasps. She could do this.

Go, Charlotte!

In a flurry, she tore the veiled hat from her head, ignoring the pain as pins pulled out hair. For once, she made no move to repair her coiffure. Gaze locked on the door, she marched across the street, heedless of the loose tresses that hung unevenly around her face. She wouldn't be tamping them down. Nor would she squelch her unbecoming emotions — her disgust of Dorchester, her rage over his involving Lily in his criminal schemes. The fetters were off and this horse was about to run roughshod over anything she found in her way.

Her stride quickened until she actually ran. Ran up to the door and burst through without a single knock to announce her arrival.

"Where is she?" Charlotte yelled, her throat scratching at the volume she'd never before attempted. She glanced quickly around the foyer, spotting Stone, Dorchester, and a third man standing to the right of the large central staircase. All three men turned to stare at her, Stone with cold indifference, Dorchester with shock dulling to impatience, and the third man with a smirk.

Charlotte ran at Stone like a bull toward a matador. "Where's my daughter, you cold-hearted scoundrel?" She collided with his chest and pummeled him with her fists, wishing he were Dorchester.

The third man chuckled. "Guess she's not so sweet on you after all, huh, Stone?"

"Shut up, Franklin." Stone shoved her away from him and directly into Dorchester's path.

"Franklin? The man who kidnapped my Lily?" Charlotte screeched and lunged toward him, claws bared. "I ought to scratch your eyes out for what you did!"

Franklin sidestepped her reach, so she altered course. A porcelain vase filled with red roses stood on a small mahogany table beneath a large mirror. It looked delicate, expensive. Charlotte smiled. Good.

She snatched the vase from the table, flowers and all, and hurled it at Franklin's head.

"Watch it, lady!" Franklin dodged to the side and threw up an arm. The vase cracked against his elbow with a satisfying *thunk* before smashing upon the marble floor. Shards flew everywhere. Spilled water splashed the trousers of both Dorchester and Franklin, setting off a string of curses foul enough to put her to the blush. But the vulgarity only fueled her indignation. So she went for the table next, grabbing it up by the leg closest to her and flinging it with all her might at the men — men who no longer included Stone, she was happy to see.

Dorchester ducked, narrowly avoiding the table edge as it whipped past. "Crazy she-devil! What do you think you're doing?"

"I'm making a mess of your life just as you've made of mine!" She ran across the hall toward the matching table on the opposite side. It supported a rather ugly sculpture of a swan that looked as if it were about to lay an egg. "Close down my school . . ." *Crash!* The swan's neck broke off, and the headless body skittered across the floor. "Make me flee my home then hunt me like a criminal . . ." She grabbed up the table.

Sensing the men closing in on her, she whirled, gripping the top of the table and swiping the legs in front of her to keep them back. They advanced as if to surround her, one on either side, arms extended, palms out as if she were a wild animal. Perhaps she was. Charlotte grinned. Who knew acting the shrew could be so invigorating?

Best of all, she had captured their full attention and drawn them away from the study. A quick glance told her Stone had not yet emerged. She needed to prolong the distraction. But how? She was running out of objects to smash and furniture to wave around.

The men edged closer. Too close. She needed to —

Franklin lunged. Charlotte flung the table at him and clipped his jaw with one of the legs. He jerked backward with a grunt, giving her just enough room to scamper along the wall out of his reach. Spying a slender bentwood coat and hat stand in the corner near the front door, she dashed in that direction.

"Stop her, Franklin!" Dorchester bellowed. "Do what I pay you for, man!"

Charlotte crowed in triumph when her fingers closed around the tall rack. She brandished it like a weapon, jabbing it in Franklin's direction. Only, the man was smart enough not to come within striking distance this time. Yet neither did he give her room to escape her corner. He rubbed at the red mark on his jaw, his eyes narrowing into dangerous slits.

"I'll take care of her," he promised, his voice low, his eyes never leaving hers.

Charlotte swallowed. She didn't like the way his hand twitched near the handle of his holstered revolver. He wouldn't shoot her, would he?

Blood rushed in her ears, but this was no time to retreat. Stone was counting on her. She had to give him more time.

"You stole my daughter from me, you fiend!" Charlotte jabbed the bottom of the coat rack at Franklin's middle.

He grabbed hold of the curved wood with both hands. Charlotte yanked her weapon back, but he held fast. "She ain't even your kid, lady. Quit your belly-achin' before I have to hurt you."

Charlotte continued pulling at the coat rack, the tug-o-war straining her arms. But she was fighting for Lily. She wouldn't let go.

"That's right," she sneered. "Hurt me. That's what you do, isn't it? Hurt innocent women and children." She gave another hard yank. "And you!" she screamed at Dorchester when she caught him looking around as if only just noticing that Stone was missing. "Randolph Dorchester! You're a vile, greedy man who'd corrupt your own granddaughter in order to line your pockets. You sicken me."

The ploy worked. Dorchester turned back

to glare at her and stopped glancing about for Stone, but it proved her undoing as well. Franklin took advantage of her shift of attention and snatched the coat rack from her with a jerk. Unprepared, Charlotte lost her grip and staggered forward as he wrested her weapon away.

Franklin flung the rack behind him. A loud *crack* sounded when it hit the floor, but Charlotte was more concerned about the meaty fist Franklin had raised. Pressing her body back into the corner, she brought up her arms to shield her face and head. She closed her eyes, but the blow never came.

"You never did know how to treat a woman, Franklin."

Stone!

"And you do?"

Charlotte pulled her hands away from her face to see Franklin struggling to tear his arm away from Stone's grip.

"You don't see her throwing the furnishings at *me,* do you?" The smug grin on Stone's face seemed so foreign, so . . . arrogant. Like a rogue bragging of his latest conquest.

"Only because you cowered in a corner somewhere far away from her," Franklin retorted, finally yanking his arm free.

"She wouldn't hurt me, would you, love? Not after all we've shared." For a heartbeat, Stone reminded her of her father strutting about in front of an audience, flaunting his young lover in her mother's face. And of the faithless Alexander, so confident in his charms, toying with her affections while betrothed to another. Betrayal speared through her chest, sharp and deep. Until Stone glanced at her, concern evident in his eyes. Concern and a bit of goading.

Remember to play your part.

Charlotte straightened and turned on Stone, ready to blast him with feigned temper. But what stirred in her breast wasn't feigned at all. No, the memories of past betrayals mixed with her anger and fear of the present circumstance combined in a combustible formula. All the words she'd kept bottled inside since her father left suddenly exploded.

"You . . . you Lothario!" She struck out at Stone, burying her fist in his gut. Air whooshed from his lungs as he bent slightly. "You never really cared about me at all, did you? All you care about is yourself. Your perfect record. Your money. You seduced me with pretty words and stole my child. How could you? How *could* you?"

Unexpected sobs rose to choke her.

Alarmed, she tried to stuff the emotion back down, but once it gained its freedom it would not be contained. She sagged against Stone, her strength depleted as she wept out the bitterness that had been trapped inside her for more than half her life. Her father's betrayal. Her mother's abandonment. Alexander's perfidy.

Strong arms scooped her up like a babe with a tenderness that only made her weep harder.

"The fight's gone out of her now, boys," Stone said, his voice still grating with that obnoxious cocksure manner he'd adopted. "Dorchester, send your carriage around. I'll give the lady some funds and send her on her way. She knows she's lost this battle. She won't be botherin' you anymore."

"Better make sure of that," Dorchester grumbled. "I'll have the hussy arrested for vandalism and assault if she shows her face around here again."

Stone nodded, his jaw rubbing against the top of Charlotte's head as he carried her toward the front door. "I'll take care of her. But if you don't have my payment ready for me by the time I get back, I'll be taking care of you next."

"I don't take kindly to threats, Hammond." Dorchester's hard voice penetrated Charlotte's fog, making her stiffen in Stone's arms.

But Stone never wavered. He responded in a tone so deadly, unpleasant shivers coursed down the length of her back. "And I don't take kindly to employers who try to cheat me out of my fee."

35

As soon as the door slammed behind them, Stone bent his face close to Charlotte's. "Are you all right?" he whispered. Her sobs had cut him to the quick. "You know I didn't mean any of the things I said in there, don't you? It was all an act, Lottie. I swear it."

"I know," she said between sniffles as she fought to put the lid on her emotions. "I'm afraid I don't have much experience with full-blown tantrums. I only intended to let my anger loose, but once the gate opened, old hurts surged to the fore as well." She patted his chest with her palm, the touch causing his heart to twitch. "I'm afraid I took them out on you. Sorry about that."

Lothario. You never really cared about me at all, did you? All you care about is yourself. Your perfect record. Your money. How could you? The words in Charlotte's broken-hearted voice replayed through Stone's mind. Her father. Had she ever given voice to that lingering hurt in all these years? Somehow he doubted it. She didn't like to deal with the messiness of ugly feelings. She'd rather push them down, ignore them, never realizing that they would fester into bitterness and distrust. If pummeling his chest and throwing a few accusations around had rid her of some of that poison, he'd volunteer to go another round.

Stone smiled down at her. "At least you didn't hurl a table at my head."

Pink tinged her cheeks. "You saw that?"

"I kept an eye on you from the other room." He winked as he strode down the steps and onto the walkway. She fidgeted as if ready to get down, but he didn't release her. She felt too good in his arms.

All at once, as if she'd suddenly awoken from a faint, she lifted her head and latched onto the fabric of his shirt. Her eyes, intense and nearly feral, searched his face. "Did you find the ledger?"

He gave a brisk nod. "In my coat pocket."

Stone brushed a quick kiss against her forehead, sure the broadness of his shoulders would block the view of anyone who might be looking on from the house. Then he reluctantly set her back on her feet, keeping an arm about her waist for support until she stood securely on her own.

"Here. Before the coachman arrives." He reached into his inside pocket and pulled out the small black leather book. He'd quickly scanned the first couple pages before leaving the study and knew it was exactly what Lily had suspected it to be. A record of business transactions — transactions one wouldn't list with his usual accounts.

Hiding the book between their two bodies, Stone flipped to a page near the beginning and tore it free.

"Give the book to Ashe for safekeeping, but hang on to the single page. I'll need it later."

She nodded and stuffed both into her skirt pocket.

The *clip-clop* of horses' hooves echoed from behind the house. Stone glanced in that direction. The carriage would be out front in less than a minute.

"Ashe will rendezvous with you, lock up the ledger, then return here to keep an eye on the house until night falls. I'll linger as long as I can, hammering out the fee with Dorchester."

Charlotte bit her lip. "Remind me again why we can't just take Lily with us now. Surely Mr. Ashe could —"

"We can't risk tipping Dorchester off, Lottie. You know that." Stone clasped her arms in a firm grip. "We have to secure the book first, secure our leverage. If we take Lily now, Franklin will come after us — and who knows how many others. You don't want her caught up in that. Securing the book means securing her freedom. It has to be this way." He glanced at the approaching carriage, set a scowl on his face for appearances, then whispered a final assurance. "Mrs. Johnson is with Lily. She'll watch over her."

Charlotte met his gaze and nodded her acceptance before wilting her posture in projected defeat as the carriage pulled abreast of them.

Heavens, but he was proud of her. She'd been magnificent. Charging through the hall with all the fire of an avenging angel. Focusing the wrath of two powerful men upon herself in order to buy him the time he needed.

It had almost been too long. Stone's throat convulsed. When he thought about Franklin's raised fist . . . He'd wanted to shoot the blackguard, or at the very least tackle him to the floor and bloody his face until it resembled pulverized meat just for thinking about hitting her. Only the knowledge that he'd halted the intended abuse had allowed him to keep his temper in check and his manner cool.

The driver hopped down from his perch and moved to open the carriage door. "Where to, miss?"

"The Sunny South Boarding House at Milam and Franklin, please," Charlotte answered in a weary tone.

Stone held out a hand to her and assisted her into the carriage.

"Ah." The chipper driver nodded. "Down by the bayou. That's a pretty part of town."

"I suppose." She sounded so broken, Stone suffered a flicker of alarm. But when the driver closed the door and hustled back up onto his seat, Charlotte favored Stone with a wink and the barest hint of a smile. The woman must have inherited a flare for acting from her mother. She was a natural.

Stone wanted to grin his relief, but aware of the watching coachman, he forced his features to hold their stoic line. "It's over, Miss Atherton." He curled his fingers over the edge of the open carriage window. "The girl is with her family. Where she belongs. You'll only bring grief upon her and yourself if you pursue this matter further. Dorchester's threat is real. He *will* have you arrested if you try to make any more trouble.

You're lucky he's not calling the law down on you now after all the havoc you caused."

"Thank you for your concern." Scorn laced each word she uttered. "However, since our association has come to an end, I find I no longer need to listen to your advice." She dismissed him with a haughty sniff. "Driver? Let us be off."

The man gave Stone a sympathetic shrug then clicked his tongue and set the team in motion. Stone stepped away from the carriage and moved back toward the house. A dark figure separated itself from the hickory trees lining the right side of Dorchester Hall and disappeared around the back. Ashe. He would follow the carriage on horseback, ensuring no harm came to Charlotte. Stone wasn't about to take any chances.

Striding up the front steps, he set his jaw. Stage One was complete. On to Stage Two.

By the time Charlotte reached the Sunny South Boarding House, she finally had her emotions back under control, though her concern for Stone and Lily still ran close to the surface. She had spent the majority of the carriage ride in prayer for their safety and was determined to leave their care in God's capable hands, yet her hard-won peace felt as fragile as a dew-drenched spider's web.

She thanked the driver then headed up the steps and into the boarding house parlor. A young woman who'd been sitting on the sofa near the hearth jumped to her feet. "Is it done, then?"

Charlotte smiled at Belinda Ashe, completely sympathetic to the worry etched along her brow. "The first step is finished," she said with a nod. "Your husband should be along shortly."

Belinda's petite shoulders relaxed. "Thank heaven." She shook her head at herself. "I don't know why I worked myself up into such a state. Robert's been on much more dangerous missions than this with the Rangers. It's just that this was the first time since his injury, and I worried . . . well . . . it seems foolish now."

Charlotte crossed the room and clasped the woman's hand. "It's natural to be concerned for a loved one's safety. Even if that loved one is a highly trained Texas Ranger. It simply means you care."

"Do you worry for Mr. Hammond?" Belinda asked, peering at her with a look that was far too perceptive.

Charlotte squirmed slightly, her borrowed mourning dress suddenly feeling a touch too tight. "Of course," she admitted, ducking her head. "He is risking much to help us. But it is Lily's safety that weighs heaviest on my heart. Leaving her in that house was the hardest thing I've ever done."

"My Robert will look after her," Belinda stated emphatically, squeezing Charlotte's hand. "No harm will come to her on his watch."

"Lindy's right, as usual." A masculine voice rumbled from the doorway.

"Robert!" Belinda squealed, dropped Charlotte's hand, and ran to her husband. He swept her up in an embrace so strong it took her feet from the floor.

"You haven't been sitting in the parlor frettin' all morning, have you?" Robert Ashe set his wife on her feet and gently tweaked her nose. "A less confident man might find such a thing insulting."

"Confident?" Belinda made a noise that sounded suspiciously like a snort. "Arrogant, more like. Sometimes I'd swear that limp of yours exists solely to increase your swagger."

Charlotte looked away from the pair. Despite their playful banter, she could sense the true affection they shared. It exuded from their hidden glances, from the way she looked him over to assure herself he was hale and whole, the way he couldn't seem to stop touching her — the finger skating down the slope of her nose, the hand to her back, his leg brushing her skirt. It stirred a troublesome longing in her heart and pictures of Stone in her mind.

"I have the ledger," she blurted, needing to do something to escape the uncomfortable feelings welling inside her. She stepped toward Ashe and pulled the small book from her skirt pocket, careful not to disturb the single page that sat deeper within.

Ashe moved to meet her, his limp slightly more pronounced after the morning's activities than she remembered from the previous night. He collected the book and tucked it into a pocket inside his coat. "I'll take it to the Ranger office and have it locked in the safe. Then I'll return to Dorchester Hall to stand guard."

"Not before you eat something," his wife countermanded. "I won't have you collapsing from hunger because you were too stubborn to spare five minutes for a sandwich. I'll see if the cook has any ham left over from breakfast." She spun out of the room before he could argue, presumably heading to the kitchen.

Ashe rolled his eyes at his retreating wife, but the smile on his face spoke only of love. "The woman can't stop tending me. Thinks

I'm still her patient."

"Let her fuss," Charlotte said softly. "It's her way of showing she cares."

Ashe sighed. "I know. That's why I'll eat whatever she puts in front of me." He winked at Charlotte. "Wouldn't want to wound her tender feelings."

Because *he* cared. It was lovely to behold, Charlotte had to admit. Two people so obviously in love. She prayed it would last, that they would grow old together — Belinda still bringing him sandwiches and fussing over his scrapes, Robert still playing along.

What would she and Stone look like if they married? Would they still take sunset walks? Would she play Beethoven's "Moonlight" for him on their anniversary? The image of them sitting in matching rockers on the porch of her home back in Madisonville, holding hands and laughing over the antics of the children scampering about the place rose unbidden, the image so powerful her chest actually ached at the picture it made.

"I-I'm going up to my room to change," she said by way of excuse as she swept past Robert. This was not the time for dreams. Lily sat in a room in Dorchester's house, waiting to be rescued. Charlotte's dreams could be examined later, when her family was whole again.

Besides, she couldn't breathe right in this stiff mourning gown. She needed her gored skirt and comfortable shirtwaist. And her mother's cameo. Her fingers lifted to the place at the base of her neck where the brooch usually rested. She'd feel more herself when she was dressed in her usual attire, more like Lily's teacher. No — her *mother.* She smiled at the thought as she maneuvered up the stairs to her room.

But after she had washed and changed, thoughts of Stone continued to intrude. Every time she thought of Lily, her mind also drifted to Stone, the child's protector. And every time her mind drifted to Stone, a dark feeling settled over her, one that felt less like idle worry and more like foreboding.

36

Stone gripped Charlotte's hand in the night as they crept through the hickory trees to reach the side of Dorchester Hall. She'd put the dreary mourning dress back on in order to better conceal herself in the darkness, but her face was pale enough to reflect the half moon's glow.

He signaled silently to Ashe with a few quick hand gestures. The man nodded and split off from their little group to climb the tree that would take him back up to the second-story veranda. Stone would follow. But not until he made sure Charlotte was all right.

"Stay behind the trees," he whispered, wishing not for the first time that he had forced her to remain behind with Belinda at the boarding house. Unfortunately, he'd given his word that she could be a full partner in this endeavor, and he wouldn't break a promise to her. However, that didn't mean he wouldn't do everything in his power to keep her out of the fray.

"No matter what you hear or think you see, you stay put. Understand?" He glared the command at her. "I'll have your word on it, Charlotte. I can't afford to be distracted by my concern for you." He added one final statement, guaranteed to garner her cooperation. "Lily's welfare might very well depend upon my ability to focus."

"It's *your* welfare that has me concerned, not Lily's. Dorchester needs her alive, and she's tucked away in her bedroom. Ashe confirmed as much when we arrived. *You're* the one who'll be threatening Dorchester. And if Franklin's still around, you might be battling two instead of one." She reached out and clasped his forearm with her free hand, her long, slender fingers digging almost painfully into his skin through the fabric of his dark shirt. "I've seen the way Franklin looks at you, Stone. Jealousy. Loathing. He's played second fiddle to you for too long. It won't take much to tempt him into ridding himself of his competition."

Stunned by her pronouncement, Stone could only stare at the woman before him. She was more concerned for *him* than for

Lily? That couldn't be right. Yet the earnest way her blue-green eyes peered up at him and the grip she had on his arm shattered his denial.

Love surged through his core, strong and unconquerable. And with a single motion, he yanked Charlotte up against his chest and claimed her mouth in a deep, short kiss. Tearing his mouth away from hers before she could tempt him into forgetting his mission, he clutched her fingers tightly within his fist.

"Promise me you'll stay in the trees no matter what happens," he demanded in a harsh whisper.

She nodded, her gaze never leaving his. Satisfied, he extricated himself from her hold and stepped away.

"I love you, Lottie."

Moisture glistened in her beautiful eyes, but then her lashes lowered and he took that as his cue to go. A soft sigh whispered on the breeze behind him as he grabbed a lower limb and swung himself up into the tree — a sigh that almost sounded like *I love you, too* but was surely just a gentle rustle of leaves.

Closing off his heart in order to focus his mind, Stone narrowed his eyes and tautened his muscles. Time to take care of business.

By the time he reached the veranda, Ashe already had the window to Lily's room propped open and one leg over the ledge.

"Took you long enough." Ashe smirked. "Thought you might've gotten stuck in the tree."

Stone crossed the balcony on silent feet then grabbed the man's head, bent it down, and shoved him through the open window. Ashe tucked and rolled, bouncing back to his feet in a silent blur even as he glared at his partner.

Stone shrugged. "Sorry. I thought you'd gotten yourself stuck in the window."

The two men shared a muffled chuckle as Stone stretched a long leg over the sill and ducked into the room. His gaze immediately went to the bed and the small shape under the covers.

Lily lay curled on her side, one hand beneath her cheek. A tiny ruffle of a snore slipped through her parted lips as she slept peacefully on while two intruders infiltrated her bedroom. Such innocence. Such trust. It only solidified Stone's resolve to bend Dorchester to his will, to guard Lily's future and preserve her innocence.

He moved to her side and lowered himself to the edge of the mattress. Placing a hand on her shoulder, he gave her a gentle shake.

"Wake up, squirt. Time to go."

She groaned and rolled to her back, her eyelids slowly lifting. "Stone?"

He smiled. "Yep. I need you to get up and get dressed, all right? We'll be leaving as soon as I have a little chat with your grandfather."

Her eyes, now wide, blinked up at him. "You're going to tell him to let me stay with Miss Lottie, aren't you?" Her gaze flitted briefly to the guns he wore then back to his face.

"That I am, squirt." Not wanting to answer any more questions for fear of the answers he might have to give, Stone patted her shoulder a final time then removed himself from the bed.

"Stay by her side," he murmured to Ashe as he strode to meet him by the door.

His friend nodded. "I will." Ashe slowly tuned the knob. Pulling the door back a few inches, he glanced out into the hall. "Looks clear." He turned back to Stone and gave him a hard-eyed stare all men in their line of work understood but never spoke aloud. *Be on your guard.*

Stone held Ashe's gaze for a moment then slipped through the door and into the hall. Hugging the shadows of the wall, he stole along the rear hall, turned left, then halted

451

in front of the corner room. The master suite.

Checking behind him a final time to make sure no servants had stirred, he drew the pistol from his right holster, held it at the ready, then silently let himself into the room and closed the door behind him. Wouldn't want anyone disturbing them, after all.

Little light penetrated the room. Dark outlines of black on gray depicted a sitting area to the right of the door. Stone moved cautiously around it, his attention focused on the large four-poster bed deeper in the room. Stealthily, he crept forward, softening his footfalls.

Dorchester never moved. Not until Stone pressed the cool metal of his pistol's barrel into the man's temple and cocked the weapon. The gentle click echoed through the room like cannon fire. Dorchester's eyes flew open.

Without turning his head, Dorchester angled his eyes to the right. "Hammond!" he rasped. "W-what are you doing here?" He swallowed, his throat working up and down. "We concluded our business earlier today, did we not?"

"That we did. Your payment was much appreciated." Stone had made sure to cash the bank draft that afternoon.

"Then why the devil are you in my room holding a gun to my head?" The man had found his backbone, it seemed. His voice spat indignation.

Stone pressed the pistol a little harder against Dorchester's head. No use letting him forget who was in charge. When the covers trembled a touch, Stone grinned. "I've got a new deal to broker. One I believe will be mutually beneficial."

"I'll have you hanged for this, Hammond," Dorchester blustered, though Stone was wise enough to recognize the threat wasn't completely idle. A man as rich and powerful as Randolph Dorchester had ways of getting things done. Especially when he had influence over key officials. It hadn't escaped Stone's notice earlier today that several of the names included in Dorchester's ledgers belonged to state judges and prosecutors.

"We'll see." Keeping his gun hand steady, Stone reached for his insurance. He pulled it from his trouser pocket and shook out the folds in front of Dorchester's face. "Recognize this?"

"Recognize what?" the man grumbled. "It's the middle of the night and dark as a cave in here. If you want me to look at this paper you're waving in front of my nose, you're gonna have to let me light the lamp."

Stone nodded but jerked the paper back. He wasn't letting it anywhere near a match. His gun trained on Dorchester, Stone backed up a step. He checked the bedside table drawer and found a Colt .32 pocket pistol, which he quickly confiscated and tucked into his waistband.

"Light your lamp, Dorchester."

The man scowled up at Stone, obviously disgruntled that he'd been thwarted. Nevertheless, he removed the chimney of the fancy brass lamp on the table, turned up the wick, and struck a match. Dorchester shot nervous glances back at Stone throughout the process, his eyes constantly straying to the pistol now pointed at his chest, his hand shaking as he lit the wick. Once he had the lamp adjusted and the chimney back in place, he propped his back against the headboard and glared at Stone, one hand outstretched.

"All right. Give me the blasted paper."

Stone handed it to him. When Dorchester's eyes went wide and his ruddy face lost its color, Stone's chest expanded in satisfaction.

"How . . . how did you get this?"

"Doesn't matter." Stone eyed him with a hard stare. "What does matter is that you understand I am in possession of the entire book of which that page is only a sample. A book safely stashed away with an associate. A book that will be turned over to the Texas Rangers as evidence of your . . . shall we say . . . less than savory business dealings unless you turn Lily over to Miss Atherton's custody as the child's rightful guardian and cease your pursuit of her. If you agree to these terms, the book will remain in my possession under lock and key, and your secrets will remain hidden."

"And if I do give up custody of my grand-daughter, what's to keep you from turning my ledger over to the authorities anyway? I'd be a fool to agree to such a deal!"

"I have as much motivation to hold to the agreement as you," Stone assured him. "If I break the deal, there's nothing to stop you from coming after Lily. Besides, unlike some businessmen, I actually have a reputation for keeping my word." He narrowed his gaze, and Dorchester's face turned almost purple.

"Let Lily go, Dorchester. Honor your daughter-in-law's wishes. If you don't, I'll see to it that book of yours goes straight to the authorities. The authorities *and* the press. All they would have to do is interview a handful of the names on that list, find one or two willing to testify against the man who blackmailed or swindled them. The press will run with the story even if you persuade the prosecutors not to try your case. I'm sure the public will find it vastly entertaining to see one of Houston's elite brought low. Your credibility will be ruined. Respectable men will stop doing business with you, and your blackmail accounts will dry up because the men you've had in your pocket will turn their backs on you. They'll want to put as much distance between themselves and you as possible to save their own skin. And once your power is gone, so is your ability to keep your blackmail victims in line. Shoot, one or more of them might even try to get a little revenge. A bullet in the back is a bad way to go." He shook his head, *tsk*ing.

Dorchester fumed, yet he made no denial of Stone's allegations, verifying the truth that Stone and Ashe had only theorized when they'd examined the book's contents that afternoon at the Ranger office. Names and itemized accounts of repetitive payments, some going on for years. Nothing in particular proved blackmail in the book itself, but it provided a lengthy list of names from which to seek witnesses and testimony.

"Give up the girl, Dorchester, and the additional income she might bring you in the future," Stone pressed, "or lose everything you have now. Your choice."

"Lily's my granddaughter. She belongs with her family."

Stone had had enough of the circular argument. "The girl belongs with the guardian her mother selected for her." He bent down until he was mere inches from Dorchester's face. The man shrank back against the headboard, a decided tremble in his shoulders. "Make no mistake," Stone growled. "I'm taking Lily with me tonight, no matter which option you choose. All you get to decide is whether or not you keep your business interests."

Dorchester's gaze darted from Stone to the door and back again. Looking for escape? Help? Stone tightened his grip on his pistol.

Then all at once, Dorchester sucked in a huge breath and screamed. "Fraaaanklin!"

Stone didn't hesitate. He clocked the old man on the chin with his fist and ran from the room. Getting Lily out safely was all that mattered now.

A door slammed against a wall somewhere behind him as he raced down the hall. A shot rang out. Wood splintered from the railing beside him.

"Ashe!"

"Got him." The ranger knelt in the opening to Lily's room and laid down cover fire as Stone dove through the doorway. Shrieks from awakening servants filled the air.

Trusting Ashe to watch his back, Stone holstered his gun, scooped up a half-dressed, wide-eyed Lily, and shoved her through the window onto the balcony.

The girl started crying, covering her ears when another shot rang out.

Stone leaned out the window and gently pulled her hands away from her ears. He pointed toward the front of the house. "Run down to the tree. I'll be right there."

Tears rolling down her cheeks, she nodded and scampered away on stockinged feet that hadn't had time to find shoes. Stone turned back to Ashe, who had just closed the door. With a grunt, Stone shoved the bureau in front of the portal. Then the two men ran for the window. It wouldn't take long for Franklin to figure out where they were headed. And since stairs were much faster to descend than trees, any lead they had would vanish in a flash.

Stone's boots pounded against the veranda as he closed the distance to Lily. He lost sight of Ashe, but he had no time to worry about his friend. The man could take care of himself. Lily couldn't.

He grabbed Lily to his chest. Her legs automatically wrapped around his waist. "That's it, squirt. Hold tight. Like a monkey. I'll take you down the tree."

She clasped his neck, closed her eyes, and burrowed her face into his chest. Stone swallowed hard and launched himself over the railing. *God, see us through.*

He latched onto a head-high branch and planted his feet on the one right below the balcony. Hand over hand, he climbed down, making sure to keep his back facing the house at all times so Lily would be out of the line of fire if Franklin showed up again.

Charlotte's pale face stared up at him from below. No tears. No screaming. Just determined grit etched into her features and outstretched arms ready to take possession of her child.

Ten feet from the ground, a gunshot cut through the night and rattled the leaves near Stone's head.

"Stop!" a voice shouted. "You'll hit the girl."

Dorchester? Did the man actually care about what happened to Lily or just to his investment?

Stone didn't have time to ponder the answer.

"I'm not letting him win!" Franklin yelled,

even as he fired another shot from somewhere around the corner, out of sight.

Charlotte's assessment had been right. Stone could hear the twisted resolve in the tight tone of Franklin's voice. All he cared about was proving himself the better enforcer.

Stone dropped down two more branches. Then another. Almost there.

A third shot rang out.

Time slowed.

His gut vibrated a warning.

He knew. Knew the bullet would strike its mark.

"Lottie!"

He thrust Lily away from him with all his strength, tearing her short limbs from around his neck and waist. As the bullet pierced his back, he saw Charlotte catch her daughter and tumble backward.

Thank you, God!

Then his leaden body fell from the tree. He slammed into the ground, and everything went black.

37

Charlotte immediately rolled her body on top of Lily's. Scant seconds after the gunshot that felled Stone, a second one blasted from somewhere near the roof.

Oh, Stone. She'd felt the earth vibrate when he hit the ground. She prayed he'd get up. Come to them. Wrap his strong, sturdy arms around her and Lily and reassure them he was all right. That he'd only lost his balance and toppled. The fall hadn't been too high. Surely only the wind had been knocked out of him. That's why he hadn't gotten up. That's why she felt nothing more than cool night air blowing against her back when she longed for his warmth.

Even as she rationalized, hot tears scalded her cheeks. *Please, God. Don't take him from me. Please don't —*

Footsteps thumped overhead as a man ran across the roof, cutting off her prayer. Charlotte lunged awkwardly to her feet, her skirt

a tangled mess around her legs. Lily's clinging weight threw off her equilibrium.
Stone's unmoving body tugged at the corner
of her vision, but she forced her gaze
upward. Was it friend or foe advancing on
them?

A familiar hitch in the man's running
stride soothed her fear a moment before he
dropped from the overhang onto the front
veranda. A scuffle ensued. Charlotte
clutched Lily to her chest and dragged her
behind the tree.

Should she wait on Ashe or make a run
for the horses while he battled with Franklin? And where was Dorchester?

"Give me the girl," a voice rasped from
behind her. Charlotte whirled, instinctively
shoving Lily behind her. Dorchester stood
on the lawn in his nightshirt, his hair standing on end, his eyes wild, and a pistol
clutched in his hand.

"Never," she vowed.

"I need her. Just for a month or two, then
you can have her back."

Was he actually bargaining with her?
Charlotte was so astonished, she could think
of nothing to say.

"I lost another ship. Right before Rebekah
died. That's why I bribed Sullivan to close
the school. Why I sent men looking for you.

I needed Lily back to help me recoup my losses." He advanced a step. Charlotte retreated, shielding Lily. "But you hid, and no one could find you. Not even Hammond. For months! Do you know how much money that cost me?" He advanced another step. And another.

Charlotte backed away, careful to do so at an angle that would take her closer to the horses. If all else failed, she could send Lily running in that direction while she lunged for Dorchester.

"I was counting on the funds from that cargo," he rambled on. "Had moved ahead with other investments — investments made with powerful men who don't take kindly to a partner who can't fulfill his monetary obligations. I've held them off with paltry payments, but they've grown impatient. The girl is my ticket out. All I need is a little leverage on one of the men in the investment pool. She can ferret out a secret for me, and I can broker a trade. My silence in exchange for the remaining funds to cover what I owe. It's simple."

"It's sinful." Charlotte ceased backing away and glared at Dorchester, heedless of the pistol aimed at her chest. "For pity's sake. If you're short on funds, sell your house. Don't endanger your granddaughter.

463

What kind of man are you?"

Suddenly a dark shape loomed behind Dorchester. "An unconscious one," Ashe announced as he brought the butt of his own pistol down on the man's head.

Dorchester crumpled to the ground. Lily whimpered. Charlotte immediately turned to gather the girl in her arms.

"Franklin?" Charlotte asked Ashe as he bent to retrieve Dorchester's weapon.

"Tied up and waitin' for the cavalry. Got a bullet in his shoulder and a few bruises for his trouble. Stone's the one I'm worried about, though." His face clouded. "Took me a few seconds too long to find the right vantage point to take Franklin out. The rat was protected by the overhang of the porch. Got to Stone before I could get to him."

Before Ashe could even finish his explanation, Charlotte had spun and hurried around the tree to the spot where she had seen Stone fall. She found him. Still facedown. Unmoving. She wasn't even sure he was breathing. The utter stillness pierced her soul.

I'll pursue you until a parson either joins us in marriage or speaks words over my grave.

The vow he'd spoken in love rushed through her memory with the strength of a hurricane. No! There'd be no speaking

464

words over his grave. Not when he didn't even know how much she loved him in return. Oh, why had she ever let fear still her tongue? She shouldn't have whispered the words to his retreating back when he went to confront Dorchester. She should have shouted it from the rooftops until the neighbors all came out to gawk.

With arms gone limp, she lowered Lily to the ground then knelt by Stone's side. Holding her breath, she lightly placed her hand atop his back. It rose and fell beneath her touch, the movement shallow, but it was there.

"He's alive." *Praise God!*

Lily knelt beside her and stared down at her hero. "Is Mr. Hammond gonna be all right?" her voice sounded so small and scared, nothing like the brave adventurer she'd been just that morning.

"I've seen him take bullets before and pull through." Ashe had come up behind them, leaving Dorchester to rot where he'd fallen. "The ruckus is bound to have woken the neighbors." He hunkered down by his friend's head, scanning Stone's body, lingering over the blood-soaked spot where the bullet had entered his back. He reached for a handkerchief then pressed the folded square atop the wound. "I'll have to stay to

465

give an accounting to the lawmen that show up. But Stone can't wait that long. You need to get him to Lindy as fast as possible. She's as good a sawbones as her old man. She'll pull him through."

"We'll need a wagon," Charlotte said without glancing up, her mind spinning with all the details of what needed to be done. "And clean cloths from the house." What other injuries might he have sustained that she couldn't see? Broken ribs from his fall? Internal damage from the bullet? They needed to get him to Belinda as quickly as possible. "And servants to help us move him."

"I'll be right down with a batch of clean towels, miss," a feminine voice called from somewhere overhead. "And I'll send Oliver to fetch the carriage."

Charlotte glanced up. "Mrs. Johnson?"

The housekeeper held a lantern aloft and leaned over the railing. She nodded. "Saw the whole thing from my window, I did. When the shooting was done, I came out to take a look. Heard what the master said. Tell that Ranger down there with you that I'm willing to testify against the man. Not just about tonight but about a host of other things as well. Any man that would put his own welfare ahead of his grandchild

466

deserves no loyalty. As of this moment, I'm turning in my resignation."

Charlotte's eyes misted. "Thank you."

A weight lifted from her shoulders, but another remained. One that grew heavier with each moment that passed without Stone reviving.

Charlotte pressed down on the handkerchief, trying to staunch the flow. He'd lost so much blood already. He couldn't afford to keep leaking the vital fluid.

After what seemed like hours but was surely only minutes, Mrs. Johnson bustled around the corner, her arms full of clean towels and bandages. "Here, miss." She handed a white towel to Charlotte along with a small ewer of water.

Charlotte gave the items to Lily then stretched down to retrieve the knife from Stone's boot. Memories assailed her of the first time he'd revealed its hiding place to her. He'd been injured then, too, though only slightly. He'd recovered from the knock on the skull Dobson had given him. From his tangle with the bobcat, too. Even the men who'd attacked them on their way to Marietta's ranch had been unable to take him down. *Please don't let this bullet finish him.*

She cradled the short hilt in her hands then moved back to the site of the injury. Lifting the handkerchief carefully away from the wound, she dipped the tip of the blade through the hole in his shirt and slit the fabric wide open. She bathed the area with water, flushing the wound as best she could, then placed the towel against the hole in Stone's back and pressed firmly, leaning her weight into her braced arm.

Charlotte bent her mouth close to his ear. "Lily's safe, Stone. We've won. All you need to worry about now is getting yourself well."

He made no sound. No movement. Just lay there. Lifeless.

"Don't leave me," she whispered. "Please, Stone." A sob rose in her throat, but she refused to let it out. She had to be strong and goad him into being strong as well. She stiffened her spine and sat up. "This pursuit of yours isn't over yet. Do you hear me?" She badgered him with her best headmistress tone, the one she knew he hated. "There'll be no quitting. You will fight, Stone Hammond, and you *will* recover. I insist upon it."

A hand on her shoulder halted her harangue. She twisted her neck and glanced up into Ashe's concerned face.

"The carriage is here."

Charlotte nodded. "Good."

The coachman who had driven her earlier in the day hurried forward when Ashe beckoned. "I'll help you get him into the carriage, sir." He bent and circled his arms about Stone's knees.

Ashe levered his friend's torso and Charlotte rose to walk beside them, holding the now-saturated towel in place. Mrs. Johnson pushed the remaining towels into Charlotte's free hand then wrapped her arm about Lily's shoulders and followed the procession toward the carriage.

It took some jostling to get Stone inside, but they finally managed, draping his long body across the seat while Charlotte knelt on the floor beside him. Mrs. Johnson settled Lily on the rear-facing seat and gave her a quick squeeze before stepping back. She clasped the door handle then paused to look approvingly at Charlotte.

"You were right to come back for her, miss. Ever since her mama whisked the young thing off to school, I suspected something was amiss. Now that I've heard a hint of the truth from Dorchester himself, well, I'm just thankful someone was willing to go toe-to-toe with the old buzzard for the child's sake." The carriage shifted as the driver hoisted himself into position. The housekeeper stepped back to close the carriage door. "I'll be praying for Mr. Hammond's recovery."

"Thank you, Mrs. Johnson."

Then the door closed, and the coach lurched into motion.

I'll be praying, too. Charlotte bowed her head over Stone's back to do just that. *Every step of the way.*

38

The ride to the boarding house stretched interminably long. The jostling of the carriage kept throwing Charlotte off balance, making it difficult to keep consistent pressure on Stone's wound. After one particularly brutal jounce, she fell backward, and Lily had to throw herself across the gap to brace her arms against Stone's side to keep him from rolling onto the floor. Thank heaven for the girl's quick reaction. The last thing the man needed was another set of bruises.

The only signs of life Charlotte had to sustain her were the quiet moan elicited when Lily crashed into his side and the warmth of his skin when Charlotte's little finger strayed from the toweling to stroke the exposed skin of his back. Her finger strayed regularly, reinforcing the connection she needed so desperately.

"As soon as we get to the boarding house,"

Charlotte instructed Lily, "I want you to rush inside and alert Mrs. Ashe. Don't wait on the coachman, just open the door and run inside as fast as you can. She'll be waiting in the front parlor and will have the door unlocked for you."

"I will."

The girl proved as good as her word. The instant the driver pulled the team to a halt, Lily burst out of the carriage and ran for the door. By the time the coachman climbed down from his perch and arrived at the door, Belinda was on the scene, giving orders.

"Carry him into the kitchen," she ordered the driver. "Grab his upper half. Charlotte and I will each take a leg."

Charlotte's limbs tingled like fire as she finally unbent from her kneeling position, but she ignored the pins and needles. "Bullet to the back," she recounted. "He also fell about five feet from a tree and landed facedown. I didn't notice an exit wound or blood on his front when the men moved him, but it was dark, so I can't be sure."

Belinda shot her a glance. "Are you up to assisting me?"

Charlotte met her gaze without hesitation. "Whatever you need."

"Good."

The woman offered no sympathy, no soft-ness, just straightforward instruction. Exactly what Charlotte needed — a way to be useful.

She worked with Belinda through the night. Wiping away blood as Mrs. Ashe dug out the bullet, spraying carbolic acid solu-tion over the wound to fight infection, clip-ping off sutures when the stitching was done. Only after they had finished did Char-lotte spare the time to change out of her soiled mourning clothes, and even then, she hurried back to Stone's side without doing more than washing her hands and splashing a bit of water on her face.

She vaguely recalled Mr. Ashe coming into Stone's room at some point during the night to let her know that Walt Franklin and Ran-dolph Dorchester had both been arrested. She supposed she should feel relieved. Lily was safe. The battle for custody was over. But as she sat by Stone's bedside, all she could concentrate on was the rise and fall of his chest. She watched each inhale lift his ribs and each exhale deflate them. She breathed with him, matching his rhythm, as if by doing so she could somehow make it easier for him. Never once did she close her eyes.

Dawn's light streamed through the boarding house's curtains and reflected off the white of Stone's bandages. He lay on his back now, bared to the waist except for the wide bandages wrapped about his middle to protect his fractured ribs and keep his wound clean. Belinda had not wanted him to lie on his stomach, more concerned about his breathing than his comfort. The bullet had nicked both his liver and right lung. Too much weight on his ribcage could turn a fracture into a break and puncture the lung the bullet had weakened.

Charlotte dreaded the pain he would feel when he finally awoke, but she prayed fervently for him to wake anyhow. She wanted to see his eyes open, to witness recognition light the amber depths as his gaze landed upon her, to revel in the love that shone there — a love she'd been too fearful to glory in before but one she was now ready to return a hundredfold.

Stroking her mother's cameo in indecision, she scooted to the edge of her chair and hovered on the brink for a moment as desire battled propriety. She wanted to be closer to him, to touch him, to feel the warmth of his skin. She needed the connection that holding his hand always brought. Her spine stiffened.

Propriety be hanged.

Without so much as a glance to the door to ensure the moment was a private one, Charlotte slid from the seat of her chair and knelt on the oval rug beside the bed. Adjusting her skirt to allow movement, she inched closer to the mattress until her chest rested flush against it. Then she took Stone's hand in hers and gently brought it toward her face. She kissed the tanned, weathered skin, tracing the lines age had wrought there, the scars experience had left behind. She pressed her lips against each of his roughened knuckles and savored the feel of his palm once again nestled with hers. It was a strong hand. A capable hand. A hand that could bring comfort with as much skill as it could wield a gun or take down an outlaw. A hand that had brought her back from the brink of loneliness and taught her to trust again. A hand she wanted to hold for the rest of her days.

Charlotte closed her eyes and lifted Stone's hand to her cheek as she spread her elbows atop the mattress and settled in. She stroked her face back and forth along his hand like a kitten giving affection. After a moment, she stilled. A sigh slipped from her parted lips.

"I love you, Stone," she whispered. Frowning at the timid sound of her voice, she cleared her throat and tried again as her eyes squeezed together more tightly in concentration. "I love you, Stone." There. That was better. Firm. Convicted. Loud enough to be heard out in the hall should anyone be strolling by. "I love you, and I want to be with you for the rest of my days." The words came easier now. Stronger.

Charlotte opened her eyes and stared at his hand. Such vows should not be made when one's eyes were closed, after all. One should be well grounded in reality when offering one's heart. Although she couldn't quite bring herself to look at his face. His lack of awareness reminded her too much of all she might lose if he didn't recover.

"I need you to wake up, Stone," she pleaded. "Wake up and tell me I'm not too late. That you haven't given up your pursuit."

His fingers twitched against her hand.

Charlotte gasped and lurched backward. She stared at those beautiful, blunt-tipped fingers as her heart thundered. *Please move again. Please!*

But they didn't. Instead, a hoarse, gravelly voice croaked into the silence of the room.

"Never . . . give up . . . on you."

Charlotte's gaze shot to his face. Amber eyes met hers. Eyes brimming with love.

476

"Stone!" She jumped to her feet and hurled herself at him, barely catching herself before she grabbed his shoulders and embraced him with a fierceness that would surely tear his stitches. She settled for cupping his beloved face between her hands and dropping a tender, barely perceptible kiss on his mouth.

When she pulled back, his lips quirked at the corners. She beamed at him in response.

"I love you, Stone." The words burst from her, needing to be heard, needing to prove to him that she was no longer afraid. "I love you with all my heart."

"Told you . . . I always . . . retrieve . . . what I . . . set out for."

A joyful tear escaped the corner of Charlotte's eye. "That you did, sir. That you did." She dropped her forehead to rest against his. "Only the most tenacious retriever in the country could have accomplished such a task. You own my heart now. A heart you brought back to life. It's yours for as long as you want it."

Stone's eyes slid closed, unable to fight his exhaustion any longer. But as his lashes fell, a single word breathed out of him. "Forever."

EPILOGUE

Six months later
Madisonville, Texas
The Hammond Academy for Exceptional
  Youths

"Hammond! Help me hang this infernal sign. This foolishness was your idea," Dobson groused from the roof of Charlotte's cottage.

Stone crossed the front porch to where his wife was busy cleaning the windows and handed her the glass of water he'd just fetched from the kitchen. Leaning close, he kissed her cheek and circled her waist with his arm. His fingers splayed wide over the barely rounded womb that housed his child.

His child. He still couldn't quite believe it. Charlotte had worried that she'd be too old to conceive, not that he had cared. They had Lily and John, family enough. Yet they'd only been married for three months when Doc Ramsey had given her the joyous news.

478

Charlotte turned to him and smiled, her eyes bright and carefree and so beautiful he just had to brush his lips against hers.

"Hammond!"

Stone sighed then winked playfully at his wife. "The gnome calls."

Charlotte swatted him with the rag she'd been using to clean the panes. "Hush," she scolded, but the giggle that followed stole all the heat from her tone. "You shouldn't call him that. Mr. Dobson's a loyal friend."

"And a gnome." Stone dodged away from Charlotte's snapping rag, his deep chuckle resonating between them.

Reluctantly turning away from Lottie, Stone grabbed hold of one of the porch pillars and jumped atop the railing. He reached for the eaves of the roof, fighting back a grimace at the soreness that still radiated down his back whenever he stretched overhead. It had taken two weeks for him to regain his strength after Franklin's bullet had taken him down. Two weeks for him to recover enough to stand up as Charlotte's groom.

They'd been married in Marietta Hawkins's parlor at Hawk's Haven. Dan had stood at Stone's side, Marietta with Charlotte. Ashe and Belinda had attended as well. John had played the piano. Lily had

recited a love poem by Elizabeth Barrett
Browning — completely from memory, of
course. And Stephen had rigged a set of
poppers from rolled paper and some kind
of plunger mechanism. He'd filled them
with dried flower petals and bits of paper
pilfered from Miss Hawkins's stationery
box, and the moment Stone and Charlotte
had stepped out onto the porch, he and the
rest of the guests had shoved their plungers
upward and showered the happy couple
with a burst of colorful blessing.

Charlotte's mother had been unable to
get away since her opera company was mid-
season in Vienna, though the woman
promised to come for Christmas to meet
her new son-in-law. Charlotte had known
her mother wouldn't be able to attend when
she'd agreed to the early wedding date, but
it had been obvious to Stone that she'd still
felt the loss. He'd vowed that day that
Jeanette Atherton would be in Texas for
Christmas, even if he had to cross an ocean
and retrieve her himself.

"C'mon, Hammond. I haven't got all
day," Dobson grumbled.

Stone set aside his thoughts and pulled
himself up onto the roof. Once he had his
feet beneath him, he ascended the slope to
where Dobson crouched between two

L-shaped support brackets that had been nailed into the roof beams.

"Hold that end there," Dobson said, pointing to the bracket on the right, "while I nail this side in. I can't keep the dad-blamed thing straight with one hand."

Stone picked up the far end of the long, narrow sign that had been delivered that morning and held it flush against the bracket. Looking around him, he located Dobson's crate of tools and grabbed the level. He placed it atop the sign so he could make the necessary adjustments to ensure everything was straight as Dobson fastened his end with a few well-struck nails. They couldn't have "The Hammond Academy for Exceptional Youths" sign sitting crooked on their roof. Wouldn't be very exceptional. Even if the Farleys were the only ones they intended to impress.

When Stephen's parents had finally arrived to collect their son last summer, Charlotte sat them down and told them the full truth of all that had happened. Mrs. Farley had been outraged to learn that her son had been subjected to such dangerous scenarios and vowed never to let him out of her sight again. Mr. Farley, on the other hand, kept staring at Stone with an odd, calculating gleam in his eye.

Mr. Farley, as it turned out, had made his fortune by manufacturing rifles. The Henry repeater in particular. The same rifle a certain pair of bounty hunters were reported to have used during the escapades published in a series of exceedingly popular dime novels. When Stephen had begged his father to let him stay and be schooled by Miss Lottie, Mr. Farley had made him a deal. Get Stone to endorse the rifles coming out of the Farley manufactory, and he could spend the school terms with his teacher and friends. It had only taken one look at the wistful expressions on both Stephen's and Charlotte's faces for Stone to give in. He'd let his photograph be taken holding one of Farley's rifles and proclaimed it "the most reliable gun on the frontier." Not that there was much frontier left these days. But it *was* a fine weapon, so he didn't begrudge the man a little aggrandizement.

Mrs. Farley had protested at first, until her husband reminded her of all the society engagements they'd already committed themselves to for the upcoming year. In the end, she had agreed on the condition that the school have a formal name, one equally as prestigious as the one that scoundrel, Dr. Sullivan, had established.

Hence the sign.

Dobson, four nails between his teeth, hobbled over to Stone's side and hunkered down behind him. "Hold 'er steady now."

Stone grinned. As if that wasn't what he'd already been doing. "Got it."

Dobson pounded the nails into place then grabbed the sign and gave it a strong tug. It held. "What do ya think, Mrs. H?" he called down to Charlotte, who stood in front of the house, a hand upheld to shade her eyes.

Stone held his breath. His wife had rather exacting standards, and the gnome knew it. If she didn't think the sign straight enough, Dobson would gleefully cast the blame on the assistant holding the level.

"It looks splendid," she called, a bright smile illuminating her features. "Mrs. Farley is sure to be pleased when they arrive next week with Stephen. Be careful coming down, now." Her warm gaze lingered on Stone, roaming from his face to his chest, over his bent legs and down to the toes of his boots. His pulse accelerated. "You've gathered enough scars in my service. I'd rather you not collect any new ones today."

"Crazy female. Always making a fuss when there's no need," Dobson grumbled after Charlotte disappeared back under the porch overhang. He tossed his hammer into the tool crate and grimaced. "As if a man can't get himself down off a roof without falling on his head —"

Just then, a loose shingle slid out from under his foot. Dobson's leg shot out from under him. In a blink he was sliding toward the edge.

Stone lunged after him, throwing himself flat against the roof. One hand clasped the top of the sign, the other snagged Dobson's wrist at the last instant. The gnome's legs dangled over the side, leaving only his shoulders and head visible.

Grunting against the pain radiating through his stretched back, Stone strained and slowly pulled the older man away from the edge.

"Stone?" Lottie's voice drifted upward from the porch.

Dobson had just gotten his thighs and knees back onto the rooftop.

"Hurry, man," Stone grit out between clenched teeth. "If she sees you danglin', she'll never let . . . either one of us . . . up here . . . again."

Stone gave a final tug, and Dobson scrambled up. He flipped at the last moment to a seated position and Stone matched him, yanking on the sign to give him the leverage he needed to spin himself around and plant his boot heels in front of him. By the time Charlotte emerged from the porch and peered up at them, they sat companionably side-by-side as if nothing were amiss.

"Everything all right?" she asked, her brow furrowed. "I heard a dreadful scraping sound from up there."

Stone waved off her concern. "We're fine. Just testing out the sturdiness of the sign. Looks like it's gonna hold well."

She frowned, obviously not convinced that there wasn't more to the tale. But since they were both safe and sound at the moment, she couldn't really challenge them, could she? "Don't stay up there too long," she finally conceded. "It'll be suppertime soon."

"Just gonna enjoy the view for a minute or two," Stone assured her. "Then we'll be down."

Once Dobson had his breathing under control, he turned to Stone. "Testing out the sign's sturdiness, huh?"

Stone chuckled and thumped the old caretaker's back. "If that board can support the weight of two grown men, I figure it deserves to pass the sturdiness test. What do you say?"

Dobson grinned up at Stone. "I say, I'm a right fine carpenter!"

The two broke into laughter, releasing the

last of the tension of the near miss to float away on the autumn breeze.

When the laughter died down, Dobson turned to Stone, a cautious look in his eyes, as if he wasn't sure he should ask what was on his mind.

"Spit it out, Dobson." Stone thumped him on the shoulder again. "I won't bite."

The man stared at him for a moment then finally broke the silence. "I noticed you got a letter from that Ranger friend of yours down in Austin. Should I be expectin' more trouble up this way? Don't seem right to welcome the Farley boy back if Dorchester is gonna be causin' us more grief."

Stone met the man's gaze. "There'll be no trouble. Dorchester's got enough on his plate with all the charges piling up against him. Walt Franklin's been released, though. Ashe wanted me to know."

Dobson scowled, his bushy white brows nearly erasing his eyes. "Will he come after ya, do ya think?"

Stone shook his head. "I doubt it. Ashe convinced him to testify against his former employer in exchange for a reduced sentence. He's been sharin' all he knows about Dorchester's business dealings, helping them build a case for fraud, blackmail, and extortion."

Dobson harrumphed. "About time that old goat got his comeuppance. Still, that's no guarantee Franklin won't try something against you and the missus when he's done spillin' his beans to the Rangers."

"I expect he'll be busy with other occupations." Stone pushed to his feet and held out his hand to help Dobson up as well. "With me retired from the retrieving business, Franklin's now at the top of the pecking order. No more competition." Stone dusted off the seat of his britches then picked up the tool crate. "And if a job offer with an attractive price tag happened to have been passed along to him on my recommendation, well, that should go a long ways toward soothing his temper."

Dobson eyed him dubiously. "Where's this job located, exactly?"

Stone winked. "Montana."

Dobson grinned. "I knew I liked you, boy."

"Was that before or after you clocked me on the head with your rifle butt?"

"After." Dobson chuckled. "Though your noggin did have a good, solid feel to it when I butted you. Sturdy. Kinda like my sign."

Stone guffawed and then, together with Dobson, made his way — *carefully* — back down to the ground.

His feet had been connected with the

earth for only a handful of seconds when Lily's excited voice drew his head around toward the parlor window.

"Stone! Come see. Hurry!" She waved him over frantically, her shoulders and head thrust through the open window as she knelt backward on the sofa cushions. She held out the latest novel in the Dead-Eye Dan series, her finger pointing to a page at the end of the book. "See? It's you!"

Stone took the book from her and frowned down at Mr. Farley's advertisement. Somehow the man had gotten Stone's likeness with the Henry repeater transposed into the back of the book. He bit back a sigh. If Dan ever got a gander at this, he'd take Stone's head off. Oh well. Family took precedence, and Stephen was family.

Stone glanced over at his daughter. "I don't suppose you could forget you saw this, could you, squirt?"

She grinned. "For you? Sure."

"That's my girl." Stone tossed the book back to her, his heart full of fatherly affection. An affection that only grew when he saw John standing quietly in the shadows of the porch, his eyes following Stone's every move.

Months of puzzling out the boy had finally started paying dividends. He was learning to read the quiet kid like he would a Comanche's trail. And right now the little Comanche wanted to fly.

"Come here, you!" Stone swooped down and snatched John out of the shadows. Holding the boy aloft, he ran down the porch steps and into the sunlight. He tossed him in the air then spun him in circles until his giggles made a finer music than any piano ever could.

When the play ended, Stone hunkered down so the boy could clamber onto his back. With John's arms around his neck and legs around his waist, Stone headed up to the house and the supper that would be nearly ready.

Charlotte met him in the doorway, smiling. She ruffled John's hair then helped him dismount before sending him off to wash his hands. Stone she kept in the doorway, one dainty palm pressed against his chest.

"You can't go in yet."

He raised a brow. "No?"

She shook her head. "Not until you pay the toll."

"Ah." He snaked an arm around her waist and drew her close. "And what toll does the lady require?"

Her blue-green eyes lit with desire and love and a trust so deep it wrapped around his heart like an unbreakable tether, binding them together, making them one. "I think a kiss would suffice. For now."

Stone's lips curled upward in anticipation. "Then a kiss it shall be."

As his lips met hers, he thanked God for the circumstance that had set him off in pursuit of this woman so many months ago. She'd turned his life upside down, filling it with music, a ragtag bunch of kids, a grizzled gnome, and a love so profound he'd be forever changed.

No longer was he the hardened man who lived from bounty to bounty. No longer was he the orphaned boy who craved only a piece of land and enough money to keep it. He'd learned the joy of pursuing a greater prize. The prize of love, family, and a woman who would hold his hand through good times and bad and never let him go. A most worthy pursuit.

ABOUT THE AUTHOR

Two-time RITA finalist and winner of the coveted HOLT Medallion and the ACFW Carol Award, bestselling author **Karen Witemeyer** writes historical romances because she believes the world needs more happily-ever-afters. She is an avid cross-stitcher and shower singer, and she bakes a mean apple cobbler. Karen makes her home in Abilene, Texas, with her husband and three children.

To learn more about Karen and her books and to sign up for her free newsletter featuring special giveaways and behind-the-scenes information, please visit www.karenwite meyer.com.